D1645754

DILLON'S RISING

F/2348377
County Library

Dillon's Rising

Published by A G Lyttle
154 Hermitage Woods Crescent
Woking, United Kingdom, GU21 8UH

Copyright © 2016 A G Lyttle

A G Lyttle has asserted his right in accordance with sections 77 and 78 of the Copyright, Designs and Patents Act 1988 to be identified as the author of this work.

This novel is a work of fiction, although closely allied to the historical facts of the period; all characters, other than those clearly in the public domain, are fictitious and any resemblance to actual persons, living or dead, is purely coincidental. Other than a few quoted statements in the public record from some of the historical characters, the spoken words attributed to them are from the imagination of the author.

All rights reserved. No part of this publication may be reproduced, stored in a retrieval system, or transmitted, in any form or by any means (apart from short quotations embodied in critical articles and reviews) without the prior written permission of the publisher, nor, by way of trade or otherwise, be lent, resold, hired out, or otherwise circulated without the publisher's prior consent in any form of binding or cover other than that in which it is published and without a similar condition, including this one, being imposed on the subsequent buyer.

Third Edition, June 2016
Printed by CreateSpace
4900 Lacross Rd, North Charleston,
SC 29406, United States

ISBN: 978-1-5237-9994-7

To my wife, Anita, for her gentle cajoling and encouragement to finish the book and for her patience and perseverance in reading and re-reading the various drafts that paved the way to publication.

WHO'S WHO

All the main characters in Dillon's Rising, both historical and fictional, are identified in an Appendix on pages 345 - 347

Funeral oration given by Padraig Pearse, over the grave of Irish *Fenian* leader, O'Donovan Rossa, 1st August, 1915, closing lines

"The Defenders of this Realm have worked well in secret and in the open. They think that they have pacified Ireland. They think that they have purchased half of us and intimidated the other half. They think that they have foreseen everything, think that they have provided against everything; but the fools, the fools, the fools! - they have left us our Fenian dead, and while Ireland holds these graves, Ireland unfree shall never be at peace."

DILLON'S RISING

A G Lyttle

PLAN OF WEST CENTRAL DUBLIN, 1916

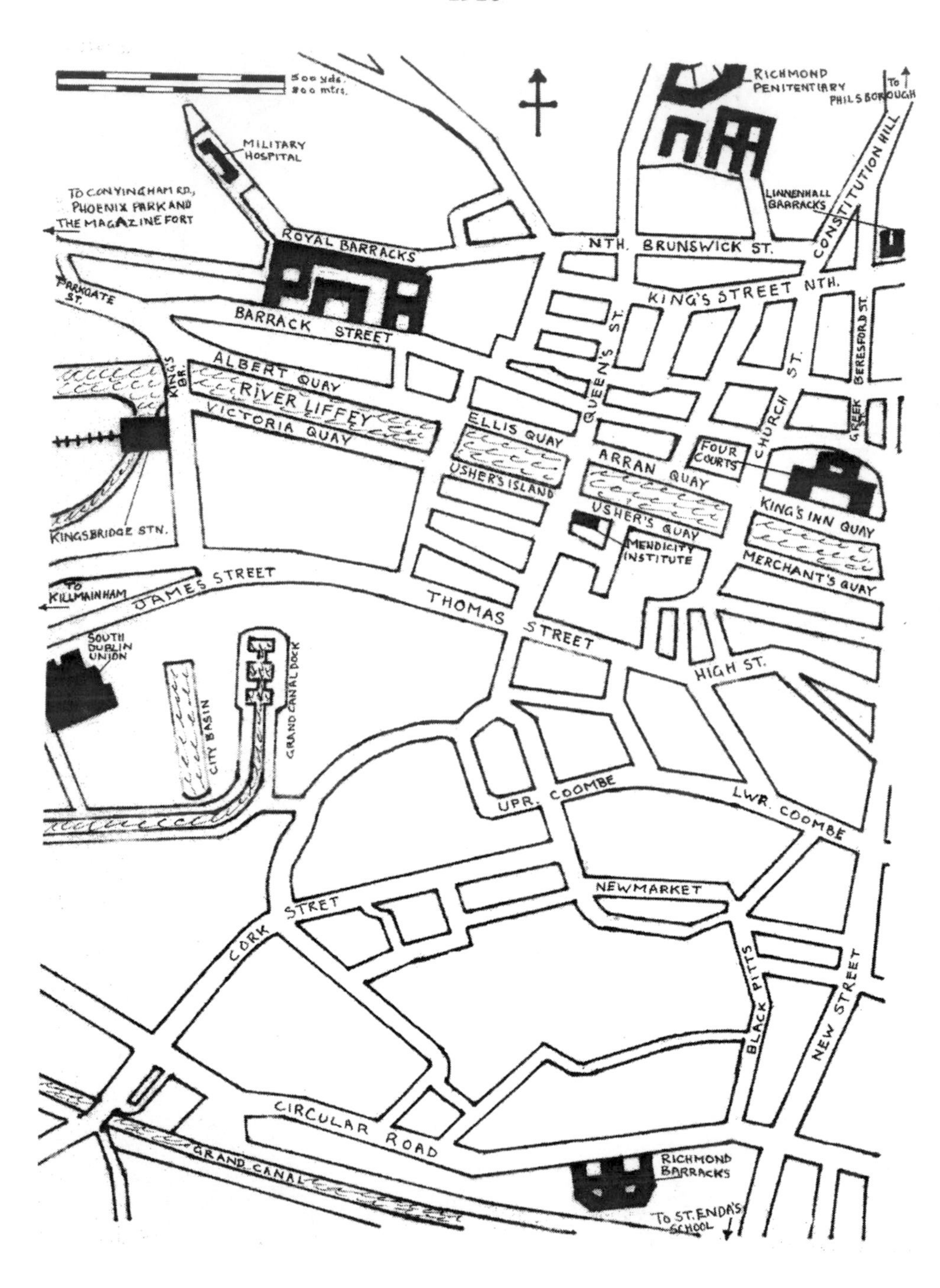

PLAN OF EAST CENTRAL DUBLIN, 1916

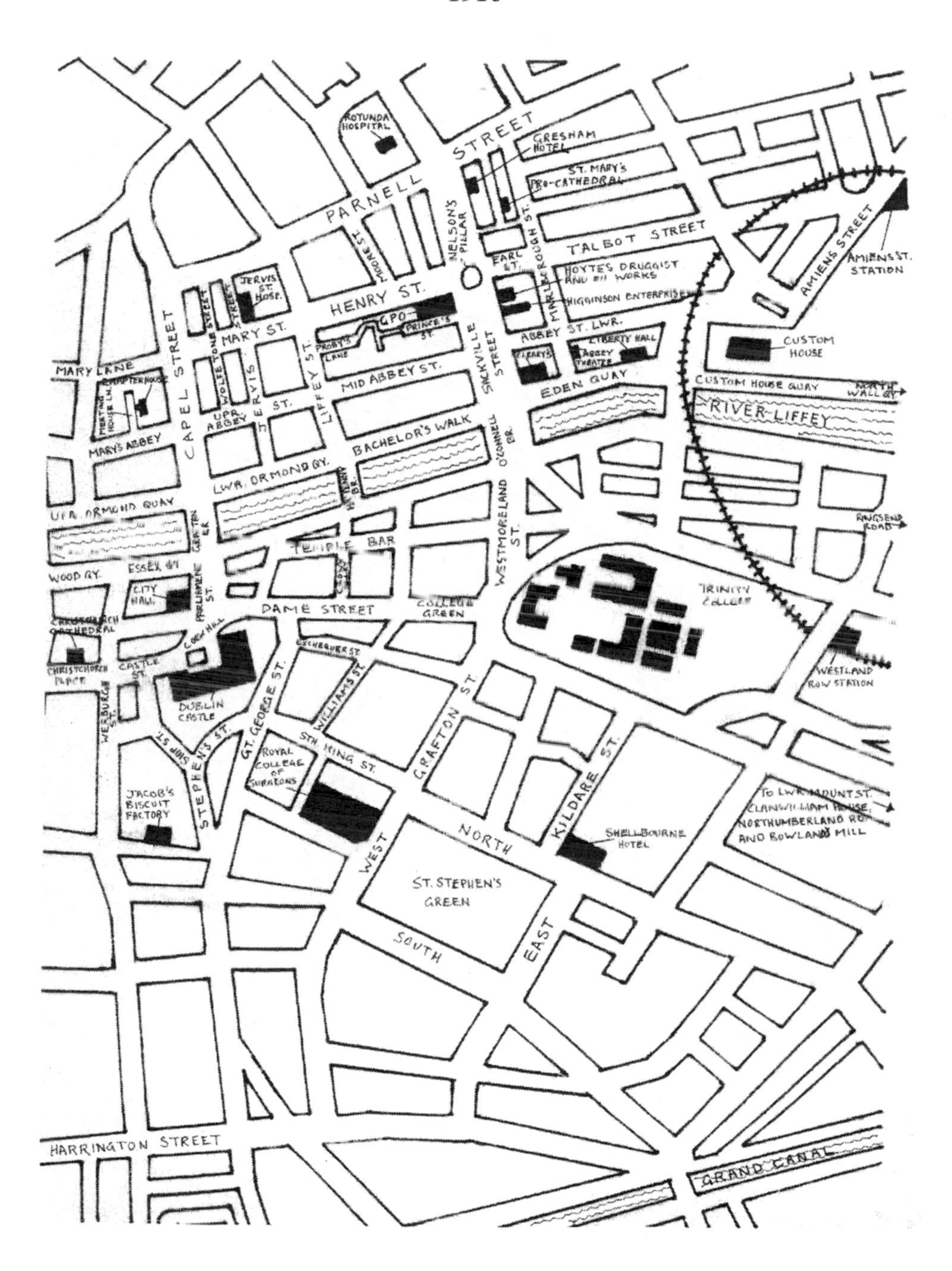

MAP OF IRELAND, 1916

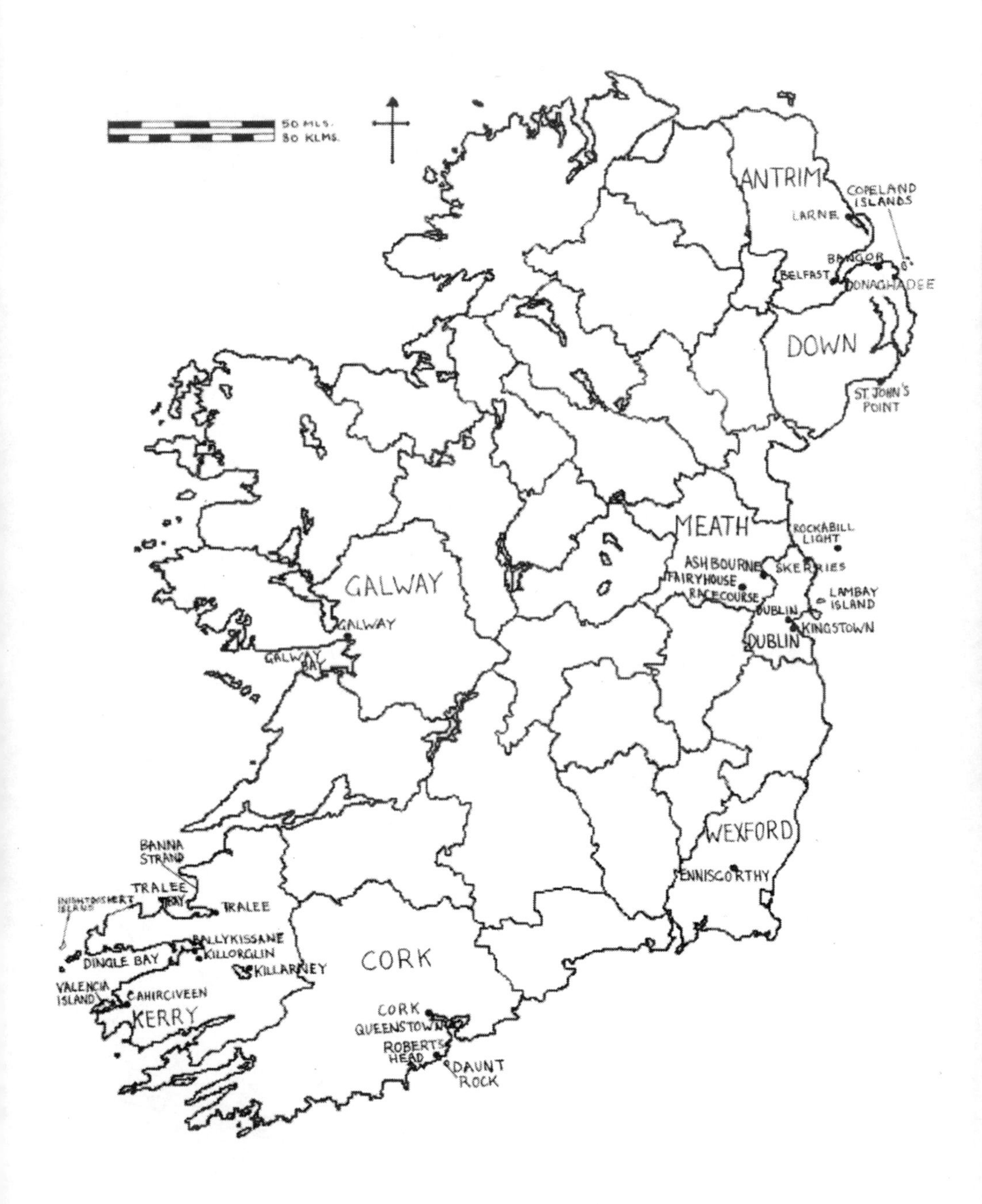

PART ONE

THE GATHERING STORM

Chapter 1

Frightened seagulls wheeled in the night sky, their raucous cries muted by the howling winds and thrashing rain. The percussive boom of the maroon that had startled them into wakefulness carried on through the darkness from the storm-lashed quayside at Donaghadee.

It carried to the ears of thirty-year-old Will Dillon as he washed down a lonely supper with his customary pint of the oul black stuff. Now the Guinness remained half-finished on the table as the volunteer lifeboat coxswain, glad to have his mind distracted, grabbed his oilskins and dashed out into the night.

Others around the town, honest County Down fishermen for the most part, were also rallying to the explosive summons, though some stout-hearted Irishmen, who would have been numbered among them, were missing. They had already responded to a higher call and gone to fight alongside their English cousins in the trenches of Mons and Flanders. Those remaining took a quick leave of loved ones who wished them a safe return as they prepared for the ordeal ahead. Each man knew that was by no means guaranteed.

Peggy Maguire was proud that both her father and brother had signed up for Kitchener's New Army and didn't think much of her husband using his need to man the lifeboat as an excuse for not joining them.

'Well, go on then, Jude Maguire, you heard the maroon. Go, man the lifeboat. If you won't fight for your country, you can at least fight for your fellow seamen.'

Jude eyed his wife as he finished spreading his piece with strawberry jam. 'I'll be off in a minute, woman. Pour me another drop of scald to see me on my way.'

Peggy saw in his face the reluctance to venture out on such a night, but he'd missed the last two call-outs: the first, fair enough, because he was struggling to get his own fishing smack back to harbour when the call went out, but the second time his excuse was pitiful. Peggy had not hidden her disgust. How could she face the other fishermen's wives whose menfolk regularly risked their lives while her Jude stayed at home because he said he was feeling none too grand? Her declaration that she would leave him if he didn't go out the next time 'and be a man' was no idle threat.

Jude took his time with his bread and jam and swallowing his tea, but then he got up from the table and collected his wet weather gear.

'That's me off, then. I hope you're happy.'

Peggy's lips pursed as her husband headed out to make for the harbour. Her thoughts were of a marriage long since devoid of any tenderness or desire, as the door slammed behind him.

The unmistakable demand of the maroon also brought a first ray of hope to the crew of the *Wild Bittern.* Fighting the late March gale – one of the fiercest 1916 had produced – they had been caught in the Ramharry tidal race and lost the battle to keep their boat from being pounded against the rocks off the Copeland Islands. A huge sea crashed relentlessly over her. Heavy equipment was being swept overboard like empty cartons. Any attempted movement on the sloping deck was perilous. The sound of splintering wood competed with the roaring wind and rain to chill the bravest of hearts on board.

As he saw the bright flash and heard the boom from the shore rocket, the skipper yelled, 'They've seen our flares, boys! They've seen us! If we can just hang on 'til they get here.'

The ship juddered from stem to stern as her timbers rasped against jagged outcrops. The crew, hardened sailors to a man, were quite unable to reef in the sails such was the fury of the gale. All they could do was loose all sheets to the wind and pray their rescuers would be in time.

William James Dillon – Willie James to his family, Will to his friends – grew up amongst the boats and the fishermen of Donaghadee and had been out on many a stormy night in his youth as an unpaid extra hand.

When war broke out he was in charge of telegraphic communications at the local Post Office and was discouraged from kindling any thoughts of joining up. What he did do was move up from bowman to coxswain of the *William and Laura* when the previous cox went off to fight the Hun.

So he was sensible of the hazards they were about to face, but he welcomed the diversion, nonetheless. From amongst the little crowd of volunteers on the quayside he counted off the men he wanted and they clambered down the steps in the harbour wall to where the *William and Laura* was moored. Will still had an element of pride at coxing the first lifeboat in Ireland to be fitted with an auxiliary motor, even if her extra weight precluded her from being kept in a boathouse and manhandled into the surf like in the old days.

We'll have a brave wheen of years between us tonight, he thought, mentally totting up the ages of the men descending to the lifeboat. Will pondered for a moment on some of his friends – men more his own age – over the water playing at soldiers. Och, maybe it's not much of a game. Good luck til them. And good luck til us; we'll be needing it before the night's out.

A seventh volunteer started down the steps.

'I need one more!' Will turned to look at those left huddled on the quay – now mostly wives and sisters of the men already in the boat. The icy rain lashed his cheeks.

Jude Maguire was just arriving, but young Alec Nelson had been amongst the first to reach the harbour. Too young yet for the British navy, he was always anxious to be included in the crew. It was Dillon, himself, who had first suggested that young Kicker Nelson, as he was known to his friends, should volunteer and the lad had needed little persuading.

'Come on, Alexander; you're due a trip.'

'Ah, houl' on there, Will,' called out Jude as he hurried over. 'I'm here now. You'll want all the experience you can get on a filthy night like this.'

Alec was at the top of the steps.

Maguire used his considerable bulk to push past Will and grab Alec's shoulder. He pulled him back and started to climb down to the waiting lifeboat. Will's hand shot out and gripped Maguire's wrist. A quick twist and the larger man yelped as he pirouetted and ended up with his left arm pinioned behind his back.

‘The lad’s experienced enough, Jude. Sure he’s never out of a boat. You should have got here sooner. I’ve got my crew.’ Will released his grip on Maguire and shoved him back onto the quay.

‘No, but – you don’t understand. I’ve got to go with yous. Peggy will…’ The wretched Maguire’s voice trailed off as he rubbed at his left arm.

Will let Alec precede him down the steps. He called over his shoulder, ‘Next time be quicker off the mark. Away off back to your missus with you.’

As the coxswain descended to the boat that was rising and falling alarmingly with the swell of the sea even within the shelter of the harbour, he was spared the dark glare from Maguire who seemed reluctant to return to the warmth and dryness of his own home.

* * *

A wall of water towered above the *William and Laura*. Spindrift whipped off the white crest, battering Dillon’s oilskins and stinging his face. It seeped under his sou’wester and trickled down his neck. The wall teetered and crashed over the gunwales. The deck flooded. The crew was drenched. Each gripped his oar and life-line. At the wheel, Dillon was thrown forward against his own life-line as the boat pitched down into the next trough. He struggled with his grip, the lines to the rudder straining as the power of the sea tried to wrench it first one way and then the other. He watched the seawater on the deck drain away through the scuppers, which barely cleared it before the next swell, the height of the mizzen mast, toppled and crashed, swamping the deck yet again.

The coxswain was already soaked through from the relentless downpour lashed by the gale into sheets of rain that penetrated even the sturdiest of garments. His knuckles showed white on the wheel as he grappled to hold their course and his mind on the job in hand.

The *William and Laura* was tossed up onto a peak and one of the crew yelled out, ‘I can see her light!’ before they plunged again and took in more salt water.

With a shake of his head, as though to dispel an unwanted image Will called, ‘Where man? Where?’

‘Dead ahead. Hold your course. Two chains – maybe less.’

A flash of lightning lit up the sky. More shouts. 'There she is!' 'Floundering dead ahead,' before they were drowned out by the growls of thunder rolling around the hostile heavens.

'Drop the mainsail!' Dillon yelled, worried they could be blown right past. He figured he'd take her in on the oars. Use the motor, if he needed to. He was pleased enough to have 40 HP of petrol engine at his disposal, but given the right conditions, he'd back the traditional twin sails and sturdy oars of these Watson boats against the unproven mechanical power any time. He was at home with sail and he trusted the strength of his men's arms to haul them close in to the wreck.

With the wind no longer in the sail, the men were struggling to make headway in the furious sea. 'Start the motor, Will?' young Kicker called out, showing more keenness than his coxswain to trust in modern technology.

'Aye, start her up, lad.' I've dropped the sail too soon. For Pete's sake, concentrate on the job, Dillon.

The lifeboat plunged again into another trough and as she rose once more the sound of the engine coming to life could be heard above the roar of the gale. The propeller gripped the sea and the boat surged forward, until it topped another towering crest and the engine raced as the blades came free of the water, only to revert to its steady chug as the prop re-entered the brine and brought them nearer to the stricken vessel.

They drew close to the wreck of the *Wild Bittern* – and close to the treacherous rocks that had been her downfall. Will wrestled with the wheel to stay seaward of the wreck and avoid the same fate themselves. They were going too fast; the sea was going to carry them past. Swinging to port, he called out to Kicker to cut back on the throttle.

'Deploy the drogue!' he yelled and a couple of men played out the line that let the cone of canvas trail astern. The drag on the *William and Laura* pulled her round perpendicular to the waves and allowed Will to steer nearer to their quarry. They could distinguish members of her crew clinging to the superstructure, their free arms making wild gesticulations to grab their attention. If they were shouting, too, no sound of voices reached their would-be rescuers, as their words were whipped away on the gale.

'Get a line aboard,' Will called to a crewman as the lifeboat continued to pitch and toss on the broiling waters. The seamen all set about doing what they were trained to do – what they had done on countless other storm-filled nights before – to rescue lives in peril on the sea.

* * *

They laboured long and hard, fighting wind and waves, rain and rocks until each man was exhausted but the last of the *Wild Bittern's* crew was brought safely on board. Will knew that each man, too, had that deep-seated feeling of triumph over the elements and elation that their mission had not been in vain. The *Bittern's* first mate had a broken arm and another crew member had bad lacerations to his face and temple where a falling spar had caught him a glancing blow, but all would survive to go to sea again.

There was still the journey home, which would not be easy, but Will was confident that the sturdy lifeboat could make it and more so that his trusty crew, tired as they were, were more than capable of bringing her to harbour in one piece. He let off a green flare, requesting a doctor to be standing by when they landed.

The rain had stopped some time ago and the swell of the sea abated a little. Salt water on the men's faces began to dry leaving a fine white crust on their chins and cheeks and the black of Will's bushy beard was turned to grey. In the pale light of a valiant half-moon that fought its way briefly through scudding clouds, it was a ghostly-looking crew that staggered up the stone steps to the quayside and into the grateful arms of waiting loved ones.

The church clock was striking the hour – a solitary peal, when Will returned alone to lift the latch on his front door. Wearily, he shrugged off his dripping oilskins in the vestibule and ran his fingers through his thick, damp hair. Exhausted, he stumbled into the parlour and switched on the electric light. A wasted expense. What does a man on his own need with electric light? A dim glow from the bulb over the table revealed the half-finished Guinness where he had abandoned it, leaving the rest of the roughly-furnished room in shadow. It was a space that lacked a woman's touch ever since his oul Ma had passed away half-a-dozen summers since and now was no longer likely to benefit from another. Will sank onto the chair where he had eaten his supper almost seven hours before. His right arm trembled with fatigue as he raised the glass to his lips.

And then he froze.

Behind him an armchair had creaked and now a voice spoke from the shadows, 'I was beginning to think you weren't going to make it back, Mr Dillon. And that wouldn't have suited our purposes at all.'

Chapter 2

It was a voice with a cultured Belfast accent. A voice Will thought he recognised – and disliked. A voice, he quickly recalled, he had last heard two years ago and had no wish ever to have heard again.

Will knew the words emanated from a man high in the echelons of the Royal Arch Purple, an organisation that most Orangemen believed simply to be a higher level within the Orange Order. It was an organisation to which Will, himself, had been elected a few years ago, even though then still in his twenties. He was therefore well aware that, although its membership was recruited exclusively from within the Orange lodges, it was nevertheless a separate organisation and not at all subject to the rules and regulations of the Order.

Hearing again this unwelcome voice from the past caused Will's stale Guinness to remain untasted, as his mind flashed back two years…

* * *

It was in the spring of 1914 when he first heard that particular brogue and had taken an instant aversion to its owner. Will was attending his lodge in Donaghadee – "Remember Ore" Loyal Orange Lodge 151. The meeting had been "raised" – meaning that the business of the Orange Order had finished for the evening and those Orangemen not members of the Royal Arch Purple had left the room. After preliminary matters of the raised meeting were dealt with, a visitor from a Belfast lodge was introduced and given the floor to address the members of the Royal Arch Purple 151.

Edmond Boyd was a small man whose purple sash looked oversized, reminding Will of a youth dressed in his father's clothes. But when he opened his mouth the visitor spoke with an authority that dispelled any such misapprehensions. His subject was one close to the hearts of well-nigh every Irishmen at the time and one that divided some as much as it united others.

'We can no longer rely on the House of Lords throwing out the Bill as it did in '86 and '93.' Boyd had been speaking for some time and he paused to push his spectacles back up the bridge of his nose. His close-set eyes peered through them at his audience as he continued. 'Not now the 1911 Parliament Act has abolished the Lords' veto. The best they can do is delay its introduction.

'Since John Redmond's Irish Nationalists are propping up the Liberal government, Asquith has been forced to agree to this third Home Rule Bill to appease him so he can hang on to power, though I doubt the PM wants Home Rule for Ireland any more than you or I. But this time, brothers, it could very well become law.'

There were cries of 'Never!' and 'No surrender!' from his listeners.

'I admire your spirit. But it will take more than shouts of defiance if we're not to end up under the thumb of the Catholics in Dublin which is the same as saying, the Pope in Rome.'

Again he paused and adjusted his spectacles. 'I expect most of you in this room are among the 471,000 odd who signed the Ulster Covenant. Am I right?'

Calls of affirmation.

'So on the 28th day of September, in 1911 you all pledged yourselves to "use all means that may be found necessary to prevent Home Rule being imposed on Ireland." '

Will's lips were pressed tight as many of his brothers confirmed this, too. He remembered when he attended one of the religious services held all over the Province at eleven o'clock on that first Ulster Day. He got all fired up like the rest of the congregation by the rhetoric from the pulpit. He joined the queue at the end to sign the Covenant. "Use all means to prevent Home Rule being imposed on Ireland." The queue inched forward. "*All* means." He thought of the self-defence classes he ran for young lads and how he was sure some of them were itching to put their new skills to uses above and beyond the realms of defence. Three people still ahead of him in the queue.

Sitting now in the Orange Hall Will recalled how, two-and-a-half years before, he had quietly stepped out of the line in the church and headed for home.

He returned his attention to the little man from Belfast, who was continuing. 'And there'll be Brothers here, I have no doubt, who are amongst the 100,000 of those signatories who answered the Unionists' call to join the Ulster Volunteer Force at the start of 1913 to defend our territory from Home Rule.' Another groundswell of agreement.

He went on to talk about how the UVF was going to be needed now, more than ever. When the Nationalists, in *support* of Home Rule, had responded the following November by forming the Irish Volunteers, an eventual conflict seemed inevitable. Edmond Boyd explained how it would be up to the UVF to take action, if necessary, to defend their land from Popery and from the clutches of the Catholic Nationalists. He spoke at some length and left his listeners in no doubt that the time was coming, and coming soon, when their courage and determination would be put to the test.

The guest speaker gave a brief inclination of his head in acknowledgement of the rousing applause that followed his speech. He pushed his spectacles back up and returned to his seat. Soon afterwards the meeting adjourned and Will and his brother Royal Arch Purplemen started to leave the hall.

'Have you a moment, Brother Dillon?' the Worshipful Master called over to him. Boyd was with him and it appeared to Will that George Gibson, the Master of the Lodge, had just been pointing him out to their distinguished visitor.

'I have, George, aye. What's up?' Will joined the other two at the front, well apart from the few remaining Brothers still filing out the back.

'Edmond, here, would like a wee word. Have you met? William Dillon – Edmond Boyd.'

The visitor extended his right hand and with the briefest hesitation, Will overcame his perhaps irrational dislike for the man and shook it.

'You're not a Volunteer, I hear.'

The man's bluntness wasn't calculated to overcome Will's reticence.

'I didnae pass the entrance requirements.'

'I beg your pardon?'

'I'm no a signatory to the Ulster Covenant.'

'Oh, I see. And why would that be, if I may ask?'

'Well, you have, haven't you? I would have signed it, right enough; I've no desire to see Home Rule brought in. But it was that phrase, "to use all means" to prevent it. I'll decide what I will or won't do to prevent it. I wasnae going to sign my soul away to let someone else dictate what I have to do.'

'But you were happy to swear the oath of a Royal Arch Purpleman, "on pain of death, to aid any fellow member…" '

' "…in all just and lawful actions," ' Will quoted. 'I was, aye.'

Boyd smiled. 'I see you're a man who knows his own mind. But you might be prepared to take action against Home Rule? If it seemed right, I mean?'

'I… suppose I might.'

'Good. We've got a big training exercise coming up. The UVF are a fine body of men and by now they are well trained.'

'Oh, aye. I've seen them drilling with their wooden rifles and broom handles.'

'That's temporary,' said George Gibson. 'That's going to change.'

'Yes, all right,' Boyd cut in. 'The point is, this is going to be a full-scale exercise, involving every Volunteer –'

'All hundred-thousand of them?'

'Everyone. Right across the Province, and more besides. Men like yourself. In key positions. We want to make it as authentic as possible. A real test of our readiness, should we ever be called to action.'

'I told him you were the very man for the job,' said George.

'Well, just what, exactly, would you be wanting from me?' Will asked, not yet convinced that he wished to oblige the little man from Belfast, despite George Gibson's apparent endorsement.

Edmond Boyd pushed his glasses up the bridge of his nose and in the now deserted Orange Hall proceeded to explain just what, exactly, he would be wanting from Will.

* * *

Three weeks prior to Dillon's first meeting with Boyd, on 30th March, 1914 the island of Langeland in the Baltic – on the Danish side of the border with Germany – was being lashed by a gale. Because Danish customs officials were concerned about Icelandic militants seeking independence from Denmark, they had just seized the papers of a Swedish coal boat, the *SS Fanny*, which was loading at the dock. They

F/2348377

County Library

suspected its cargo might consist of more than just the carboniferous fuel the papers claimed.

As the storm raged, reducing visibility to less than fifty yards, the *SS Fanny* slipped her moorings and ploughed her way out through heavy seas. In the foul conditions she managed to evade pursuit until she was outside Danish territorial waters. During the days that followed she worked her way around and up past the northern tip of Denmark. There she sailed west out into the North Sea and turned south.

Sometime later the *SS Clyde Valley* out of Glasgow was also sailing south, through the Irish Sea. On the night of the 19th and 20th April she and the *SS Fanny* rendezvoused off the coast of Wexford by the Tuskar Light. Later, the *SS Clyde Valley* started to make her way northwards once more. For most of her journey she kept within a few miles of the Irish coastline.

* * *

'It's not often I see you doing the nightshift, Will.'

'I could say the same about yourself, Jude Maguire. What are you up to, out at this hour?'

'I'm sworn to secrecy. We all are.'

'All?'

'The UVF.'

'Oh, the training exercise.'

'You know about it?' The pitch of Jude's voice rose in tandem with his eyebrows.

They were standing outside the Post Office on Friday 24th April, 1914. Will had arranged to take the night duty himself on that particular evening as a result of his chat with Edmond Boyd a few days before. Boyd had assured him that the police and army were being kept in the picture and had given the UVF permission to practice a full-scale mobilisation.

Largely on the strength of that, but partly because he couldn't help feeling a grudging admiration for the pains the planners were obviously taking to make the exercise as realistic as possible, he agreed to play a small part himself in his role as the Donaghadee Chief Telegraph Officer. They've even included the intercepting of telegraphic communication around the Province in their training exercise, Will thought; they're nothing if not thorough.

'Aye, I've heard rumours; that's all,' he said to Maguire. 'No details.'

Jude's eyebrows resumed their normal elevation. 'That's because no one knows the details. Every man's been told only what he has to do. Where to be and when. Nothing else.'

On a need-to-know basis, was how Boyd had put it to Will. So he knew only that he was to monitor any calls to the police and a few individuals who acted in an official capacity in one way or another, and he was to hold delivery of all telegrams until the next day. Of the rest of the exercise he was told nothing, though to help persuade him, George Gibson let slip that his counterparts in Bangor and Belfast and even up the coast at Larne would be doing the same thing.

Jude said, 'I must be off down to the harbour. Good night to you.'

'Aye, goodnight, Jude. I hope it keeps fine for you.' Will turned and let himself into the Post Office. In the dim glow filtering through from the street he groped his way to the telegraph room. There he flicked the switch for the electric light and made himself comfortable; it was going to be a long night.

So, the harbour is it, Jude? There's harbours in Bangor and Belfast, too. And Larne. What are them boyos up to?

Will opened a book of poetry he had brought to help pass the time. It opened at the flyleaf and he gazed at the inscription that he loved to read: *To dear Willie James with much affection, Annie.* He couldn't help feeling a tinge of resentment that he had had to cancel their usual Friday night rendezvous to oblige Edmond Boyd. He thumbed through the anthology until he found a short poem entitled "A Drinking Song"

Wine comes in at the mouth
And love comes in at the eye;
That's all we shall know for truth
Before we grow old and die.
I lift the glass to my mouth,
I look at you, and I sigh.

and he raised an imaginary glass to the image of his love, and sighed. He thought of walks in Ward Park in near-by Bangor town. Ducks on the pond. Annie's slender hand in his, fingers intertwined. And laughter. Always laughter. He turned the pages until he came to the "The Green Helmet," a mythological play in verse about Cuchulain, and started to read.

The few calls Will had to put through eventually dwindled to none at all as the hour grew later and the room grew chillier. He got up and put a kettle on the gas ring. He needed a warming cup of tea.

Sipping his sweetened brew he turned his attention once again to W. B. *Yeats' "The Green Helmet and Other Poems,"*[1] a birthday present from the loveliest girl in all of Down. But before he could read more of the Laegaire, Conall and Cuchulain, his peace was shattered by a loud banging on the street door.

* * *

Customs officers at Belfast docks noted the number plate of the large truck, which appeared to be awaiting an incoming shipment. A contingent of Ulster Volunteers had also invaded the quayside. The officers watched as the *SS Balmerino* manoeuvred alongside. Their colleagues had already boarded her on her approach up Belfast Lough. They reported that they found her crew particularly obstructive in answering their questions. With the smuggling of arms a constant threat the revenue men were convinced they had stumbled on a major haul.

It was approaching midnight on Friday 24th April, when they called in reinforcements from nearby ports to search the *Balmerino* from stem to stern and from funnel to keel.

* * *

Twenty miles to the north, at 1:00 a.m., on Saturday 25th April, in response to their need-to-know instructions, the UVF Motor Corps in Antrim started to arrive at the approaches to Larne harbour. It wasn't long before the headlights of 500 vehicles lit up the sleepy town in a three mile long queue to the docks. The police knew about the planned exercise and took no action.

The lights of the motorcars at the head of the procession illuminated the name on the side of a vessel just mooring at the quayside – *Mountjoy II*. The symbolism of the name was not lost on the Unionist drivers of the motorcade. To a man, they recalled the original *Mountjoy*, the ship that finally broke through the boom across the Foyle estuary to bring desperately needed provisions to the beleaguered loyalist citizens of

[1] The Green Helmet and Other Poems, William Butler Yeats, 1911; The MacMillan Company, 1912

Derry in 1689. By so doing, it ended the longest military siege in history to that date. Its brave action heralded the beginning of the end of the catholic King James II's attempt to regain his English throne, and made it possible for William of Orange – King Billy to all the Volunteers waiting in Larne – to confront the Jacobite king and defeat him the following year at the famous Battle of the Boyne.

As the ship started to unload her cargo, unhindered by customs officials, all called away to assist their Belfast colleagues, the UVF men saw that the ship's name was painted on large canvas sheets hung so as to obscure her real insignia. They were not aware – need-to-know – that they were actually helping to unload the *SS Clyde Valley* of a cargo that had been transferred to her at sea a few days earlier from under the coal on the *SS Fanny*, which she herself had taken on board from an arms dealer in Hamburg.

Colonel Frederick Crawford, Director of Ordnance of the HQ staff of the UVF and a true blue protestant who claimed to have signed the Ulster Covenant in his own blood, had been tasked by the Ulster Unionist Council to equip the wooden rifle-toting UVF with the real thing. His remit was to turn them from a well-disciplined but toothless tiger into a powerful beast to be let loose if the Home Rule monster ever reared its head in earnest. There were many rich sympathisers – among them, men like Rudyard Kipling, Waldorf Astor and Viscount Halifax – who were happy to finance the operation.

A great army of Antrim men beavered away transferring rifles, bayonets and ammunition to the waiting vehicles to be spirited off to secret arms dumps around the Province. And there were some who later swore they recognised among the workers that night the features of staunch supporter, Bonar Law, leader of the UK Conservative Party and future Prime Minister. While they worked, the *SS Roma* and the *Innishmurray* came alongside the *Clyde Valley* and took on board thousands of the weapons before heading out to sea to make their way round the coast, one to Belfast and the other to Donaghadee. The *SS Clyde Valley*, herself, having delivered the Larne consignment, sailed once more and headed for Bangor to discharge the remainder of her lethal cargo there – all still unharried by any customs officials who were spending a fruitless night searching through the innocent cargo of the *Balmerino*. Operation Lion, as this vast exercise was code-named, was playing out precisely as planned.

* * *

Will Dillon put down his tin mug and hurried through to see what the racket was at the street door.

'Who's there,' he called. He wasn't about to let anyone else into the Post Office at this hour of night.

'It's all right, Will. It's me.'

'Me who?'

'It's Jude. Maguire. I've been assigned to act as runner with any messages.'

Will wasn't expecting any messages. Wasn't it just a training exercise, for Pete's sake? 'You cannae come in here,' he said. 'This is government property. No civilians.'

'Sure don't I come in every time I need a stamp?' Jude's logic was impeccable.

'That's different. Opening hours is nine to six. Public aren't allowed in at night.'

'You have to let me in. You have to let me do my job.'

'I have to do nae such thing. I'm in charge here. Get off back to the harbour or wherever you're supposed to be "exercising".'

'Aw, come on, Will. I wudnae touch anything. Just open the door.'

Will was about to tell his annoying visitor to push off when he heard a familiar click-clacking sound from the telegraph room. He hesitated. 'Wait there a minute.'

He made his way back through the shadowy Post Office.

Will quickly scanned the paper tape spewing from the machine. He recognised the addressee as Donaghadee's head coastguard, a brother lodge member. The message read:

`Big op going down Belfast. Be extra vigilant. Could be others. Phone lines down maybe telegraph too so details en route by dispatch rider.`

The signatory was designated, Chief Customs Officer, Belfast.

Will tore off the paper strip and began cutting it into lengths and pasting them on a telegram form. Full-scale mobilisation exercise, my Aunt Fanny. What's to be done about this? I've agreed not to deliver any messages until the morning, but will that be enough? A fast dispatch rider from Belfast could make the journey in less than half-an-hour and there's no way of knowing when he started out. There could be fifteen minutes or maybe less than five.

Will didn't know for sure what the UVF were up to that night but he could make a fairly good guess. If he was right, the arrival of the coastguards at the harbour would be about as welcome as a Fenian at a lodge meeting.

He grabbed a notepad and pencil and quickly copied out the message. He tore off the sheet and rushed back to the street door. The key turned quickly in the lock and he pulled back the bolts.

'Here! You'd best get this to whoever's in charge. There's not a moment to lose.'

Jude's eyebrows did their levitation act again as he clasped the note and turned in the direction of the harbour.

'And you better come back and join me when you've delivered it,' Will called after him. 'I suppose there could be more messages.'

He relocked the door and went back to the telegraph room.

His tea was cold.

His thoughts regarding Edmond Boyd were colder.

Chapter 3

Dispatch riders were much in demand that night back in 1914. The Ulster Volunteers had their own on standby to help keep the leaders in different locations informed of progress. With the unloading well underway in Larne a rider was sent to report to Sir George Richardson, the UVF Commander, who remained in Belfast throughout the night. As the UVF biker slewed to a halt on the loose gravel outside Richardson's quarters, a number of Government riders at the docks were setting off with warnings to various coastguards stationed around the shores of the Province.

Harry Wilson was one of the first to leave and he made swift progress out of the city along the Upper Newtownards Road. He hurtled through Dundonald village and instead of following the main road that bends sharply to the left at Quarry Corner he kept on along the straight country road that switchbacked its way towards the little market town of Newtownards. At the tops of the hills his bike almost left the asphalt before plunging him down into the next hollow, but he saved precious minutes and he was soon leaving Ards behind as he climbed up towards Six Road Ends. His headlamp picked out the crossroads ahead and no approaching lights were visible on any of the other roads.

Harry held the throttle open to shoot through the junction. At the last moment a shadowy figure emerged from behind a hedge, one arm raised in an unmistakable fashion requiring him to halt. It was far too late to stop the bike. Harry caught a glimpse of the man's balaclava-covered head as he swerved round him, started to lose the back end, wobbled crazily and somehow managed to accelerate out of the skid over the crossing and onto the last leg of his journey.

As he throttled back on approaching the outskirts of the fishing village of Donaghadee he glanced at his watch. Nineteen and a half minutes. He reckoned he could be heading for a new record. Looking ahead once more he was alarmed to see another dark figure looming up in the beam of his headlight, again signalling that he should stop and this time standing in front of a road barrier. Harry had heard about the UVF exercise planned for this night and he had rightly concluded that the sentry at Six Road Ends must have been part of that. He had to assume that the men in front of him – for he could see now that there were two – were also Volunteers. He had no reason to suppose that they would interfere with the King's business, but neither had he ever been asked to stop before when dispatch riding. He made a swift decision and hurled his bike right, down a side road just before the roadblock.

The shouts of the men rung in his ears even above the roar from his exhaust. His grin as he sped on soon faded, though, when he heard the distinct kick-start of another bike. Glancing behind he saw a single headlamp swing into the side road and speed after him.

* * *

James Craig, MP for East Down and one of only twelve men in the Province who knew in advance the true nature of the night's UVF exercise, scanned the scribbled note Jude Maguire handed to him.

'And this was received when?'

'About three minutes ago. I ran all the way here. Sir.'

'All right. Good man. Corporal West!' he turned in the direction of a thickset man in his thirties with fair, unruly hair. 'Take three men and get up to the coastguard cottages in double-quick time. At all costs stop a dispatch rider delivering them a message. He could arrive there any minute. Go!'

'Sir!'

Jude watched his friend Geordie West set off at a trot, commandeering three others as he went. Soon they had left the quayside and were out of sight. Jude retraced his steps at a more sedate pace, wondering what reception he would get this time as he knocked on the door of the Post Office.

* * *

Harry Wilson took the first turning on the left that he came to and then a quick right and left again. He glanced behind but couldn't be sure if he'd managed to throw of his pursuer. He relied on his sense of direction to negotiate the side roads heading towards the sea. At one point he caught a flash of headlight in his mirror and at this ungodly hour in the morning he had to assume he was still being chased. But he felt sure he was close to his destination. If he could just keep ahead.

He swung his heavy machine right, onto a main route that he realised must be the coast road. The coastguards' cottages would be up on the left, set back from the road with their rear aspects facing the sea. After having seen not a soul since leaving Newtownards, apart from the UVF sentries he was startled to spot four men jogging up the incline ahead of him. He slowed down as he was going to have to let them go past the entrance to the cottages before he could turn in. Then three things happened at once.

The joggers reached the first cottage and turned to face Harry just as he pulled up, blocking his path and shouting at him to stay where he was. Behind him, the second bike pulled out of the side road and roared up towards him. And in the cottage, a light came on in an upstairs window.

* * *

Later, at the Post Office, Will Dillon was seeing Jude off back to the harbour. Another message had come through, this time for Captain Craig advising him of the safe departure of the *Innishmurray* which was expected to make Donaghadee by 5:45 a.m. He was to be standing by with his vehicles to offload and distribute its cargo as soon as it arrived.

Will needed no more guessing as to the nature of the cargo. From what Maguire had told him of the scene at the harbour: hundreds of men sealing it off from unwanted onlookers; trucks, motorcars and carts lining up; the steam crane commandeered for unloading. It was clear to Will that a major gunrunning operation was in progress. Which was fine by him. The Volunteers need to be able to defend themselves. Or were they expected to club their foes over the head with wooden rifles? But Will hated the subterfuge. That man, Boyd, swore it was just an exercise. The bastard knew exactly what it was. I don't mind helping, but I don't like being lied to.

Back in his seat, Will realised his teeth were grinding. Yeats' anthology lay abandoned on the table beside him. His thoughts raced around what he suspected was going on all over the Province that night and what the consequences might be. Would there be fighting? Bloodshed? Is Edward Carson going to lead the Unionists into a civil war to stop Home Rule being imposed upon us? Not a good time to be a member of the UVF even if I do know how to defend myself. I reckon I'm well out of it.

Just then the sound of the returning Maguire reminded him that he wasn't that far out of it. He let the man in and lit the gas under the kettle again.

They supped their tea and Jude talked about the price of fish.

'It's getting to be that it's hardly worth taking the boat out. If we dinnae get a decent catch I cannae cover my costs.'

'Is that a fact? I thought the fishing wasn't too bad at the moment.' Will couldn't help thinking there must be an element of exaggeration in Maguire's lament.

'Och, it's not like the old days. I tell you, I'm thinking of chucking it in. If it weren't for the few bob I get from manning the lifeboat we'd be struggling to make ends meet.'

Their conversation turned to sea rescues they had been on and the many adventures they had had on the *William and Laura*.

Sometime later, after a pause in the chat, Will asked, 'How's that brother of yours? We never see him on the lifeboat these days.'

'Who, Seth? He and Molly moved down to Dublin. Did you not know that?'

'Did they, now? No, I hadnae heard. But that would explain it, right enough.'

'Oh, aye. Got himself a good job, too. Jacob's Biscuit Factory.'

'So he's left the fishing behind?'

'Well the boat can hardly support me, never mind the two of us. But sure his heart was never in it, so it wasn't. He's landed on his feet, but – the same lad. Sometimes I think I could do worse than go and join him.'

'You'd give up the fishing?' Will asked.

'I don't know. Maybe one day. Maybe I willnae have a choice.'

The ever hospitable kettle was boiling again and with more tea and more idle chatter the two passed away the small hours of Saturday morning. It was another message for Craig click-clacking through on the telegraph that eventually sent Jude scurrying off once more. When he had gone Will picked up his book and started to read again from Yeats' poems. But he'd only scanned a verse or two when a call came through. He grabbed his headphones and inserted the jack plug and spoke.

'How can I connect you, caller?'

A voice, sounding at once urgent and yet very quietly spoken, said, 'Put me through to the police. Quickly, please.'

Without any conscious thought Will reacted with professional speed and inserted the appropriate plug into the right jack. The ringing tone went on for some time before a sleepy voice answered.

'Royal Irish Constabulary, Donaghadee. Sergeant McBride speaking.'

His headphones still connected, Will picked up a pencil and pulled the pad towards him.

'Sergeant, this is the Divisional Officer of the Donaghadee coastguard.'

'Lieutenant-Commander! What can I do for you?' Listening in to the conversation, Will could imagine the police sergeant almost standing to attention while still rubbing sleep from his eyes.

'I need you to get a constable up here straight away. I'm being held under house arrest by some form of militia. They claim to be UVF men. There was a dispatch rider outside earlier and they wouldn't let him through to deliver an official message. The chap called out to me that it was from the Chief Customs Officer in Belfast before he was forced to ride away escorted by a UVF motorcyclist. That was near on four hours ago now. Ever since then they've stood guard outside my house with one of them in the hall keeping me incommunicado – '

'In where, sir?'

'In – never mind. He's finally gone outside for a smoke. I refused to let him light up in the house. Filthy habit. But I can't speak for long. How soon can you get someone here?'

'That might not be possible, Lieutenant-Commander.'

'Not possible? Why not? These men are acting illegally.'

'My constables are all down in the harbour area observing this UVF mobilisation exercise tonight. I don't have anyone to spare.'

'The harbour area! Why the harbour, man? What's going on?'

'Nothing, sir. We are assured it's just an exercise.'

'An exercise, my Aunt Fanny!' Will smiled, hearing the coastguard utter the same expression he had used himself. 'If the harbour is a point of interest you can bet your pension there's contraband involved.'

'I wouldn't know, sir.'

'Well you ought to know. It's your job to know.'

'Well, contraband, sir – isn't that your –'

'Don't be impertinent, Sergeant. Are you going to send someone up here, or not?'

'I'm sorry, sir. I can't see as how I can; not straightaway.'

'It's not good enough.' There was a pause before the Divisional Officer continued. 'Well listen here. I've got Painter with me, one of my men. Lives next door. Sneaked round the back way to see what all the fuss is about. UVF thugs don't know he's here. I'm going to send him down by the cliff path to find out what's happening at the harbour. I shall expect your men to see he comes to no harm. Is that clear, Sergeant?'

'As crystal, Lieutenant-Comman – '

There was a click as the customs officer hung up.

' – der,' finished the sergeant. After a slight pause, another click and the line fell silent.

Will glanced at his pad. "Painter," "cliff path," "harbour." He knew Painter, vaguely. The man hadn't long been posted to Donaghadee, but was one of the more pleasant coastguards. Married, with a couple of kids. Always stopped to pass the time of day. But a coastguard was a coastguard. And this coastguard was about to head down to the harbour. Will consulted the large wall clock – 5:40. The guns were scheduled to arrive at any minute.

Dillon didn't hesitate. He couldn't wait for Jude to get back. He rushed out of the Post Office and set off for the harbour.

He gave an involuntary shiver and hunched his shoulders against the cold morning air. Dove-grey tinged with red streaked the sky, heralding an imminent dawn. It added a rosy tinge to the white of the lighthouse standing sentinel at the head of the harbour wall. Will's eyes, always first drawn to its regal lines, quickly took in the rest of the scene. The vast throng of people milling around on the quayside; the lines of vehicles of all types queued up; the uniformed bobbies – he spotted at least three pairs – standing, hands behind their backs, "observing." As he drew closer, the air of expectancy about the place was infectious; pent-up excitement shone in the eyes of everyone he passed.

'Will Dillon! Is it yourself?' George Gibson loomed out of the shadows from behind the cab of a flatbed truck.

'Aye, it's me, George.'

'But what are you doing here, man? Who's at the Post Office?'

'There's no one; this couldn't wait. Who's in charge?'

Gibson glanced around, but said, 'You better tell me. What have you got?'

Will explained how the coastguard was on his way to check up on what was going on and could catch them red-handed if the boat arrived on schedule.

Gibson gave him a sly look and said, 'Catch us red-handed? Not sure what you're implying, Brother Dillon.'

'Come off it, George. We all know this is no exercise. Not with all these trucks lined up. How many guns are you expecting?'

For a moment George Gibson looked shocked and then he threw back his head and guffawed. 'You always were the sharp one, Will, and you'll know soon enough anyway.' In a lower voice he added, 'Thousands, Will. Thousands. How will we know this Painter fellow? You're right we need to stop him coming onto the quay.'

'Well I know him to say hello to; I could point him out.'

Will was dispatched back to the barrier where the road joined the quay. He had a corporal and two other UVF men detailed to keep the coastguard in check. Will stood, hands in pockets, shoulders shrugged and shuffled his feet to keep warm. There was no sign of Painter.

'You sure there's a coastguard coming?' the corporal said, lighting a fresh cigarette from the butt of his last one.

'He's coming,' said Will. The white cloud of his breath was visible in the growing light.

Silence. More feet shuffling.

'There!'

'Where?'

'There. Just passing the green cart. That's him.' Will stepped back into the shadows as the corporal waited for Painter to reach the quayside.

'Sorry, sir. No one's allowed on the harbour wall without permission.'

'I'm a coastguard. My name is Painter. I have permission to access the harbour.'

'Not today, you don't.'

'Don't be ridiculous. Let me through.' Painter pushed past the UVF men who immediately grabbed him and swung him round so they were between him and the harbour once more. 'I demand to be let past!' he said.

'Not possible, Mr Painter. Now, if you'll just be on your way.' The corporal took his arm to lead him back onto the road.

Painter snatched his arm away and immediately two of the Volunteers grabbed both his arms and frog-marched him off the quay.

Will was aware that he ought to be getting back to the Post Office, but stayed and watched as they left the coastguard standing some yards beyond the barrier. He felt a little sorry for the man who was only trying to do his duty, but he also felt relieved that the expected boat must be running late. He had been keeping an eye on the entrance to the harbour in the murky light. Will noticed Mr Painter's eyes were focused on the same point and he didn't look as if he was planning on going anywhere.

Men on the quayside, who weren't shuffling their feet or stamping them, were pacing up and down. One standing next to Will pulled out a pocket watch. 'Almost ten to six. What's keeping them?'

Even as he spoke, Will saw the prow of a small ship nudge round the harbour wall opposite the lighthouse. It chugged its way over to the quayside and willing hands caught the mooring ropes. No sooner was she secure than the unloading began. Will watched as bale after bale, each about four-and-a-half feet in length was hauled up by the steam crane onto the quayside. He could see the muzzles of rifle barrels protruding at one end and the end of stocks at the other. Fascinated, he watched as scores of the heavy bales were manhandled onto the waiting trucks.

A raised voice behind him said, 'I've seen enough. You're all involved in illegal activity. My superiors will hear of this.'

Will spun round in time to see Mr Painter turn away from the bustling scene at the harbour. A man nearby grabbed at him. He shrugged him off. Another shoved him and he stumbled but managed to keep his feet. Two more lunged after him, but Will called out, 'Leave him be. Sure what can he do? The UVF have this all sewn up; no one's going to stop you.' Will eyed two of the RIC officers who were keeping well back and lifting not a finger to intervene.

Painter was allowed to hurry on his way. He got about a dozen yards before he stopped. Will saw him seem to lean forwards and bring his arms up across his chest. He stumbled and then collapsed on the road. Dillon sprinted after him and dropped to his knees beside the prone coastguard. A crowd gathered around them as he tried to find a pulse.

'Is there a doctor here? Quick! This man needs help.' Will's eyes scanned the crowd and saw an older man push forward.

'I'm a doctor. Stand back.'

Will made way for the medic to examine Mr Painter where he lay on the ground. Behind them, on the quayside, hundreds of bales were being quietly and efficiently transferred to land vehicles; thousands of rifles, as George Gibson had predicted, would soon be smuggled away to all parts of County Down. A highly successful night's work.

The Doctor looked up and said, 'He's suffered a massive heart attack. This man is dead.'

Chapter 4

Will could still remember, two years later, the look on the doctor's face as he pronounced the coastguard dead. With a slight shudder, he brought his mind back to the present and to his uninvited guest seated in the shadows of his parlour. Without getting up from the table, or turning round, he said, in response to his remark, 'I was hoping never to cross paths with you again, Mr Boyd.'

He raised his glass to his lips and took a gulp of the stale Guinness, as all these past events flashed through his mind . He had run into George Gibson again at The Railway Arms on the Saturday evening. The Worshipful Master bought him a pint and couldn't hold back from talking about the tremendous success of the UVF exercise. The whole thing had been meticulously planned from start to finish, no detail overlooked and everything had gone without a hitch. Will had to admit, it did seem an amazing achievement. According to George a total of 216 tons of guns and ammunition had been landed at Larne, Belfast, Bangor and The Dee and all were distributed safely to hiding places around the province. The UVF, George said, were now the proud owners of 11,000 Mannlicher rifles, 9,000 ex-German Army Mauser rifles, 4,600 Italian Vetterli-Vitali rifles and five million rounds of ammunition.

Aye, an amazing achievement, right enough. Will gave another involuntary shudder in the dim glow of the electric light bulb in his parlour at the thought of all that fire power. He slowly turned to face the man who had persuaded him to play a part in its acquisition.

Ignoring Will's comment, Edmond Boyd said, 'We were very pleased with the assistance you provided back in the April of '14, Mr Dillon. Very pleased, indeed. With the help of men like yourself and the entire membership of the Ulster Volunteer Force, Operation Lion went entirely to plan. Since then, the UVF have been armed and ready to defend our country, and not a drop of blood was shed in the doing of it. We can all be proud of what was achieved that night.'

'Aye, no blood. That must have been a great consolation to Mrs Painter and her two weans.'

'Who? Ah – yes. I heard about the coastguard. Very regrettable, but we can't be held responsible for a man having a weak heart, now can we?'

Will jumped to his feet and his chair tipped over, He took two steps across the room and stood in front of his uninvited guest. Edmond sat bolt upright. His eyes narrowed and for once his spectacles remained where they had slipped down the bridge of his nose. His right hand moved towards the pocket of the overcoat he was still wearing.

'Regrettable!' Will's face was red. 'I'll give you regrettable.'

Will's hands lunged forward and grasped Boyd's lapels, but with a swift, easy motion the Belfast man produced a revolver from his pocket and Will's midriff felt the prod of its muzzle.

'Back off, Dillon. No need for violence.'

Will released his grip on the man and started to straighten up. But his right arm plummeted and the straight edge of his hand chopped hard on Boyd's wrist. The gun clattered to the floor and Will kicked it out of reach.

'Well, we won't be needing that then, will we?' he said. 'I'll thank you to get out of my house. It's been a long day; I'm going to bed.'

Edmond Boyd rose. 'Indeed it has and I apologise for intruding at this late hour. But it is imperative that we two should not be seen together, because of the nature of what we have to discuss.'

'We have nothing to discuss, but I'm more than happy never to be seen together with you. Now will you please leave?'

'I will. I will. It was just… George and I have been discussing… certain matters, late into the evening and it seemed the ideal opportunity when I left him to pop round here to sound you out. We'd seen your green flare earlier from George's bay window so we figured you ought to be back about now.'

'George? George Gibson?'

'The very same.'

Will had a great respect for the Worshipful Master of his Orange Lodge. George was a good friend. If he was somehow involved, perhaps

Will ought at least to hear what it was about – and then he could throw Boyd out.

'What's George got to do with this?' he asked. He couldn't imagine what his old friend and this… this *gentleman* had to talk about into the wee hours that might involve himself.

'Our mutual friend, as you know is much revered within the Orange Order and The Royal Arch Purple. He has for some time been privy to the thoughts and plans of a group of powerful individuals that includes myself and certain other… captains of industry, senior clergymen, politicians and professional men – all with the best interests of a protestant Ulster at heart. An interest which we believe you share, Mr Dillon.'

'My belief in Protestantism is as staunch as the next man's, but – '

Boyd interrupted, 'But are you prepared to take action to defend our rights to live in a protestant country? If Home Rule ever becomes law, for example? Our northern, protestant counties would be swamped by a catholic government. Would you stand for that?'

Will hesitated, 'I… well, I wouldn't like it. I'd – '

'You'd what? Join us in taking a stand against such a violation of our religious freedom?'

'Aye. I'd play my part.'

'You're a good man, Will – if I may call you that.' Boyd continued without waiting for confirmation, 'But what if I were to tell you that there are certain elements in Dublin who are plotting to bypass Home Rule altogether and make a clean break from Britain? Men who will stop at nothing – bloodshed, betrayal, mayhem – whatever it takes to establish Ireland as an independent Catholic state.'

'I'd say you and oul George have been knocking back too many Bushmills between yous, tonight. Who are these men? When are they going to do this?'

'We're not sure who. And we've no idea about the timing of any uprising.' Boyd paused. 'That's why we want you to move down to Dublin and keep your ear to the ground. Try to get close to some of the leaders. There are so many groups: the Gaelic League, the Irish Citizens' Army, the supposedly secret Irish Brotherhood, Irish Volunteers – you name it…'

'And the leaders of these groups are planning a rebellion?' Will asked.

'Maybe, maybe not. Maybe the leaders, maybe others. That's what we want you to find out before the British are caught napping. Over the next few months we would like you to talk to anyone and everyone. If anything's going to happen it'll likely be in the summer. Maybe June. Although there's precedent for August, of course –'

Will nodded. 'The '98. The United Irishmen.'

Boyd adjusted his spectacles and Will thought he detected a glint in his eyes as the man continued, 'George tells me you are descended from a certain Jamie Dillon who lived back then? I believe, at great cost to his own standing amongst his neighbours, he provided vital information to help the British army put down that rebellion.'[2]

'He was my great-great-grandfather.'

'Well, there you are. Isn't it in your blood? Find out if they *are* planning a rising, and if so, when? Could you do that for us, Will? For your country? To protect your protestant heritage?'

* * *

'Ah, it was a tragedy, indeed. A tragedy,' said George.

Will had called to see his friend, George Gibson, the next day, following his encounter with Edmond Boyd. He remained silent, sipping his whiskey and soda. From the wide bay window he could just distinguish the ghostly outline of Big Copeland through a late wintry mist and across a grey sea of white horses. In his inner eye he sees the sunshine from two summers ago and Annie, skipping and dancing over the heather, laughing and calling him to catch up as they wander over the island. He draws level with her and catches her around the waist. They have been walking out for a few months, having met the previous Christmas. Now in the beauty and seclusion of the island they glory in their first kiss, before gazing down, arm in arm, on the north beach where seals bask on the warm rocks and mewling terns are silhouetted against the blueness of the sky above.

'A lovely lass. Lovely.'

George Gibson's comment broke into Will's reverie and his lovely lass melts from his vision, but only to reform beneath the mistletoe at the party at her parents' home six months later. By that time Will is quite sure she is the one. She yields willingly to his embrace and allows him to steal a Christmas kiss. He pulls the ring from his pocket and, on one

[2] Read an account of Jamie Dillon's exploits in *Betsy Gray – a Tale of Ninety-eight* by W. G. Lyttle, re-published in 2015 by Books Ulster, ISBN 978-1-910375-21-1

knee, offers himself to her with the seal of the solitaire set in its golden band.

The whiskey burned the back of his throat as he sat in George's bay window and knew again for a fleeting moment the euphoric feeling of a shared, unbounded happiness; the totality of being in love and planning for their wedding and their future.

A long engagement is expected, a year at least, which would take them to Christmas, but Annie sets her heart on a spring wedding. So they set the date for their big day for Monday, 24th of April, 1916.

Will sipped his drink. Easter Monday. We were to be married next month. A dark shadow fell on him as it so often did in recent weeks.

He drained his glass. 'I wouldnae mind a refill, if that's all right, George.'

'Certainly.' His host reached for the decanter and replenished his tumbler. 'They haven't caught the driver, have they?'

'They haven't, no.'

It was early last January, two weeks after celebrating the anniversary of their engagement. Will recalls the ice around the edge of the pond as they walk, arm in arm, through Ward Park; Annie throwing breadcrumbs to the ducks confined to the middle of the water; the delicate curve of her neck and the little black curls that caress it; the dark clouds threatening snow; trees, still skeletal, held in winter's grip; her hand now in his as they stroll on; the feel of his ring upon her finger; the dog that has slipped its leash, frolicking past them as they are leaving the park; stopping on the pavement and looking back at the peacock that has chosen this moment to raise his magnificent fan of tail feathers as though to wave them goodbye; the sickening squeal of brakes behind them, the yelping of the dog and the slithering of tyres on an icy road as the green Crossley 15 mounts the pavement; Annie snatched from his hand and thrown to the ground.

Will drops to her side where she lies still, a dark stain spreading beneath her head. 'Help us,' he cries, as he finds a weak pulse. He looks over his shoulder where the open topped motorcar has come to a stop at a crazy angle half on the pavement, half on the road. The dog is running off, seemingly none the worse. The driver, large and bulky and wearing a chauffeur's hat, bears a look of horror, his gaze fixed on the girl he has hit. But Will's pleading look is directed to the man seated behind him, whose supercilious features survey the scene with a look of mild annoyance.

'She needs the hospital,' Will calls out. 'Quick. Help me lift her into your motorcar.'

For a moment the man in the back seat continues to stare, a coldness in his eyes, a look of complete indifference. The man's head turns to address his chauffeur and Will notices a livid scar snake down from the top of his left cheekbone to his jaw.

'Drive on, man; I'm already late. And pay more attention to the road.'

Astounded, Will shouts, 'Wait! Stop. We must take my fiancée to hospital straight away. You can't just leave us.'

In George's front room Will spoke again to his friend, 'I dinnae hold the driver to blame, but. Not fully. It was an accident. Just one of those things. Swerving on an icy road to avoid a stupid mongrel. It was the bastard who owned the motorcar, who refused to take Annie to the hospital. He could have saved her. They said that – if she'd been treated sooner. But we couldnae get her there in time.'

Holding his sweetheart's cold hand in his, Will gazes at the receding Crossley. Passers-by are offering assistance. Local residents come out to help. One of them rushes off to where his own vehicle is parked on a side road and finally Annie is driven to Bangor hospital.

Too late.

Will keeps seeing those dark, uncaring eyes in the face of the man in the back seat of the Crossley. He'll know him again, the Crossley man can be sure of that. He pictures the receding motorcar and tries to recall the vehicle registration number. He sees IK followed by three digits. Was the last one a 3?

'Ah, a sad business, Will,' said George. 'A sad business and no mistake. It's why I think you need a break. Get away from North Down for a while. Even if you don't feel you can take on the job we have for you, you should still get away. You need a complete change in order to forget –'

'I'll never forget her!'

'No, no. I didn't mean forget Annie. Of course not. But you need to put the trauma of losing her behind you. Forget the pain. Remember the good times.'

It was over two months since Annie's funeral but he still couldn't accept she was gone. He gulped down more whiskey. Was George right? Change of scenery. Is that what Will needed? He was dreading Easter. Annie's parents had booked Bangor's Royal Ulster Yacht Club, the perfect venue for the big Easter wedding reception. Cancelled now. It doesn't matter. Nothing matters. Not anymore. Maybe he did need something to take his mind off… the emptiness. The void that ached, like an amputee who could still feel pain in the limb he no longer owned.

He had no particular desire to oblige Boyd but George had explained to him more thoroughly what they wanted and he had no qualms about helping out his old friend. Could this clandestine job for Boyd and his shadowy group be just the thing to occupy his mind? He supposed it might. But he would never forget Annie.

And he would never forget the face of the brute who drove off, leaving her to die.

So, a move to Dublin? Will allowed himself a grim smile. Why not? He recalled once more the green Crossley 15 with its IK registration – and the fact that IK numbers were only issued to motorcars sold in the Irish capital.

Chapter 5

It was the exquisite art work and calligraphy. It was the beautiful colours and penmanship. But even more, it was the centuries of history encapsulated in the vellum pages displayed before him that left Will Dillon awed and in wonder at the ancient skills and dedication of the monks of Colum Cille, or St Columba, as he became known. Will read that they had laboured for years on the island of Iona off the west coast of Scotland to produce this work of love and art. Then, to protect it from raiding Vikings, they transported it to the Abbey at Kells to finish the illuminated text of the four Gospels based on the Latin Vulgate. Since the mid-nineteenth century this, now world-famous Book of Kells has been on display within the hallowed sanctuary of Trinity College in Dublin.

Will stepped back from admiring the volume, thinking how much Annie would have loved to have seen it and he felt a renewed pang of heartache, not for the first time since moving south. He started to retrace his steps across the cobbled Library Square overlooked by the imposing Portland stonework of the university buildings. From a plaque, Will had just learned that this was one of the oldest universities in Europe, founded by Queen Elizabeth I to further the education of Ireland's protestant youth.

Suitably impressed, he pulled his coat tighter as a weak spring sun ducked behind a growing bank of cumulus. He headed back out to College Green and Westmoreland Street, making for O'Connell Bridge. He had been in Dublin for less than a week and the width of this crossing over the Liffey still amazed him each time he saw it. His new boss at the General Post Office assured him that the 48 yards long bridge was fully

54 yards wide – the only bridge in Europe that was wider than its length. Will wondered why its designers thought that such a wide crossing would ever be needed. As he strode over it now he was accompanied only by a solitary motor vehicle – a two-seater Swift – along with a few horses and carts and a number of cyclists. His fellow pedestrians that included a couple of officers of the Royal Irish Constabulary, were the majority users.

The bridge was as broad as Sackville Street (O'Connell Street) that it fed into, which was where Will was returning, his lunch hour almost over. He strolled past the windows of Cleary's big department store, admiring the gaiety of their spring displays, and then crossed towards the towering columns of the GPO's imposing façade.

'Would you be after buying a lovely bunch of daffodillies, Mister?'

He was passing by the great plinth of Nelson's Pillar in the centre of the street. From a little group of dishevelled flower girls congregating there, one stepped forward with her basket of blooms, hoping to earn a few pennies. A curl of black hair caressing her neck reminded him a little of Annie. Will gave her a thrupenny bit but declined the flowers.

He wondered for a moment whether she might have been the inspiration for the local writer, Bernard Shaw's play that had opened in London a few years ago. Well – her mother, maybe, before Shaw moved to London as a young man. Will could remember reading the reviews at the time. Shaw's story was all about a young London flower girl learning to talk like a lady. He raised his eyes from the flower basket and craned his neck to glance up at the figure of the English admiral that dominated the Irish capital's fine shopping thoroughfare.

'A fine monument, is it not?' he remarked to a man crossing the street beside him.

'A fine *English* monument. He'll be the first to go, come the revolution.'

The man had a distinctive Dublin brogue and Will turned to see he was about his own age and half a head shorter. A little startled at this openly declared observation, particularly in the light of the approach of another pair of the RIC's finest – though perhaps still just out of earshot, he nevertheless laughed and said, 'I dare say you could be right about that.'

'Oh aye,' came the reply, and then, 'You're not from Dublin.'

'That I'm not. I'm a County Down man.'

‘Thought I detected a northern twang. Here for your Easter holidays, is it?’ The shorter man matched his stride to Will’s as they both continued across to the opposite pavement.

‘Ah, it’s no holiday, I’m afraid. I’ve just moved here with my job. I work for the Post Office,’ Will nodded towards the fluted Ionic columns, ‘and I must get back in; my lunch hour is up. Nice talking to you.’ He stepped towards the great portico entrance.

‘Sure, aren’t I headed there myself? I’ve got to send a telegram and me without a shadow of an idea on how to go about it. Maybe I could ask you to help me?’

Will stood back and allowed his new acquaintance to enter in front of him. ‘Certainly you may. That’s my job. Telegraphic communications, they call it. Come over to the counter while I go round behind.’

Apparently it had been a simple task for one of Edmond Boyd’s highly-placed Shadows, as Will had come to think of them, to arrange a transfer for Dillon to the Dublin GPO’s telegraphic staff. It was a front office, clerical position, but they agreed to top up his pay to the level he was on before, plus 20% and added living expenses. He was not going to be out of pocket, they assured him.

He found himself some respectable lodgings at the good end of Mary’s Lane within easy walking distance of Sackville Street which lay to the east. Further west, Mary’s Lane ran into one of the run-down parts of Dublin. Dillon had been astonished to learn, from a piece he read in the Irish Times, that it contained old and dilapidated tenements where hundreds of families lived in one room each. And such squalor was not unique to this area just north of the magnificent Four Courts on the river. The article was commenting on a report about Dublin housing that claimed no less than 28,000 Dubliners were living in dwellings condemned by the Corporation as unfit for human habitation. Dublin, for all its architectural heritage of fine buildings, could make the shameful boast of having the worst slums in the whole of the United Kingdom of Great Britain and Ireland.

Will knew that it was this, together with having the lowest wages and higher rents than in the rest of the UK that resulted in the Irish Transport and General Workers Union organising a series of protests for better conditions and wages a few years back. It had led to the infamous lock-out by employers when police were particularly brutal in dealing with the protesting workers. Men, women and children were felled by police baton charges and beaten where they lay on the street. Hundreds were admitted to hospital. Some strikers died at the hands of the Dublin Metropolitan Police. It was to protect the workers from further assaults that the ITGWU founder and leader, "Big Jim" Larkin, ably abetted by the outspoken union activist, James Connolly, felt obliged to form an Irish Citizens' Army. For the employers, though, the lock-out had the desired effect and after a few months of near starvation, groups of workers started drifting back to work with nothing to show for the stand they had taken.

The Citizens' Army, however, remained and on Will's second evening in the capital when he was walking by the Liffey opposite Liberty Hall, the ITGWU's headquarters, he was intrigued to see a squad of men being drilled outside its frontage. Many bore rifles but some shouldered what Will was pretty sure were hurleys. They were observed by a small group of uniformed RIC officers who made no attempt to intervene.

'What's going on over there?' Will asked another passer-by who had likewise paused to watch.

'That's Connolly's Citizens' Army boys. You often see them out training.'

'With hurley sticks?'

'Tipperary rifles, they call them,' the man laughed. 'Sure it does them till they all get the real thing.'

Will chuckled. 'I always said hurling is a ferocious game.' But he was thinking back a couple of years to the landing of many thousands of guns up north for the UVF and asked, 'Did I not hear that the best part of a thousand guns were smuggled in through Howth some time ago?'

'Oh, you heard right, sure enough. But those were for the Irish Volunteers. That's not these boys – at least not many of them.'

'I don't follow you.'

'Aye, well they say that some Volunteers signed up for the Citizens' Army, too, to keep an eye on what Connolly is up to. But sure I don't know if that's a fact. It's just what I heard.'

Will was thinking of Connolly's army and the Volunteers as he handed a telegram form to the short man with big plans for the future of Nelson's Pillar. He explained how to fill in the form and how it was charged.

'Well, you make it all sound very simple. Thank you. I feel a bit of an eejit, not knowing how to send a telegram.'

‘Well, if you’ve never had to send one before there’s no reason why you should.’

‘No, you’re right there. Indeed there isn’t. And if that crazy cousin of mine hadn’t upped sticks and taken himself across the water to find fame and fortune and then fallen in love with an English lass I wouldn’t be having to send one now. It’s his wedding tomorrow.’

‘So it’s a greetings telegram, is it?’

‘It is, aye. With all them German U-boats patrolling the Irish Sea none of the family felt inclined to turn up in person.’

Will wasn’t sure about any threat of U-boats in the Irish Sea, but he could understand the man’s reluctance to risk it. The message was duly completed, the words counted and the appropriate charge passed over the counter. Will noticed the sender’s name and said, ‘Right ho, Mr Doloughan. I’ll get that sent off straight away.’

‘Oh, call me Ryan. Mr Doloughan was me old man! I’m very grateful to you for helping me – er…?’

‘Dillon. Will Dillon.’ He reached out his hand and Ryan Doloughan shook it rather like a terrier might shake a rat to break its neck.

Before letting go, Doloughan said, ‘Listen, Will, you say you’re just arrived in Dublin?’

Retrieving his fingers back to the safe side of the counter, Will said ‘This is my first week; started Monday.’

‘Well it’s Thursday, now. Have you any plans? We’ve got a ceilidh on at the League, tonight.’

‘League?’

‘The Gaelic League.’

‘Oh yes, of course. And they’re holding a dance? I thought they were all about encouraging the use of Irish in schools.’

‘Not just in schools; in literature and all over the place. But we also promote Irish culture, generally. We hold ceilidhs and concerts, too, from time to time. Would you like to come tonight? Meet a few people. Let your hair down.’

‘Sounds grand – Ryan. I don’t have anything else planned. Perhaps I’ll take you up on that.’

Which was why, later that evening, Will found himself on a tram heading west. The address Ryan Doloughan had given him was out near Phoenix Park and, following his new friend’s directions, he found the hall easily enough. The ceilidh band was already in full swing and a crowd of dancers were cavorting around the floor. Will immediately thought of the last dance he had attended. It was on New Year's Eve. With Annie.

He paused inside the entrance. This was a mistake. He shouldn't have come. The pang of heartache he had felt earlier in the day had returned. He hesitated as a very pretty girl approached him to take his coat. He turned back towards the door.

'Eh, I'm not… Sorry, er… I've got to…'

'Will Dillon! The man himself.' Ryan Doloughan seemed to appear from nowhere and grabbed his hand to give it the frenzied terrier treatment. 'This is the man I was telling you about, Maeve. Helped me out this afternoon. There's not a thing he doesn't know about telegrams. If you ever want to send one – he's your man. I can't recommend him highly enough. Will, this is my little sister, Maeve. Maeve, meet Will Dillon.'

'I'm pleased to make your acquaintance, Mr Dillon. Let me take your coat. Ryan, I do wish you would stop calling me your little sister; I'm a grown woman.'

In spite of his earlier misgivings, Will allowed Maeve to help him out of his coat and, handing her his hat, he heard himself reply, 'And grown in all the right places, too, I can see.'

Maeve blushed scarlet. 'Mr Dillon!'

'Will, please. Call me Will. May I call you Maeve?'

The girl recovered her composure and gave a brief curtsey. 'You may – so long as you promise to behave like a gentleman. And partner me in the next dance.'

The band was striking up again with The Gay Gordons and Will found himself being led by the hand onto the dance floor by Ryan's "little sister." Her russet hair hung in a fringe across her broad forehead and in flicks on each rosy cheek. Wide-eyed and full-lipped with a slim body, she looked every inch the grown woman she claimed to be. Will reckoned he probably had four or five years on her.

She was quite unlike his black-haired Annie, whose pale complexion and fuller build still haunted Will's inner thoughts. Perhaps because Maeve was so different – not really the type that would normally attract him – Will didn't feel any guilt in the enjoyment he got from dancing with her. He delighted in a number of turns around the floor with Ryan's pretty sister over the course of the evening and felt no sense of betraying his love for Annie. This mild diversion was just that – a bit of fun.

A bit of fun, he thought, in a rare moment when he was sitting down to catch his breath. It dawned upon him that it was the first time since the terrible accident three months ago that he could honestly claim to be having fun.

'Having fun, Will?' Ryan plonked himself down on the next chair, breathing heavily.

'Indeed I am. It was good of you to invite me. Just what I needed.'

'Ah, that's what I like to hear. Have you moved permanently to Dublin, then, or is the Post Office just a temporary transfer?'

Will paused before answering. 'Well, I guess it's permanent enough – for as long as I want it to be. I can always transfer back up north if I dinnae like it here.'

'Sure what's not to like about Dublin? You've the dance and the music, the Guinness and the crack. What more could a man want?'

'Aye, if it's all like tonight, I'd think seriously of staying on. One thing I've noticed, though, there seem to be a lot more police around than at home.'

'Ah, sure enough. That's 'coz of the Volunteers and the Citizens' Army. The RIC like to show they're still in charge. Not that they interfere much with the exercises these big groups carry out. It's the smaller ones like the Gaelic Brothers and Force Erin and the like – gangs of thugs, mostly. Jumping on the bandwagon to give a legitimacy to their thieving and robbing.'

'How can thieving be legitimate?' Will thought it was a fair question.

'"Contributing to the Cause" they call it. "Patriotic duty." If people don't care to contribute they get beaten up and still end up lining the coffers of the thugs, as well.'

'Is there a lot of that going on, then?'

'Ah, a fair amount. But the Peelers keep on top of it in the city centre. You're quite safe, Will. I've seen them up our way sometimes.

'And where's that?' Will asked

'We're out here near Phoenix Park.'

'We?'

'Maeve and me. We lost our elder brother and then Father died a few years back. So we both live in the ancestral home to keep an eye on our old mam.'

'Oh, sorry about your loss. It sounds very grand, though.'

'Ah, sure I'm only kidding. It's just a house in a row of other houses, in an area that's none too salubrious.'

'Because of the gangs of thugs?'

'Aye, but enough of this sort of talk. We're here to enjoy ourselves. A drink?'

'Sure. I could do with wetting my whistle.'

Ryan hopped up and without waiting for Will headed for the bar. By the time Will got there Ryan was ordering a lemonade. 'What'll you have?' he asked. This is a Temperance Hall so it's all soft drinks, I'm afraid, but they're cool and refreshing.'

'Same as you, then,' said Will. 'Thanks.'

The barmaid handed him his tumbler of brown lemonade and Ryan nodded towards the far end of the bar.

'See those two?'

Will glanced down the bar.

'The one with the moustache like a bedraggled ferret is the president of the Gaelic League and the gentleman he's talking to, with the glasses, is the League's co-founder. Come on, I'll introduce you.'

They took their drinks and moved along to where the older men were conversing.

'Mr Hyde,' said Ryan, 'May I present Will Dillon, a friend of mine from the North.'

Will shook the proffered hand.

'Douglas Hyde. A pleasure to meet you, Dillon.' The ferret on the man's upper lip seemed to come alive. 'Are you a League member?'

'Not yet, sir,' said Will. 'I must say I am no linguist. I find the Irish tongue quite impossible, but I love all things Irish and am all for promoting the culture; even the folk culture, like tonight.'

'Good man, yourself. It's not just about our beautiful language (though you really should try to master it), but our literary and cultural heritage, too. We shall hope to look forward to welcoming you among our number soon. Isn't that right, Eoin? Eoin MacNeill. This is Doloughan's friend, Dillon.'

As he, in turn, shook hands, MacNeill said, 'Indeed. We would be pleased to welcome you as a member. We live in exciting times, Mr Dillon. We do have our cultural past to preserve, but we also have some of the finest contemporary writers and poets in the world.'

'That we have,' said Will, 'but they follow in a grand tradition. Haven't we always produced great writers? Wasn't it the sixth century when our monasteries were spreading light and learning throughout Ireland and Great Britain?'

'Aye, and even into Europe. They were indeed. A land of saints and scholars. Will you have another drink, Mr Dillon? What'll it be? ... Mr Doloughan?'

Will and his new friend accepted refills from Eoin MacNeill who, Ryan told him later, was Professor of Early and Medieval History at University College Dublin. Ryan took a sip of his drink and said, 'You'd go a long way to better the likes of Swift or Goldsmith, or Maria Edgeworth.'

'Bram Stoker,' said Will, 'or Oscar Wilde.'

'A rich heritage we have, surely,' said Hyde.

MacNeill said, 'But those great Irish legends are all dead now, God rest their souls. What about the today's writers? Shaw, Edith Somerville, Joyce, Yeats...?'

'Ah yes, Mr MacNeill, I do like Yeats,' said Will. 'I have an anthology of his, "The Green Helmet and Other Poems".' *With much affection, Annie*. Will's face clouded, but MacNeill was speaking again:

'Have you, now? Yes, Willie is another great writer and good friend, too. As a matter of fact he's reading some of his latest stuff at a little soirée on Saturday evening. I'd be happy to take you along as my guest, if you'd like to meet him.'

'Would you? That would be grand,' said Will.

'You too, Mr Doloughan, and bring that pretty sister of yours.'

Ryan said, 'That's very kind of you, Mr MacNeill. I'm not sure that we should impose upon your – '

'Nonsense, Mr Doloughan. You and Miss Doloughan do a splendid job in helping run this Gaelic League branch. I'd be honoured to have you as my guests.'

So it was that when Will finally left the ceilidh after thoroughly enjoying the evening and a few more dances with Maeve, he agreed to meet up again with Ryan and MacNeill on Saturday.

On stepping outside the Temperance Hall he saw that the threatening rain clouds of the afternoon had dispersed and the evening had turned quite mild. He decided not to wait for a tram and started walking back to his digs. It was some distance but he made his way down to the Liffey and enjoyed strolling along Albert Quay (Wolfe Tone Quay) listening to the lapping of the water against the side. Reflected lights from buildings opposite shimmered on the surface in contrast to the shadowy hulks of nearby moored barges. Even at this time of night Will heard the occasional quack of an insomniac duck or the squawk of a moody moorhen.

He nodded and wished a pleasant, 'Good evening,' to the few people he passed on the quay. Most gave a friendly response, though two police constables stared straight ahead and continued their beat in silence.

Just before he reached the Four Courts he turned away from the river and made his way up Church Street towards Mary's Lane. As he crossed Chancery Street he noticed the change in the state of the buildings. He'd left behind the modern, well-maintained premises bordering the river and moved into the slum area. Rendering was falling from walls and paint peeled from doors and window frames, many with broken panes. Litter strewed the pavements and gutters. He passed a row of houses where one had collapsed from neglect and the rubble was left like a festering gum between two rotting teeth.

It was a depressing place and Will quickened his step as he turned into Mary's Lane. He had only gone a few yards when a young woman standing in the shadows of an alleyway stepped out.

'Fancy a good time, dearie?'

She allowed her coat to hang open to reveal that her blouse, too, was unbuttoned. She was a skinny girl but whatever form of corsetry she wore contrived to push up and display a considerable portion of her small breasts.

Will took this in at a glance and, mumbling a 'No thank you,' kept walking. But she caught his arm and said, 'Please, mister. Only five bob.'

Only? thought Dillon. Rather than simply wrench his arm free from her grip he stopped and turned to look at her again. She might have been pretty once, but her face was drawn and scrawny, her wispy hair unkempt. Will guessed she was probably about the same age as Maeve but she looked older than he was. He lifted her hand off his arm and repeated, 'I said, no, thank you. Go on home to your bed.'

'I can't go home, mister. Not with no money, I can't. He'd kill me. Here, you can have a nice feel for half-a-crown?' She lifted her skirts up from mid-calf to reveal two bony knees and white thighs. She wore no undergarments.

'No! Stop this. Cover yourself, woman.' Will hesitated. 'Look,' he took out his purse and extracted four half-crowns, 'here's ten shillings. Take them and go home. Will you do that?' He could always claim it on expenses.

Her eyes lit up. 'Oh, thank you, sir. You're a gentleman. We can have a lovely time for that.' She moved closer.

Will stepped back. 'No, I said. You are to go home. You've got money, now. You'll be safe.'

The girl moved forward again and he felt her hand groping around his groin area.

'Stop it!' Will turned on his heel to find himself face to face with an ugly-looking ruffian in a dirty green rugby shirt. From the size of him he could easily have played prop forward for Ireland.

'This boyo causing you a problem, Elsie? Trying to get away without paying, is he?'

Elsie had shuffled right back into the alley and was saying nothing.

'Quite the contrary,' Will said and moved to step around the newcomer, only to find a second bloke, shorter but looking if anything, tougher than his companion, emerging from the alley to block his path.

'I'm sure yous dinnae want any trouble, lads.' Will made his voice maintain a quiet confidence.

'We're not the ones in trouble, boyo; that would be you. Pay the girl and you can go. A pound.'

'A pound!'

'The extra is a collection fee and count yourself lucky it's not more.'

'It's nae going to happen, lads,' said Will, shifting his weight onto his right leg.

'Oh, I think it will. There's two of us.'

'No there isnae. There's only you.'

Will's left foot shot out and landed a well-aimed kick just below the shorter guy's right kneecap. He let out a howl as his leg gave way and he collapsed on the pavement. Before Rugby Shirt could react, Will spun round bringing up his right elbow. He used his momentum to crash it against the side of the man's skull who staggered sideways. Will hammered his left fist into his solar plexus. His antagonist doubled up, gasping for breath. A final swift rabbit punch to the back of his neck saw him sprawling on the pavement next to his mate.

Will glanced around for the girl but couldn't see her. He hoped she wouldn't be in any trouble, but her two minders, or pimps or whatever they were had brought it on themselves. He walked on down Mary's Lane towards his lodgings. Those ruffians wouldn't be in any state to follow him; in fact the shorter one would be needing treatment for a dislocated kneecap.

Will had had a long day and he was grateful to sink into his bed. He'd already forgotten about his encounter with the two thugs. He thought about his "undercover" work and decided he had made an acceptable start. He'd established himself at the GPO, made a good impression and been accepted by the other staff. He was to work a four day week, Mondays to Thursdays. This was explained to be because of a weak heart, but in reality it would allow him more free time for any other activities that might prove necessary.

He'd picked up a bit about the Irish Citizens' Army and now he'd met up with Ryan Doloughan. He kept recalling the first thing that man said to him – about getting rid of Nelson, '*come the revolution.*' Ryan could prove to be a useful contact. He'd already introduced him to the leaders of the Gaelic League and he'd have the chance to cultivate his acquaintance with Eoin MacNeill on Saturday evening. And he'd met Maeve, Ryan's pretty little sister. He thought of Annie – and then he thought of the man responsible for her death. It irked him that he hadn't had a chance yet to make any progress on that front but he planned to start putting that to rights on his day off, tomorrow.

Chapter 6

Friday morning broke fair and the mildness of the previous evening persisted. The man, who was still wearing the dirty green rugby shirt, stood in front of a set of ornate, wrought iron gates. He was reluctant to go through them and it wasn't just because of his raging headache and the dull throb from the bruise on his right temple, but he pushed them open and approached the front steps of the big house. He was out of place in the posh South Dublin suburb with open paddocks separating the residences. He'd been before, of course, but always with Eamon. His friend may be a shorty but he was the one who took the lead. Rugby Shirt wasn't relishing having to report to the Boss on his own.

Mostly when he'd been here before it wasn't business. The Boss threw some great parties and all his underlings got invited. The drink flowed, the dance music played, the girls obliged. There were always girls – Eamon and he made sure of that. He remembered the mid-summer party last year. Dancing on the terrace by the big pool. All the girls in bathing suits. Long bare legs everywhere, including one particular pair, he recalled, that were wrapped around his own for a good part of the evening. In fact, wasn't she the one who left him for the Boss when he came out and then had the misfortune to tip her drink down the great man's shirt? It was just an unlucky chance that when he back-handed her, her head hit the side of the bathing pool as she fell in. Getting rid of the body was just one more job for him and Eamon. It had been a great party, though. He hoped for many more.

But today was business; business that Eamon would normally be doing. Rugby Shirt forced himself to rap using the ornate door knocker. The Boss's man showed him in. He knew the Boss liked to call Kelly his butler, but he was just another heavy like himself – his minder-cum-butler-cum-chauffeur.

'Wait in the library,' said Kelly, pushing open a door off the large hall and moving on, presumably to inform his master that he had a visitor.

Rugby Shirt stood awkwardly in front a huge oak fireplace. Above it, a splendid stag's head was mounted on a shield. Leather-bound volumes lined the room on wooden shelving that matched the fireplace and there was a carved oak desk, too. The sumptuous leather armchairs remained empty; he chose to stand.

His wait was brief. The door opened and the Boss strode in.

'Gregson! I was expecting Moore. Why are you here? Where's Moore?'

'I'm afraid Eamon has had a bit of an accident, sir.'

'Accident? What happened?'

'He's dislocated his knee. Had to go to hospital.'

The Boss made an annoyed click with his tongue, 'And in the meantime the prosperity of my housing empire and my,' his pause was only momentary, 'entertainment industry lies in your hands?'

Buster Gregson, as he was known, assured the Boss that all his business interests were quite safe. 'You can trust me and the lads, sir; sure you know they're safe with us.'

'I know what will happen to you if they're not, and I hope *you* know *that*.'

'I do indeed, sir. Don't you worry about a thing, sir.'

'Oh, I'm not worried. That's what I pay people like you to do. Anyway, you've brought last night's takings?'

'I have, sir,' he handed him a small leather bag; 'it's all there.'

The Boss stepped across and emptied its contents on the desk and said, 'Of course it's all there. You'd never walk out of here alive if it wasn't.'

Buster blanched and watched as the Boss counted the money.

'This is all we got? What are the little tarts doing – giving it away?'

'Business is slack, boss. There's a lot more police patrols around of late. Scares off the punters. And there's less of them about, too, what with all these Volunteers meetings and Citizens' Army and whatnot. Éamonn's brother Ewan's a Volunteer but I was never one for politics. These *Sinn Féiners* aren't doing our business any good at all.'

'You let me take care of politics. Your job is to see that the girls pull their weight. Don't I house them, clothe them and feed them. What do they think I am – a charity? Tell the slackers to smarten up their act or they'll be out. And I mean permanently. D'you hear me?'

'Boss.'

'And the same goes for you. What happened to your face? Was that something to do with Moore's "bit of an accident," too?'

Buster shuffled his feet. 'It was a punter. Didn't want to pay. We had to rough him up a bit.'

The Boss rarely laughed but he did now. 'You had to rough him up a bit and you end up with the mother of all shiners and Moore's in hospital! The guy's dead, I trust.'

'Not yet. We – '

'He's not! What, he walked away?'

'We know where he lives; I got Elsie to follow him.'

'Elsie. The little scrubber? Why didn't *you* follow him?'

'I was in no – I mean, I had to take Eamon to hospital, didn't I?'

The Boss sighed. 'All right, all right. So you know where he lives.'

'We do. Me and the lads will be waiting for him tonight.'

'Well make damned sure he can't walk away this time. He's costing me money, putting Moore in hospital.'

* * *

About the time Gregson was entering his master's mansion Will was eating a leisurely breakfast of eggs, bacon, sausages, fried tomato and mushrooms with fried bread and potato-bread. There were slices of hot buttered toasted wheaten farl and grapefruit marmalade to follow. He washed it all down with plenty of hot, sweet tea from an earthenware pot with its own hand-knitted cosy that sported a fully fashioned rooster's head and cockscomb. The matronly Mrs Rafferty liked to ensure her 'boys', as she called her lodgers, started the day with a nourishing Irish breakfast.

'More toast, Mr Dillon? And let me freshen that pot of tea.'

'Mrs Rafferty, you'll have me putting on the pounds. It's very tempting but I have an appointment to keep, so I'm going to have to say, "No". Thank you. That was grand.'

On leaving his digs Will turned right along Mary's Lane and continued into Mary Street. But instead of carrying on along Henry Street towards the GPO as he had done on the previous four mornings, he turned right again down Liffey Street, pausing to let a pony trot past pulling a jaunting car along Abbey Street. He paid the halfpenny toll and crossed the river by what was officially called the Liffey Bridge although the humped-back walkway was known to everyone in Dublin as the Ha'penny Bridge. Navigating the little streets in the Temple Bar area he headed towards Dublin Castle.

He strode past the striking pillared frontage of City Hall before turning down Cork Hill to Castle Street. Ignoring the entrance to the main forecourt of the castle he continued until he reached a smaller arch further on. An armed sentry asked him his business, and directed him across an open area to a green doorway set in a stone wall.

'I've come to see Mr Geoffrey Bradshaw,' Will told the clerk sitting at a reception desk inside.

'And you are?'

'Dillon. William James Dillon.'

The clerk checked a list that he took from a drawer and was apparently satisfied. He directed him up a flight of stairs. 'It's the third door on the right.'

A few minutes later Dillon was seated in a small room in front of a green metal desk. A framed portrait of King George V hung on a pale green plastered wall. A window behind the desk afforded a glimpse of City Hall but the only other feature in the room was a green metal waste paper basket that must have come as a job lot with the desk.

'So, Mr Dillon. It's good to meet you. You come highly recommended.' This, from the tall, austere figure who had risen to greet him as he entered and was now seated behind the desk. He spoke with a crisp Oxbridge accent.

'Oh well, I dinnae know what you've heard, Mr Bradshaw, but I wouldnae believe the half o' it.'

Edmond Boyd had supplied Will with Bradshaw's name and set up this initial meeting at the end of his first week on the job. Geoffrey Bradshaw was to be his contact to report whatever findings he came up with while he remained in Dublin. Ostensibly, Bradshaw worked as a Clerical Officer, Archives. This gave him access to all sorts of information held on the good citizens of Ireland, and on the not so good. He was a useful man to know and the 'Shadows' in Ulster had for some time been augmenting his remuneration in exchange for his keeping them informed of anything that he learned about certain activities amongst the republican elements and the more radical nationalists in the country.

Will's brief was to try to get close to some of these 'elements' and supply Bradshaw with insider knowledge which could be helpful to the English and which he would also pass on via the 'Shadows' in the North.

'How are you settling in, William? May I call you William?'

'It's Will, actually. Sure, by all means.'

'Fine, Will. Call me Geoff.

'So how do we do this?' Will had never been a "secret agent" before; he smiled at the concept.

'Just tell me if you pick up any interesting snippets – no matter how trivial they may seem – you'd be surprised how useful apparently irrelevant information can prove.'

'So I pop in here once a week with an update?'

'No. Not after this initial meeting. Can't risk your being spotted making regular visits to the Castle. Could compromise you with any new republican friends you might be cultivating. And don't wait for next Friday before you contact me again if you have something for me. The sooner it's passed on, the better.'

'Quite. So how will I – '

Bradshaw handed Will a card. 'When you want to see me call this number. I'm usually here; if I'm not leave a message with whoever answers. Just say, "There's a good show on at the Abbey tonight." Don't leave your name. I'll come and meet you in St Stephen's Green at 12:30 in the afternoon, or 6:30 in the evening, depending on when you contact me. Do you know the Green?'

'I know where it is. I havenae taken a walk in it, but,' said Will.

'Oh, you must; it's a delightful enclave in the heart of the busy city. There's a little humped-back bridge over a narrow part of the lake. We'll rendezvous there? Clear?'

'Perfectly. "There's a good show on at the theatre, tonight," 12:30 or 6:30 at the bridge, St Stephen's Green.'

'At the Abbey. Might as well stick to the script. Otherwise, fine. So – how has your first week been?'

'I met someone who's planning to blow up Nelson's Pillar, so I did.'

'You what!'

'Well, maybe not personally, but I'd certainly put him down as a republican sympathiser.' And Will went on to fill Geoff in about his new friend Ryan Doloughan and being introduced to Hyde and MacNeill at the Gaelic League. 'They seemed awful keen for me to join,' Will said.

'It mightn't be a bad idea to do just that. Eoin MacNeill may be passionate about preserving Irish culture but he is also responsible for establishing the Irish Volunteers. It's widely believed that he's their Chief of Staff and there are those who suspect the Gaelic League, whatever else it might be, is a fertile recruiting ground for the Volunteers. He'd be a good man to get to know.'

Will told him that's what he was planning to do. They were meeting tomorrow evening, in fact.

'Excellent, excellent.'

The two men talked some more until Bradshaw said, 'Fine, that will be all for now – unless you have any questions?'

'Just one more thing,' said Will. 'There's something I hope you can help me with.'

'Surely, what is it?'

'Car registration numbers. Are they issued from here?'

'Registration numbers? No, they're handled by my colleagues at City Hall?'

'Ah. Do you know if they keep a list of who is allocated which number?

'It wouldn't be "who". The numbers are allocated to vehicles – motorcars and trucks. What's this about, Will?'

'I don't want to say just at the moment. It may well be nothing. But I'd like to trace the owner of a particular motorcar. Might be a useful lead.'

'Right. Lead to what, if I may ask?'

'Rather not say more at present. I'll let you know if I find out anything. But it looks like you can't assist me, anyway.'

'Well, if you give me the number, I could ask a colleague at City Hall to find out what make of motorcar it was allocated to.' Bradshaw seemed to want to be helpful.

'That's just it. I know what make of motorcar it was, but I'm not sure about the number. It was IK followed by three digits. Pretty sure the last one was a 3.'

'IK something, something, three? That's not much. At least you know it's a local motorcar – from the IK. What make was it?'

'A Crossley 15. Green, open top.'

'Right. Can't be too many of those around. Shall I get my friend to draw you up a list of all the numbers allocated to Crossley 15s? Maybe you'll get lucky and there'll only be one ending in 3.'

'Hmm. Not too likely. But that would be a start. Thank you.'

'What you really need to do is go round the dealerships. They keep their own records. More than likely they'll have the new owners' names against the make of motorcar and registration. But first, you'd need the number. I should imagine it will take a while to go through all the card indexes and copy out every Crossley 15.'

'Are they not filed alphabetically?'

'With all the Crossley's together? 'I'm pretty sure they're not. That would be too easy. I believe they are in alpha-numerical order. Of registrations. Pop in on your lunch break on Monday and I'll have the list for you.'

Will didn't want to waste the weekend. 'Or...,' he said, 'If you could arrange it, I could go through the records myself and save your colleague having to spend time on it. I don't mind doing it if you can provide me with the necessary introductions.'

Bradshaw had been told to afford Dillon every assistance and that he was completely trustworthy. So with barely a hesitation he offered to walk Will over to City Hall right away and arrange for him to have access to the appropriate records.

The pillars in front of the Dublin Corporation's headquarters reminded Will very much of the GPO building, but ornate as the GPO's interior was, it had nothing to approach the splendour inside City Hall. The great circular rotunda with twelve massive pillars supporting a gilded dome must have been spectacular when originally built as the Royal Exchange by rich merchants in the late eighteenth century. But when it became the municipal building in 1852 office partitioning was installed which to Will's mind ruined the impact of the original design.

Bradshaw found the right clerk, a local government officer called Seán Connolly, and explained what Will needed. He then left them as the officer led Will down a corridor to a large room that was lined with packed shelving and had double rows of filing cabinets down the middle. A musty odour of old documents and papers hung in the air like the cheap cologne of an elderly aunt. There was a big mahogany table at one end with a couple of chairs and a bright electric light over it, which was essential as the way the Corporation had partitioned the building had left the room with no natural light. The clerk showed Will the card index boxes and quickly checked through them until he found the IKs. There were three boxes of them, all stuffed with cards. The two men carried them to the table and Will sat down to start his search.

'Take as long as you need, Mr Dillon. I'll be in my office next door if you need anything,' said the clerk, looking relieved to be stepping out from the stuffy archive room into the fresh air of the corridor.

In the event it took Will two and a half hours, but at the end of that time he was confident that he had a list of every Crossley 15 with an IK number plate. He thanked Seán Connolly as he left and then made his way back over to Temple Bar to get some lunch in one of the little cafés there. As he munched on a cheese and pickle sandwich he studied the list of numbers which he'd written down in columns. With a pencil he underlined the ones ending in 3.

IK 20	IK 111	IK 148	IK 185	IK 215
IK 31	IK 112	IK 153	IK 189	IK 222
IK 65	IK 113	IK 172	IK 196	IK 223
IK 91	IK 114	IK 179	IK 197	IK 237
IK 92	IK 122	IK 183	IK 200	IK 258
IK 93	IK 143	IK 184	IK 206	

He was pretty sure the number on the motorcar that killed Annie had had three digits but he thought he better include IK 93 to be safe; he was just glad the Crossley 15 was a fairly new model and there weren't that many on his list – 29, of which he was probably only interested in five or six. That was manageable.

Before they left Dublin Castle Geoffrey Bradshaw had looked up the addresses of Dublin motorcar showrooms that were likely to be selling Crossleys. It turned out there was only one main dealer with the Crossley franchise, so Will hoped he would strike lucky at Munster's New and Used Motorcars.

He found a little second-hand shop on Grafton Street and bought a cheap attaché case and then, in a newsagent's, purchased a small selection of the thickest magazines on their shelves. With these safely locked in the case he re-crossed the Liffey and caught a tram by Nelson's Pillar that said "Rathmines" on the front. This took him south over the river again and across the canal by Portobello Bridge. The tram went right past Portobello Barracks where Will was surprised at the amount of activity going on. A platoon of soldiers was being drilled by a fearsome-looking sergeant-major, while others were hurrying this way and that on their various errands. Heavily armed sentries guarded the gates. Expecting trouble? Will wondered where it was likely to come from, if it did. He turned his thoughts back to the matter in hand and shortly afterwards he spotted Munster's coming up on the left. He stayed on the tram, still keeping a sharp lookout as it drove on.

As he had hoped, he soon spotted what he wanted and hopped off the tram opposite another used motorcar lot under a banner that read, "Mick's Motors." He crossed over and was struck at once with the smell of oil and a faint odour of petrol fumes. Will didn't find this disagreeable; it reminded him of the *William and Laura* with her newfangled engine. This, in turn, reminded him of the life he had left behind in Donaghadee – at least temporarily. His thoughts were of Annie, who he should have been marrying on Monday-week, as he pretended to inspect one of the second-hand models on display. Soon a smartly dressed young man approached him.

'That's a little beauty, sir. Runs like a dream,' the man said.

Will eyed the rust on the running board and the passenger door that didn't seem to close properly and imagined the salesman probably had meant nightmare. The price on the windscreen said, 'Only £99'. Cheap, but probably still over-priced.

'Got anything better?' he asked and Mick, as Will assumed him to be, there being no one else around, visibly straightened and his grin grew wider in anticipation of a lucrative sale.

'Sure we have, sir. Right this way.'

He preceded Will, weaving between other vehicles in various states of decay, to stop in front of a rather fine looking Prince Henry Vauxhall – with a rather fine looking price to match.

£299? I could get a new motorcar for that, thought Will. Not a Prince Henry, of course, but that seems pretty steep for a second-hand motorcar. 'I'll take it,' he said.

'Grand!' the salesman looked as though he couldn't believe his luck. 'I'll get the paperwork.'

'Fine,' said Will, 'provided she runs smoothly.'

'Ah, she runs grand. I'd buy her myself if I could afford it.'

'Well, I'll just give her a wee spin up the road and back and if she's half as good as she looks, we've got a deal.'

Mick looked doubtful and said, 'Well, I really can't leave the lot; I'm on my own here today.'

'Oh, that disnae matter. I dinnae mind trying it out on my own. Test the engine; listen to the transmission; that sort of thing. If I've any questions, sure I can ask you when I get back.'

'It's just that… I don't think I can let you drive off by yourself – '

'No, of course not. I hadnae expected you to be on your own, here. But I must try it out before agreeing to purchase.' Will tapped his case and said, 'Look, I'm a salesman myself. I have all my customer contact details in this attaché case. It's worth a lot more than £299 pounds to me, I can tell you. How about if I leave it with you while I take a spin in the Vauxhall? I can trust you to look after it for me?'

'Of course you can,' said the proprietor, quick to confirm his honesty and thereby finding himself already half conceding to his customer's request.

'Very good! Here you are, then,' Will handed over the case. 'Crank the handle, will you?' he added as he climbed in behind the wheel.

A few minutes later Will pulled out into the traffic – what there was of it – heading back the way he had come. A glance over his shoulder from the open-top showed him a bemused Mick watching him go, and clutching the attaché case as though it contained the crown jewels.

Will didn't have far to travel before he reached Munster's. He pulled across the road and parked on the forecourt next to a brand new Shelsley, the recently introduced sporting version of the Crossley. He got out and strode across to the showroom. No odour of oil in here, only the lingering fragrance of new leather.

Unlike Mick's Motors, Munster's boasted no less than three salesmen, one of whom was occupied with another customer. Wearing a radiant smile, one of the others approached Will as he entered.

'Sir, how can I help you? You're interested in a Crossley?'

'I am indeed, yes,' said Will, 'though not, unfortunately to buy.'

The radiance of the smile reduced by a few hundred lumens but remained perceptible. 'I see,' he said, although it was obvious that he didn't.

Will explained, 'What it is – it's a bit embarrassing, really – the thing is, I was manoeuvring my Prince Henry,' he nodded back out to the forecourt, 'out of a tight space. Not an easy motorcar to manoeuvre, I'm sure you know. And – accidentally, you understand – touched an adjacent motorcar. Well, I say touched; it was quite a scrape, actually. I feel terrible about it. And the point is, there was no sign of the owner for me to arrange to pay his repair bill. So, of course, I thought the best thing to do was to take a note of the registration number and trace him that way.'

'Very sensible and, if I may say so, very commendable, Mr...eh...?'

'Lynn. James Lynn,' said Will.

'Well, Mr Lynn, I take it the other vehicle was a Crossley?'

'Yes, a Crossley 15, with an IK number.'

'The 15. Ah, a lovely motor. And if the registration is an IK it was almost certainly bought from us. You're in luck, Mr Lynn. We keep full details of all our sales: customer, make of motorcar, registration. So if you'll give me the number I'll just check our records.'

'Ah... yes... well. This is the really embarrassing bit. I don't know about you, but I have a hopeless memory for numbers, which, of course, is why I wrote it down. Keep it safe. But somehow... it wasn't safe enough. I've lost the dratted note I made. Honestly, I'd lose my head if it wasn't screwed on.'

'Oh dear. Well, I can't help you without the number, I'm afraid,' said the salesman.

'But I do have some possible numbers.'

'You do?'

'Yes. You see, I can remember it started with IK and I'm pretty sure that was followed by three digits ending in a 3. I have a friend up at City Hall and from their records I have been able to list all the Crossley 15s with IK registrations ending in 3. There are only five, plus a two digit one, but I don't think it could be that one.' Will handed his shortlist to the salesman who took it and asked him to take a seat while he went to check his records.

It seemed to take a long time before he returned, but in reality it was just over ten minutes. He was all smiles again as he gave Will back his list of numbers. Against each one he had written the names and addresses of the purchasers. Three had telephone numbers, too, but Will wasn't interested in phoning.

'This is marvellous. Thank you so much. My man must surely be one of these. You've been so helpful.'

'It is my pleasure. Be sure to tell the owner, when you find him, that we can arrange a re-spray of the affected area for him – and you'll find our charges very reasonable, Mr Lynn.'

Pleased with his investigations so far, Will drove the Vauxhall back to Mick's Motors and saw the look of relief that flooded the proprietor's features as he turned into the lot. He was still gripping the attaché case.

'You've been over fifteen minutes; I was beginning to think – '

'What? That I wasn't coming back! Ha ha, and leave you with all my client contacts. I don't think so.' He took the case from Mick and continued, 'No, I liked the motorcar very much so I wanted to make sure and drove a little further than I had intended. But I'm afraid there is definitely a knocking sound in the engine. You can't hear it while she's idling. Anyway, reluctantly, I'm going to have to turn this one down. Sorry.'

Mick said, 'In that case you must have a look over here' I have just – '

Will stopped him before he could get into a new sales spiel and with a brief word of thanks made a swift departure. He waited for a tram back to the city centre where he planned to find a pub with live folk singing for a leisurely evening meal and a bit of crack while he considered how he would proceed with his quest to find Annie's killer.

The singing was good and the crack convivial. As a result it was already dark by the time Will started back to Mrs Rafferty's boarding house. He turned into the east end of Mary's Lane and wondered idly what the little knot of men were doing further up on the pavement just opposite his digs.

Chapter 7

Elsie didn't sleep much Thursday night. Buster Gregson had made her follow the gentleman who had given her ten bob for nothing. Find where he lives, he said; we've a score to settle. Let me down and I'll skin you alive, he said. Elsie could still hear the menace in his voice as she crept along Mary's Lane in the dark, trying to keep up with the man without getting too close and risk being seen. She noted the number of the house he entered and retraced her steps with a faltering stride. She didn't want to tell Buster, but she'd have to. If she didn't he'd hurt her bad.

She went back to her room that she shared with six other girls in the damp tenement block in Beresford Street owned by the man Buster called the Boss. She hated it but where else could she go? And there could be no complaining about the conditions. There used to be eight of them sharing the room. Megan complained once and they never saw her again.

Buster had told Elsie to wait in the room for him. She supposed it was better than standing around in alleyways. He came back eventually and she told him the address. She's been a good girl, he said. She deserved a reward, he said. So she had to lie on her back while he climbed on top to reward her. Afterwards, she didn't sleep much.

But in the morning she had the makings of a plan in her head. She kept seeing the kind gentleman lying in a pool of his own blood and that wasn't right. In the evening, when it was time to go to work she reached the alley near the corner of Mary's Lane and Church Street, her usual pitch; the police seldom came down there. Tonight, she kept on walking. Past the doorway where she had seen the gentleman enter the previous evening, well before Buster and his cronies would get there. She went on to the end of Mary's Lane, the posher end. She saw two RIC men a little way off and slipped into the recessed entrance to a darkened building. She mustn't get moved on.

* * *

Will didn't alter his pace as he walked towards his digs. He could see four men now, hanging around smoking. They were obviously trying to look casual with the result that they looked anything but. They pretended not to notice him but were all watching his approach under hooded eyes. As Will got nearer he recognised the man in the dirty green rugby shirt from the night before. It was too late to turn and run, which would have been the sensible thing to do, but he was too close now.

Will carried on walking. The door to his boarding house was ten yards away. Rugby Shirt and his gang stepped off the pavement and to his consternation Will realised there were five of them. The one at the back that he hadn't noticed and one of the others veered left to come up behind him. Rugby Shirt and the other two reached his side of the road between him and the door. Will stopped. He needed to see in both directions. He moved so his back was against the wall. And waited.

* * *

In her darkened doorway Elsie waited. Punters walked by but she didn't emerge to offer business. Every now and then she noticed police patrolling their beat further east and she made sure she remained concealed. She could see down Mary's Lane and she saw Buster Gregson and his gang arrive opposite the gent's house. She saw them light up and she saw them throw away their stubs and light up again. After an absolute age, she saw the gentleman from last night coming up from the direction of the river. He turned into Mary's Lane.

She wanted to rush out and warn him but she didn't dare. Buster would see her and she recoiled with the thoughts of what he would do to her. She waited. And watched. Another punter was approaching.

* * *

Along the Lane two men closed in on Will's position from either side. He found a grim humour from the fact that Rugby Shirt was hanging back. Had enough yesterday, had he? In his peripheral vision he saw one of the men on his other side shift his weight so Will was ready for the kick that was launched towards his groin. He couldn't move back. Instead he caught the booted foot and deflected its aim. He held on, making its owner dance about on his other leg to keep balance. Will scythed his own left leg hard against his opponent's hopping limb and the man crashed to the ground. Will could have released the foot that he held as the man fell but he didn't want him to get up again to join the fray. So he held on to it just long enough to hear a satisfying crack and the man yelling out.

All this action happened in the space of two seconds and meant the other man on his right was unable to get at him, but the two on his left rushed in and grabbed his arms before he had a chance to use them to his advantage. Their grip was savage and the other bloke on his right stepped over his fallen comrade to aim a heavy fist at Will's solar plexus. Will lifted both feet off the ground, ably supported by the men holding his arms, and launched a two-footed kick hard into his attacker's chest. The man staggered back and fell in the gutter.

But Rugby Shirt had come in close with a hefty swing at Will's jaw. He didn't see it coming and the force snapped his head sideways. He struggled to free an arm. He kicked wildly at the shins of the man holding him on his right but the grip on his arm only tightened. He felt a sickening blow to his midriff and tried to double up, fighting for breath. He couldn't bend forward because of the men holding his arms. He had to lift his legs off the ground again, bending his knees into a foetal position to protect his stomach.

Then he felt himself falling. His arms had been released and pain shot through his coccyx as he hit the unyielding pavement. Immediately the toe of a heavy boot landed hard to the base of his skull and bright light filled the front half of his brain. This was bad. He curled up even tighter and brought his hands and arms up to try to protect his head. Two more kicks landed on his upper thigh and on his back. Another slammed into his head. His brain felt like it was being tossed about in a turbulent sea. It bobbed around, registering only vague shapes and sounds. Feet all around him. Cold paving slabs beneath. Grunts from his attackers. Pain all over. A shrill whistle.

* * *

Elsie had stepped out of her doorway as the punter approached. 'Looking for business, love?'

The man stopped. Elsie let her coat hang open so he got an eyeful.

'Like what you see, dearie?'

'How much?' said the man.

'Only ten bob, seeing as you look so handsome.' She needed a prolonged negotiation.

'Ten shillings! Seems a bit pricey, darling.'

'Come on. We can have a real good time for that,' she said, leaning forward to ensure the punter could see just how good a time he could have.

'I'm sure we could, but there's plenty of girls'll give me a good time for five bob.'

Elsie was glancing up and down the road. She said, 'Well, seeing it's you, I'll let you have it for seven and six. That's a real bargain.'

'Five bob,' said the man.

Glancing about her again, Elsie finally saw what she was looking for. She raised her voice, 'I'm not some cheap tart. Do you want to have me or not?'

'Not at seven and six, I don't.' The man made as though to go.

'Here, don't go, dearie.' Elsie's raised voice sounded a little desperate. 'All right, five bob and I'm all yours. Happy?'

'That's more like it, darling.' The man slipped his hand around her waist inside her coat just as the sound of two pairs of heavy boots approaching made him look up. 'Blimey, it's the Peelers!'

Elsie was amazed at how quickly he seemed to vanish in the darkness. She drew her coat tight around her.

'Now then miss, what would you be up to? As if we didn't know.'

'Nothing, officer; the gentleman was asking directions,' said Elsie.

'Sure he was. I could arrest you for soliciting – '

'Oh, officer, look!' Elsie point up Mary's Lane. 'What are they doing to that poor man?'

The RIC man who hadn't spoken had already seen the fracas and whipped out his whistle. 'Come on!' he shouted at his colleague, 'leave her.'

The two rushed down Mary's Lane with a shrill blast on the whistle.

Buster “Rugby Shirt” Gregson saw them first. ‘Coppers, lads! Leave him. Make yourselves scarce.’

Two of the gang helped their friend with a broken leg to stand and they supported him between them as they hurried away. Rugby Shirt flung a last barb at Will, ‘We haven’t finished with you, Blackbeard. You’re a dead man.’

Chapter 8

Mrs Rafferty fussed over her "boy" who was sitting in her parlour while she dabbed gently at the nasty abrasion on the side of Will's head with a cloth soaked in warm water and disinfectant.

'Those uneven paving slabs will be the death of someone one of these days,' she said. 'The Corporation never do a thing about fixing them. That was a terrible fall you had, Mr Dillon. But there, I've cleaned up the wound as best I can. At least it's not bleeding anymore.'

'You've been very kind, Mrs Rafferty. Very kind. I'm feeling a whole lot better already.' He took another sip of the hot, sweet tea she had made for him when he stumbled in and explained that he had taken a tumble out on the pavement.

The two constables had helped him to his feet as his assailants ran off. His breathing was returning to normal by then and he made light of the whole thing. He told them that the gang hadn't managed to get hold of his wallet, thanks to their timely arrival, implying that it was a simple attempted robbery. The officers wanted to take a full statement, but he assured them it wasn't necessary. He certainly had no wish to have his name registered with the local constabulary. He thanked them once more and proceeded to the boarding house and the tender ministrations of Mrs Rafferty.

As she was cleaning him up on the outside, he felt the warm drink reviving him from within. What to do? He had no doubt that Rugby Shirt and his gang would try to make good their threat. These digs were no longer safe.

'Mrs Rafferty,' he said, 'you've been kindness personified. I've been grand here over this past week. Most grateful to you.'

'Ah, isn't that lovely to hear, Mr Dillon. I like my boys to be happy.' The landlady straightened up and started to clear away her cloths and towels and enamel bowl of disinfectant.

'But I fear I must now settle my account. After tomorrow my business requires me to move on.'

'Oh, I am sorry to hear that,' said Mrs Rafferty.

'I'll be sorry to go. I'll miss your wonderful breakfasts.'

'Well, I'll make sure you get a good one tomorrow morning, if it's to be your last.'

Will grimaced inwardly at the aptness of her choice of words. The condemned man ate a hearty breakfast. He climbed the stairs to his room, wincing as various bruises around his ribcage objected to the exercise, but he was pretty sure none was broken. He stumbled into bed and despite a bad headache he must have dropped off quickly. It only seemed like moments later that light was streaming through a gap in the curtains and the delicious aroma of frying bacon caressed his nostrils. He arose carefully. There was a bit of stiffness in sundry limbs and his jaw was a little tender, though his thick beard had absorbed much of Gregson's savage blow. His right thigh felt badly bruised but his head was clear. The rest had done him good.

He pulled back the curtains to reveal a bright sunny morning. The low rays were slanting in over the corrugated roof of a ramshackle outhouse built against the high wall at the rear of Mrs Rafferty's back yard. In the other corner, by a door in the wall that led to the back lane, he saw the chickens strutting around in their coop. His face relaxed in an expression of pleasant anticipation of the bacon and new-laid eggs that awaited him.

* * *

In his prestigious office not far from Clery's on Sackville Street, Michael J Higginson was seated behind his ostentatious mahogany desk. The expression on his face suggested he was far from pleased at having to be there so early on a Saturday morning. The man seated opposite him could not have been more dissimilar. Short in stature, undernourished, shabbily clothed, calloused workman's hands – a sharp contrast to the affluent appearance of the man who had summoned him to present himself at the office at nine. The only mark of similarity at all was that the visitor's face, too, betrayed its owner's desire to be anywhere else but in this office. The great bulk of a third man, who had admitted him, was ominously blocking any possibility of retreat by the office door.

Higginson had kept him waiting until nine fifteen and since then had been listening, with increasing impatience, to the man's pitiful excuses for failing to clear the back rent that he owed by yesterday's mid-day deadline.

'I'm not interested in sick children or mothers who have to miss work to look after them,' he interrupted; 'they're your responsibility. Mine is to see that all my tenants pay their rent.'

The tenant opened his mouth to speak but Higginson hadn't finished.

'In full.'

'But –'

'And on time!' The crash of Higginson's fist on the desk caused even the big man at the door to raise a surprised eyebrow.

'But I will, Mr Higginson, I will. I just need a little *more* time.'

'I've been more than generous in giving you time to pay. Have you got my money?'

His visitor hung his head.

'No money. Well I have no more time, either. You and your family will vacate your room by six o'clock this evening.'

'But... but where will we go?'

'That's not my problem. We agreed, did we not, that you would pay in full what you owe by mid-day yesterday and if you didn't your tenancy would cease?'

'Yes, but I was hoping – '

'Hope is a much over-rated commodity – as you are learning.' Higginson opened a buff folder that was on his desk and extracted a typed sheet. 'Sign this. My men will be round this evening to receive your keys and secure the premises after you have left.'

'But – '

'Sign.'

The wretched man took the proffered pen and wrote his name at the bottom of the lease termination. Higginson replaced it in the folder.

'That will be all.' Higginson consulted his Half Hunter pocket watch. 'I have another appointment now. Kelly will see you out.'

The big man at the door opened it for the visitor. As they left the room Buster Gregson stepped in to keep his nine thirty appointment with the Boss.

'Come in, Gregson.' Higginson felt no need to offer his employee a seat. 'Got a job for you and Mick this evening. Go to this address,' he handed Buster a slip, 'and make sure the premises are vacated by six o'clock.'

'Er… I'm afraid Mick's broken his leg.'

'He's what! How did the fool manage to do that?'

'Had a bit of a set-to last night. With Blackbeard.'

'Who?'

'The bloke who tried to cheat Elsie.'

'Him! The bastard who put Eamon Moore's knee out. You're not telling me he's now broken Mick's leg?'

'Well… '

The desk shook as Higginson's clenched fist slammed down again. The man's face was red and turning redder. A twisted scar on his left side cheek looked purple. 'Blast that man to hell! I trust that is now his permanent abode?'

'It would have been. Definitely. We had him, but – '

'But! I'll not have "buts". Don't you "but" me.'

'The Peelers turned up before we could finish him. It was just bad luck. Don't worry, we'll get him tonight. He won't be going anywhere; we gave the bastard a right going over.'

'You still haven't got rid of him! What am I paying you for? Don't wait until tonight. Change of plan. You know where he lives. It's early yet, he'll still be licking his wounds. Round up a couple of the lads – if you've got any left – Kelly will drive you and provide extra muscle. I want him brought back here. Alive. This is personal. Bring him in by the back alley to the basement. I'll pull his beard out one whisker at a time, the trouble he's caused me, before we send him on his merry way to hell where he belongs.'

Buster shuffled his feet.

'Are you still here? Go! I'll expect you back within the hour.

* * *

Replete after one of the best breakfasts he had ever eaten, Will finished packing his meagre belongings into a canvas holdall. He was donning his coat when he heard Mrs Rafferty call up the stairs.

'Oh, Mr Dillon, there are some men here. Friends of yours, who are looking for you.'

Will froze. Friends? One friend – it was just possible that Ryan might have taken it into his head to call on him – but friends? No mention of a pretty little sister, just men. This didn't sound right.

He crossed the room to where the slope of the ceiling matched the roof and hinged up the pane of the skylight that overlooked the street. He stretched so that he could look down to the road and was surprised to see a green Crossley parked outside the house. He had seen two or three during his first week in Dublin – none with registrations ending in three, but each time he spotted one his heart missed a beat and memories of Annie flooded back. He read the plate on this one and his heart positively leapt: IK 253 – oh, wait, no. It was 258.

He turned his attention to the burly bloke standing by the vehicle and looking towards the house. Was there something familiar about him? One of the ruffians from last night, maybe? Will couldn't be sure, but he wasn't going to take the risk.

He traversed the room, again, with three quick strides and eased up the sash of the rear window. Leaning out, he could see a cast-iron drainpipe was fixed to the wall about a foot to the right. Will slammed his hat on his head grabbed his holdall, stuck an arm through both handles and shifted the bag right up onto his shoulder. He climbed out onto the windowsill and then heard Mrs Rafferty calling again.

'Mr Dillon?'

He leaned back into the room and called, 'Tell them I'll be down in a moment, Mrs R.'

He should have kept quiet. He heard heavy boots on the stair and Mrs Rafferty's voice protesting. He didn't wait to hear more. Leaning out to the side, he gripped the drainpipe and, ignoring his bruised thigh, shinned down it as quickly as he could. He was halfway across the yard when he heard a voice from the open window above.

'Stop right there!'

He risked a glance back up and was rewarded with a view of the ugly face of Rugby Shirt – now wearing a black polo neck that, if anything, made him look more fearsome. What most concerned Will was the Colt automatic in his right hand aiming down into the yard.

Will zigged to his left and zagged back right to wrench open the door in the rear wall. He launched himself through as he heard a sound like a motorcar backfiring and a bullet thudded into the wooden frame of the chicken coup just by where his right shoulder had been an instant earlier.

He slammed the door behind him to the sound of some indignant squawking from the hens and raced down the alley.

Veering out into Arran Street, he cursed as he heard shouts behind him.

'There he goes! Come on.'

Will was never going to be able to outrun his pursuers carrying his holdall. He was passing the building that housed the city's wholesale fruit and vegetable market. There were a number of great stacks of empty wooden crates piled up outside an entrance. By crouching, Will managed to squeeze himself between two stacks and found a bit of space at the back where he could crawl under some loosely piled boxes. He couldn't see out to the pavement, so he couldn't be seen either. He realised his pulse was racing and he was breathing hard. He tried to calm himself, fearful that his panting would be heard.

A moment later the sound of running feet told him his 'friends' were still after him. They stopped and Will heard the voices of their owners.

'Where's he gone?'

'He couldn't have made it to the end of the street.'

'Did he go the other way?'

'We'd still have seen him. He must have gone through the market.'

'Or be hiding in among all these crates.'

Will heard the sound of boxes being pulled off the tops of the stacks over the thumping of his own heart.

'Leave it, we're wasting time. He's getting away; come on. The Boss will be livid if we don't bring him in. Spread out and search the market.' This last, fading, and accompanied by the sound of retreating feet.

Will's heart felt like it was being used by an over-enthusiastic timpanist. He stayed where he was for two minutes as his heart rate reduced to something approaching normality. As he regained his strength he was pondering on the identity of 'the Boss.' These men are serious. They're not giving up and now, it seems, there's a Boss who they're supposed to bring me to.

Cautiously, he crawled out of his tunnel. There was no sign of his attackers. He set off, keeping mostly to side roads until he found what he was looking for and entered the premises. Twenty minutes later he emerged, clean-shaven and with his hair trimmed shorter than it had been since he was a boy, but long enough at the side to hide his abrasions.

He needed to find new lodgings and change his clothes to complete his fresh look. He'd already ditched his felt hat. He made his way to Sackville Street and crossed over to Clery's, where he bought himself a cloth peaked cap. On exiting the department store he turned north. He paused for a moment by the window of a toy shop that displayed a large Ferris Wheel made out of Meccano and clockwork model railway engines. Tearing himself away from these, he passed Hoyte's Druggist and Oil Works and then a prestigious office building with a brass plaque that said, *Higginson Enterprises*. He turned the corner into Talbot Street that ran down to Amiens Street (Connolly) Station. As he expected, he found a number of dwellings in that area with cards in their windows that said "Rooms to let" all still within easy reach of the GPO, which would now be to the west of his lodgings rather than the east.

He declined the first couple of rooms he was shown as they didn't have a rear aspect and he realised now that that could be a vital factor in his future safety. He got lucky at his third attempt. A kindly looking woman wearing a blue, wrap-around pinny offered him a room very similar to the one he had been forced to vacate. It commanded views of both the street and the back yard.

'I'll take it,' said Will. 'This'll do grand.'

'Right you are, then, Mr... er?'

'Lynn. James Lynn.' Will shook the hand of his new landlady.

'And I'm Mrs Gilpin. If you need anything, just let me know. I'll leave you to settle in.'

As the door closed behind her Will felt himself relax for the first time since Mrs Rafferty had called up to him that he had visitors. Finally he reckoned he was safe once more to go about the business that had brought him to Dublin.

He was looking forward to meeting William Butler Yeats tonight although he realised he should use the evening to get to know Ryan Doloughan better and cultivate his acquaintance with Eoin MacNeill, too. However, that was tonight. Before then he had work to do on his self-imposed mission to find Annie's killer.

Chapter 9

By the time Will was riding the tram out to the district where the poetry reading was to take place, he was grateful for the chance to sit and relax. His aches and pains no longer bothered him but he had spent a tiring few hours tracking down owners of Crossley 15s. He had hired a bicycle and, armed with a good Dublin street map, set off to find the first address on his list – the second, actually, as he decided to leave IK 93 to the last, hoping to strike lucky with one of the others first.

He was lucky, in one sense, when he got to the home of the owner of IK 113, in that the motorcar was parked on the driveway in plain sight. It was blue. Back on his bike, he had some difficulty in locating the next address and when he did find it – a large, rambling cottage-style house set well back from the road – there was no sign of any Crossley. There was a separate garage to one side of the house with its doors closed but whether it contained the vehicle Will was looking for he had no way of determining. He cycled on up the road a little way and then turned and cycled back past the house a short distance. He found a mossy bank on a bend where he wouldn't be too conspicuous from the house, set back as it was, but from where he could keep it under observation. With his bike pulled in and propped against a tree he sat down and lay back on the bank.

The sun came out from behind some receding clouds and Will quite enjoyed the first half-hour of his surveillance, but by the time he had been watching for an hour he was becoming distinctly bored. He had one brief moment of excitement after about forty minutes when a green Crossley drove by but even before he realised that it was not going to turn in at the drive he was watching he saw that its registration number did not end in a three. Nor did the driver bear any resemblance to either the chauffeur or the passenger he remembered from the accident.

When he had been sitting on the bank for an hour and twenty-five minutes and was telling himself that he would give it five more minutes he thought he spotted some movement up at the house. As he watched, someone came around from the side of the cottage and went to the front of the garage. Will found himself holding his breath as the double doors were opened. It was too dark inside for him to see anything at this distance. He had another frustrating few minutes after the figure disappeared inside until the sound of the engine being cranked preceded the distinctive purr of the motor ticking over that only a Crossley 15 can make.

The motorcar reversed out into the sunlight. It was green. Will decided to risk getting closer. Standing up, he rubbed his joints to relieve the stiffness after his lengthy inactivity and jumped on his bike. He cycled slowly towards the house where the motorcar had stopped by the porch. The front door opened and an elderly gentleman emerged while the driver climbed out to help him over to the passenger side. Will's face dropped. Although the motorcar was registered to a man, the driver was a woman. It couldn't be the one he was looking for. Resolutely, he climbed back on his hired bicycle. This was going to take some time. He made a mental note to look out for a cheap second-hand bike. No point in wasting money on hire charges even if he could claim it on expenses.

Leafy suburbs were trundling past the tram window as Will recalled the feeling of dejection that had come over him when he realised his long vigil had been for nothing. But he chided himself that it was not for nothing: he had eliminated another possibility and shortened the odds on finding his quarry at one of the remaining addresses. He had managed to cross one more from the list before he had to return to his new digs and dress for his much anticipated meeting with William Butler Yeats.

In the tram, a toddler with a lady Will assumed to be his mother stood on the seat in front looking back. Will stuck his tongue out and the child giggled and ducked back behind the seat. When he reappeared, Will pushed his tongue into his cheek and then pretended to burst the 'bubble' with his forefinger. More squeals of laughter were followed by the mother insisting that her son sit down and stop bothering the gentleman. Will felt a twang of guilt at getting the child into trouble. He glanced at another fellow-passenger seated across the aisle – a middle-aged man with a high forehead and a bushy walrus moustache. The man looked preoccupied and didn't appear to have noticed the brief disturbance. Laughter came from the back of the tram where it sounded as though three or four young people were bantering and joking with one another.

Will yawned – it had already been a long day. His mind turned to his imminent meeting with the famous poet and writer. It was going to be such an experience. Spending time with Eoin MacNeil could be useful, too. He'd try to garner whatever he could on the Volunteers. And then there was his new friend Ryan Doloughan – and Maeve.

It was the image of Maeve in carefree mood, dancing in the Temperance Hall that lingered in his mind as he turned and directed his attention out the window. He must be nearing his destination, so in the failing light he tried to make out the names of the side streets. As they crossed a major intersection, Will caught sight of a road name and realised that he wanted the next stop. He reached up to pull the leather cord but the gentleman across the aisle beat him to it and when the tram pulled up Will followed the older man out and down onto the road.

His travelling companion stepped onto the pavement and set off at a leisurely pace in the wake of the retreating tram. Will stopped and consulted his street map. After orientating himself he worked out that the avenue where Eva Gore-Booth had her Dublin residence was a little further on. He hurried off in the footsteps of the gentleman with the walrus moustache.

The distance between them was diminishing when a motorcar drove past and pulled up just ahead of the man in front. A short individual got out of the passenger side and two other, thickset types emerged from the back. They approached the gentleman up ahead who stopped as they crowded around him. Will hesitated. He thought he caught the words 'contribution' and 'Force Erin' and then, quite clearly, 'Come on, hurry it up.'

Will quickened his pace but it wasn't until he came right up to the man from the tram that he saw the revolver prodding into his ribs as the short man berated him. Amateurs, Will thought. Never hold a gun close to your victim. Though it didn't look like this particular victim was the sort who could take advantage of their mistake and Will couldn't risk starting anything physical with the gun where it was.

'Stop this at once!' he commanded, stepping to one side and forcing Shorty to half-turn to look over his shoulder at the newcomer.

One of his companions shoved Will. 'Keep out of this!' he said, 'We'll have your contribution next.'

'You'll have no contribution from me,' said Will. 'I'm going to call the police.'

'Stay right where you are.' Shorty spun round and Will felt the muzzle of the revolver in his own side. Now he could deal with these louts without risking injury to the other gentleman.

'Take that pea-shooter out of my ribs,' he said.

Shorty cocked the gun. 'You don't get to make demands,' he said. 'Move and you're a dead man.'

In one lightning action Will twirled through ninety degrees, his right arm knocking the gun away from his body. In the same motion his left hand came up and grabbed the barrel high up near the butt. His forefinger slipped between the cocked firing pin and the base of the bullet in the chamber, rendering the firearm useless. Without pausing, he pulled the gun down hard and to the right. Shorty's body twisted in that direction as he tried to hold on to the weapon and Will's right fist slammed into the fleshy part of his nose.

Shorty swore and his grip on the revolver slackened momentarily. Will twisted it violently from his grasp as he felt one of the other men grab him round the neck. Will gripped the man's forearm with his right hand, lowered his centre of gravity and leaned forward. The man was forced to lean, too, off-balance. The next moment he was flying over Will's shoulder to land in an unceremonious heap on the roadside. Will sprang back, switching the revolver to his right hand. Well out of reach, he levelled it at the attackers.

All these manoeuvres had taken about two and a half seconds and Shorty's other henchman had not even started to react before all three found themselves facing the barrel of their own gun.

'Get back in that jalopy you came in and get out of here,' said Will, indicating their motorcar with a slight jerk of the barrel.

The men hesitated.

'Now! Before this thing goes off accidently.'

Shorty grunted something to his pals and turned away. Will kept them covered as they climbed into their vehicle and drove off.

Only as the motorcar was disappearing round a bend did the man with the walrus moustache find his voice. 'Sir, I am very much indebted to you. These thugs – they call themselves Force Erin but they're nothing more than a gang of thieves – would have emptied my wallet, and yours, too. I was most impressed with how you handled them.'

Will said, 'Well, I could see they were up to no good and I don't like shooters; dangerous things.' As he spoke he checked the chambers of the revolver. Full. He removed one bullet and left the empty chamber at the top. He slipped the gun into his overcoat pocket as he introduced himself, 'I'm Will Dillon, at your service. Only too glad to have been able to help.'

The other man took Will's outstretched hand and shook it warmly. 'Connolly, James Connolly. Very pleased to make your acquaintance, Mr Dillon.'

Chapter 10

The applause was polite but genuine as William Butler Yeats concluded another of his poems and removed his wire-framed pince-nez. Will clapped as enthusiastically as the rest of the gathering as he watched the poet glance around the elegantly fitted out salon full of elegantly fitted out admirers.

Pocketing his spectacles, Yeats said, 'That'll have to do you for now while I lubricate my throat. Did I hear somebody mention a Jameson?'

A handsome lady, a decade or more older than Will lifted a decanter from a fine walnut sideboard and poured a liberal portion into an antique crystal tumbler. 'Oh, Mr Dillon, come and let me introduce you to our distinguished guest. Willie, that last poem was truly delightful. Where do you get your inspiration?'

'From life, dear Eva, in all its idiotic irrelevancies – and not a little from this fiery amber nectar, too,' Yeats added, lifting the proffered glass to his lips.

Eva Gore-Booth had already made Will feel most welcome when he arrived at her door in the company of another of her favourites poets, James Connolly, for it transpired that the notorious advocate of the Industrial Union and founder of the Citizens' Army that Will had unwittingly rescued from the Force Erin thugs was also invited to the evening's poetry reading.

As they had walked together down the avenue to the Gore-Booth home, Connolly said, 'Do I detect a northern accent, Mr Dillon?'

'You do, aye, but call me Will.'

'Well, Will, I can see you're a handy man to have around. What brings you to Dublin?'
'The Post Office. I'm working in Sackville Street. Telegraphic communications.'
'Is that a fact? That sounds a responsible position. You must be well schooled?'
Will smiled to himself. The subtle question. Not, Are you Protestant or Catholic, Will? Just, What school did you attend?
'Oh aye, the Christian Brothers did me proud, right enough,' he said. No matter that as a staunch Orangeman he would never have set foot in a Catholic school, even as a lad, but he had an image to engender here and that's what he aimed to do.
'Good, good,' said Connolly, 'and are you active in the Gaelic League, at all?'
'Not yet, but it was Eoin MacNeill, himself, who invited me to tonight's do. I'm hopeful of joining up, if they'll have me.'
'Of course they'll have you. The more people who have the love of Ireland in their belly the sooner we'll be free of the English yoke for good and all.'
'Right you are, then. I'll talk to Mr MacNeill tonight, or maybe Ryan Doloughan; I think he runs the central Dublin branch.'
'You know Doloughan, do you? He's a good man.'
'He seems a decent chap. You know him, then.'
'Oh yes, I know Ryan.'
They walked on in step for a few yards before Connolly spoke again.
'I could use a man with your skills in the Citizens' Army. The men are well drilled now in handling rifles but in hand to hand combat I doubt there's many of them could put up much of a fight. Would you ever think of helping us out in that line of things, Will?'
Will couldn't believe his luck. 'Oh, I'm not sure,' he said. 'Handling a few ruffians in the street is one thing, but teaching martial arts to proper soldiers? I'm not sure that's me, Mr Connolly.'
'Well, to be brutally honest with you my "proper soldiers" as you call them are not much more than a bunch of ruffians, themselves – albeit a bunch of ruffians with rifles. Some of them, at any rate.'
'Aye, I watched a troop of them drilling outside Liberty Hall the other day. I could see they were short a few guns.'
'More than a few, I'm afraid. I'm hopeful that will change soon. But, listen,' he went on, quickly, 'you think about what I said. No need to

make your mind up on the spot. But I'd be very grateful if you decide you could give us a few evening training sessions. I'll talk to you later.'

They had reached the steps up to the rather grand house where the soirée was to take place. The big glazed door was ajar and it was opened wide, as they approached, by their hostess, herself. Will had been enchanted by her open friendliness. Eoin MacNeill was amongst a group of guests milling around, drinks in hand, in the spacious hallway. After a swift double-take, MacNeill came over to introduce him to Miss Gore-Booth.

'Dillon! I almost didn't recognise you. You've lost your beard.'

'I have. Decided to shave it off for the summer.'

'Well – you certainly look... different. Eva, allow me to introduce Will Dillon whom I took the liberty of inviting along this evening. He's keen to meet Yeats.'

'Well, he's come to the right place, then. You're very welcome, Will.' Eva put a hand on his arm. 'Do sign our visitors' book, won't you?' she added, indicating a leather bound volume that lay open on a rosewood table in a recess near the foot of a sweeping staircase. 'Can I get you a drink? And James! Lovely to see you. What will you have?'

Someone relieved the two new arrivals of their hats and coats and Will soon found himself regaling Eva and a small group of her guests with an entertaining account of some of his exploits at sea. He was an accomplished raconteur and won much acclaim from his largely female audience, although it was MacNeill who took him aside when he finished.

'I thought you said you were with the Post Office, Mr Dillon.'

'Oh I am, right enough. The lifeboat work is voluntary,' said Will.

'And a lover of poetry. I can see you are a man of hidden depths.'

'Och, I wudnae say that, Mr MacNeill, but I like to do my bit for the oul' country. Indeed, I'm thinking of joining the Gaelic League.'

'I'm pleased to hear that. We'd be very glad to have you. What about the Volunteers? Would you be interested in signing up for the Irish Volunteers, at all?'

'Oh, well now, I hadnae thought about that. I don't know too much about them, to be honest.'

'Well, of course it started because we were worried about the Unionists – you'll know about them, coming from County Down – worried they might take up arms when Home Rule is introduced. They've got their Ulster Volunteer Force and we felt we had no option but to form our own Irish Volunteers to counteract those that would deny us our freedom for self-determination.'

'So that's the reason for the Irish Volunteers: to defend against a militant UVF should Ireland ever be granted Home Rule?'

MacNeill's hesitation was barely noticeable. 'That's its role, as I see it, and it's an important role. We need to be ready. In fact we've got large-scale manoeuvres planned for Easter Sunday. We're taking the opportunity of the holiday to really put them through their paces. I'm determined my men will be ready should they ever be called upon to defend their country.'

'Admirable sentiments, Mr MacNeill,' said Will, as the pair of them joined the others still in the hallway in the general shuffle into the salon where, they were told, the guest of honour was about to read.

* * *

Now, as Yeats sipped his "fiery amber nectar" Eva said, 'Willie, this is Will Dillon from Donaghadee. He's a big admirer of your poetry – when he's not out fighting force ten gales to rescue shipwrecked mariners.' Then, having performed her duty as a hostess, Eva Gore-Booth moved on to see to other guests.

Will extended his right hand. 'So pleased to meet you, sir. I really enjoyed that last piece you read.'

'Very kind, very kind. Do you write, yourself, Mr Dillon?'

'No, no, no. I can spin a good yarn, but writing it down or putting it in verse – that's beyond me. That's why I was so grateful for the invitation to come and meet a man who can do both with such mastery.'

Yeats raised his glass in mock salute and ran the fingers of his free hand through his tousled hair. 'You flatter me, Mr Dillon, but do go on; I love it!'

Both men laughed and Will asked, 'Does Eva – Miss Gore-Booth – hold many of these gatherings?'

'Oh, from time to time, but she's always got something on the go, her and her big sister, Constance – campaigning to have the provision of school meals extended to Ireland, running a soup kitchen in Liberty Hall during the workers lockout a couple of years ago. Anything to help the poor or downtrodden. They are a very pleasant, kindly, inflammable family.'

Will didn't have a chance to ask what he meant by inflammable, as Yeats went straight on:

'Eva is an accomplished poet, too, you know. It was I who first encouraged her to develop her writing – way before she was published.'

'I didn't know. I must get hold of some of her work,' said Will.

'Do. You won't regret it. We need more good Irish literature. There are some wonderful writers in the Gaelic and those that can read it are well catered for but we need more good Irish works in English for the world to read. And not just judged 'good' because of its political rhetoric – that has its place – but 'good' because it can stand up against the best literature in the English language.'

'Absolutely,' said Will. 'I'm planning on joining the Gaelic League. They're all for supporting good Irish literature, aren't they?'

'The League paints a broad picture. Literature, sport, politics – everything Irish. Good luck to it. It's doing a good job, I've no doubt.'

'But?' Will could sense his namesake had more to say on the matter.

'But merely building up the fine Irish tradition, I fear, will never rid us of the parasites that rule in Dublin Castle.'

A new voice broke in, 'Nor the parasites who own the factories, run the industries, exploit our fine Irish working class.' James Connolly had wandered over and caught Yeats' last remark.

'Hello again, Mr Connolly,' said Will. 'You want the British out of Dublin Castle, too?'

'I want the honest working Irishman free to decide his own destiny and not have to line the pockets of rich factory owners intent on bleeding the country dry. And I doubt that's ever going to happen under British rule.'

'And Connolly, here, is the man to change all that,' said Yeats. 'Hasn't he established the largest industrial union in the land with enough muscle to stand up to the oppressors?'

'And the Citizens' Army to protect them, I gather,' said Will with a grin.

'An army that I'm hoping Will is going to instruct in unarmed combat. He's something of an expert. What do you think of that, Willie?'

Yeats ran a hand through his tousled hair again and said, 'Isn't that grand? So Dillon's one of us, is he?'

'Us?' said Will.

'The Brotherhood. The IRB.'

Will looked blank.

'Irish Republican Brotherhood. We tend to keep a low profile. Took over late in the last century where the Fenians left off – '

Connolly interrupted, 'Dillon is a good Irishman, as we all are. Which is enough. Right, Will?'

Will noted the slight tone of annoyance in Connolly's voice as he stopped Yeats in full flow. 'As good as the next man,' he said. 'But listen, I haven't actually agreed yet to give lessons to your soldiers.' He was still being canny. Didn't want to appear too eager to get closer to the heart of what was going on.

'But you will, I feel sure. Do say you will,' said Connolly.

'Do not hesitate, young Dillon,' said Yeats. 'Ireland needs men of your calibre.'

'Well, I suppose I could come along once or twice and see how it goes.'

'Excellent, Dillon; excellent,' said Connolly. 'I can't be there Monday evening; got a meeting. Come along on Tuesday evening.'

'Isn't it the fine fellow you are, right enough?' Yeats shook his hand once more and Will couldn't help feeling a tinge of guilt that his motives weren't quite as altruistic as these men assumed.

Just then, from across the room, a voice called, 'There you are!'

Will glanced over and saw Maeve making her way towards him, auburn hair flicking delightfully around her rosy cheeks, just as he remembered her. He excused himself from Yeats and Connolly and turned to her with an ear to ear smile on his face.

'Hello. Lovely to see you again,' he said.

'My, you do look different without your beard. Mr MacNeill had to point you out to us. I like the new you. You look younger; quite dashing,' said Maeve. 'What have we missed? Ryan got held up on some Gaelic League business or something, so we've only just got here.'

'Well, you've got some catching up on drinks to do and the guest of honour has completed one reading session, but he's promised there'll be more.'

Maeve leaned close to whisper in Will's ear, 'Is that *him* behind you?'

'That's him. And a very pleasant fellow he is, too.'

'You've met already?'

'Just been chatting to him and James Connolly, there.'

'Name dropper! You know Connolly, too?'

'We met on our way here. I did him a bit of a favour and he wants me to teach unarmed combat to the Citizens' Army.'

'He what?' Maeve looked incredulous. She put her arm through his and said, 'Take me through to the buffet and tell me all about it.'

An archway at the side of the salon near the back led through to the dining room where a long rosewood table covered in fine Irish linen took pride of place under a magnificent crystal chandelier that matched a similar one in the salon. The flicker of flames refracted by the cut-glass danced around the room as though excited to be illuminating such an august gathering, which Will had discovered included playwrights and poets, intellectuals and philosophers, professors and politicians as well as simple admirers like himself. And for them, their hostess had laid on a splendid cold collation of slices of ham, roasted turkey and beef as well as jellied chicken, vol-au-vents, tiny sausage rolls and a variety of dainty sandwiches – all with their crusts removed, Will noticed, as he cast his eyes over the spread. They were drawn on to the confections further along the laden table: meringues, cream-filled choux pastries, profiteroles and sponge cakes. On a side table a selection of Irish cheddars was on display alongside a lead crystal decanter of ten year old tawny Port.

'What a feast,' Will said to Maeve. 'I'm surprised our hostess is able to be so lavish, with the war and all.'

'Sure all this is from our own green fields. There's nothing the Kaiser can do about that, now, is there?'

'I suppose not, but I've read that the Germans are having their food rationed.'

'Oh, how terrible,' said Maeve, eying the spread. 'I hope that doesn't happen here.'

'Well, just in case it does, can I tempt you to a mushroom pâté right now?' He held one out to her.

'Vol-au-vents. I love them,' said Maeve and allowed Will to hold it as she took a bite.

Then Will bit off a piece.

'Hey, that's mine!' she laughed, pulling his wrist over to bring the pastry case back to where her delicate white teeth could take another nibble.

'So what's all this he-man stuff with James Connolly,' she asked and Will explained what he had agreed to do. Maeve looked impressed and concerned in equal portions.

'Don't get yourself hurt, Will.'

‘Och, dinnae worry about me, I can look after myself.’

‘Well I hope you can, Will Dillon. I’ve only just met you. I don’t want to be visiting you in hospital.’

‘You’d do that?’ Will felt a flutter in his stomach.

‘Of course I would. But don’t make me! I’d never forgive you.’ She took his hand as she added, ‘You will be careful?’ He grinned at her and she went on, ‘Now what are you doing after mass tomorrow?’

Will had forgotten tomorrow was Sunday and he wasn’t ready for her question. ‘Oh, eh… you know, I’m not really a mass sort of person. Not really a practicing catholic so much these days.’

‘Not even on Palm Sunday?’

‘Is that tomorrow? Aye, I suppose it must be. Do you go, then?’

‘I do on special days like Easter and Christmas and certain of the saints’ days. But no matter. How would you like to come for a picnic lunch tomorrow. We’re taking a jaunting car to the beach to eat our sandwiches watching the waves lapping the sand. There was red in the sky tonight – shepherds’ delight – so it will be a good day tomorrow.’

‘Well… er… that would be my delight, too. I’d love to join your party.’

‘I thought I might find you at the food, little sister.’

‘Cheek! And don’t call me – ’

‘Will! What’s happened to your beard?’ Ryan ignored Maeve’s protest as he joined them at the table. ‘Was it a false one? It had me fooled.’

‘No, no. A poor thing, but mine own,’ said Will. Maeve took a plate and wandered off round the table selecting from its delectable offerings, and Will added, ‘I actually needed a change of appearance.’

He told Ryan about his run-in with the pimps and their boss who apparently “wanted him alive.”

Ryan’s eyes narrowed. ‘That’s bad, my friend. Would you like me to arrange some protection for you?’

Will glanced at Ryan as he put a slice of ham on a plate and couple of sausage rolls. Who exactly was his new friend? He remembered Connolly – *Oh yes, I know Ryan.* ‘That’s kind of you,’ he said, ‘but don’t worry about me. I can look after myself.’

‘Well, if you’re sure. We’re on the telephone if you ever do need any help.’ Ryan produced a pencil stub and wrote his number on a paper doily; he jotted down his address, too. Will folded it and slipped it in his breast pocket.

‘I see the drinks are over there.’ Ryan nodded in the direction of a rosewood cabinet displaying both Jameson and Bushmills whiskeys, a selection of vintage wines – red and white, and a number of beers and bottles of Guinness; there was both brown and white lemonade and some other soft drinks, too.

Will cracked open a Guinness and poured it carefully into a half-pint tankard, holding it at a slope to avoid too much froth building up. Ryan helped himself to a generous tot of Jameson.

‘So you’re thinking of helping the cause, I hear?’ said Ryan.

‘I am?’

‘Unarmed combat training for Connolly’s boyos.’

‘Oh, that. Well, I’ve said I’d give it a try. Not sure what I can teach them.’

‘Quite a bit, from all accounts. James was telling me how you saw off a Force Erin gang tonight.’

James, is it? *Oh yes, I know Ryan.* ‘Och, I was lucky, so I was. They didn’t know what they were doing. But how come you know?’

‘I was repor– chatting to James earlier and he mentioned it. Asked me if you were all right.’

‘All right?’

‘Trustworthy. Heart in the right place. I told him any man who could keep up with my little sister in an Irish jig was all right in my book.’

‘Ah, good man, yourself. Although I’m not sure what I’m getting myself into.’

‘You’re helping the cause, like I said, and not a moment too soon.’

Will risked a slight probe: ‘But the Citizens’ Army won’t be doing anything more than defend the workers for a brave while yet surely?’

‘You can never be too sure about that. Who knows?’

Who indeed. ‘Connolly?’ suggested Will.

‘Ah sure, how would I know?’ Ryan was topping up his Jameson’s. ‘It won’t be up to the Citizens’ Army, anyway. There’s not enough of them. They need the firepower of the Volunteers and that means keeping their Chief of Staff, MacNeill, happy.’

Will was fairly sure that wasn’t just Ryan’s second whiskey. He probed again while his friend was in the mood for indiscretions. ‘Have they got the firepower, but? The manpower, yes. But don’t they need more weapons?’

Ryan touched his forefinger to the side of his nose. ‘Don’t worry on that score. It’s why I was late this evening, as a matter of fact.’

'Oh yes?' Will occupied himself with selecting a delicious meringue and appeared not to show much interest in Ryan's revelations.

'I'd placed a long-distance phone call earlier and I was waiting for the operator to call me back and put it through.'

'Long-distance, eh? Where were you calling?'

'Washington.'

'My! That sure is a long distance. And you actually spoke to someone in Washington this evening?'

'An embassy.'

'It never fails to amaze me, our modern technology.'

'Come on, you two. Mr Yeats is about to give another recital.' Maeve came over and hustled them back through into the salon.

Eva Gore-Booth was sitting with her sister on a chaise longue and moved up a little to make room for Maeve beside her. Ryan made his way further into the room and Dillon stood at the back, leaning against the thickness of the archway wall.

Yeats read three more of his poems, which Will appreciated along with everyone else. Afterwards, a fairly large lady in an ankle-length gown was introduced. She proceeded to entertain the gathering with a selection from the operettas of Gilbert and Sullivan, sung *a cappella*. A number of people started talking in low voices, content to have the mezzo-soprano as a background to their conversations. Will took the opportunity to slip back to the drinks cabinet for his second half.

While he was in the deserted dining room he picked up a profiterole and popped it into his mouth whole, relishing the taste of fresh cream and chocolate. Then, as he approached the archway between the rooms he was fairly sure he heard the walrus moustachioed, James Connolly's lowered voice saying:

'...and you have that direct from our man at the German embassy?'

'Not an hour since.'

Will froze. That was Ryan. His new acquaintances must be standing near the rear of the salon against the wall next to the arch. Will silently took up a similar position on his side of the arch and sipped his Guinness. The conversation continued *sotto voce* against the singer's unlikely assertion that she was called Little Buttercup, but he could follow the gist of what they were saying.

'20,000. And she sailed 9th of April?' Connolly again. 'What about –'

'A million rounds. Sir Roger has done us proud.'

‘The Council was hoping for a lot more, but we can’t complain. Casement has done a good job. And due off the Kerry coast on Good Friday, you say. Perfect timing.’

Applause from the salon signalled the end of the singer’s contribution to the evening and some people started to drift through to the dining room once more. Will moved out from the wall as though he’d just come through the arch himself. Eva’s sister, Countess Markievicz, was with a tall, bespectacled gentleman with a long, sharply-defined nose. She caught sight of Will and came over.

‘Mr Dillon! Have you met Eamon? He’s a professor of mathematics.’

The tall man extended his right hand. ‘De Valera. Pleased to meet you, Dillon.’

Will shook his hand. ‘An uncommon name.’

‘My father was Spanish. Met my Irish mother in the States, where I was born.’

‘I see. Well, pleased to meet you, too. I’m afraid I was never much good at sums at school.’

De Valeras’s lips twitched almost imperceptibly and the Countess quickly changed the subject:

‘That was a most exciting tale of your adventures on the high seas you gave us earlier. I’m sure you must have many more thrilling accounts.’

‘Oh, one or two, I dare say,’ said Will, ‘one or two.’

‘I’d love you to come and speak sometime to my boys about your adventures in the lifeboat service.’

‘Your boys?’

‘Constance founded *Na Fianna Éireann* some years ago,’ explained de Valera. ‘The *Sinn Féin* Boy Scouts, they call them.’

Constance frowned. ‘I don’t know who “they” are, but I call them what they are – the youth movement of the Irish Republican Brotherhood,’ she said.

Will’s spying antenna buzzed in his brain. An opportunity to get closer to Dublin’s republican circles? Perhaps this could be a back door into the secretive IRB.

‘Och well, if you think they’d be interested I dinnae mind coming along sometime,’ he said.

‘That’s splendid, Will – if I may call you that? I don’t suppose you’d be free next Monday evening? It’s very short notice, I know, but we had Padraig Pearse booked to come along to talk about becoming a barrister and he’s had to cancel; some important meeting he has to attend.’

Before Will moved to Dublin, Edmond Boyd had supplied him with a list of names to memorise. Names of people from various walks of life who may or may not be involved in any clandestine plotting that may or may not be going on. Connolly was on that list – not surprising, given his Citizens' Army connection. So was one, Padraig Pearse, barrister, educator, poet and editor of *An Claidheamh Soluis*, the newspaper of the Gaelic League.

Will had planned to do some more sleuthing of his own after work on Monday to try to track down the owner of the Crossley 15 that killed his fiancée, but he said, 'Monday's fine. I'd be happy to come along and have a wee chat with the lads.'

Constance Markievicz was profuse in expressing her gratitude and how she was sure her boys would be captivated by Will's adventures. But Will's mind was elsewhere. *Some important meeting has come up.* He flashed to Connolly – *I can't be there Monday evening; got a meeting.* And the conversation he had overheard by the archway. He had an uneasy feeling that he might not have until sometime in the summer to figure out what was being planned and by whom. Good Friday was just a week away.

He needed to contact Geoff Bradshaw – without delay.

Chapter 11

The white beak of a coot contrasted sharply with its black plumage as the bird slipped in amongst the reeds at the edge of the lake in St Stephen's Green. Two men leaning on the parapet of the little bridge that was like an isthmus between the two halves of the lake watched it disappear. Still gazing at the green reflecting water, the taller of the two spoke. The other gave no outward sign of listening, yet spoke in response, his own eyes, too, directed resolutely at the lake. A nearby church clock chimed the half-hour.

'I wasn't sure you'd come, it being Sunday.'

'I always have messages passed on to my home number, no matter when. You have something for me?'

Will proceeded to tell Geoff Bradshaw what he had picked up so far and about his plans to learn more about the IRB and the Citizens' Army.

With James Connolly seemingly expecting his men to be fully armed soon, Ryan's reference to "20,000 and a million rounds" could only mean guns and ammunition, surely. To be landed somewhere on the coast of Kerry next Friday. Then there was the meeting that Connolly and Pearse are attending tomorrow night, apparently arranged at short notice. And lastly, was Geoff aware of the Irish Volunteers' "large-scale manoeuvres " planned for Easter Sunday?

'We know about those; they've been planned for some time. The police are aware; they'll be keeping a close watch on things.'

'Well, as long as they do.' Will sounded uneasy.

'We're really not expecting anything this soon. Still looking towards the summer. Weapons can come any time and be stock-piled until they're needed. But I'll pass on what you've told me. At least we might intercept those guns arriving off Kerry. You've done well. Keep in touch.'

Bradshaw turned and walked back over the bridge the way he had come leaving Will still gazing at the spot where the coot had vanished among the reeds.

* * *

The plan was to meet in Sackville Street where the tram on the Doloughans' route drops off its passengers. Half-an-hour after meeting Bradshaw, as the church bell announced the hour of one o'clock, Will saw Maeve's trim figure as she stepped down from the tram. She wore a white, close-fitting blouse embroidered with little blue flowers, a long pale green skirt and a little flowery bonnet with a matching pale green ribbon tied under her chin. She was carrying a picnic rug and a small hamper.

Will rushed over to relieve her of her burden, wondering why Ryan wasn't carrying them, but Ryan was nowhere to be seen.

'Maeve! I do like your bonnet; very fetching. Where's your big brother?' Will was trying to look further down inside the tram.

'Ryan? Oh he's off on some League business; no rest for the wicked. But he wasn't coming today. This is our picnic. Did I not make that clear? Are you disappointed that it's only the 'little sister'? Maeve's full lips pouted.

'No, no,' said Will, 'not at all. It's just… em… I suppose I was expecting... But no, I cannae think of anything I'd enjoy more than an afternoon with you, Miss Doloughan.'

'Really?' Those delicious lips and hazel eyes were smiling again. 'You're not just saying that?'

'I wudnae do that. I want to get to know all about you.' She's so unlike Annie; much more forward. Annie would never have dared to suggest going off for the afternoon on our own together when we had just met, much as both of us would have liked to.

'And I, you,' Maeve replied.

'Och, there's no much to know about me. You're the interesting one, with your work for the Gaelic League and all.'

'Sure most of that is just boring administrative stuff.'

'But you must meet all sorts of interesting people?'

'Sometimes.' They were walking towards the corner with Abbey Street to pick up a jaunting car and she started to tell him how James Joyce on a rare visit back home to his native country came to give a talk a few years ago. And both Padraig Pearse, the poet and his brother Willie, an accomplished artist and sculptor had spoken at League meetings.

'Padraig, of course is on the Executive Committee of the Gaelic League,' said Maeve. 'Oh, and we had Countess Markievicz, no less, quite recently. You met her last night.'

'I did. She and Eva were excellent hostesses. How come Constance is a countess, but?'

'Because she married a count, of course,' Maeve laughed.

'He wasnae there last night, was he?'

'Casimir? No. Sadly, he's gone. She met him in Paris and fell madly in love. They got married and lived here for a while but their relationship had been effectively over for some years before the threat of war gave Casimir the excuse he needed to leave Dublin and go back to Poland. They've got a daughter named after me,' Maeve added in a matter-of-fact tone of voice.

'Really?'

She laughed. 'Not really. I only got to know Constance recently, but I've met her daughter, Maeve. She's being brought up by her grandmother on their estate at Lissadell in Sligo. She visits her mother in Dublin every now and again.'

They had reached the rank of Jaunting cars and Will was less than impressed with the mangy looking ponies that were harnessed to the two-wheeled cars. Each horse stood between the shafts, head down and the picture of dejection. The jarveys hanging around smoking and chatting to each other looked little better in spite of the sunny day that this Palm Sunday was turning out to be. One soon brightened up, though, as Maeve called to him and started to haggle over the price of taking them out to Clontarf.

Having reached an amicable compromise with the driver, Maeve asked Will to put the hamper on one of the two bench seats that were arranged back to back and facing out sideways.

'Now be a gentleman and help me up, please,' she said.

There was a footrest that ran the length of each two-seater bench seat that made mounting a simple task, but Maeve took Will's proffered hand

and used it for extra support, continuing to hold him until she was comfortably settled on the padded leather seat next to the hamper.

The jarvey said, 'If you wouldn't be mindin' popping round t'other side, sir. Balance things up, like. It makes it easier for Ruby.'

Will readily obliged, taking the seat diagonally behind Maeve so that, leaning back, they could turn to face each other like in a Kissing Chair.

Ruby, as Will had guessed, was thc horse and their driver, in his greatcoat and bowler hat, introduced himself as Seán. He climbed up and perched high on a dickey at the front. His long whip flicked Ruby's ear and she obediently moved forward. The iron-rimmed wheels started to bump over the uneven road surface but much of the vibration was absorbed by the car seats' mounting springs.

'This is surprisingly comfortable,' said Will, as they got up to speed – a brisk walking pace.

'Have you not ridden on a jaunting car before?' asked Maeve, her head turned towards him, eyebrows raised.

'My first time.' Will found her eyes to be quite startling, soft but determined. 'And I'm so glad my first time is with you,' he added.

Maeve's rosy cheeks flushed a deeper hue and she quickly averted her gaze. 'Oh, look!' she said, 'That poor donkey.'

Will followed her pointing finger and saw an ass with two pannier baskets heavily overladen with peat. The turves were piled high on each side of the beast, towering above the small boy who was leading the animal. He directed it as close to the side as he could to let the jarvey squeeze the jaunting car past the wide load. Then Maeve pointed out the Abbey Theatre on their right.

'Mr Yeats founded the Abbey; him and a few others,' she said.

'I'd heard that, yes,' said Will.

Ruby trotted on and her passengers sat in silence for a while. City streets gave way to suburban roads and finally to open countryside. From time to time, one or other of them would remark on the scenery or something else that caught their eye and they would chat some more, only to allow the gentle rocking of the jaunting car, the clop-clopping of Ruby's hooves and the pale warmth of the April sunshine to lull them into silence once more.

Jolted, as one wheel hit a pot-hole, Will shifted in his seat. He said, 'You have no told me where we're going yet; you just said the seaside.'

'Oh, haven't I? No. Well it's an island, but there's a wooden bridge out to it. It's called Bull Island and it has three miles of strand. I haven't been there for years, but I used to love going as a girl. I wanted to take you.' Again she averted her eyes.

'That sounds grand, so it does.'

'Bull Island, you say?' Seán spoke over his shoulder.

'Yes, we thought you could drop us at the wooden bridge, please,' said Maeve.

'Sure that's all closed off to the public, now. Has been since the start of the war. Did you not know that?'

'Oh no. We didn't know,' said Will. 'So what, you can't go on the island at all?'

'Not this last two year, you can't. British army's using it for training. Learning how to dig trenches on the beach, or so I'm told.'

'Oh, Will, I'm so sorry;' Maeve looked on the verge of tears, 'I wanted our picnic to be on the strand. It was to be so perfect.'

'Ah, never fuss yourself, Maeve. We'll find a nice spot for our lunch that will be just as perfect.'

'If it's the sea you're wanting, I can set you down at Dollymount where the Irish Sea comes in between Bull Island and the mainland.'

'But there's no sand there as I recall; it's all reeds and if the tide's out, mud. Oh, I'm sorry, Will.'

'Maeve, please. Don't worry. You're giving me a wonderful time just taking me on this picnic outing. We can go to another beach another time.'

'Maybe there won't be another time.' All the sparkle had gone from her eyes and the hazel seemed to have paled to match her skirt.

'Don't say that. I'd like there to be another time. Lots of other times.'

'So would I, Will, only – '

'Only what.'

Maeve sat up straight and smiled at Will. 'Nothing. I'm being silly. Seán, will you take us a few hundred yards further to St Anne's Park. That's where we'll have our picnic; lying on the grass in the shade of the trees with bees buzzing in the blooms and the far-off sound of breakers crashing on the strand.'

* * *

They lay side by side on the rug, the remains of their picnic scattered about, an empty bottle of Chardonnay on its side next to two glasses. Will couldn't think of a better way to spend a Sunday afternoon. The sun was warm but not hot, so they didn't need the shade of the trees that were beginning to come into leaf. They'd chosen a spot not far from some ornamental flowerbeds and the scent of spring blossom was in the air but so far they had not heard the buzz of a bee. However, if they lay still and held their breath they could just make out the distant sound of breaking waves on the far side of Bull Island.

'You have to imagine the strand,' whispered Maeve; 'it's a really beautiful stretch of sand backed by dunes all the way along the island.

Will hadn't been impressed by the landward side of the island as they drove past the Wooden Bridge and causeway that led out to it, but he was happy to take Maeve's word for it about the splendour of the beach beyond the low sand hills.

He recalled the look of boredom on the faces of the two armed soldiers standing guard at the turn-off for the bridge as they passed them in their jaunting car. There were trestles with barbed wire stretched between them, blocking access. Maeve had turned right round to look at the soldiers. She waved at them as they approached.

'Don't they give you Sunday's off, then?' she called out.

Both soldiers brightened up to be addressed by a pretty colleen in her Easter bonnet. 'No, miss. Twenty-four hour guard here, miss.'

'Twenty-four hours! You can never stand there for twenty-four hours, can you?' The concern in Maeve's voice sounded genuine.

'Oh no, miss. There's three shifts. We're here 'til six o'clock.'

'Well, I hope it keeps fine for you,' she called with another wave. The soldiers and the Wooden Bridge retreated behind them as Ruby plodded on.

St Anne's Park was a little further on the left and Seán set them down by the entrance. Ruby immediately started to graze at the grassy verge.

'You're sure you don't want me to wait, at all?' said the Jarvey.

'No, no. We're fine, thank you. We'll catch a tram back later,' said Maeve, extracting an apple from their picnic hamper. 'Can I give this to Ruby?'

'You can, surely. She'll be your friend for life, she will.'

Will took the rug and hamper and Maeve held out the apple to the mangy animal that had brought them all the way from central Dublin. Ruby peeled back her great lips and then closed them delicately over the fruit. She crunched on it as Seán flicked her ear with his long whip. The horse moved off and executed a tight U-turn before trudging back in the direction of the city, paying scant regard to her new friend for life waving at the roadside.

The couple spent a lazy afternoon picnicking and chatting, or just lying in the sun. Will found Maeve easy to talk to. He loved the Dublin lilt in her voice and she said she could listen to his Down accent all day long. He told her some of his stories about lifeboat rescues, which had her listening, wide-eyed. Maeve told Will about her acting ambitions and how the Countess had introduced her to people at the Abbey Theatre. Will talked about his love of poetry and how great it had been to meet W. B. Yeats. Maeve talked about her work for the Gaelic League and how, when her brother had joined the Volunteers, she had too.

Will sat up, leaning on his hands behind him. 'You're in the Irish Volunteer Force? I didnae know the Volunteers took women.'

Maeve bridled at that and raised her head. 'And sure why wouldn't they? Tell me that, I'd like to know.'

'Oh, no reason. No. Why not, indeed?'

'Right. I'm in the *Cumann na mBan*, the League of Women; we're the woman's Volunteers. It's not just men who can fight for liberty. Sure, isn't Constance in the Citizens' Army?'

'She is? I didnae know that either.'

'She is, sure enough. I expect you'll see her there when you go to teach them your one-armed combat stuff.'

'Unarmed combat!' Will laughed. 'No need to make it harder than it is.'

'Oh, right. Yes, well, she's been drilling the men and teaching them marksmanship. She's a fine shot, they say. Brought up hunting on her father's estate in Sligo.'

'Well now. Seems quite a woman, does Constance.'

'Aye, she is that. Between the two of you there'll be no stopping our soldier boys, come the revolution.'

They lay back once more to the sound of the quarrelsome chirping of some sparrows and blue tits until a song thrush high on a branch added a more melodious note to the symphony. Will was thinking about his forthcoming self-defence sessions with the Citizens' Army. *Come the revolution*. That's what Ryan had said the first time they met at the foot of Nelson's Pillar. Is it just an expression? Something people say about some vague, far-off time when things will get better? Or does it have a more immediate significance? And would Maeve be involved? She's a

Volunteer; that surprised him. But perhaps it shouldn't. What she'd told him about Constance didn't. He'd learned at last night's soirée that the Countess and her sister were strong supporters of women's suffrage. In fact, it had been Eva, when working over in England, who had introduced Christabel Pankhurst and her daughter Emmeline to the movement.

Constance, apparently, had gone on to be a militant supporter of Trades Unionism, inspired by the passion of people like Alexander Bowman and the rather more radical Jim Larkin, actively supporting him during the infamous Dublin lockout in 1913. So, no, it didn't surprise him to learn of her involvement with the Citizens' Army. Why, therefore, should he be surprised that Maeve, an equally feisty individual, should have become a Volunteer?

He lifted his head and looked at her, lying at his side. Her eyes were closed against the sun; her hair kissed her cheeks from under her bonnet; her lips curled at the corners in the suggestion of a smile. Her small breasts and narrow waist gave enticing shape to her tight blouse. (The blue flowers were gentians, she said.) Her ankles, partly concealed by the flow of her skirt, were slim, delicate, also enticing. Will realised that he felt, not surprise, but concern about her involvement with the Irish Volunteers. He didn't want any harm to come to Maeve.

Was anything imminent? Or was he adding two and two and making five? He wondered what Edmond Boyd would make of him assisting the Cause by teaching the lads to fight and chuckled to himself. His mind, pulled back up North by thoughts of Boyd, flashed to Annie and other picnics; other days spent in the sun in Ward Park and on Copeland Island. Now here he was in another park, by another island.

With another girl.

He shut his eyes to cut off his view of Maeve and lowered his head back onto the rug. The brightness of the sun through his lids made circles of colour on his retinas as he tried to summon up a picture of Annie. He had loved her fuller figure, still beautifully proportioned but it was the slender shape of the girl lying beside him whose image he saw. He loved Annie's black hair against the paleness of her skin and how its little curls caressed the back of her neck but what he saw was a russet fringe under a bonnet and Maeve's rosy cheeks.

With difficulty he concentrated hard until he could visualise his beautiful Annie. The image was fleeting and was replaced by one of her lying in a pool of her own blood outside Ward Park in Bangor and a green Crossley 15 driving callously off down Hamilton Road, its muddy number plate in plain view, as though mocking him: IK something something 8.

Beside him Maeve stirred.

'We ought to start clearing up,' she said; 'we mustn't miss the tram back. Ryan is coming into town to meet someone at Liberty Hall and I'm supposed to join him there. Have you ever seen the Union headquarters?'

Will wasn't listening. Scenes were flashing through his mind like scratchy Pathé News films at the picture house. Ducks on the pond, the little dog off its leash, eyes displayed in the peacock's tail, Annie on the pavement, the look of horror on the face of the burly chauffeur and the disinterested, annoyed look of his passenger. And then, again, the retreating motorcar and its number plate. At the time he hadn't remembered the splatters of mud, but his subconscious had. It probably explained why he couldn't recall the first two digits. They were obscured by the mud; mud that slightly obscured the last digit, too.

Making an 8 look like a 3.

Another newsreel flash. Looking down from Mrs Rafferty's skylight at the Crossley 15 that had brought Rugby Shirt and his thugs to hunt him down. Will had made the same mistake then, when he looked at the number plate. Thought it ended in a three and then realised it was an eight. He remembered the familiar look about the burly driver. And he knew.

It was the same car.

The Crossley 15 that knocked down Annie.

Whose owner had left her to die.

And to find him Will realised he was going to have to track down the very men he had gone to such lengths to escape.

Chapter 12

Will turned onto Eden Quay carrying the picnic hamper. At his side, with the folded rug over her arm, Maeve trailed her free hand along the railings that fronted Liberty Hall until they reached the steps up to the central doorway. Before entering Will stepped back and glanced up to the parapet on the roof and then lowering his eyes to read the name that ran the full length of the imposing two-storey building above the ground floor windows. It read:

HEAD OFFICE IRISH TRANSPORT AND GENERAL WORKERS UNION

And, above it, a banner had been fixed which proclaimed:

WE SERVE NEITHER KING NOR KAISER
BUT IRELAND

Between the last two first-floor windows on the right were the words, "Irish Women Workers Union". On the left, between the first two windows, a matching sign read, "Office Irish Worker Newspaper."

'That was "Big Jim" Larkin's newspaper,' said Maeve, following the direction of Will's gaze.

'The union leader?'

'Yes. The Government banned it so he produced a new paper called "The Worker" but they banned that one, too.'

'Bit too controversial, was he?' said Will, eyeing the banner.

'A bit too truthful, he was. But they're still publishing. Mr Connolly has taken over since Mr Larkin went to America and handed over control of the Citizens' Army to him. He calls the paper the "The Workers' Republic" now.

The pair trotted up the three steps to the front door and weren't surprised to find it locked, being a Sunday. Will knocked and after a few moments it was opened by someone in the dull green uniform of the Citizens' Army. Maeve asked for Ryan and he stood back to allow them in. He appeared to have been expecting them, or Maeve, at least.

'I'll inform Mr Doloughan you're here, Miss,' the soldier said.

Placing the hamper on a reception desk, Will asked if he could use the lavatory and he was directed down a dark corridor where he found what he was looking for about halfway along. He entered a cubicle and had just locked the door when he heard the door from the corridor open and a voice he recognised at once as James Connolly's echoed around the tiled bathroom.

'… and I say we're better off without the likes of Seán O'Casey. His leaving us was a blessing in disguise.'

'How's that? He's a good man.' Will didn't recognise the second voice.

'He is. And he wrote a good constitution for the Army – for Larkin's Army, but we've moved on. We're no longer a workers' self-defence militia. What we have under our command, Michael, is a revolutionary organisation. You've got to grasp that. It's going to help create an Irish socialist republic. Seán was never up for that; at any rate, not for the physical force that it'll take to bring about.'

'Aye, it was the IRB convincing you to join their Military Council that decided O'Casey to quit,' the man addressed as Michael replied.

Will carefully and silently sat down and hardly dared breathe as he heard sounds of the two men going about their business at the urinals while continuing their conversation.

'They made it difficult for me to do otherwise,' said Connolly. 'I was more or less held captive. I'm convinced if I hadn't agreed to join their Executive I would not have left there alive. What it boiled down to was they were scared I'd initiate something with the CA before they were ready to start what they were planning.'

'Well, you made the right choice, James, I'm sure of that.'

‘Except I didn’t have a choice. But it was an easy decision to take. The Republican Brotherhood wants the same thing we do. It makes sense to go after it together.’

Will heard taps running and squeaking as they were turned off again.

‘But do the Irish Volunteers?’ said the man addressed as Michael. ‘Eoin MacNeill may not be another O’Casey but he sees the Volunteers as very much a defensive force. And as long as Bulmer Hobson has his ear he’s unlikely to change his attitude.’

‘Which is why the Chief of the Irish Volunteers and their entire executive must be told nothing. MacNeill is happy for the manoeuvres to take place and that’s all he need ever – ’

The rest of the sentence was lost to Will as the door to the corridor slammed and he was left with his mind spinning about the significance of what he had just heard.

‘There you are!’ Maeve greeted Will as he returned to the foyer where she was still waiting for Ryan. ‘I thought you’d got lost.’

‘No no. Sorry to keep you. I’ve been admiring the architecture. It’s a grand building.’

‘The building’s fine, but it’s what goes on in the building that is making Ireland a better place. Or will do. It’s only through empowering the people – the working people, the real people of Ireland that our country will ever truly prosper.’

‘Well said, little sister, well said!’ Ryan arrived in the foyer in the company of James Connolly and another gentleman as Maeve was speaking.

For once, Maeve let the “little sister” soubriquet pass unchallenged and addressed herself instead to Connolly. ‘These fine walls must have witnessed some momentous debates and seen many a far-reaching decision taken to better the Irish people.’

‘Indeed they have, Maeve, indeed they have,’ Connolly acknowledged.

Ryan held his hand out, ‘Will, good to see you again. Did you have a nice picnic in the park?’

‘It’s been a beautiful afternoon. Yes, thank you. A very enjoyable picnic in very enjoyable company,’ said Will, retrieving his hand from Ryan’s vigorous shake.

‘Ah, that’s grand. Now, Connolly you know. Let me introduce Michael Mallin. He and Countess Markievicz have been drilling the brave lads in the Citizens’ Army. Mallin’s in charge so he’ll sort you out on Tuesday evening for your first training session. Michael, this is Will Dillon.'

As soon as Mallin spoke Will recognised his voice as the second person he had overheard in the lavatory, 'Very pleased to meet you Dillon and more than grateful to take you up on your offer to give my lads some training in hand-to-hand fighting.'

'Happy to oblige, Mr Mallin, though I'm not sure what good I will be.'

'From what I hear from James, you're just the man we need. A timely arrival. Come and I'll show you where we can hold the class. See what you think.' Mallin headed off and Will followed with a nod to the others and a big smile for Maeve.

'This way,' said Mallin, holding a door for Will that led into what looked like a small gymnasium or fitness training room.

As the door swung to behind them Will caught the sound of Ryan's voice, 'So, the Wooden Bridge; what were you able to find out?'

* * *

That night, in his new lodgings off Talbot Street, Will couldn't sleep. His mind was too active and he kept going over the day's events. Making contact with Bradshaw. Feeling that he hadn't fully conveyed to the Englishman his sense of something imminent. Then the wonderful afternoon spent in Maeve's company. He was growing fond of Maeve – but what were her feelings for him? He thought there was a mutual attraction and that scared him a little but not enough to cause him to do anything to discourage it. But Ryan's voice kept popping into his mind: *Did you have a nice picnic in the park?* Will had been quick to affirm that they had, because it had been very pleasant indeed. It was only later that the significance of Ryan's question had hit him like a thunderbolt; later, when he heard him ask his sister about the Wooden Bridge.

The question Ryan should have asked was: Did you have a nice picnic on the beach? That's where Maeve told him they were going and should therefore have told Ryan, if she mentioned it at all. Yet Ryan knew they went to St Anne's Park.

So, the Wooden Bridge; what were you able to find out?

The whole trip had been to check out what security the British army had set up at Bull Island. Maeve already knew they wouldn't be able to picnic on the beach. She had used him as cover to spy for the Irish Volunteers. He hadn't felt so betrayed since the Crossley 15 had driven off leaving Annie to die. There was an empty feeling in the pit of his stomach. He had thought – just maybe – Maeve could have helped to heal the void left by Annie. And now to discover this.

He turned over in bed, eyes tight shut, and tried to will himself to sleep but his mind wouldn't let him.

Which is why the Chief of the Irish Volunteers and their entire executive must be told nothing. Connolly's voice. Nothing about what? What must Eoin MacNeill and Bulmer Hobson and the others not be told? Not about the manoeuvres planned for Easter Sunday; they were organising them, so that wasn't it. Unless... Will's mind flashed to the image of the *Innishmurray* nosing its way into the harbour at Donaghadee; the steam crane hoisting bales of rifles onto the quayside; the dozens of vehicles heading off to distribute them around County Down. Just a UVF exercise, they'd all been told. Only twelve people, George Gibson let slip afterwards, knew the truth beforehand.

Which is why the Chief of the Irish Volunteers and their entire executive must be told nothing. So what is the truth? Over 10,000 Volunteers – all armed, unless next Friday's landing can be thwarted – on training manoeuvres throughout the country. Training manoeuvres? Don't tell Eoin MacNeill. Tell him what?

Then Maeve again. Her pretty face, her slim body. Will lying beside her on the rug, watching her. With a sudden feeling of guilt, he realised the hypocrisy of his indignation at her ulterior motive for selecting the destination for their picnic. His whole life since arriving in Dublin has been a deception. He had his own ulterior motives for even befriending the Doloughans. But his growing feelings for Maeve transcended those. Could he dare to believe that perhaps hers for him did too?

Will finally fell into a fitful sleep where he dreamed he was driving a jaunting car at the head of a long column of Volunteers marching to the Wooden Bridge. There a whole platoon of British soldiers was holding Maeve hostage and blocking access to Bull Island.

He awoke far from refreshed on Monday morning and called Bradshaw first thing when he got to work. They met up again in his lunch break and he passed on his latest discoveries.

'OK, good stuff, but still all a bit vague, Will. We need proof of what they're planning, if indeed they are,' Geoff had said. Will promised to find it.

He remained preoccupied throughout the day. He had Constance Markievicz's "Boy Scouts" to regale in the evening with stories of derring-do on the high seas and he was looking forward to that. Before then, however, he wanted to get back to Munster's New and Used Motorcars to get addresses for the two Crossley 15 registration numbers that ended in 8. That would be the easy bit. Tomorrow, or as soon as he could, he would have to check out the addresses without running into Rugby Shirt and his merry band.

* * *

Buster Gregson – the man Will knew as Rugby Shirt – was, as it happened, rather preoccupied himself that Monday morning. He had to report to the Boss with the weekend's takings from his girls. He wished Eamon's dislocated kneecap would hurry up and mend. He wished he was visiting the posh home of Michael J Higginson for a bathing pool party, not on business – especially as he knew the Boss was bound to ask him about progress on finding Blackbeard. Which was precisely nothing.

Which was why Buster had decided to delay his visit to the Boss until after he had paid another visit first. To a house in Mary's Lane.

Mrs Rafferty opened her front door in response to a demanding thumping on the panel. Gregson pushed her back into her hall as he barged in and slammed the door behind him.

'In there,' he commanded, shoving her again, this time through an open door that led to a room containing a number of tables waiting to be cleared of breakfast things.

Gregson pulled out one of the chairs. 'Sit,' he said and enjoyed the look of terror in the old woman's eyes as she obeyed.

Until now she hadn't spoken; she'd hardly drawn a breath. But she found her voice which trembled as she said, 'What do you want? I know you. You're that friend of Mr Dillon. Only I don't believe you are his friend. Who are you?'

This is going to be easy, thought Gregson. So his name's Dillon. 'Shut up! I'm asking the questions.' His left hand slapped her hard across her right cheek.

Mrs Rafferty gasped and stifled a sob.

'Where's Dillon?

The old lady held a hand to her cheek as it turned bright red.

'Do you want another slap? Where is he?'

'He's not here,' Mrs Rafferty said, quickly, her eyes glistening. 'He's gone.'

'Gone where?'

'He didn't say. Only that his business here was finished and he was moving on.' She cringed as Gregson raised a hand to deliver another slap. 'It's the truth; I don't know where he's gone. Please don't hit me again.'

'He must have said something.'

'He didn't. He came in on Friday night – he'd had a nasty fall; he tripped over on the uneven pavement. That was when he told me.'

'Told you what?'

'That he'd be leaving in the morning.'

'And no forwarding address?'

'No'

'I don't believe you. You're holding back.' Gregson's right hand shot out and Mrs Rafferty reeled from the blow to her other cheek. She started to weep.

'I'm not; I've told you everything I know,' she sobbed. She cowered as Gregson raised his hand once more.

'No don't!' she shouted. 'Maybe the Post Office could help you find him. I think he said he was working there last week. Please don't hit me again.'

Gregson lowered his hand and gently patted the old woman's glowing cheek. 'There's a fine girl,' he said. 'Don't bother to get up, I'll see myself out.'

Buster Gregson would have no opportunity to check out the Post Office that day. After reporting to the Boss out at his South-Dublin mansion, Kelly was driving him on to Kingstown (Dun Laoghaire) to pick up a couple of new girls freshly shipped in from Liverpool. They were expecting to start jobs as nurse maids in one of the posher suburbs, but by the evening they had both been raped twice by Gregson and one of his henchmen and been left in no doubt about what their new jobs actually entailed. That night the girls were locked in a room in the rundown tenement in Beresford Street. When Elsie returned in the small hours, tired from servicing five punters, she heard their sobs and knew that her living quarters would soon be more cramped again.

So it wasn't until after lunch on Tuesday that Buster Gregson made his way to Sackville Street and, full of pent-up anger at the trouble this Dillon bloke was causing him, strode up to the big central doors of the General Post Office.

Chapter 13

Will was in a much better frame of mind when he got to work on Tuesday. It was a quiet morning as far as telegraphic communications were concerned, and he had plenty of time to lose himself in his own thoughts. *Na Fianna Éireann* were a fine bunch of young lads who had seemed to enjoy his unique brand of storytelling last night. Their discipline and enthusiasm were a tribute to Constance Markievicz and Bulmer Hobson, her co-founder of the nationalist scouting movement. It was Hobson who introduced Will to the boys as their speaker for the evening – after they all settled down, that is, following a session of target practice with air rifles led by the countess herself. Will could quite see in their eager faces a fruitful recruiting ground for the Irish Republican Brotherhood.

Prior to turning up for his session with these *Sinn Féin* Boy Scouts, as Éamon de Valera had called them, Will had managed to get the two further addresses he needed from Munster's New and Used Motorcars. He had cycled out to their sales rooms on his 'new' black Raleigh that he'd picked up cheap in a junk shop. He explained that his motorcar was in for repairs. One of the registration numbers ending in 8 showed an address out Clontarf way, where he had been on Sunday with Maeve, but the owner was a lady in her late 60s. The salesman remembered her well as he had thought her a little old for a Crossley. Will decided to discount that one. The other had been allocated to a Michael J Higginson who lived in one of the smarter areas in South Dublin and Will planned to make a visit out there on Thursday evening, since Tuesday and Wednesday would be taken up with his unarmed combat classes.

When he arrived to speak to her boy scouts, and Constance discovered that he had not had time for any dinner beforehand, she insisted on driving him back home with her afterwards in her open-topped Rover. Eva would have a meal ready, she said, and people were always dropping in; there would be plenty for an extra guest.

And so it proved to be. Enough for two extra, as it happened. Bulmer Hobson, who had left the scouting meeting on other business after introducing Will, had dropped round with a book he had promised Constance she could borrow and Eva had persuaded him to stay to dine with them.

Will spent a most enjoyable evening in the company of the two older women and the Secretary of the Volunteers' provisional council and sometime member of the Supreme Council of the IRB, as he learned from Hobson during the evening's conversation. The four discussed poetry, politics, the theatre and, inevitably perhaps, man's perennial battle with the sea. Will and Bulmer shared reminiscences of life in the north, Hobson being a Belfast man, while Constance told them something of her time in Paris with Count Casimir and how he had once fought a duel with swords to defend her honour. They talked well into the small hours before the conversation started to ebb. Eva insisted on driving the two men home, dropping Hobson off at his house on the way into the city centre with Will.

In his lunch break the next day, as it was bright and sunny again, Will walked down past Trinity and entered St Stephen's Green to explore more of this haven of peace within the busy city. As he strolled beneath the trees, he thought how much he was enjoying life in Dublin. His true purpose for being there wasn't proving to be too onerous so far and he was meeting the most interesting and stimulating people. Eva Gore-Booth liked much of the same sort of poetry that appealed to Will and she had even signed a slim volume of her own work and given it to him as he was preparing to leave last night. The countess was the more militantly political of the two and as well as talking about her earlier love of the stage and her appearances at the Abbey, she also enthused about the wonderful preparation her *Fianna Éirann* boys were getting and how much she enjoyed helping to organise and train the Citizens' Army. Will got the distinct impression from a few brief asides she had with Hobson that, despite her being a woman, this feisty female was more than just a training officer for the CA.

His stroll through the park took him diagonally to the far corner. Will turned north and continued up Monks path to the lake before making his way around it back to the entrance gate. As he walked, grey squirrels scuttled out of his way and shot up the trunks of nearby trees. From the branches overhead he heard many varieties of bird song that lightened his heart, although he had no idea which voice belonged to which species. He recognised a blackbird that he spotted on a bush and a thrush that was pecking at something in the grass but he couldn't put names to most of the smaller birds that were flitting about. Maeve could have. She had enjoyed pointing out blue tits and great tits and long-tailed tits during their picnic on Sunday. And sparrows, but he knew them – except some that he thought were sparrows were dunnocks, Maeve told him with a friendly laugh.

Maeve. Pretty little Maeve. He wondered, could she feel some attraction towards him. She had been such wonderful company and she would touch his arm in her enthusiasm to draw his attention to another bird, or a flower. There was a nuthatch – small bird with a long pointed beak, he remembered. And he remembered the touch of her hand on his arm. He couldn't hold it against her that her Irish patriotism had caused her to join the women's Volunteers, nor that, as a member, she could be asked to report on British army sentry posts. Especially considering his own reasons for being in Dublin. Perhaps he had been wrong to assume she had been using him – any more than he had used her. Maybe she did hold a little affection for him. The sudden warm glow he felt wasn't just the spring sunshine on his face, as he got back from his lunchtime perambulation and headed under the portico to the big double doors of the Post Office.

There was something familiar about the back of the man entering the vestibule in front of him, but it was not until the individual revealed his profile as he turned to go through into the main concourse that Will pulled up short and remained motionless. His old adversary, Rugby Shirt was only feet away. Will tilted his head forwards so that the peak of his cap would hide his features and held back until the man had gone through the swing doors.

Now what? Why was he here? Did he want to buy a stamp or send a telegram? Or was he looking for Will Dillon and, if so, what were his intentions? He could hardly plan to start a fight in the GPO or expect to abduct him without a fight. Will didn't want to be late back from lunch but he decided he had no alternative. In spite of his changed appearance he couldn't risk being seen up close by this man who had so recently promised to kill him.

He walked a little way along the front of the building and took up a position where one of the pillars hid him from view from the Post Office entrance but from where he could keep watch on who was coming out.

It was almost five minutes before Rugby Shirt re-emerged. He stood at the door and looked up and down Sackville Street. Was he searching the faces of the crowds? Had he found out that Will worked there and was due back from lunch? At last, he appeared to give up and move away. He crossed to the centre of Sackville Street and Will moved, keeping the column between them. Now, instead of continuing across the other half of the thoroughfare Rugby Shirt stopped by Nelson's Pillar and stood facing the GPO. It seemed he was determined to await Dillon's arrival.

Will couldn't delay his return much longer but if he walked up to the door now, the man couldn't fail to see him, it was just a question of whether he would recognise him without his beard. But since he must have enquired about him and now knew he was due back, he might also know that he no longer had the bushy black beard. Will couldn't risk being recognised. Keeping the columns between him and the watcher by Nelson's Pillar, he hurried to the far end of the building and slipped round the corner into Prince's Street.

Now really late, he sprinted down the side of the GPO until he reached the slip road used by the postal delivery vehicles emerging from the back of the building. He had been introduced to Brian, the gatekeeper on his first day but hadn't had occasion to speak to him since. On being challenged, Will told him who he was and that he'd decided to go clean-shaven for a while. Brian scrutinised Wills features.

'You look different, but I'd recognise that County Down accent anywhere. In you go, Mr Dillon.'

Will was breathing hard as he took his place behind the counter.

'You're lucky the boss seems to be on an extended lunch break, himself, today,' said a colleague.

'Yeah, sorry. Got held up. It willnae happen again.'

'Ah, don't worry about it. You missed your friend, though.'

'Oh?'

'Aye, Buster, he said his name was. Buster Gregson? Was looking for you. It seemed quite urgent.'

‘What did you tell him?’

‘Well, it was about a quarter of an hour ago and I told him you’d be back any minute. Silly me, thinking you’d stick to your allotted hour for lunch.’

‘I’ve said I’m sorry.’

‘Hey, I’m just kidding you. Anyway he said he couldn’t wait and off he went.’

‘He asked for me by name, not description?’ Will ventured.

‘No, he asked where Mr Dillon, who was working here last week had moved on to. I said to him you hadn’t moved anywhere; you still worked here. That’s when I told him you were due back any minute. Then he said he couldn’t wait and left pretty sharpish. I thought it was a bit odd, to tell you the truth.’

‘Aye, well thanks for telling me.’

‘Is everything all right?’ Will’s colleague looked concerned.

‘Oh aye. Nae problem. I’ll lose nae sleep over having missed him, but.’

Will turned to deal with a customer who had come up to his position, his mind racing through the implications of this Buster fellow having traced him to the Post Office and knowing his name. He wasn’t going to give up. Will would have to stay vigilant.

When it was time to go home, he played it safe and left the GPO by the ramp at the rear of the building.

‘Goodnight, sir,’ old Brian spoke to him as he passed the gatekeeper’s hut. ‘Doing anything interesting this evening?’

‘Oh, nothing special, Brian. You take it easy, now. Goodnight to you.’ Will thought it wiser not to publicise his planned extra-curricular activities with the Citizens’ Army.

Emerging onto Sackville Street, he turned south towards the river without looking back at the GPO main entrance; he had no wish to attract the attention of anyone still watching there. When he got to Liberty Hall he was expected and a man in a dull green uniform took him through to the mini-gymnasium Mallin had shown him on Sunday. Before long it was filled with about twenty CA members. Will wasn’t sure whether to refer to them as soldiers or citizens.

‘These good citizens are soldiers to a man,’ said Michael Mallin by way of introduction, which didn’t help at all. However, the evening’s practical lessons proceeded without any need for Will to refer to the participants' status.

'When you're faced with someone trying to kill you,' he explained, 'it doesn't matter two hoots whether you're an ordinary citizen or a man in uniform; or whether your antagonist is a British soldier or common thug.'

'Same thing,' someone called out from the back.

'You're right!' said Will. 'Same thing insofar as it's your life or his and in war there's only one rule. Kill or be killed.' Will cringed inwardly that he was advocating the killing of British soldiers but he added a moderator. 'However, having said that, it's not always necessary, or indeed desirable, to kill your opponent. The fact is, it's often much quicker and easier and tactically more advantageous to disable him; put him out of the fight for the duration. The wounded soldier that needs rescuing, doctoring, hospitalising, is a lot more bother to the enemy than a dead one.'

By the end of the evening the first twenty all knew the rudiments of self-defence and a second and a third batch had also gone through the same training in the basic manoeuvres. About half-a-dozen from each session, who showed particular aptitude, were selected for another session the following evening of more advanced moves and techniques. These included a number of officers; men like Michael Collins, Cathal Brugha, Thomas MacDonagh.

Constance Markievicz popped in halfway through, her face registering approval as she watched for a few minutes.

'I imagine you'll be here until quite late,' she said to Will as he stepped back to allow two opponents to practice a new move, 'so I won't offer you dinner tonight. Maybe tomorrow, if you finish a bit earlier?'

'That's very good of you, Constance, but I can't keep sponging off you and Eva.'

'Nonsense, dear boy, we'd be delighted to have you. Besides there's something we need to discuss. I'll drop by about this time tomorrow. I mustn't keep you from your good work. Goodbye.'

Will tried to return his concentration to his coaching but his active mind kept turning over just what it could be that Constance might need to discuss.'

* * *

He was still pondering that conundrum on Wednesday evening when the countess looked into the gymnasium as he was concluding his session of advanced training.

'I'll be in the foyer as soon as you're ready, Will,' she called and left him to finish off.

As she went out of the room, Michael Mallin came in. He had been keeping a watching brief on the men's progress under Will's instruction over the last two evenings.

'Well, Dillon, on behalf of my men I'd like to thank you for your time and expertise. I think I can safely say that the Citizens' Army is in better shape because of your efforts. What do we say, lads? Hip, hip!'

'Hooray!' The room echoed to the men's enthusiastic response and did so twice more as they repeated their cheers, much to Will's embarrassment.

'Och, away on with yous. Sure it's all good fun. I only hope yous dinnae have any call to put your new skills into practice any time soon.'

Will had half expected Mallin to ask him if he could spare them more time next week, judging by his appreciation of what had been achieved so far, but there was no mention of any further training. Just a grateful handshake as he was leaving.

'I'm very much obliged to you, Dillon. Now, I believe you are off for a chat with the Countess Markievicz. We'll meet again, I'm sure.'

'Goodbye, Mr Mallin. I hope we shall, indeed.'

* * *

Thirty-five minutes later Will found himself back, once more, at the home of Eva Gore-Booth. There was a most enticing smell of Irish stew coming from somewhere to the rear of the big entrance hall but, after removing their coats and hats, Constance showed Will into the resplendent salon where he had met Yeats on his first visit.

The room was not filled with elegantly dressed guests as on that previous occasion but nor was it empty. A man turned from admiring some exquisite pieces of Wedgewood in a walnut display cabinet and extended a hand of greeting to the new arrivals.

'Constance, lovely to see you. And Will! Good to see you again, too.'

Will braced himself for the demented terrier handshake and said, 'You too, Ryan. I wasn't expecting to see you here.' He glanced around, half hoping to see Maeve somewhere but there was no sign of her. Ryan was continuing:

'Did Constance not mention that. Tut tut. She's a great one for the secrecy, she is. Not a bad trait to have, though.'

'All she said was, there was something she needed to discuss with me. I'm intrigued. What's this all about?'

'I apologise, Will, but Ryan is involved in what we shall talk about. Not until we have had something to eat, though. There are delicious smells coming from the dining room. Please. Come through.'

They moved to the rear of the salon and went under the arch in time to see Eva pulling the cork from a bottle of claret. Will noticed another on the sideboard behind her, already uncorked and left to breath. They all took their places and he had to restrain his curiosity throughout the meal of mutton, exquisitely stewed with chopped carrots, turnip, parsnips and potatoes and well-seasoned with bay leaves and relish.

It was not until the last of the fine claret had been poured that Constance returned to the subject that had been occupying Will's mind for the past twenty-four hours. Even catching a glimpse of Gregson hanging around the main entrance of the GPO, while returning from his lunch break, had only displaced for a few moments his continual thoughts about what on earth Constance might want to discuss.

Eva passed the cheese board around. Will helped himself to some ripe stilton before handing it on to Ryan, as Constance spoke.

'I expect you've been wondering, Will, what it is we needed to discuss.'

Eva stood up. 'If you're all going to talk business, I'll just take these things out to the kitchen. She piled empty dishes and used cutlery on a tray and left her sister with the two gentlemen.

'I have wondered, off and on, I must admit,' said Will.

Constance looked at Ryan. 'Perhaps you'd like to explain,' she said, putting her little finger to her lips to push an errant crumb of Irish cheddar into her mouth.

'I will, indeed,' said Ryan. 'The thing is, Will, we could do with your help tomorrow evening.'

'More unarmed combat lessons, is it?'

'Ah no. I heard those went down well with the boys, though. No it's not that – though it could involve a spot of combat, sure enough. I hope not but it's better to be safe than sorry.'

'We would like you to accompany some IRB men on an important mission tomorrow evening,' Constance cut in. 'It's vital they get to… a certain place to carry out some IRB work in the early hours of Friday – '

'And we'd like you to ensure they get there unmolested.' Ryan again.

'Be a sort of bodyguard, you mean.'

'Exactly. And with your skills you're just the man for the job.'

'But – these men are IRB? Weren't in my classes, then? Can't they look after themselves?'

'They are specialists. Radio ops, telegraphic communications. So fighting… self-defence – not really their thing.'

'Not that we expect there to be any. Fighting,' said Constance. 'But just in case they meet with any opposition we'd feel much happier if you were with them.'

'It's essential they get where they need to be to set up their equipment very early on Friday morning.'

'Good Friday,' said Will.

'The day after tomorrow.'

'So where would we be headed?'

'Can't tell you that, precisely. Not yet, but you'll be travelling across to the west coast. You'll have to call in sick on Friday, I'm afraid, unless you've got it as a holiday.'

'Actually, I don't work any Fridays, so that won't be a problem.'

'Perfect. So you'll do it for us?' Ryan pushed back his chair and stood up.

Constance said, 'Come to Liberty Hall tomorrow night at 9:00. It should be an easy walk from your digs, according to Eva. You'll be told everything you need to know, then.'

'Is that not a bit late for a journey across Ireland?'

Ryan said, 'You'll be catching the last train to Killarney. That's all you need to know for now. Travelling through the night there'll be fewer nosey police around, or soldiers.'

'Now just hould on there a minute. Why would the police be interested in us?' asked Will.

'Sure, aren't they getting paranoid with their random stop and searches, especially the closer we get to the manoeuvres coming up on Sunday,' said Ryan

'Well, why not wait until after Sunday, then?' asked Will with apparent innocence.

With barely a moment's hesitation, Constance said, 'We're on a fixed timescale, Will. I'm afraid after Sunday wouldn't do at all.'

* * *

'Just tell him there's a good show on at thc Abbey, tonight.' Will rung off and tried to concentrate on his Thursday morning work at the Post Office. He'd had another fitful night trying to piece together everything he was picking up from his republican friends; certainly enough to warrant another report to Bradshaw. *After Sunday wouldn't do at all.* What did Countess Markievicz mean by that? Sunday. It has to be related to the manoeuvres but in what way? Radio operators; the west coast. Kerry? It has to be Kerry. To contact the ship bringing in guns? But telegraphic communications? And if it's only manoeuvres why is it so important to have the guns?

He must have finally dropped off sometime in the small hours and as a result found he'd overslept in the morning. Because he was running late he had to risk using the main Post Office entrance, slipping in among a small crowd of early shoppers.

Having left his message for Bradshaw, he hung up the phone's earpiece and, without looking up, accepted a telegram form that the next customer handed to him over the counter. He totted up the words and made a quick mental calculation.

'That will be 2/6, please,' he said, glancing now at the customer.

Staring back at him was the ugly face of Buster "Rugby Shirt" Gregson.

Chapter 14

Karl Spindler eyed the off-centred blue and white cross that stood out against the red material being whipped and slapped against the mast-head of the *Aud Norge* by a North Atlantic squall. His ship, flying the Norwegian colours had passed, unchallenged, through the Royal Navy blockade between the Faeroes and Iceland but had been forced to shelter in the lee of Rockall until high seas dropped sufficiently for her to continue safely. However, he was still in good time which was fortunate as he continued to make heavy weather all the way down the west coast of Ireland as far as County Kerry and was glad to reach his rendezvous point where he anchored off Inishtooskert Island.

He remained there for some time. Although he had arrived a day ahead of schedule he still hoped to make contact with the shore. Seeing no sign, he sailed slowly into Tralee Bay and then turned to head back to Inishtooskert.

'British vessel approaching our starboard side, Captain,' said the first mate in faultless Norwegian.

Damn. He could do without this. Spindler's irritated glance to his right confirmed the presence of a navy auxiliary ship fast overtaking them and closing. He took a pragmatic look around the wheelhouse. He and his First Mate, like the rest of the crew were dressed in typical Scandinavian seamen's gear, all purchased in second-hand shops in Oslo. Charts and other documents lying around were all in Norwegian. There was even a trashy novel by a popular writer from Bergen sitting, half-read, by an empty Pilsener glass.

Spindler throttled back, his grim features set. 'Let them come,' he said.

Five minutes later *HMS Shatter* had a line on board the *Aud Norge* and an armed boarding party had transferred to Spindler's ship. A British Lieutenant was examining the papers that the captain proffered, readily enough.

British Intelligence knew from intercepted Irish communications with the German embassy in Washington that a consignment of guns was expected at some stage. The naval officer's instructions were to be on the lookout for a German ship trying to smuggle rifles into Ireland. The size of the delivery was not known but he was expecting something much bigger than the *Aud Norge* and one heavily armed, so he wasn't surprised when he found nothing untoward about this small ship that belonged to a neutral and friendly country.

The Lieutenant folded the papers and handed them back to Spindler. He glanced around the wheelhouse as he said in a mixture of English and rather poor Norwegian, 'These all seem to be in order. We'll detain you no longer.'

Captain Spindler watched *HMS Shatter* sail away. His grim expression remained but the corner of his mouth now turned up slightly. He recalled how a Hull ship, the *Castro* had been captured by the Germans and renamed the *Libau* and how it had been loaded with 20,000 rifles, ten machine guns and a million rounds of ammunition following negotiations with the Britisher, Sir Roger Casement – a staunch Irish Nationalist, from all accounts, even though the son of a British army officer. The man had wanted much more but that was all he was to be allowed. Karl Spindler was, nevertheless, proud to have been given the job of transporting these arms to help the Irish in their fight against the hated English.

He patted the highly-polished wooden wheel of his ship that had been renamed yet again and disguised as Norwegian as he set his course once more for Inishtooskert.

* * *

Just about the time Spindler was taking back his expertly forged papers from the British naval lieutenant, Will Dillon's heart missed a beat as he glanced up at the customer on the other side of the counter in the General

Post Office in Dublin. Their eyes locked for less than a second before Will snapped his gaze away.

Less than a second, but time enough for him to recognise the man who had sworn to kill him. The question was, had Gregson recognised him without his beard? And if he had, what would he do? Did he have a gun concealed under his jacket? Did he have backup with him? Would he risk taking any action in such a public place? These thoughts flashed though Dillon's mind in the time it took him to divert his gaze from the ugly features of the pimp and refocus on the telegram form.

He stole a glance around the concourse trying to spot any of Gregson's henchmen as he accepted the half-crown his customer offered him without showing any signs of recognition.

In spite of his raised heart-rate, Will had the presence of mind to put on a southern brogue as he said, 'Thank you, sir. That'll be sent off straight away.'

Buster Gregson turned and, without a backwards glance, left the Post Office. Will Dillon took a deep breath and with a controlled, slow release allowed his heartbeat to regain some semblance of normality.

In his lunch break he took extra care as he emerged from Prince's Street and headed for the bridge and St Stephens Green. He felt sure no watchers by Nelson's Pillar could have seen him.

At 12.30 precisely, he saw Geoff Bradshaw wander onto the little hump-backed bridge and stop a pace or two beyond where he was watching a pair of ducks on the lake. Without looking at him, Bradshaw asked, 'What have you got for me?'

Will didn't look up but told Geoff about his intended trip across Ireland to the west coast and how postponing it until after Sunday would be "too late" according to Countess Markievicz .

'It can only be to rendezvous with a ship bringing guns,' he said, 'and something serious is going down on Sunday.'

'The day of the Volunteer manoeuvres?'

'Exactly.'

'Good work, Will. If you can get anything more precise, let me know.' Bradshaw seemed to lose interest in the ducks and continued on across the bridge.

Dillon pulled out his pocket watch and glanced at the time before turning and walking back in the direction of the General Post Office.

With the Easter weekend ahead only a skeleton staff would be on duty and Will felt obliged to clear as much work as he could since he wouldn't be in again until Monday. As a result it was much later than usual when he stood and stretched his limbs, finally able to call it a day. He took his usual precautions, leaving by the Prince's Street exit and taking a roundabout route to his digs.

* * *

Ewan Moore stepped out from a narrow alleyway at the end of Prince's Street. He was the younger brother of Eamon Moore who had only just, with the aid of a pair of wooden crutches, been allowed to put any weight on his right leg, which now sported a fine cast made of plaster of Paris. The younger Moore had been concealed in the shadows of the alley for some hours on the instructions of his brother, who, the previous evening, had berated Buster Gregson for a fool for not realising that the GPO would have a rear entrance.

Before starting his shift he conferred with Gregson who was still watching the front.

'We've got the bastard at last!' Gregson told his crony. 'I thought I spotted him going in this morning, though it was a back view so I couldn't be sure.'

'So how do you know it's him?'

'Didn't I go in after him, myself? I waited a bit until there were plenty of customers inside – '

'And you spotted him?'

'Not right away. I scanned all the counter staff and thought he wasn't there. Thought I'd made a mistake. Then I looked again at the bloke on the telegrams. It was Dillon! But without the big black beard. As clean-shaven as a baby's arse, he was, but he didn't fool me.'

'Did he see you, at all?' asked Ewan.

'Oh, he did, right enough. Didn't I scribble out a telegram and ask him to send it for me?' Gregson chuckled.

'You did what!'

'Put the fear of God into him. We locked eyes for a brief moment and I showed no sign of recognising him, but he knew me all right. He looked away pretty damn quick but I saw it in his eyes in that fraction of a second. He knows his days are numbered.'

'Eamon wants to be there when the Boss deals with him,' said Ewan.

‘I know he does. Don’t we all? We’ll have a jolly little party in the cellar over there one day soon.’ He nodded across Sackville Street to the offices of Michael J Higginson.

Ewan made his way round to the alley where he relieved another of Higginson’s men who had been on surveillance all morning and trailed their quarry on an apparently random walk to St Stephen’s Green at lunchtime.

Now he was walking about ten yards behind as Dillon made his way through the evening crowds of office workers, all homeward bound or bent on various other diversionary activities. He had been expecting to see him using the rear access after his colleague told him of his lunchtime sortie and when he saw him come up the slip road he recognised him with the help of Gregson’s updated description, as the man in Mary’s Lane whose arm he had held rigid while Gregson punched him in the stomach.

As he followed him through the Dublin streets, he was thinking about the last ‘jolly party’ he had attended beneath the offices of *Higginson Enterprises*. The walls of the stone basement were thick. The screams of a wretched employee who had been caught siphoning off funds collected from local small businesses as protection money could not be heard beyond them. Higginson was fairly sure the man had been acting alone but to be certain he had Éamon Moore use a pair of secateurs on the man’s fingers. By the time the third one was removed just below the second knuckle and the writhing and bloodied creature strapped to a big wooden upright supporting the ceiling was still protesting that no one else was involved, Higginson had been inclined to believe him.

Quickening his pace to come out into Talbot Street, Ewan glanced each way before he spotted Dillon again, crossing to the far side. There were less people on these pavements so he had to drop back further to ensure he wasn’t detected.

As he dogged Dillon’s footsteps, his mind was still back in the cellar. He shuddered as he recalled how Higginson had taken a flick-knife from his pocket and thrust it into the prisoner’s gut, twisting it and slicing upwards before pulling it out and wiping the blade clean on the man’s trouser leg.

‘Clear up this mess,’ he said, striding over to the wooden stairs to return to his office.

Ewan and the others had the job of disposing of the man's body once the bleeding from his belly had stopped along with his heart.

Twenty yards in front of him he saw Dillon turn into a side street and Ewan hurried forward to get eyes on him once more. He stopped at the corner and peered round.

The road was empty.

Nothing. No one.

Ewan's mind raced. He daren't lose Dillon now. Gregson's perennial threat to have his guts for garters loomed large. He hurried forward, his heart racing. The man can't have just vanished.

* * *

Up in his room Will heard the rapping on the front door and out of idle curiosity he went to the front bay window where he could see down to whoever was calling. The sash was raised a crack to air the room and he heard Mrs Gilpin's voice saying, 'Sorry, no vacancies. Did you not see the sign?'

What he heard next caused him to duck back sharply out of sight.

'Ah no, I'm not after a room. I'm looking for a Mr Dillon. I believe he might be staying in your guesthouse.'

'Dillon, you say? No. No one of that name here. Try Mrs Flannigan two doors up.'

'I'm much obliged to you, Missus,' came the reply.

'Ah, sure it's nothing at all. I hope you find your friend.'

Will heard the click of the front door closing and the footsteps of the caller making his way further along the road. He shifted the lace curtain and took a cautious look through the window, thanking his lucky stars that he had thought to give a false name to Mrs Gilpin when he had booked in.

The caller was standing sideways on, knocking on the door next but one. Will felt sure he recognised him as one of the gang that had set upon him last Friday night. His hand went involuntarily to his bruised thigh that still ached from time to time. Will watched the thug speaking to someone at the other guesthouse before turning away. He trudged further up the road and eventually down the other side, knocking on each door in turn and Will could only assume that he had somehow managed to follow him back home but hadn't seen which house he had entered. A lucky break.

By now it was getting on towards nine o'clock and, between keeping an eye on the progress of his stalker, Will had made himself ready for his journey to the west coast but he could still see the man loitering up near the Talbot Street end. He decided to take his trusty Raleigh which was in the back yard. He could leave by the lane at the rear. The trouble was it made a right between two houses and joined the side road a bit further up. Will was relying on the extra speed of the bike to avoid any unwelcome confrontation with Gregson's thug if he should spot him slipping away.

As it happened, as far as he could tell the man had no idea the cyclist riding off down the street was his quarry and Will made it safely to Liberty Hall a few minutes before nine. He was shown into a small conference room that contained a table that had seen better days. Apart from chairs around the table, the room held nothing else. A number of men were already there, some standing, some seated. Ryan Doloughan was near the head of the table talking to a resolute-looking young man who looked to be in his mid-twenties. His smart suit and neatly parted hair spoke of a meticulousness that would shortly be confirmed.

'Come in, Will,' Ryan called out as he saw him enter. 'Take a seat; I think we're all here.' He raised his voice, 'Sit down, everyone, and we'll make a start. This won't take long. Michael, over to you. You all know Michael Collins, I'm sure.'

Will opened his mouth to speak and Ryan quickly added, 'Except, possibly, Mr Dillon, here.' Will and Collins exchanged nods. 'Tonight's little exercise is all Michael's idea and a damn fine one it is, I think you'll agree when you've heard it. Michael.'

'Gentlemen. You're here this evening because each of you has a specific part to play in a special operation. Con Keating, here, is our radio expert. Charlie Monaghan, mechanic and wireless installation expert. Donal Sheehan, you've worked at the War Office and know the Admiralty codes.'

Each man, as his name was mentioned, nodded in acquiescence to the description given.

'And Will Dillon,' Collins continued; 'a handy man to have by you in a punch-up, I'm told. His job is to protect you along the way from any unwanted attention. I cannot overstress how important it is that you succeed in your mission. Nothing and no one must be allowed to get in your way.'

Will wondered if he was the only one who, as yet, had little idea of what the mission was about, but Collins was still speaking.

'And that just leaves Ryan Doloughan.' He placed a hand on that worthy's shoulder. He'll be co-ordinating things at this end. You can contact him by phone at any time of the day or night.'

'So what exactly is our mission, Mr Collins?' It was the wireless installation man, Charlie Monaghan who raised the question.

Will smiled. So there were others in the dark, too.

'We couldn't tell you before. Only the Military Council of the IRB know the details and have approved them. Not even the Supreme Council know of this, which is why not a word of what you are about to be told must be discussed with anyone who is not part of the mission.'

Collins went on to outline the plan and by the time he finished Will's mind was in a whirl. As soon as he heard it he knew he had, somehow, to pass on the information. No time to lose. But how? And to whom?

There was no way of contacting Geoff Bradshaw so late in the evening. Who else could he tell who could inform the authorities, or – and a sudden idea flashed into his mind – or who had the power to get the whole thing called off?

Will realised Ryan was talking. 'There's a pony and trap waiting to take you and your equipment to the station. Any questions?'

There were none. They all rose from the table and Will said to Ryan, 'I wasnae expecting to go straight off. I've a couple a things I need from my lodgings. But I'm on my bike so I'll nip back and then cycle to the station. By the time they load the trap and plod through the streets, I'll probably be there before the others.'

'Well, mind you are, then. Hurry up, man.' Ryan slapped his back as he went out the door.

* * *

Bulmer Hobson placed aside his book and thought about retiring for the night. He couldn't concentrate on what he was reading as he found his mind going over and over all sorts of trivial details that he had picked up over the last week or so. Scraps of conversations that he overheard; requisition slips for various items; a heightened sense of expectancy among certain of his IRB colleagues. He regretted now resigning from the Supreme Council, a move rather forced upon him over his allowing John Redmond, the Irish Parliamentary Party leader, to gain a strong influence in the running of the Irish Volunteers. He couldn't avoid the feeling that something was up, although he admitted to himself that most of his friends still on the Council showed no particular awareness of any matters of concern.

Along with the Irish Volunteers Chief of Staff, Eoin MacNeill, Hobson had had a busy day with the administrative organisation involved in readying the Irish Volunteer Force for their big exercise on Easter Sunday; he'd had no time to ponder the rumours or idle chatter that could mean something or nothing. Not until now, when he sat down to relax and tried to read. Now, his nagging thoughts wouldn't let him settle.

So it was almost a relief – although in other circumstances it might have caused some alarm so late in the evening – when he heard what he imagined were bicycle tyres skidding on the gravel outside, followed moments later by the persistent rapping of the front door knocker.

He went into the hall and opened the door to find Eva Gore-Booth's friend, Dillon, looking flustered and short of breath. Before he could say a word, Dillon spoke:

'Hobson, I have the gravest of news. Let me in, please.' And without waiting for an invitation, his visitor pushed passed him and turned in the middle of the hall to address him further. Hobson closed the door and listened to what Dillon had to say.

'I've come straight from Liberty Hall and I haven't a moment to spare. I've got to be at the station by ten o'clock. Four of us are being sent to Kerry to take over the wireless transmitter on Valencia Island.'

'You're what?'

'Just listen, Bulmer, please. The plan is to broadcast a warning to the Royal Navy that a German fleet is about to invade the North of Scotland – to divert vessels from patrolling off the west coast of Ireland.'

'With what purpose, Mr Dillon?'

'They also have to radio to a German ship in the vicinity that is bringing guns for the republicans. It is due to unload them this weekend in time for the Irish Volunteers exercises on Sunday.'

'But why the urgency? They don't need to be armed any better than they are at present to carry out the planned manoeuvres.'

'But that's just it – and why I decided I had no option but to come here to tell you. The manoeuvres are a cover. There's to be a Rising on Easter Sunday. With the military backing of the Volunteer force and the

Citizens' Army, Plunkett, Pearse and Connolly and others are going to declare a Republic!'

'Hell's bells, man, is it the truth you're telling me?'

'As true as I'm standing here. You've got to tell MacNeill and get him to cancel the Volunteers exercises or there'll be mayhem on the streets of Dublin. I'd have gone straight to him, myself, if I'd known where he lives. But I need to get to the station; I must go.'

'I could drive you to where he lives,' and Hobson mentioned the house number and the name of the road, 'it would be much better if he heard this from you.'

'I'm sorry, I haven't another minute to spare. I hope you can convince him to act.'

Hobson opened the door for him and said, 'Very well. I'll do my best. I'm very grateful to you, Dillon, for the information. I shall go straight round to Eoin's now. Get him out of bed, if I have to. And listen. One other thing.'

'What's that?'

'Our lads need those guns, to be sure. But now isn't the time to be declaring a republic. If you were ever to get a chance to scupper their plans and delay their landing at all, they'd have to postpone any thoughts of a rising and there are a lot a people in Ireland who'd be mighty grateful to you.'

'I'll bear that in mind, my friend.'

Bulmer Hobson watched as Will Dillon jumped on his bicycle and scrunched off through the pebbles back down the drive.

Fifteen minutes later it was Hobson's turn to play the late-night visitor. He drove to the Irish Volunteers Chief of Staff's residence and had to knock for a considerable time before a dishevelled Eoin MacNeill, dressed in a red silk dressing gown, drew back the bolts and opened his front door.

'Bulmer! What in the world do you want at this hour?'

'Grave news,' Hobson found himself repeating Dillon's words. 'I need to come in.'

In a few brief minutes Hobson acquainted the Chief of Staff with the true intentions of the IRB to use the Volunteers' manoeuvres to support a break with British rule and declare a republic. As MacNeill listened, Hobson saw his cheeks suffuse with blood and his fists clench. His speech was barely coherent when Hobson had finished.

'But... but... what... why wasn't I told of this? It can't be true. This is an outrage!'

'I fear it's the truth, Eoin. All Dillon told me fits with the snippets I've been picking up. I was sure there was something in the air; I just didn't know what.'

'I'm going straight to Pearse. Right now. Demand to know his true intentions. I'm not having this. I will not allow it. Will you drive me there, Bulmer?'

As soon as Eoin had got dressed the two drove through the darkened streets of Dublin for a momentous confrontation upon which the very future of Ireland could hinge.

* * *

Kingsbridge Station (Heuston Station), where the Killarney train was waiting to depart at ten o'clock, is south of the river and so not that far from Bulmer Hobson's house. Which was just as well, as Dillon made it with only a few minutes to spare. He dumped his bicycle in a rack which was otherwise empty at that time of night.

His companions were there before him and Donal Sheehan was leaning out of a window of the rear carriage watching for him. They had bagged two pairs of facing seats and a couple of holdalls with their equipment had been slung up onto the racks. The four men settled themselves as they heard the guard blow his whistle. There was a great whoosh of steam as the engine filled its pistons and they felt the first clunk and jerk as the carriages took up the slack.

Just then the door between their seats was yanked open and two men running along the platform clambered in and slammed it behind them. Without a word of apology, they pushed between the legs of Will and the others and stood in the aisle surveying the passengers. Their RIC uniforms and Webbley revolvers prominent in their holsters gave them all the authority they needed to command the attention of everyone present.

Chapter 15

Will and his confederates, Con Keating, Charlie Monaghan and Donal Sheehan shifted uncomfortably in their seats. Will noticed Con glancing up at the holdalls and hoped the policemen hadn't. These weren't members of the Dublin Metropolitan Police force who don't carry arms. These were RIC men and clearly meant business.

'Just sit quiet, lads,' he breathed. 'Easy does it.'

The officers moved to the back of the carriage and Will, facing that way, watched them scrutinise the passengers on each side of the aisle as they moved slowly forward. They didn't seem to be interested in any women but they studied the faces of every man as they advanced. They reached the seat before Will's party and studied two men on the other side of the aisle.

Will took a pack of playing cards from his pocket. 'What'll it be, lads – stud or draw?' he said, and proceeded to deal out cards in turn to each of the others. He was aware that the policemen were now staring at them. He continued to distribute the cards without looking up. After what seemed an age, one officer turned his attention to someone on the other side but his colleague remained looking first at Donal Sheehan and then across at Will Dillon. Back to Sheehan. Finally he turned to follow the other RIC man down the carriage.

And stopped.

Will felt a hand on his shoulder and froze.

The policeman spoke for the first time since his precipitous entry into the train. 'You've dropped the five of diamonds – down there at your feet. Enjoy your game.'

'We will, officer,' said Will. 'Thank you, sir.'

The policemen moved on, leaving the four to their poker – and to try to regain some measure of composure. Their adrenalin levels gradually subsided as the rhythmic clackety-clack of the wheels on the joints between the lines effected its calming influence upon them. Later, when the train stopped at Kildare they caught sight of the uniformed officers alighting from further along the train with a dishevelled-looking individual in handcuffs.

'Looks like they got their man,' said Keating.

'I'm glad it wasn't us they were looking for,' said Monaghan.

'I'm mighty glad I had the cards to look at when we were being scrutinised,' said Sheehan. 'Yon was good move, Dillon. I don't mind telling you I was getting ready to hold up my hands and surrender. Those guys would shoot you as soon as look at you.'

'Ah well, sure now it didn't come to that,' said Keating. 'Isn't it what Dillon's here for – to keep us safe?'

'I wasnae expecting to be protecting yous quite so soon, though, I have to say,' Dillon grinned at them. 'But your man, Collins did say nothing must get in the way of your mission, so I expect that includes the Peelers.'

The men had given up their card game; it was difficult without a table. They chatted on about the planning Ryan Doloughan had put into Michael Collin's brainchild. They were to be met at Killarney by an IRB man from Limerick called Tommy McInerney who would drive them down the Dingle peninsular to Cahirciveen where Con Keating used to work at the big radio installation before it was moved over to Valencia Island. They would make their way to the island by fishing boat where the three experts, with the help of some local IRB men would set about commandeering the transmitter and adapting it for their own purposes.

'I've been thinking,' said Sheehan. 'When we contact the gunrunners do we speak in English, German or Norwegian?'

'Norwegian?' said Will, 'Why would you speak that?'

'Because their ship's flying a Norwegian flag and the crew are all disguised as Norwegians to fool the Royal Navy,' said Keating.

'Right, of course' said Dillon, thinking that bit of information needed to be passed on as soon as possible. Could he get a chance to put through a phone call from the station? He found it difficult to imagine how he could without the others knowing. 'I'd stick to English, if I were you,' he said. 'Yous don't want to be broadcasting in German and run the risk of it getting picked up by the authorities.'

After a while, as the hour grew late, their conversation lapsed and the men dozed to the soporific sound of the train snaking its way through a sleeping Tipperary and Limerick.

Will stirred at a change in the sounds penetrating his consciousness. He opened his eyes in time to see the name, Rathmore, on a country station platform that was rushing past. He nudged, Donal Sheehan, 'We've crossed into County Kerry. It willnae be long 'til we're at Killarney.'

* * *

As the train came to a halt in Killarney station, it huffed and puffed like some giant cast-iron wolf eager to get at one of the three little pigs and then let out a long sigh of steam as though grateful for this brief respite from its exertions.

As Will and the others stepped down onto the platform they saw that only two other passengers were alighting at this ungodly hour of the morning. One looked to Will like a commercial traveller with his brown leather suitcase of samples. The other could well have been a local hotelier. He was supervising the unloading of two large wicker hampers from the guard's van that Will imagined might contain fancy foodstuffs purchased in the capital to augment the Easter menu for his customers.

The commercial traveller was quick to leave the platform. Will and his friends followed more sedately, leaving the hotelier talking to a porter who was loading his purchases onto a handcart.

The four emerged from the station and stood under its wide canopy as they got their bearings. The moon was a few days past full and shed its light on the darkened road but as yet there was no hint of any lightening of the sky to their left; dawn was still a long way off. A solitary jarvey stood by his jaunting car, his horse probably asleep on its feet. The man watched the commercial traveller, who had declined his offer of a ride, stride off in the direction of the Station Hotel just up the road heading west.

Probably where those hampers are headed, thought Will, as he looked around in vain for anywhere that might have a telephone. But the ticket office was closed and there didn't seem to be anywhere else apart from the hotel. He had been to Killarney before, one summer when he had arrived at a respectable hour in the afternoon, and seen a score or more jaunting cars lined up waiting to take holidaymakers to their various destinations around the beautiful lakes that were one of Ireland's most famous attractions. But in the middle of the night the place was dead. He'd have to bide his time and hope an opportunity would present itself later on.

'That'll be Tommy up yonder,' said Keating, who had spotted an open topped motorcar parked well up the road but visible because of the night lights of the hotel.

They set off in that direction, disappointing for a second time the poor jarvey who must have drawn the short straw that evening to meet the night train.

They walked away from the light of the station and into the shadows and were suddenly aware that they were no longer alone. From out of nowhere, it seemed, four big hulking ruffians confronted them in the darkness.

'You'll be wanting to contribute to the local branch of the Gaelic Brothers before you get off to your beds, now, won't you?' said their leader.

Con Keating had been in front of the others and the demand was addressed to him. He hesitated, took a swift glance over his shoulder towards Dillon and said, 'We don't want any trouble. Please stand aside.'

'Oh, hark at him. "Please stand aside." What about it, lads? Do you want to "please stand aside"?'

'Nope,' said two of the toughs, producing a couple of nasty looking knives.

'Not me,' said the fourth drawing his own knife from his belt.

In one swift movement the leader stepped up to Keating and Will saw the point of a fourth blade held close to Con's throat. 'Your wallets, gentlemen – *if you please*.'

The other three took up threatening positions next to Sheehan, Monaghan and Dillon.

Will sighed inwardly. He was tired. The last thing he wanted was a fight with four thugs armed with knives – in the dark. His hands were in his coat pockets against the chill in the night air – a big disadvantage if you need to make fast sudden moves. Precious time is lost freeing your hands from their confines. Precious time he didn't have – but didn't need, either.

A muffled retort broke the stillness of the night. Behind them the jarvey's horse awoke and whinnied loudly. In front of them the man holding a knife to Keating's throat staggered backwards clutching his left thigh as dark blood seeped through his fingers. Will's coat sported a neat, singed hole by the right pocket.

His hands were now clear of his pockets. He stepped back and covered the other three would-be attackers with the revolver he had acquired during his previous brush with one of these thieving bands.

'No good bringing knives to a gun fight, lads. Now beat it.'

The thugs hesitated.

'Now!' Will pointed his weapon at their leader's other thigh.

'Come on. Leave these homos to please themselves,' snarled the leader, turning and starting to limp away. Two of his cronies took an arm each to help him and all four were soon lost in the shadows again.

'Let's go,' said Will. He started to jog towards the waiting vehicle with the others close on his heels.

Thomas McInerney got out of his 20 horsepower Briscoe American open touring motorcar as the four men approached. He said, 'Keating?'

'As I live and breathe,' said Con. 'You must be Tommy.'

'I suppose I must.'

'You know Donal Sheehan, I believe,' Keating indicated his friend.

'And I'm Charlie Monaghan,' said Charlie.

Tommy acknowledged the other two. 'And who's this?' he said, looking at Dillon.

'This is Will Dillon, providing a bit of muscle.'

'I was told there'd be only three of you,' said Tommy.

'Ah, well I think Dillon was a bit of an afterthought, but he's proved very useful to have with us. Did you see our little contretemps back there with a gang of Gaelic Brothers?'

'I saw something but I couldn't make out what was going on. Have they robbed you?'

'They would have,' said Sheehan, 'but Will, here, soon sent them packing, didn't you, Will?'

'I did what needed to be done,' said Will.

'Aye, well never mind that. My problem is that I've only got room for three of you in the motorcar,' said Tommy.

The men looked at the front passenger seat in the Briscoe and the small bench seat behind, big enough for two at the most, and saw the problem.

'Look,' said Will, 'you guys are the important ones. The mission depends on you. I don't mind dropping out. I'll hang around here and catch a train back to the city later.' And in the meantime find a telephone, he thought.

'No, no. I'm sure we can squeeze you in some way,' said Keating.

'I really don't mind,' said Will.

'Couldn't he sit on your wee luggage rack contraption at the back?' said Monaghan.

Thomas McInerney had had a chromium platform installed on the rear of the Briscoe designed to hold cases. It was a sturdy rig and looked like it could hold the weight of a man, if somewhat uncomfortably. A travel rug was laid upon it and Will had no choice but to continue with the Republican Brotherhood men. He sat on the rack facing backwards, legs dangling and took a secure grip on the bars to reduce the risk of being jogged off as they traversed the country roads of Kerry.

McInerney got the engine started and shortly after that they were off. For all the grandness of the American model the headlights were none too bright so he kept to a moderate speed where he could stop in an emergency within the distance that he could see. This made Will's position more tenable, less bumpy.

He was pondering about what he had intended to be doing this evening – well, Thursday evening. The Briscoe was the same colour of green as the Crossley he was trying to locate, and that had reminded him. He flashed and saw his beautiful Annie lying on the pavement back in Bangor. He wondered if he might well have found her killer by now if he hadn't been commandeered into riding shotgun on this operation. But he should get back to Dublin in time to get on with his own mission tomorrow, or Sunday at the latest, and check out this owner called Higginson.

Thinking of Sunday, Easter Sunday, pulled his thoughts right back to the present operation, which was all part of the secret plan to start an uprising on Sunday. Had Bulmer Hobson managed to persuade Eoin MacNeill to cancel the Volunteers manoeuvres on Sunday? Or would the peace of Easter be shattered by gun battles all over Dublin? Using guns he was in the process of helping to procure.

He needed to do two things: warn Bradshaw that the guns were on a Norwegian vessel, and see if he couldn't, as Hobson had put it, scupper their plans to land the guns later today.

They'd left Killarney far behind and were now approaching a village. The motorcar came to a halt at a T-junction.

'Where are we?' Will turned round to communicate with the others.'

'I'm not rightly sure,' was the unsettling reply from their driver.

'Well, if it's any help,' said Will, 'we've pulled up by "Milltown General Stores",' he said, reading the sign above the shop.

'Milltown?' said Tommy. 'Oh, heck, we must've taken the wrong road out of Killarney; this should be Killorglin.'

'Are we lost?' asked Sheehan.

'Ah no,' said Tommy, 'sure we know where we are. We're just not where I thought we were.'

'That sounds lost to me,' said Sheehan.

'Not at all. Sure we've just joined the road to Cahirciveen a tinge further north than I meant to. It's left here and that'll run us down into Killorglin and then we're back on route.'

'Well, so long as you know what you're doing,' said Monaghan.

'You carry on, Tommy,' said Keating. 'Never mind the boys. We're very grateful to you for driving us at all.'

Before too long they were at the little market town of Killorglin but approaching it from an unfamiliar direction. Once more, Tommy was unsure which way to turn.

There was the smallest hint of a lightening in the sky behind them promising that daybreak hadn't abandoned them altogether and with it some early risers had begun to stir. They had passed a couple of men half a mile back and just now a girl with her shawl pulled tight around her was walking a little way off.

Will hopped down from his perch, grateful to stretch his legs and ease the numbness in his buttocks. 'I'll ask this wench for directions.' And off he strode.

Catching up with her, he said, 'Excuse me, miss.'

The girl looked startled, but stopped and looked at him, waiting.

'We're a bit lost.' He nodded in the direction of the motorcar. 'Can you tell me which road we want for Cahirciveen.'

'Cahirciveen, is it? Aye, sure you want to turn right over the bridge. At the crossroads you could go straight on along Lower Bridge Street but it's not a grand road for motorcars; you'd probably be best to stick to the main road that goes right. After a wee while where the road ahead takes you to Ballykissane you turn sharply to the left and stay on that main road. You can't go wrong.'

'I'm much obliged to you, Miss. Good morning.' Will headed back to the motorcar. He remembered Ballykissane from his holiday in

Killarney: a charming little hamlet on the River Laune where it flows into Dingle Bay.

He reported back to the others, 'Tommy's doing fine; we're right on course. Over the bridge up ahead, turn right at the crossroads and it's straight on all the way.'

Which instructions, in the continuing darkness, Tommy McInerney duly followed.

Tommy was used to not seeing too far ahead and so he relied on the houses on both sides of the road he had just turned down to keep him straight. Then, quite abruptly the ones on the right were set way back off the road. Tommy assumed there must be a sizeable village green between the road and the houses whose dark roofs he could just make out against the greying sky. He felt the road surface change beneath his tyres, a bit bumpier, as the houses on the left petered out and Tommy could see nothing in that direction, fields he presumed. He tried to keep a straight course judging by the far-off homes to his right.

Ahead, the road surface beyond the range of his headlamps was lit only by moonlight. It looked different; smoother, he hoped.

That was when the front wheels suddenly dropped. The Briscoe lurched forward at an alarming angle. Its chassis scraped on the road. Tommy's passengers were tipped headlong. They clung on to whatever they could as the tilt increased.

Will found himself high off the ground on the rear luggage rack, which had somehow come loose with the impact. He heard Sheehan yell, 'What have we hit? What's happening?' There was an answer from Monaghan, 'The road's just opened up; we're slipping into a hole. Don't anyone move, for all our sakes.'

But from where Will was poised he could see the "hole". The "road surface" beyond was not asphalt or stone. What he saw from his vantage point was the silver moonlight glinting on water. He realised that the far-off houses which, like Tommy, he had assumed were beyond an open grassy area, were in reality on the other side of the river. Tommy had driven onto the pier at the mouth of the Laune – and then he had driven off the end of it, thinking they were still on the road to Cahirciveen.

These thoughts flashed through Will's mind in a single moment. It was no more than a second or two since the Briscoe's front wheels had gone off the pier and Charlie Monaghan had shouted, 'Nobody move!' But for

Will that was going to be difficult. One of the brackets holding his makeshift seat had broken, pitching him sideways. He grabbed it tight as his feet scrambled to try to get a purchase.

For the other thing he now realised was that it was only his weight on the back that was stopping the motorcar from tipping further and sliding right off the pier into the swirling waters of the Laune River.

Chapter 16

Hobson had barely brought his motorcar to a standstill before Eoin MacNeill was out and banging on the door of the home of Padraig Pearse. When, eventually, it was opened by the owner, bleary-eyed and dressing gowned as MacNeill, himself, had been an hour earlier, he barged into the hall, proclaiming: 'I'm here for an explanation, Pearse. The truth. Out with it, man. What are you planning for Sunday?'

It wasn't until MacNeill's mention of Sunday that any sign of comprehension appeared in Pearse's expression. Then his face took on a hardened look. He stood back to allow Hobson to enter before ushering his unexpected and, no doubt, unwelcome guests into the front room.

'I'm not sure what you mean, Eoin,' he said, but before he could continue MacNeill interrupted:

'You know exactly what I mean. I mean the Volunteers manoeuvres on Sunday. What do you plan to do with *my* men?'

'Let us sit down and talk about this calmly.'

'I'm fine standing and I'm perfectly calm. I want to know why I haven't been informed of your true intentions.'

'If, by my true intentions,' said Pearse, 'you mean the declaration of an Irish Republic backed by a redoubtable force of patriotic Irishmen, I fear it would seem that you have already been thus informed, or perhaps partly so. It is regrettable, I admit, that until now, the plans of the Irish Republican Brotherhood's Military Council have had to be a carefully guarded secret shared only by those with an absolute need to know.'

'And the Chief of Staff of the main body of fighting men for your… your… your what? coup? rebellion? – doesn't need to know! This is outrageous. I'm not having it.'

'Eoin, allow me to explain.'

'What's to explain? You're going to throw the country into a bloody war with England that you can't possibly hope to win for... for what? Some poetic vision of a free Ireland. A republic that you or I will never live to see?

'Whether we live or die,' said Pearse, 'we can at least try. This war in Europe has given us the chance for which we have been waiting for generations. Are we not to have the sight to see, or the courage to do? Or is it to be written of this generation, alone of all generations of Ireland that it had none among it who dared to make the ultimate sacrifice?'

'Now is not the time,' said MacNeill. 'We're not ready. Not yet strong enough or well enough armed. You are mad even to be contemplating a call to arms. I shall do everything in my power, short of ringing Dublin Castle, to stop you. You cannot succeed and I will not allow you to put my men in danger to satisfy your own foolhardy utopian vision.'

MacNeill turned to Bulmer, 'I should be obliged, Mr Hobson, if you would be kind enough to drive me home. I've nothing more to say to this... gentleman.'

* * *

Back in his own home, Eoin MacNeill could not sleep. He paced his room in the dim light filtering through the curtains from the streetlamps. Up to the fireplace, back to the window, over and over. His anger prevented clear thinking. Anger, both with Pearse and his cohorts who were behind this thoroughly misguided venture, and with himself for not having realised what was being planned behind his back. Hobson had had suspicions but only now when it was too late – or almost too late – had the truth come to light. Well, he would make sure it was not too late. He would spend tomorrow – today, for midnight was long since passed and Good Friday had begun – countermanding the Irish Volunteers' mobilisation orders. The Volunteers were, and had always been, a defensive force; they were not there to be used in an offensive capacity by some idealistic group of poets and visionaries.

His irate cogitations were abruptly halted by a rapping on the front door that filled the darkness with its unexpected demand. MacNeill responded to the summons and for a second time that night found himself admitting unlooked-for visitors. Padraig Pearse stepped into his hallway accompanied by two other gentlemen known to MacNeill to be equally fervent revolutionaries. Pearse must have dragged them out of their beds to lend him support.

The first, Thomas MacDonagh, MacNeill knew had trained as a priest before becoming a teacher and, with Padraig Pearse, co-founded St Enda's, the bilingual School for Boys. He was another writer, not a bad poet and dramatist, Eoin thought, but perhaps a surprising addition to the ranks of the Volunteers, much less the Military Council of the IRB, but MacNeill was reliably informed that's where he was now.

The other reinforcement Pearse had brought was Seán MacDermott, or MacDiarmada, as he liked to be known. MacNeill had come across him as a member of the Gaelic League, but it was an open secret that he was also involved with the Irish Republican Brotherhood.

'You'd best come through here,' said MacNeill and went straight into his front room ahead of his guests. 'But I've nothing more to say to you, Pearse, unless you've come to agree to call off all this insanity.'

'I believe you should hear what our friends, here, have to say, before you make up your mind,' said Pearse.

'My mind is made up. There's nothing else you can say.' MacNeill stood with his back to the fireplace, the ashes in the grate long-since cooled and dead. He faced his three visitors, like a stag confronting a pack of attacking hounds.

Rather than attack, however, MacDiarmada said, 'All the secrecy during the planning was my fault, I'm afraid; I insisted upon it. I'm sorry it wasn't possible to include you, Mr MacNeill. Very few people know of our plans – which is precisely why they have such a good chance of success. The British will be caught completely off their guard. If more people had known it would have leaked out sooner and all would have been lost.'

'The element of surprise gives you no more than an initial advantage, if indeed you get that,' countered MacNeill. 'How can you hope to fight off the whole of the British army indefinitely? It's ludicrous!'

'Not as ludicrous as you seem to think,' said MacDonagh. 'The British soldiery is much depleted due to the war and we happen to know that General Lovick Friend, their Commander-in-Chief here, is on leave in England at the moment.'

'And,' said MacDiarmada, 'due to Sir Roger Casement's sterling efforts in Germany on behalf of the cause, a shipment of arms and ammunition should, at this minute, be off the coast of Kerry ready to be landed and distributed to our battalions around the country.'

Pearse broke in to sum up. 'So,' he said, 'we have the manpower, we have the firepower and – let no one think otherwise – to a man, we have the passion and conviction to end the English suppression and win back Ireland for the Irish once and for all! Come on Eoin, what do you say? Are you with us? We can't do it without the Volunteers.'

MacNeill hesitated. He couldn't help feeling inspired to some extent by the arguments. There was something in what they said. If the men were to be properly armed that did shine a new light on things. At least they would have a fighting chance. But he said, nevertheless, 'I don't know. I'm not convinced that passion and conviction are enough to defeat all that England can throw at us.'

His guests talked on, reasoning, arguing, pleading, threatening. The darkened window gradually paled as streaks of dawn breached the eastern sky over the Dublin rooftops. MacNeill grew tired, exhausted through lack of sleep and the constant effort of trying to counter Pearse, MacDonagh and MacDiarmada. He realised he was wavering. He sighed.

'Perhaps you are right. Perhaps it is time to stand and fight for what we believe.'

'It is, Eoin,' said Pearse, 'it is. You are absolutely right. So we can count on your support?'

'Reluctantly,' said MacNeill, 'but... Well, if we have to fight or be suppressed, then I suppose I'm ready to fight.'

With those words, at the end of a long and tiring night, an uneasy truce was called between the leadership of the nationalist IVF and the republican IRB.

* * *

The blackness of the night was easing into a reluctant grey as Will clung onto the back of Tommy McInerney's Briscoe. It was teetering on the end of the pier and he leaned back as a counterbalance, trying to steady the rocking vehicle. He realised the very lives of the four in the motorcar could depend on him. At almost the same instant it flashed through his mind that all the equipment they needed to take over the radio station on Valencia Island to decoy the Royal Navy away from the Kerry coast would also be lost if the motorcar went over. For a moment he was tempted to let go. *Scupper their plans, if you can.* Bulmer Hobson's voice sounded inside his head. All he had to do was let go.

These men were not his friends; he'd only just met them. Their politics were far removed from his own. Their intentions were to bring all of Ireland under what would inevitably be a Catholic controlled government. Not at all what he wanted, nor any of his pals in the Orange Order nor, indeed, the vast majority of Irish citizens living in the protestant north.

Yet they were men, fellow human beings. He dismissed any thoughts of abandoning them. He had to save them if he could. He stretched more, shifting his centre of gravity further back. Slowly, the motorcar started to right itself. Will felt his damaged perch lowering inch by inch towards the pier. The strain of holding his weight out at such a reach was telling on his arm muscles but he had to hang on. The rear wheels of the motorcar were almost back on the ground.

That was when the loud crack and metallic ripping sound broke the silence that had reigned since Monaghan's shout not to move. With it, Will felt himself fall. His back thumped against the stone pier. His grip remained firmly on the luggage rack but his former seat was no longer attached to the motorcar. The same strain that Will had felt in his arms had been too much for the single remaining bracket. To his horror he saw the back of the vehicle rearing up again before the Briscoe started to slide forward over the edge and plunge into the depths.

His lifeboat training snapped in. First thoughts were to look around for a lifebelt, but if there was one, he couldn't see it in the semi-darkness. He ran to the edge and peered into the water. The level was high. Full tide. Was that movement? Over to the right. He couldn't be sure. He knew, though, it would be madness to jump in without a rope.

He felt terrible. He had misdirected his colleagues hoping they would become lost and delay their mission until he could get a message through about the Norwegian ship. But because of his subterfuge four men were now struggling in the tidal currents of the river estuary.

Will looked all around again for a rope or a lifebelt. At the far end of the pier he saw a flickering light. Someone was approaching with a candle. He heard voices. Saw more lights. People, probably from the last cottages they had passed, who must have heard the motorcar drive onto the pier and come to investigate.

Will realised he was still holding the luggage rack with the travel rug caught up on its broken brackets. He tossed them into the dark waters of the Laune. Then he moved back from the edge and over to one side where he sat on a low wall that ran the length of the pier. He remained still in the darkness as the person with the candle drew near.

The man went to the end of the pier and gazed out over the water without noticing Will. Two others, carrying lanterns, joined the first arrival.

'It must have gone over. There's not a sign of it,' said the first man.

'What about the driver, can you see him?' said another, 'Hold your lantern up higher.'

'There! Is that someone swimming, or just the water swirling?'

Some others had arrived on the pier now and Will slipped out of the shadows and joined the small crowd of people earnestly searching the waters with their eyes for sight of any survivors.

'It is! I can see someone swimming towards the far bank.'

'I can see two. I'm sure there's two of them side by side.'

'They'll never make it all the way across the mouth of the river.'

'They must have lost their bearings in the dark. Hold, you, that lantern up high where they can see it. AHOY! THIS WAY. COME TO THE LIGHT!'

Will could now see the vague shapes of two men swimming in the water and at first they appeared not to hear. He joined with the others in shouting to them as he searched in vain for any sign of the other two.

'They've heard us!' someone called out and it was true. Will saw them pause and splash around before they changed direction and started back towards the pier.

'Guide them round the pier to the beach,' the man with the candle said.

People kept shouting encouragement as Will watched anxiously. Sometimes he could see only one person in the water. Then he would think he caught a glimpse of a second but, as the splashing drew closer to the pier he became convinced it was made by a single swimmer.

There was, by now, a large crowd of inquisitive and concerned onlookers on the pier including a uniformed RIC officer. Will pushed his way back through them all to get round to the stony beach. When he got there two strapping young lads were already wading out towards the approaching swimmer. They supported him between them as they splashed their way back out of the water.

Will was there to help them lay the exhausted man down. It was Tommy McInerney. Will leaned close as though he was checking for breathing and whispered in his ear. 'Tommy, praise God you made it.

There's a crowd of people here and a peeler. too, but they don't know I was with yous.'

'Dillon, is it yourself?'

'It is, aye. What do you want me to do?'

McInerney struggled to get his breath, 'Get as fast as you can to a telephone and let them know what's happened. Has Con made it? He was right beside me. We never saw Donal and Charlie.'

'We haven't found Keating yet. Or the others. Good luck, Tommy.'

Will stood up to see the shape of the policeman looming over them.

'Do you know this man?' he said.

'I don't, sir, no. I was checking how he was. I'm a trained lifeboat man. He seems not much the worse for his wee dip in the water. He'll be fine when he gets his breath back.'

'Right, move aside, sir. I need to question him.'

Before Will melted into the crowd he saw the constable prod McInerney with the toe of his boot and heard him ask, 'Can you stand?'

Tommy stayed where he lay.

'You two!' the policeman nominated two of the nearest bystanders. 'Lift him to his feet and hold him up, if he needs help.'

Will decided to wait to hear what would happen.

'Now then, what's your name?' said the RIC man.

'McInerney, Thomas; from Limerick.'

'And what are you doing here so early in the morning?

'Driving some gentlemen around Kerry.'

'At this hour?'

'They wanted an early start,' said Tommy.

'Who are they – or were they?'

'I couldn't tell you, officer, and that's the truth. They just asked me to drive them.'

Will chuckled to himself as he turned to go. Tommy wasn't going to give anything away. Silently, he wished him luck once more. He still felt dreadful about the other three but he told himself that they were rebels plotting against their king and country. If there ever was an uprising, a lot more than these three would lose their lives. Maybe their loss, if lost they were, might save an awful lot of others. Will hoped so as he trudged back along the road to Killorglin.

By the time he crossed the bridge over the Laune and turned left for Killarney the sun had breached the horizon. Its slanting rays illuminated

Slieve Mish across Dingle Bay behind him and threw into sharp relief the peaks and valleys of Macgillycuddy's Reeks rising up on his right. He knew there was no use trying to find a telephone in Killorglin. He could only make local calls from a little place like that. He had a thirteen mile tramp ahead of him to get to Killarney which he was sure would have a trunk line to Dublin.

As the sun moved higher it took the early morning chill out of the air and Will opened his coat. He enjoyed walking in the countryside, listening to birdsong and admiring the variety of trees and wildflowers. He realised he'd taken few walks in the months since Annie died. He could imagine her now, her arm through his, walking by his side and giving a little skip every few steps to keep up with his stride. How he wished it could be real. His thoughts turned to the Crossley owner. He was convinced that it was this Michael Higginson but he had to check him out to be sure. Once confirmed, he'd have to decide how to proceed, especially if, as seemed likely, he turned out to be 'the Boss' who wanted him dead. Whatever lay ahead, he needed to be back in Dublin to push things along.

After a while, a gentle and continuous clip-clop began to insinuate itself into Will's sub-conscious and then his conscious mind as it grew louder. He stopped and stood aside in the verge as a flat cart with an elderly-looking donkey between the shafts drew level. The man holding the reins sat on the cart, his legs dangling, and looked in human terms as old as the donkey. He touched his cap to Will as he was passing.

'Is it a lift you'd be wantin' this fine morning?' he asked.

'That's very decent of you,' said Will, 'I'm obliged.'

The cart carried a number of sacks – one filled with potatoes, to judge by its lumpy appearance, others had a variety of green vegetable leaves poking out the tops – but there was room at the edge for Will to hop up and sit at the other side from the driver. The donkey plodded on without appearing to notice the extra weight she was hauling.

'Heading for Killarney, is it?'

'I am, sir. Is that where you're going?'

'Not quite as far. I'll be turning off up the Gap of Dunloe. I've a load of vegies for Kate Kearney's Cottage.'

'Ah,' said Will, remembering his holiday, 'is that wee café still going strong?'

'Oh it is, sure enough. Do you know it?'

'I once took a ride in a jaunting-car up to the Gap to look down on the lakes. I drank one of the best cups of tea I ever tasted at Kate Kearney's.'

'Sure, I can believe that. And did you have a wee drop of the poteen in it to warm your cockles?'

Will laughed, 'I was sixteen at the time, so I doubt it, but me Mam and Da probably did, if there was any going.'

They chatted on with the ever-present clip-clopping of the donkey's hooves as a background to their conversation. The old man looked up at the height of the sun and gave the animal a touch with his whip to speed her up.

'I hope they're no needing these vegies for today's dinners; I'm running a wee bit late. There was a big commotion in Ballykissane this morning.'

'Oh yes?' said Will.

'Aye, someone drove their motorcar off the end of the pier.'

'No! How did that happen?' Will sounded suitably shocked.

'Ah, sure it's easily done. They weren't the first to have gone over and won't be the last either unless they put up some of them bollards or something. I don't know if you know Ballykissane at all, but the road makes a sharp turn to the right up the estuary, where it's straight on for the pier. It's easy to miss the turn in the dark.'

'How terrible.' Will hesitated, 'Em...and were they rescued, the people in the motorcar?'

'The driver was, as I heard, but they found the bodies of his passengers, both drowned.'

'Both?' said Will.

'Aye, a terrible tragedy. Terrible.'

'Indeed it is,' said Will, 'Terrible.'[3]

They were approaching a road on the right and, without any prompting, the donkey swung round into it.

'This is as far as I can take you,' said the driver, 'so off you hop.'

Will did just that. 'Thanks for the lift,' he called after the old man.

'You're welcome,' he replied, without looking back.

---

[3] The bodies of Con Keating and Donal Sheehan were recovered soon after the accident but it would be almost six months before the remains of Charlie Monaghan were discovered washed up on an island in the Laune river. These three became the first causalities of the Easter Rising.

Will started walking again much refreshed after his ride on the cart. But having it confirmed that two of his erstwhile companions were drowned with, apparently, no sign of the third brought back his melancholy thoughts. After half-a-mile or so he determined to think of something more pleasant and almost at once a picture of Maeve popped into his mind: Maeve laughing and dancing at the ceilidh; Maeve, listening with him, fixated by the sound of Willie Yeats' voice reading his poetry; Maeve on the jaunting car with her picnic basket; lying on the grass in the park listening to the birdsong. And always, her pretty face filling his mind, and her slender figure, and the gentle touch of her hand when she would reach out to him to draw his attention to a bird or a flower.

He wanted to see her again. Another compelling reason to get back to Dublin.

* * *

'Can I speak to Geoffrey Bradshaw, please?' Will was told that Mr Bradshaw wasn't available but if he cared to call back on Monday…

'No, it's very urgent that I get a message to him, please. Can you do that?' Apparently the person on the other end of the line could.

'Tell him I know there's a good play on at the Abbey tonight but I won't be able to go with him. Some Norwegian friends have arrived unexpectedly. Please give Mr Bradshaw that message as soon as possible.' He was assured it would be passed on straight away.

Will hung up the earpiece on the telephone in the Railway Hotel and searched in his pocket for the folded paper doily upon which Ryan Doloughan had written his address and telephone number. He picked up the earpiece once more and asked the operator to place a second trunk call to Dublin. He then sat down at a low table in the foyer where the coffee and sandwiches he had ordered were ready for him. The rich aroma from the cup filled his nostrils as he took a satisfying sip and waited for his call.

The hotel receptionist had looked up train times for him. He had several hours to put in before the Dublin train would arrive so he took his time savouring his egg and cress sandwiches. He was finishing a second cup of coffee when the receptionist told him his call had come through.

Will spent an awkward five minutes on the line explaining to Ryan how their trip had been cut short in such a tragic manner, omitting any hint of his own part in their misdirection.

Ryan was very quiet in response. 'So they're all dead?'

'Tommy McInerney isn't.'

'Our men: Con, Donal and Charlie Monaghan.'

'I'm afraid so. I'm terribly sorry.'

'Aye... I'm glad you're all right, Will. It doesn't sound as though you could have done any more. And Tommy – he's lost his motorcar, but he has his life still.'

'But the mission – what's to be done?'

'I don't know, Will. It's too late to get anyone else down there now even if we had people with the radio skills and the knowledge of the Admiralty codes. We have lads all ready to do the unloading, of course. We'll have to hope they manage to signal the ship with lights or something to guide her in. Without her cargo things here could go down very differently; we're relying on it.'

'Well, we must hope for the best,' said Will. He heard Ryan respond in his ear, 'We must,' and his grim thought was that his definition of "the best" was not at all the same as his friend's.

Ryan's voice continued: 'Can you come out here when you get back? For a full debriefing. You've got our address, haven't you? We're not too far from the station. I expect it will be latish but we could put you up for the night, if you like. Save you having to go all the way back to your digs after a pretty gruelling twenty-four hours. Have you had any sleep at all?'

'Eh, there wasn't a lot of opportunity for that. But, yes, I can come out to your place. Not sure when the train gets in. Expect me when you see me.'

Will waited for Ryan's response but the line went dead. He jiggled the hook for the earpiece to no avail. They'd been cut off. That happened, he knew. But no matter, he had reported back – to both his "contacts".

He had done all he could. The outcome of his efforts remained to be seen. Would Bradshaw pick up on his coded message? Had he thwarted the attempt to land German guns to aid a rebellion? Had Bulmer Hobson been able to persuade Eoin MacNeill to stop his Volunteers being used as gun fodder by Pearse and the other ringleaders? Above all, had he managed to foil the uprising? Only time would tell. It was out of his hands, now.

Will settled his hotel bill and decided to play the tourist and go for a stroll round the town until it was time to make for the station. He sauntered down Killarney's main street gazing in the windows of the gift shops. Thoughts of staying over at Maeve's home tonight, rather than returning in the small hours to his digs put a smile on his face and a jaunt in his step.

He could not know that he was destined never again to spend another night at his lodgings off Talbot Street.

Chapter 17

About the time Will Dillon was scanning the moonlit waters of the Laune river, desperate to spot survivors from the motorcar that had gone off the pier at Ballykissane, an inflatable was drifting towards the night-darkened beach at Banna Strand some sixteen miles to the north on the west coast of Kerry. The three men in it had been lowered from the conning tower of a German U-boat when it surfaced briefly in Tralee Bay.

Sir Roger Casement hadn't wanted to risk the possibility of capture aboard the German gunrunning ship by accompanying the arms he had procured to support an Irish rebellion. So the U-boat commander, Lieutenant Weisbach who, almost a year ago, had fired the torpedo that sank the *Lusitania* was ordered to take him back to Ireland. Robert Monteith, an IRB man from Dublin who had accompanied Casement in Germany was with him, as was Daniel Bailey one of a small group of Irish prisoners of war whom the Germans had released in return for their promise to change sides and fight in Ireland for the republicans.

None of the three could row and their light craft was at the mercy of the rolling Atlantic breakers. As they hit the line of surf the dinghy capsized and all three were drenched by the time they managed to struggle to the beach in the light of the pale half-moon. Roger Casement was already unwell and the soaking brought him close to death from hypothermia. The other two went to try to make contact with Irish Republican Brotherhood men in Tralee, leaving Casement hiding in the nearby ruins of McKenna's Fort.

Quite fortuitously, a local RIC constable came across him there and recognised him as a man wanted in Britain for treason. He was in no state to resist and was arrested. Later in the day his two submariner travelling companions were also apprehended.

* * *

While these latter arrests were happening on shore, and while Will was spending a pleasant afternoon browsing the souvenir shops in Killarney Town, the Commander of a British destroyer, *HMS Bluebell*, was patrolling off the west coast of Ireland in the Mouth of the Shannon. He was reading a signal that had just been received and turned to his Lieutenant Commander.

'More about possible German gun smuggling. Could be flying Norwegian colours. Keep a lookout.'

'Aye aye, sir.'

HMS Bluebell continued its southerly course.

An hour or so later, about the time Will Dillon was boarding the Dublin bound train at Killarney, the port lookout on the *Bluebell* was directing his powerful binoculars on the masthead of a ship sailing out of Tralee Bay. As he brought the image of the red flag into focus he could see the distinct outline of an off-centred blue and white cross.

The Commander ordered a change of course to intercept the Norwegian vessel and called her on his radio. No answer was received. The radio operator continued to call as the *Bluebell* closed on the foreign ship. With still no response the Commander fired a shot across the bow of the *Aud Norge*, whose name they could now make out on her side. The vessel hove to and the Commander tried to make contact using a loudhailer.

'Why did you ignore our radio messages?'

The captain of the *Aud Norge* replied, 'We have no radio on board.'[4]

The Naval Commander ordered the Norwegian vessel to follow him round the Dingle Peninsular and the south coast to Queenstown (Cobh) in Cork Harbour. The two ships set off in convoy.

By evening they were nearing their destination and steaming past Daunt Rock off Robert's Head south of Cork harbour. The British Commander was feeling justifiably pleased with himself when he heard what sounded like a small underwater explosion.

---

[4] This was later verified. So that part of Michael Collins' plan to guide the ship in by radio messages was doomed to failure from the start, even before the tragic accident at Ballykissane.

One of the ratings came rushing forward and, forgetting himself, shouted up to the bridge, 'The Aud, sir; she's going down! And she's flying the German ensign!'

The Commander uttered an oath under his breath and issued the order, 'Stop engines.' He sent a launch to go to the aid of the stricken vessel, which was rapidly taking on water. The *Aud* had launched her own lifeboat and her crew calmly awaited their rescuers, each one now dressed in his full German uniform. The Captain surrendered to the senior officer on the launch and all hands were safely transferred from the scuttled ship. On their way back to *HMS Bluebell* they watched as the *Aud Norge* slipped below the waterline with a gentle hissing sound. The German flag was the last of her to disappear – along with her clandestine cargo of rifles and machine guns and a million rounds of ammunition.

* * *

Will had never felt more ready to sink between the sheets of a soft bed than he did that night at the Doloughans. That the lovely Maeve lay in her own room, just across the landing, made the feeling all the more delicious. He put his head on the pillow and made a conscious effort to relax. It had been almost forty hours since he last slept and in that time he had come face to face in the Post Office with a man who had sworn to kill him; he had learned the closely guarded secret of the true intentions behind Easter Sunday's Volunteers manoeuvres – and managed to pass them on to Bulmer Hobson; he had protected three Irish rebels from being robbed in Killarney, survived a hair-raising ride perched on the back of Tommy McInerney's motorcar and then lost his three charges in the swirling waters of the River Laune. He had walked the best part of twenty miles, travelled the breadth of Ireland twice and spent an uncomfortable half-hour explaining to Ryan Doloughan most of what had happened on their ill-fated mission.

'Don't feel bad,' Ryan had said, as Will finally sat down to a very late supper consisting of a massive fry-up that Maeve and her elderly mother had prepared for him. 'You've more than justified our sending you along with the boys: protecting them from the Peelers on the train, the thugs outside Killarney station and you did your best to save them from going off that pier. You mustn't blame yourself.'

'It's kind of you to put it like that, but it's hard not to keep thinking about three good lives that have been lost. I can't get them out of my mind.' Will forked a bite of hot buttered potato bread into his mouth and reached for what was left of the Guinness that Ryan had offered him as soon as he arrived.

'It was a tragic accident,' said Maeve. 'I'm just so relieved nothing happened to you.'

Ryan must have told his sister something about his earlier telephone call, for when Will arrived at their door it was Maeve who opened it and flung her arms round him, saying, 'Oh, Will! I'm so glad you're safe. It must have been terrible.'

Will found himself returning the hug, her yielding body against his arousing all sorts of alarming sensations. He assured her that he was fine as she led him into the house, where her apparent embarrassment by her spontaneous show of affection caused her to hang back. She left Ryan to introduce him to their mother.

'It's good of you to let me invade your home at this hour, Mrs Doloughan,' said Will. 'I brought you this wee souvenir from Killarney.' And he handed her a small cardboard box.

'Och, indeed there was no need for that,' said his hostess. 'You're very welcome. Ryan tells me you've a heart for the Cause. Sure that's enough for anyone.' She opened the box and unwrapped the contents from its tissue paper.

'It's a little china replica of Kate Kearney's Cottage with a round hole in the roof to take a wee posy of flowers,' said Will.

'Och, isn't it just lovely,' said the old lady, reaching up and kissing Will on the cheek. 'I'll go and put it on the mantle over the fireplace.'

'Have you had anything to eat, at all?' said Ryan. 'I'll bet you're hungry. And a drink. What'll it be, Guinness?'

'A pint of the oul black stuff would go down a treat and, indeed, a bite to eat wouldn't go amiss either,' said Will.

Mrs Doloughan said, 'Come, you, with me, Maeve and we'll fix Mr Dillon his supper while he and Ryan have their wee chat.'

With the "wee chat" behind him, Will enjoyed his meal. Ryan had gone out, in spite of the lateness of the hour, to pass on Will's report and left him with Maeve for company. Will told the girl about their scare with the police on the train, his ride on the donkey cart, his time looking around Killarney…

'It's changed a fair bit since I was there as a kid,' he said. 'A lot more souvenir shops, that's for sure. I got you a wee present, too.'

Maeve's eyes lit up, 'Really? What is it?'

Will took another small box from his pocket and handed it to her. 'I know how much you like birds. I hope you like it.'

Maeve carefully unwrapped the tissue paper protecting her gift. 'Oh, isn't it beautiful! What a lovely present, Will; I love it.' She reached over and kissed him on his cheek. 'Thank you. I shall treasure it forever.'

'You like it, then?'

'Of course! It's lovely.'

'I wasn't sure whether to get the kingfisher or the robin, but I thought you can see real robins all the time but kingfishers, not so much.'

'It was a perfect choice and very thoughtful of you.' She looked into his eyes and Will felt a surge of warmth flood his cheeks as he gazed back. She has such a pretty face when her eyes sparkle like that.

For a moment he hesitated and afterwards he couldn't swear whether he started to lean forward first or if Maeve had made a tiny movement before he did; he only knew their faces drew closer. Will intended to return Maeve's kiss on the cheek, but somehow he found his lips brushing gently against hers and then pressing more firmly in a full but brief kiss that sent his heart racing.

The sound of the door handle turning caused them to jump apart like guilty children.

'How was your supper, Mr Dillon?' asked Mrs Doloughan as she entered the dining room, 'Have you had enough? There's half an apple pie in the larder. Will you have a wee slice of that?'

'Thank you, Mrs Doloughan, this was delicious; you did me proud, the two of you.' Will's smile embraced both mother and daughter. 'But hungry and all, as I was, I don't think I could manage another bite tonight.'

'Well, I'll leave you to clear away, Maeve. It's past my bedtime. I'll say, "Goodnight", Mr Dillon.'

Will stood and took the old lady's hand. 'Please call me Will. I'm sorry I've kept you up. Thank you again for the lovely meal.'

'You're welcome… Will. Goodnight, then.'

'Goodnight, Mam,' called Maeve as her mother retreated.

'Have you any plans for tomorrow?' Maeve asked.

'I do have some business to take care of. Not sure how long it will take me.' Will had managed to pick up his bicycle at the station, which was still where he had left it twenty four hours before. He planned to find Higginson's residence and establish once and for all if he was the man responsible for his fiancée's death. 'Why do you ask?'

Maeve looked coy. 'Well, it's Easter Saturday. I wondered if we might do something together.'

'Perhaps in the evening,' said Will. How about the theatre? I hear there's a good show on at the Abbey.' Will stopped. The phrase reminded him of the double life he was leading.

'That would be lovely. I haven't been to the theatre for ages.'

Me neither, thought Will, as he started to help Maeve clear the table. Not since last Christmas with Annie.

They took everything out to the kitchen.

'Ah, leave them by the sink. Sure I'll wash them in the morning,' said Maeve. 'I expect you want to get to bed, too.'

Will would have happily stayed up all night talking to Maeve but his body told him he'd never make it; he needed rest. So he allowed her to lead the way up to his bedroom. She opened its door and stood back in the landing for him to enter. Will went in and turned in the doorway to face her.

Neither spoke.

Then they both spoke together.

'You first,' laughed Maeve.

'No you,' said Will.

'I was just going to say that that's my room across the landing.'

'And I was just going to say how lovely it is to be here with you.'

There was another pause.

'Well, goodnight, Will.' Maeve remained where she was standing.

'Goodnight, Maeve.' Will took both her hands in his and inclined his head towards her.

She raised her lips to meet his and he felt that fervour of desire once more that their earlier brief kiss had aroused. Her hands left his and reached around him, her arms drawing him close. The tip of his tongue caressed hers as the gentle pressure on their lips increased. His arms were around her pulling her body against him. Her kissing grew more urgent as he felt her surrender to his embrace. She ran her fingers through his hair at the back of his head and his scalp tingled to her touch, just like – .

For a moment Will froze, as Annie's face filled his consciousness; just like Annie used to. He couldn't stop his body responding to Maeve's delicious proximity, but slowly, he brought their kissing to an end and, after a final squeeze, relaxed his hug. Maeve didn't seem to have noticed that brief moment. She stood on tiptoe and placed one more brief kiss on his lips.

'Goodnight, my lovely Will,' she said and went to open her own bedroom door.

Will watched her as she turned, briefly, to wave.

'Goodnight, my sweet.'

Their two doors clicked gently as they closed.

* * *

Will arose fully refreshed and came down to breakfast to find Ryan engrossed in the morning paper, his tea going cold on the table beside him.

He glanced up, 'The news is bad, Will, terrible. Roger Casement has been caught, but that's not the worst of it. A Norwegian ship called the *Aud Norge* with his arms shipment from Germany was taken under escort to Queenstown. It says rather than surrender the guns to the British the German crew scuttled the ship off the south coast. We're getting no new weapons. This is a disaster.'

Will struggled to hide his delight at the news. Geoff Bradshaw had understood his message and passed on the information. 'That is bad news,' he said. 'How will it affect the planned rising, do you think?'

'It makes a difference, obviously, but I doubt if Padraig Pearse or the others on the Military Council will allow it to alter their plans.'

'They'll go ahead, tomorrow, then.'

'All being well, they will. Eoin MacNeill somehow got wind of what we're organising and threatened to cancel the Volunteers exercises. Now that *would* have made a difference. We couldn't do anything without his ten thousand Volunteers.'

'Would have?'

'Yes, Pearse and MacDonagh and MacDiarmada managed to make him see sense. When they told him about Roger Casement's guns he agreed we might have a chance of pulling this off.'

Will's earlier elation fizzled out like a flaring match dropped in water. Even though his efforts caused MacNeill to plan on stopping the exercises, the Irish Volunteers Chief of Staff has allowed himself to be persuaded to change his mind. Will had failed after all. Ryan was talking again,

'What he'll do if he reads this, I dare not think. It was only the promise of the guns that made him agree to go along with the plans.'

Will took heart. The situation could yet be saved.

* * *

Eoin MacNeill didn't have the Saturday papers delivered so he was surprised to find a copy of the Irish Independent on his doormat as he passed through his hall after a rather late breakfast. Having missed most of his sleep on Thursday night, he had enjoyed a long lie-in on Saturday. He picked up the paper and tossed it onto a polished mahogany hall table, glancing at his reflection in the ornately framed mirror above it. He had some Gaelic League work to do and it wasn't long before he forgot all about the newspaper lying on the hall table.

* * *

Will hoped he had remembered the right house number Hobson had mentioned, as he cycled out of Eoin MacNeill's avenue before returning to his digs to freshen up and get a change of clothing. He also had to pick up his note of Higginson's address. He cycled down the lane behind his lodgings and used the rear entrance for his bike.

Up in his room, he surveyed the street from the bay window. A lady pushing a pram and an elderly gentleman wheeling a bicycle were passing. Further down, a man with a rolled up newspaper under his arm walked in the other direction, smoking a cigarette. Two youths were kicking a stone around as they walked. No one who looked like they were on a stake-out.

Will let the lace curtain drop back into place. He collected his wash bag and went to run a bath. He wasn't sure if there'd be any hot water at this time of day but there was some – enough for a tepid soak. As he dried off he studied his reflection in the mirror on the bathroom cabinet. He had a few days' growth of stubble and he decided to leave it. Buster

Gregson knew what he looked like without the beard, now, so it was no longer a disguise. Besides he felt naked without his beard.

When he was dressed he sought out Mrs Gilpin and explained that he was staying with some friends for the weekend and not to worry if he didn't come in. He paid his rent up to the end of Easter week to put her mind at rest. Back in his room, he wrapped up his good suit, a clean shirt and a few other things in some brown paper and stuck the address that went with the IK 258 registration number in his pocket.

Before leaving he checked the view from his window again. Much as before: a few people ambling by. A woman carrying a heavy shopping basket; two girls arguing as they went along; a man with a rolled up newspaper under his arm, not smoking a cigarette. Will stared at him. Was it the same man who had been on the street when he came in? He was sure it was. But he was also sure he didn't recognise him from any of his previous encounters with Gregson's crew. This was worrying. They were still looking for him and they were using fresh faces he wouldn't know.

He slipped out the back way once more and cycled off, reassured that he had gone unnoticed by the man with the rolled up newspaper.

He first headed back to the Doloughans. Maeve had suggested that, after taking her home this evening from their theatre trip, why not stay the night again. Then they could go to mass together at the Cathedral on Easter Sunday morning before coming back for dinner.

'Attend mass?' said Will.

'Oh well, if it's too much of an imposition to force yourself to come with me...' Maeve's lips pouted.

Will faced a dilemma. Not particularly religious, he was a staunch Protestant nonetheless. For a respected member of the Orange Order and the Royal Arch Purple to be seen inside a Roman Catholic chapel, much less a cathedral would be unthinkable up north. Could attending a service be justified to preserve his assumed identity? He could think of some friends in the Lodge who would never forgive him if they knew. Yet he didn't see how he could get out of it – not without denying himself the pleasure of another night under the same roof as this captivating young woman.

'No, no. That'll be grand. I'd love to stay with you again. Your Mam won't mind?' Will allowed his heart to overrule his head.

'She won't mind. You've won quite an admirer there.'

'Well, I'm glad at least one female member of the Doloughan family still likes me,' said Will.

'Just you be grateful for what you can get, Will Dillon. The female Doloughans are a choosey bunch,' said Maeve.

Will laughed, 'I'll gladly escort you home for the price of a bed and some breakfast, never mind dinner!'

'And without that incentive you'd have packed me off on the tram to make my own way back, I suppose.'

'Hey! You be grateful for what you can get, too, Miss Doloughan.' Will grabbed her round the waist and gave her a peck on the cheek. She made no struggle to be released.

So Will dropped off his package of a change of clothing and suchlike round at the Doloughans' home before setting off once more upon his self-imposed mission. He found the road to the southern suburb where Higginson's address was located and set off at a leisurely pace with the whole afternoon ahead of him.

He had been cycling for some time and thought he should be drawing close to his destination when he came to a pleasant-looking pub set back from the road where patrons were enjoying their Easter Saturday drinks at outside tables on its forecourt. It was the name – R B Doloughan's – that caught his eye and caused him to apply his brakes, deciding to stop for a pint and a sandwich since he hadn't had any lunch. Upon enquiry, however, the R turned out to stand for Rory and the landlord had never heard of Ryan Doloughan.

Patchy clouds allowed the sun through at intervals and, when it shone, Will found sipping the oul black stuff, as the world went by, to be a most agreeable pastime. But he was aware that the peaceful scene around him might look very different by this time tomorrow. Could Pearse go ahead with his plans without the guns, now sunk off the coast of Cork? Ryan seemed to think he could. But what about the Volunteers? Surely a rising would not be possible without them? What will be MacNeill's reaction to the loss of the German arms? Will wished he knew what was happening in other parts of Dublin right at this minute – Liberty Hall, MacNeill's home, Dublin Castle even. He hoped that, with his reliability as a source proven by his warning about the Norwegian gunrunning ship, the British army would now take whatever action was needed to stop tomorrow's planned uprising.

Will's uneasy thoughts were interrupted by a green open-topped motorcar pulling up beyond Doloughan's and reversing back onto a piece of open land adjacent to the pub. As it manoeuvred he could see it was a Crossley. He read the rear number plate with a start, IK 258. Buster Gregson occupied the front passenger seat.

The driver got out and held open the rear door. Even across the length of the pub's frontage Will couldn't fail to recognise the bulky frame of the man he had seen waiting by the same green motorcar outside his digs in Mary Lane, or indeed the face that had looked in horror at Annie lying prone on the pavement in Bangor.

Will sat with his left elbow on the table and supported his forehead in his hand to conceal as much of his face as possible. Through his fingers he saw the rear passenger alight from the vehicle.

Michael J Higginson wore an annoyed expression as he glanced around the forecourt full of late diners and early drinkers. It was an expression burned in Dillon's memory, quite apart from the red S-shaped scar Will could see on his cheek. Instantly, he was back on Hamilton Road, Annie at his feet, red blood pooling around her head. He was calling to this man for help and the face was turning away and ordering his chauffeur to drive on. Except now the face, closely followed by his brutish driver and Gregson, was heading directly towards where Will was sitting.

Chapter 18

About the time Dillon was wondering what was going on in other parts of the city, Eoin MacNeill was enjoying an after dinner cup of tea by the fire in his drawing room. He had remembered the newspaper on the hall stand and retrieved it to peruse while he sipped his steaming brew. As he read, the taste of the tea turned bland in his mouth. Blood drained from his cheeks. Lifting his eyes from the newsprint, he removed his spectacles and gazed, unseeing, towards the hearth.

Lost. Sunk. There were to be no new guns.

The news item said that a Norwegian vessel, The Aud, believed to be carrying German weapons intended for use by republican elements has been sunk off the coast of Cork. A separate item mentioned the arrest of Sir Roger Casement. MacNeill sat motionless, facing the fire. Milk formed a thin film on the surface of his tea.

* * *

Joseph Plunkett suffered from tuberculosis but that hadn't prevented him from travelling to Germany with Roger Casement the previous April to assist him in his initial arms procurement endeavours. It was Plunkett, along with Seán MacDiarmada and James Connolly representing the Citizens' Army, who helped develop the military strategy for the planned uprising. So although he was also recovering from a recent operation on his glands, he was at Liberty Hall that Saturday afternoon with important matters to arrange. The select group that had gathered in the small conference room included Thomas Clark, who had been responsible for revitalising the IRB a few years back, Padraig Pearse,

Connolly and MacDiarmada. There were a few others there, too, and from amongst them, Ryan Doloughan spoke up:

'It is confirmed, I'm afraid. The guns were on the Aud. There'll be no extra arms arriving for our boys. We'll have to make do with what we've got.'

'This is a bad blow,' said MacDiarmada. 'Is what we've got enough, though?'

'We have what we have,' said Pearse, 'and with it we shall do what we shall do. What alternative remains to us? Now is not the time to waiver.'

'We probably have enough weapons in Dublin,' said Plunkett, 'but what about around the country?'

'They shall manage,' said Pearse. 'When they see us rising up in the capital they will rally all over Ireland, guns or no guns. And when the Germans know we mean business they will surely come to our aid.'

It was at that point that the door flew open revealing a red-faced Eoin MacNeill, accompanied by Michael O'Rahilly.

Connolly said, 'What brings 'The O'Rahilly' amongst us so precipitously and so far from his Kerry business enterprises?'

Ryan added, 'This isn't a Gaelic League meeting you are interrupting.'

Michael O'Rahilly, or The O'Rahilly, as he was known far and wide, pushed ahead into the room. 'I may be prominent in the League, sir, but I am also Director of Arms for the Volunteers, in which capacity, I and their Chief of Staff are here "amongst you".'

'I trust you are meeting to call off the Rising,' said MacNeill. 'You've heard, of course that there are to be no new guns? So it's off. It has to be. I just wanted your confirmation.'

Pearse responded almost before the irate leader of the Volunteers had finished speaking. 'Eoin, my dear fellow, *au contraire*. We fight on. Having once put our hand to the plough, we dare not, now, look back.'

'But it would be madness to take on the might of the British army with so little weaponry.'

'We've been through all this,' said MacDiarmada; 'you've agreed to fight with us.'

'I agreed – reluctantly – on the strength of the Kerry guns. You haven't got them anymore. I'm withdrawing the support of my Volunteers. I will not have them slaughtered all around the country.'

'It may not come to that,' said Pearse, 'but better to die for one's country than to tremble in fear at the first setback and do nothing.'

'You're speaking like the poet and idealist that you are, Padraig,' said The O'Rahilly. 'Fine words, but any military-minded man knows to proceed as planned would be disastrous. Plunkett – you can't be thinking of going ahead, can you?'

Plunkett opened his mouth to answer but Connolly got in first. 'We are resolved. The Republic will be declared tomorrow.'

'Over my dead body,' said MacNeill. 'You have until ten o'clock tonight to assure me that it is all off. If I do not receive such assurance I shall cancel tomorrow's manoeuvres.' He swung on his heel and, accompanied by The O'Rahilly, left the rebel leaders to come to their senses.

'We shall hear from them well before the deadline, I feel sure, Michael.'

'Shall we?' said O'Rahilly. 'I wonder.'

* * *

MacNeill paced his drawing room by lamplight.

'Relax, man; sit down. You'll have the carpet worn through. They have a few minutes yet.

MacNeill paused when The O'Rahilly spoke but only momentarily. He resumed his pacing.

'I can't understand what they can be thinking. Without the 10,000 plus Volunteers they have nothing. A few hundred in the Citizens' Army and who knows how many in the Brotherhood? Not many. What they plan is militarily impossible.'

'That may well be, but those who plan it do not have military minds. They are writers, poets and visionaries. To such people all things seem possible, whatever the odds.'

'Do they have suicide in their vision? For that is what it will be. No! I will not allow my members to be used as cannon fodder for some misguided patriotic gesture.'

At last, the Volunteers' Chief of Staff ceased his pacing and moved to an occasional table in the bay window that contained his writing materials.

The Westminster chimes of the clock on the mantelshelf recorded the passing of Pearse's deadline.

Twenty minutes later, The O'Rahilly left MacNeill's home armed with written instructions countermanding the order to turn out on Easter Sunday morning for manoeuvres. MacNeill, had written, on sheets torn from a notebook, "*22 April 1916 Volunteers completely deceived. All orders for tomorrow, Sunday, are completely cancelled.*" For O'Rahilly it was the start of a manic drive through the night, contacting Volunteer units all around Ireland.

No sooner had Michael O'Rahilly departed on this marathon quest, than MacNeill set about calling out boys from *Na Fianna Éireann*. He needed them to cycle round all the local units in and around Dublin with the new orders. By the time the last of these left, Eoin MacNeill sank into a chair. His brain, as well as his body, cried out for rest but he had one more task to complete before he could relax. He picked up the telephone earpiece and asked for the number he needed.

Having been connected to the appropriate person, he proceeded to dictate into the mouthpiece, 'Owing to the critical position, all orders given to the Irish Volunteers for tomorrow, Easter Sunday, are hereby rescinded, and no parades, marches, or other movement of Irish Volunteers will take place. Each individual Volunteer will obey this order strictly in every particular. Signed, Eoin MacNeill, Chief of Staff, Irish Volunteers.'

The following morning, across the country, the Irish populace would read his words printed in the Sunday Independent. Exhausted, MacNeill retired to bed, feeling that he could not reasonably have done more to try to stop the inevitable bloodshed and loss of lives that Clark and Pearse and the rest were so intent on instigating.

* * *

Earlier that afternoon, outside Doloughan's Pub, Higginson seemed to be paying scant regard to people occupying the tables he was weaving past. The trio came ever closer to where Will Dillon was sitting alone at a table for four. If they were to sit down, or even if they paused to ask if the vacant seats were free, Gregson couldn't fail to recognise him. Will half turned his head away while still watching their progress in his peripheral vision.

He saw the chauffeur, still a couple of tables away, eye the empty seats beside him and nudge Gregson with a nod towards them. Will still had half a sandwich uneaten and almost half a pint of Guinness remaining but he prepared himself for a speedy and strategic withdrawal.

The approaching men pushed past an adjacent table. Will tensed his leg muscles, ready to spring up and run all in one smooth action. If he did, it couldn't fail to draw Gregson's attention to him but if he remained seated the three, as they stood over him, would have him at too much of a disadvantage. It was now or never.

Will's chair made a slight scraping sound on the paving slabs as he transferred his weight from the seat to his thigh and calf muscles. He saw Gregson glance towards the sound and at the same instant noticed Higginson make a sharp right and head towards the entrance to the pub. The other two followed him and Will, who had barely moved, let his weight relax back onto the chair.

His heart thumped in his chest. He took a deep breath and exhaled slowly as he reflected. He was close to the address of the Crossley owner. Doloughan's was most likely the man's local. Will cursed himself for being so careless. He mustn't risk still being there if the three came out again with their pints. He drained his glass in a single draft, took one last bite of his sandwich and made his way between the tables to where he had left his bike.

As Will peddled away from the danger zone he realised he now had the ideal opportunity to check out Higginson's home while the man was still at the pub. He quickened his pace and covered the remaining distance of just under a mile in five minutes. He slowed but didn't stop as he approached a pair of ornate, wrought iron gates on the left. Through them he could see a drive winding up to wide steps in front of a large front door with frosted glass panels.

A seven foot high brick wall bounded the grounds on each side of the gate. Will cycled on until the wall ended where a thick hedge of cupressus ran back from the road, delineating the boundary between the big house's grounds and an open field or paddock that seemed to belong to the next residence.

He went a little further until he came to a five-bar gate into the paddock and propped his bicycle against it before climbing over. Keeping close to the hawthorn hedge between the field and the road, he made his way back to the tall row of cupressus. A barbed wire fence separated the hedge from the field and he turned right to follow it. Here and there the thick foliage thinned a little and he was able to glimpse parts of the house and garden. He saw a wide terrace and a large rectangular area which he took to be a bathing pool judging by what looked like a low diving board mounted at one end.

How the other half live, Will thought, as he scaled the barbed wired fence that continued along a thickly wooded area behind the big house. Here a seven foot high wooden fence denied him any views of the rear of the building as he made his way through the trees. At what he judged to be about halfway along he came to an obliging oak tree with some of its gnarled branches overhanging the fence. It was a simple task to jump to one of the lower limbs, scale the tree and work his way out along the overhanging branch.

He made a careful check that there was no one about, but the place looked deserted. He let go of the branch and dropped down into the rear garden. It was only then that he thought about how he was going to get back. Glancing up at the limb he had climbed along, he realised it was a good eighteen inches higher than the fence. He tried to leap up and grab it but came hopelessly short. For the second time that day Will cursed himself for not taking more time to think before acting. He'd have to find another way out.

Beyond the house and to his right a sizeable vegetable patch with a potting shed and a wheelbarrow took up all that side of the garden. Will ran to the cover of the left hand corner of the back of the house in case there was anyone inside to glimpse him through a window. He had no plan other than a vague notion that it would be useful to get an idea of the layout of Higginson's house for when he could come back to wreak his revenge.

He stood close to the corner. The cupressus hedge was way over on his left beyond what he could now see clearly was a splendid tiled bathing pool set in a multi-level paved terrace complete with rattan garden furniture. The paved area looked like it stretched right along the side of the house to meet the front drive.

Will ducked under a windowsill as he started to explore the rear elevation. He raised his head, tipping it back so that his forehead wouldn't be visible from inside before his eyes cleared the sill. He saw a large, sumptuously furnished drawing room that ran the depth of the house. A large bow window at the far end, with heavy floor to ceiling curtains, looked out on the driveway at the front. French windows at the side opened onto the terrace and opposite that was a door that probably led to the hall. Along from the doorway was an enormous, open, natural stone fireplace with a wrought iron grate laid with turf.

Through the next window he saw a shorter room, a study or library. Shelves of leather-bound volumes lined the walls and there was a carved oak desk and some plush leather armchairs. An Adam fireplace that must share a chimney with the grate in the drawing room was surmounted by a rather splendid stag's head on a shield.

To the right of the study was some sort of cloakroom and next to that, a window with frosted glass that must be a downstairs lavatory. Next, there was a half glazed door into a lobby which had a door on the right that was partly open. Through it Will could see a big cooking range against the wall so he wasn't surprised on checking out the next window to see a spacious and well-furnished kitchen with a Belfast sink and draining board under the window. Opposite him, to the left of the range, Will saw a door that he assumed led to the rest of the house while on the other side of the big cooker was a serving hatch, so the dining room must be beyond that at the front of the house. Set between built-in cupboards on the wall on the right was a door that may have led to a larder, perhaps.

Will moved on to check the 'larder' window and was startled to find it had two vertical bars set into the brickwork covering the glass. It was also set high in the wall and he had to jump to grab the bars and pull himself up to see in. The small window didn't admit much light and Will needed to wait for his eyes to adjust to be able to make out the interior. Before he could see anything he heard a loud metallic clang and felt a tremendous thump on the back of his head. His hands lost their grip and he fell back to the ground with blinding flashes behind his forehead and a throbbing ache at the base of his skull. His eyes lost their focus but as he landed, sprawled on the ground, he vaguely registered a pair of muddy boots and the blade of a garden spade before blackness replaced the strobe lights and he lost consciousness.

Chapter 19

Throughout Saturday a series of meetings were taking place in Dublin Castle. With the arrest of Sir Roger Casement the previous day and the interception of the *Aud Norge* the British administration were aware that something was imminent. Special Branch officers who had infiltrated the ranks of the Irish Republican Brotherhood had reported rumours they had picked up about possible trouble ahead but such was the secrecy maintained by the Military Council that, just like the IRB's own leadership, the authorities knew nothing of the details regarding the timing or extent of any planned insurrection.

'There are anywhere from sixty to a hundred republican leaders known to us. We should play safe. Have them all arrested.' This, from one, Ivor Churchill Guest, the Lord-Lieutenant of Ireland, Lord Wimborne, who was confident he understood the Irish psyche. He twirled the points of his neat, handlebar moustache as he added, 'Put their top men under lock and key and any resolve they might have had will fizzle out.'

His remarks were addressed to Sir Matthew Nathan, Assistant Secretary whose job it would be to order the RIC to carry out the arrests across the country and that gentleman was wishing his boss, Augustine Birrell, the Chief Secretary was not – as was so often the case – away in London at the time. However, before he could answer Lord Wimborne the other person present, Assistant Adjutant General, Colonel Cowan spoke up.

'Trouble with large-scale arrests, they do rather stir up resentment amongst the masses.' The colonel paused, wishing like Sir Matthew, that his superior officer, Major-General Friend, commanding officer of the British army in Ireland had not taken the Easter weekend off to spend it in England. He drew a deep breath and decided to continue, 'I'm not sure I agree with you that such a course would necessarily nip any rebellious thoughts in the bud. It might just be the catalyst to set it off. There'll always be others to step into the leadership roles.'

'Not at short notice,' said Wimborne. 'Knock the stuffing out of them, is what I say. Give us more time to assimilate our intelligence and find out exactly what they're up to.'

'Well, our friends in the North are telling us their man on the ground here seemed pretty definite that tomorrow's manoeuvres are planned to be the start of an uprising,' said Sir Matthew.

'Who is this new chap? What do we know about him?'

'Very little, Lord Wimborne. He's acting, primarily, for some highly influential people in Ulster who have always had our best interests at heart,' said Nathan.

'But is the man reliable?'

'It was he who found out the German guns were coming in under a Norwegian flag. That led directly to the arrest of the crew – all German officers.'

'But the weapons were lost.'

'Unfortunately, yes, but the informant can hardly be held responsible for that, sir.'

The debate continued without reaching a decision on the question of multiple arrests. They all had evening engagements and agreed to reconvene at ten-thirty to re-assess the situation in the light of whatever further intelligence might become available.

So it was that shortly after that time the three men were again gathered in Lord Wimborne's office at the Castle. The other two accepted the Napoleon brandy that he handed round in goblets of century-old Tyrone crystal.

'So, what news? Anything fresh?' asked the Lord-Lieutenant, carefully sharpening the points of his moustache.

'The very best!' said Sir Matthew, all beams. 'This is to appear in the *Sunday Independent* in the morning,' and he handed the others copies of Eoin MacNeill's countermanding order to stop the Irish Volunteers exercises.

'Well, this is splendid news, indeed,' said Colonel Cowan. 'I don't mind telling you that I was a little apprehensive; we've only 400 men on active duty here in Dublin at the moment.

'I'd still feel happier with at least some of the more prominent Fenians – republicans, locked up,' said Wimborne.

'Surely that is no longer necessary,' said Sir Matthew. 'Without the Volunteers, there can be no possibility of an uprising. I really believe we can afford to relax and enjoy our Easter weekend. Damn good brandy, this, Lord Wimborne. Here's to MacNeill for showing a bit of common sense.' He raised his glass and the others joined him in the toast.

'Some of my officers are keen to see the Grand National on Easter Monday. They'll be cock-a-hoop now I can give them the go-ahead to spend the day at Fairyhouse racecourse.'

'Quite right, Colonel. Your men deserve some relaxation,' said Sir Maxwell. 'We can all rest easy in our beds tonight. Happy Easter, gentlemen.'

* * *

Earlier that same day, Will Dillon had opened one eye and then, with some effort, the other. He had the mother of all headaches and for a few moments couldn't focus. He realised he was lying on his side on hard tiles and for the time being he was content to remain there. His limbs felt weak but most of his concentration centred on his throbbing cranium. He raised a hand to probe gently round the back of his head and winced as his fingers touched a large bulge under his hair.

From where he lay he could now make out some tall metal cupboards. A row of them. Dark green, like Geoffrey Bradshaw's desk. Will didn't feel inclined to raise his head to see any more of the room.

He closed his eyes again and tried to remember what had happened. He had been checking out Higginson's house. And Higginson was at the pub. He remembered that. But for how long? How long had he been unconscious? He had no way of knowing. Not long, he guessed; he wasn't stiff from lying in one position for a long time. He'd been trying to see in through a high window when he'd been hit on the head. By a spade. He remembered a spade before he passed out. A gardener must have spotted him. Probably been in the potting shed.

Will decided he better find out more about where he was. He raised himself slowly until he was leaning on one elbow and gingerly moved his head to take in the rest of his surroundings. The room was narrow, not large. In the wall opposite the steel cupboards was a sturdy door that looked as if it might be steel-lined. Pretty sure to be locked. I'll try it in a minute. To the right of the door was a large wicker basket. Laundry, he thought, noting the corner of a white sheet hanging from under its lid. His guess was confirmed by the presence of another big Belfast sink, a mangle and a mop and bucket against the wall to the left of the door.

A small window set high in the narrow end wall finally told him exactly where he was. The room off thc kitchen. Not a larder; a laundry room. But not just a laundry room. All the metal cupboards had individual locks and Will felt sure he knew what they contained, given the reinforced door to the room. He got slowly onto his knees and then managed to stand up. It was as though the increased altitude sent his head spinning again. He paused to get his balance before stepping across to the door. Silently, so as not to alert anyone who might be in the kitchen, he tried the handle. Locked, as expected. The door is rigid; no chance of budging that. Against the wall opposite the window, an ageing set of wooden drawers. He pulled one open and what he saw confirmed his suspicions. Cartons of shotgun cartridges. He checked another – boxes of bullets of a number of different calibres. I'm imprisoned in Higginson's armoury. The cabinets will contain guns, and quite a few, judging by the number of them and their size. It explains the two vertical bars across the window. Probably the only secure room in the house and the gardener, another one of Higginson's thugs, will have dumped me there to await the Boss's return.

This a prospect that Will did not relish at all. He tried each of the green cabinet doors in turn. All locked. He had to escape, and soon. The Crossley had been heading in this direction and they were unlikely to remain at the pub for long. They could already be on their way.

Will looked at the door. Out of the question. Even without his raging headache and the risk of calling attention to anyone in the house he couldn't possibly kick that door open. It was built to keep people out but served equally well to keep him in. So, it had to be the window. Will eyed the spacing between the bars; not much.

Then he heard voices. Raised voices. From the front of the house, somewhere. The Boss had returned and he didn't sound pleased.

Will shoved the laundry basket over against the wall under the window. Ignoring the throbbing in his head, he grabbed the mop and climbed onto the wicker lid.

The arguing voices were louder.

Will held the mop handle like a javelin and jabbed it with all his strength against the glass pane.

* * *

'You put him in the gun room? Are you mad?'

'He was out for the count. And sure all the guns are locked up, anyway. It was the only place I could think of; he wouldn't have been long busting out of the potting shed.'

'I thought he was unconscious.'

'He was. Is. But he'll come round eventually, I suppose.'

'Oh, very well. Let's have a look at this intruder.'

In the hall Michael J Higginson pushed aside Gerry Walsh, his handyman/gardener and entered the kitchen.

He was met by the unmistakable sound of breaking glass.

'What's that?'

'It sounded like it came from the gun room, said Kelly, who had followed Higginson into the kitchen.

'Well get in there, then.' Higginson rushed across to the laundry room door. 'Hurry up, man!'

Walsh and Gregson were entangled in the kitchen doorway, Buster Gregson asserting his position in the pecking order by trying to go first, while Gerry Walsh was just anxious to placate his angry boss by producing the keys for the gun room. He managed to squeeze past the unyielding Gregson and fumbled in his trouser pocket for his bunch of keys.

'Quickly, what's keeping you?'

Walsh picked through the keys on his ring, trying to find the right one.

'Come on, come on!' said Higginson. 'Oh, give them to me.'

He snatched the bunch out of Walsh's hand and started the process afresh of finding the right key. Once identified he lost no time in inserting it in the lock and flinging open the sturdy door. He stepped aside to ensure Kelly entered first and said, 'Bring him out here.'

Kelly stepped in and paused. Higginson saw him move the door and check behind it.

'There's no one here,' he said, 'but the window's broken, sure enough.'

Higginson dashed in and stared around. 'He used the laundry hamper to reach the window. But the bars are still in place. Was he small enough to squeeze through those?'

The wretched Walsh said, 'I didn't think he was, but... I suppose he might have been.'

'You suppose! You didn't think, full stop. Moron! Get out there after him. Now! All of you.'

Gregson was already in the lobby and opening the back door. Kelly and Walsh rushed after him.

'Bring him back! Dead or alive – I don't care,' Higginson yelled after them as he strode out of the kitchen to the front door.

* * *

The kitchen and the laundry room fell quiet with only distant sounds of shouting penetrating through the open back door to the lobby and the broken window in the gun room. Will cautiously raised the lid of the laundry basket and, seeing no one about, extricated himself from under the soiled sheets and climbed out. He crossed to the chest of drawers containing the ammunition and grabbed what he needed before peering out into the kitchen.

Deserted.

He crossed to the range and, using a tea-towel that was hanging on a rail to protect his hand, he pulled open the stove door and threw in half a dozen shotgun cartridges. He ran out into the hall, ignored what he assumed to be the door to the study and opened the door that he knew must lead to the big drawing room he had seen with the French windows.

Once there, he headed straight to the bay. He crouched down in a corner below the window level to ensure he wasn't seen from outside. He was concealed from anyone inside by one of the heavy, brocade floor-length curtains.

Now he waited.

It didn't take long. The silence in the house – and indeed the shouting outside – came to an abrupt end with a single loud report like a gun shot. This was rapidly followed by three more shots. The shouting outside started again and from it Will could tell the men were running towards the house. He heard the French window open and two pairs of footsteps running through the drawing room to the hall as a fifth shot rang out.

Next came the distinctive sound of a revolver being fired, closely followed by the last cartridge exploding. Will was already at the French window, confident that all his pursuers would now be back in the house. He sprinted across the terrace and past the bathing pool towards the cupressus hedge. He aimed at one spot where the lower foliage looked a bit thinner and flung himself on the ground between two trunks. He wriggled in under the fronds and branches.

There was more shouting back out in the garden again followed by two more revolver shots. Will pulled his legs in under the hedge and prayed he was hidden. More gun fire and a bullet ripped through the branches above him. They'd spotted him. He heard running footsteps on the terrace and voices sounded nearer. He daren't look back. He crawled further into the hedge, ignoring the scratches.

More shots rang out and he flattened himself to the ground, but he realised they had hit the hedge further along. Spasmodic firing continued, seemingly at random. They couldn't have seen him after all. He crawled on until he emerged from under the cupressus behind the barbed wire fence. He couldn't risk standing and catching a stray bullet so, again, he crawled forward on his stomach under the lowest strand of the fence. There was little clearance and the vicious barbs kept catching on his clothing. Each time he had to pause to extricate himself.

By the time he made it through, the gunfire had ceased. He could still hear angry voices that sounded as though they were down by the front gate. Keeping low, he started to jog up to the field gate. He promptly changed that to a brisk walk as the jogging did his raging headache no good at all.

Walking eased the pain in his head and he was soon back on his bike and pedalling fast. The irate calls of Higginson's henchmen soon faded in his wake and for the first time since being clonked on the head by the spade Will was able to relax.

* * *

Sitting in the stalls in the Abbey Theatre with the lovely Maeve at his side was such a contrast to how he had spent his afternoon that Will could almost believe he must have dreamt his near encounter with the "Boss." His headache, though – by now mercifully subsiding – and the lump on the back of his head, told a different story.

And he had told a different story to Maeve to account for his sore head. He didn't want to go into his whole vendetta that was his real reason for being in Dublin, so he had simply said he had come off his bike and banged his head – the accuracy as to the sequence of events appealed to him, despite being decidedly misleading as to the cause of his injury. He felt bad deceiving Maeve, especially as she had shown such tenderness and concern for him when he told her. She had provided him with some tablets called Aspirin – a new German drug that their doctor recommended for her mother's arthritis. It was harder to obtain since the start of the war but according to Maeve, Bayer, the company who made it, had set up manufacturing plants in the USA in case America should enter the war and put a ban on German imports, so it was still available in Dublin pharmacies from time to time.

'It reduces pain anywhere in your body,' Maeve told Will. 'Mam says it's wonderful.'

Will was a little sceptical but had to admit his headache did diminish after he swallowed a couple of tablets. Though he did wonder whether the therapeutic effect of Maeve's gentle caresses and tender kisses, after she brought the Aspirin to his room, might not have been a contributing factor.

By the time they got to the theatre for the 'public' dress rehearsal of *Kathleen Ni Houlahan* Will was relaxed and determined to forget about his brush with Higginson and his other secret activities. He had done what he could to thwart the republicans' plans for a rising. Whether it was enough, only time would tell. He chose not to think about what tomorrow might bring.

Maeve reached for his hand to hold in hers as the house lights went down and the curtain went up. He squeezed her fingers gently and she snuggled up to him with her head on his shoulder. It felt good.

The programme stated that *Kathleen Ni Houlahan* is a play in one act, written by William Butler Yeats and Lady Augusta Gregory in 1902. The tale is set at the time of the rebellion of the United Irishmen in 1798.

Will knew that the eponymous Kathleen is a famous figure in Irish literature, usually portrayed as a poor old woman who has been dispossessed of her farmhouse and four green fields. The fields are seen to represent the four provinces of Ireland and Kathleen is the personification of the country itself. He had heard that the play is unashamedly nationalistic.

Although it was a dress rehearsal, the producer let the actors go right through to the end without interruption. As the story unfolds, it becomes clear that the old woman wants to entice a young man, due to be married the next day, to come and fight for his country, even if it should cost him his life. His fiancée pleads with him to stay but the call of Kathleen prevails and as he leaves with her, his younger brother sees that Kathleen has been rejuvenated into a beautiful young girl.

Referring to all who follow her, mostly to their deaths, the girl calls out, 'They shall be remembered forever. They shall be alive forever. They shall be speaking forever. The people shall hear them forever.'

Along with many Dublin theatregoers, Will would come to realise the supreme irony of the fact that the official opening night for the Abbey Theatre's production of *Kathleen Ni Houlahan* was to be Easter Monday – a day that was destined indeed to be remembered forever.

PART TWO

A TERRIBLE BEAUTY

Chapter 20

Easter Sunday in 1916 saw the usual crowds of soberly suited and gaily bonneted citizens of Dublin celebrating the Saviour's resurrection at places of worship all around the capital. The mood inside Liberty Hall, however, the spawning ground for months past of the republican's covert planning to break free of the English yoke, was far from celebratory. The Countess Markievicz had tears running down her cheeks.

'He has shattered the uprising. How could he? All our planning, all our preparations – in ruins. It's just too much.'

A copy of the *Sunday Independent* lay before her on the table where she sat and all those present had read the terse notice signed, Eoin MacNeill, cancelling that day's Volunteer manoeuvres around the country. It had all but dashed any hopes of victory. Tom Clarke, the man responsible for revitalising the Irish Republican Brotherhood and the chief instigator behind the planned rising, flicked the newspaper away and said, 'It's a shame. Shame! I feel like going off somewhere to cry, myself.'

Pearse said, 'We're all feeling knocked back by this unwelcome news, but what's done is done. We have a decision to make.'

Young Michael Collins, Plunkett's aide, who had helped him from his sick bed and got him dressed to be there, said, 'It's a hell of a decision, whether or not to call off the rising.'

'Call it off!' Pearse jumped to his feet. 'What sort of option is that for a true-blooded Irishman? Never. What we have to decide, and decide now, is whether or not to postpone the start of the rising.'

Clarke rose, too and clapped his hands together, ensuring the others' attention. 'Pearse is right,' he said. 'No question of calling it off. And

I'm not sure we should even be considering a postponement. Sure, once we start fighting in Dublin, republicans all over the country will rally to us.'

'But we have reduced resources, now. We need to sit down and figure out how to use them to the greatest effect.'

'I think Pearse has a point, there,' said MacDiarmada; 'our plans need to be reviewed in the light of MacNeill's traitorous action.'

'We can review them this morning and still start the rising at mid-day,' said Plunkett.

The debate continued, becoming heated at times, until Connolly stood up and said what he felt was the growing consensus.

'My Citizens' Army and the IRB are ready to move but without the backing of the Volunteers we have to reassess whether we can take and hold all the strategic positions we intended to. I say we spend the rest of today refining and adjusting our plans and make final preparations in the morning – muster the troops, print off copies of the Declaration, load up supplies ready for distribution.'

There was a general murmur of approval.

'Then we are agreed,' said Pearse. 'We march on Easter Monday. At midday our beloved Ireland will become a Republic!'

* * *

Will Dillon was eying six tall Doric columns supporting a pediment under which a stream of people were entering the place of worship. The style of the architecture reminded him of the GPO frontage where he worked, but the absence of any spire surprised him. 'So this is the famous St Patrick's Cathedral?' he asked his companions.

'Ah, bless you, Will, this isn't St Patrick's,' said old Mrs Doloughan, who had accompanied her daughter and Maeve's new young gentleman to celebrate mass on Easter Day. 'Is that where you thought we were going?'

Will was confused. 'Er... I thought, when Maeve said you always go to the cathedral on Easter Sunday, that's what she meant.'

'But we're Catholics, the Doloughans. I should have thought you'd have known that.'

'Oh yes, Mrs Doloughan, I know Maeve is a good Catholic.'

Maeve said, 'St Patrick's is a Church of Ireland cathedral. This is St Mary's Roman Catholic Pro Cathedral.'

'Wait – "Pro Cathedral"?'

'Yes, it means "acting" Cathedral; it's complicated.'

'Sure, there's nothing complicated about it,' said Mrs Doloughan. 'There were two cathedrals in Dublin – well, Christ Church was *in* Dublin and St Patrick's was just outside the old city walls.'

'So you're telling me there are three, now?'

'I'm telling you, if you'll listen.'

'Sorry.'

'When that Henry VIII fellow fell out with the Pope, the Irish bishops went along with him and the two cathedrals became Anglican and so the Pope raised St Mary's to the status of cathedral for the Catholics.'

'But why Pro Cathedral?'

Maeve answered, 'Because the catholic church has never recognised Christ Church as being Anglican. So until it's handed back to the Catholics, St Mary's is only the acting catholic Cathedral.'

'And that's likely to happen?' Will sounded doubtful.

'Oh yes. When Hell freezes over, probably.'

They laughed, but Mrs Doloughan said, 'Don't be irreverent, Maeve.'

'Sorry, Mum. But we'd best be getting inside or there'll be no seats at all.'

Will was never happier than when the service ended and he emerged again from the hallowed precincts of St Mary's. Not being overtly religious, he realised it shouldn't matter to him which particular rituals or litanies were followed by the priests or ministers. Yet during his upbringing amongst the Protestants in the North he had absorbed an ingrained antithesis to the catholic religion. At an intellectual level he was a mere observer at the Easter Mass, yet hearing the Archbishop intone that the 'host has become for us the body of Christ,' when his own Presbyterian minister would say simply that 'this bread represents the body of our Lord Jesus Christ' still grated with him. He wasn't sure how much he believed about Christianity, but transubstantiation was a belief too far.

He knew it was a major obstacle for some of his more ardent Orange brethren. "The blasphemy of the Mass," they called it, saying the Catholics were murdering our Saviour all over again each time they celebrated Mass. But, if he was being honest, Will thought this service had been reverent and worshipful, neither more so, nor less than some protestant services he had sat through.

But he couldn't help feeling he was betraying his protestant heritage by being there. When everyone filed out, one row at a time, to go forward to receive the host from the priest Will was in a quandary. This, above anything else, was the moment – the action – that could damn his soul, if he were to believe his diehard protestant pals. He followed Mrs Doloughan and Maeve for appearances sake and, struggling with his conscience with each step, inched forward towards the celebrants. Finally it was his turn and the priest placed a small round wafer on his palm – not a little cube of bread like they had in First Donaghadee Presbyterian, he thought. He moved on, raising his palm to his mouth but not inserting the wafer. He dropped his hands and surreptitiously pocketed it before returning to his seat next to Maeve and hoped his subterfuge would be sufficient to retain his place in Heaven, if such a place existed.

'Did you enjoy the service, Will?'

Relieved as he was to be out of the cathedral, Will was happy to be able to tell Mrs Doloughan that he had.

'It was a great experience,' he added.

Maeve was watching him with a slightly odd expression. 'You really enjoyed it?'

'I did, Maeve. Thank you for bringing me.'

The moment passed and they moved off towards Sackville Street to catch a tram.

Preparing the dinner was fun. Will offered to peel the spuds and Maeve scraped the carrots. They joked together and flicked peelings at each other.

'I hope you're going to pick all those up when you've finished making eejits of yourselves,' said Mrs Doloughan, as she got the chicken ready for the oven.

When the vegetables were prepared and they'd tidied up their mess, Maeve's mother said, 'Now off you go, you two young people, out of my kitchen. Sure you're just getting under my feet.'

'Are you sure we can't do anything else to help, Mam?'

'You've "helped" quite enough, thank you,' said her mother bending to pick up an errant potato peel. 'Off with you, and entertain our guest.'

Maeve led the way into the front room and chose to sit on the sofa rather than either of the matching armchairs. Will was about to lower himself into one of these.

'The sofa is more comfortable.' Maeve shifted a little to one side to leave plenty of room for Will, who came and sat beside her. She shifted back again.

Taking the hint, Will placed an arm around her. Their thighs were touching. Maeve rested her head on his shoulder and he nuzzled her hair. The tickling of the strands on his cheeks sent a thrill down his spine. She smelled intoxicating. He should find out what perfume she used and then he could buy her some.

'Ryan will be back soon,' Maeve said.

Why mention her brother, Will thought. She had told him he'd gone out early, when he came down to breakfast. On IRB business, no doubt. He wondered what was happening amongst the republican revolutionaries. He had seen MacNeill's piece in the *Sunday Independent* and, certainly, there had been no sign of Volunteer activity in the city centre when they had been at St Mary's. Throughout the morning Will's optimism was growing that the rising had been abandoned.

'So we don't have much time,' Maeve's sultry tone interrupted his thoughts.

'Time for – '

Before he could finish his question, Maeve twisted round and lay with her back across his knees. He saw her reach up to embrace him and he lowered his lips to hers. They yielded to his pressure and parted, the touch of her tongue on his, tingling like a mountain stream caressing the mosses on its banks. His hands moved over her body and she moaned, returning his kisses more fervently.

The two lost track of time; lost track of everything, save their ardent desire for each other. It wasn't Ryan's return that brought them back to reality, but Mrs Doloughan's call that dinner was ready and if they didn't come and get it, it would go cold.

They untangled themselves and Maeve stood up and adjusted her clothing.

'Is my face as red as yours?' Will asked her, coming to his feet and grabbing her around her waist.

'Let me go!' she squealed in a stage whisper. 'I'm quite sure this wasn't what Mam had in mind when she told me to entertain you, so you behave yourself when we go in to dinner.'

'Right. Absolutely. Is Ryan back? I didn't hear him come in.'

'I think your mind was on other things. I must have missed him, too.'

'Funny, that.'

Will stood back to allow Maeve to enter the dining room first. 'Be sensible,' she hissed at him.

They took their places. The table was laid for four but there was no sign of Ryan.

'No Ryan?' Will asked Mrs Dologhan.

'I expect he'll be along, shortly. He did say not to wait for him, though. Said he couldn't be sure when he'd get back.'

The three of them enjoyed the meal. They had a treacle tart for dessert that Maeve had prepared on Saturday for them.

'Well that was delicious,' said Will. 'Thank you both, so much for your hospitality. Ryan doesn't know what he's missing.'

Will missed Ryan over lunch as much as his family. He was hoping his friend would have been able to tell him what was happening, or not happening, regarding the planned rising.

In the continued absence of Maeve's brother, Will put thoughts of hostilities out of his mind and enjoyed her company for the rest of the day. They walked hand in hand through Phoenix Park and came to the Zoological Gardens, where a notice claimed it to be the third oldest public zoo in the world, founded in 1830 a year after London Zoo and two years after the one in Paris. Maeve's uncle was the deputy Head Keeper and when she was a girl she had often been allowed in free after hours. She called to one of the staff through the railings who was there on Sunday to feed the animals. He knew who she was and was happy to let them take a wander round. They laughed at the monkeys and marvelled at the giraffes. Will teased the elephant by holding out his hand as though offering it something to eat. The giant animal swung its trunk out over the railings before realising he had nothing in his hand. After the second occasion, it dipped its trunk in a pail of water for a drink. Then it raised its trunk once more in Will's direction and squirted him with water.

Maeve jumped aside from the splashes and laughed aloud. 'Ha, you deserved that, Will Dillon; teasing the poor animal.'

Will looked suitably contrite and then pulled her to him and rubbed his wet cheek against hers before running off. Maeve chased after him until he let her catch him by the penguin enclosure. He stood behind her with his arms around her waist as they watched the birds' antics. One of them slid down a smooth slope made in the artificial rock and splashed into the pool, swam around and climbed back out and up to the top of the slope to slide down again.

'Aren't they funny?' said Maeve, 'and so cute.'

'Just like you.'

'I'm not funny.'

'Aren't you? You're cute, but.'

He took her hand and said, 'Come on, let's walk some more. It looks set to be a lovely spring evening.'

With a wave to the keeper, they left the animals behind and strolled past Citadel Pond where they saw a coot with two chicks. They walked, arm in arm, round the periphery of some playing fields until they found themselves at the foot of St Thomas' Hill. They looked up to the solid, limestone walls that enclosed a large area at its summit.

'The Magazine Fort,' said Maeve.

Will eyed the sprawling fort and the rooftops they could glimpse of the old barracks buildings, kitchens, stores and residential. He saw some concrete constructions that must be the magazine itself.

'Ryan says the walls are five feet thick. One part is full of barrels of gunpowder; another has artillery, and ammunition in the third.'

'How come Ryan knows all that?'

'I'm not sure, but I think it was one of his jobs to find out about the Fort. He has a friend called Paddy O'Daly who worked as a carpenter inside the fort not long ago. I expect he got most of it from Paddy.' Maeve suddenly turned and faced Will. Her eyes had lost their carefree sparkle; her forehead was creased in a frown. 'Is there going to be a rebellion, Will? Are we going to war with the English?'

Her question took Will off guard. He hesitated. He knew how zealously the leaders had been guarding their secret, but Ryan must have known most of what was being planned. He had given Will his instructions regarding the ill-fated Kerry trip, but it seemed he didn't discuss much of what he knew with his sister, which was only to be expected, he supposed.

'It might happen yet. It might. But I have a feeling that it won't. Not in the immediate future, at any rate.'

‘What do you know, Will? Why do you think that?’

‘You saw MacNeill’s countermanding order in the paper this morning. That tells us two things: a) something had been planned involving the Volunteers and b) the manoeuvres are cancelled so whatever else was planned must be cancelled, too.’

‘I wonder are you right. Ryan has always said that we are going to have to make a stand if we are ever to gain our freedom. Recently he has been hinting that the time to do that is now, while the English are all caught up in Europe.’

‘There is that, I suppose.’

‘But if there is fighting, Ryan is bound to be involved. He could be killed.’

‘If there is fighting a lot of people could be killed. That’s what happens in war.’

Maeve took both Will’s hands in hers. ‘I know we all must be prepared for the worst, but we can hope for the best.’

‘We? It’s not your fight. If it comes to the crunch, it’s the men who’ll be battling it out.’

‘Why?’ She dropped his hands. ‘Do you think women can’t fight? Take a stand for our country’s freedom?’

‘Whoa! I didn’t say that.’ Will saw he’d touched a nerve. He went to take her hand again but she held them both out of reach. ‘I’m sure you women are every bit as patriotic as the men. But have you ever fired a gun? Taken part in unarmed combat? Gone for days and nights without sleep?’

‘Constance Markievicz is the best shot in the Citizens’ Army, I’ll have you know.’

‘I think the Countess is rather special, though, don’t you?

‘Maybe, but there are hundreds of us in *Cumann na mBan* – ’

‘The women’s Volunteers. I know; you told me.’

‘We’re separate from the Irish Volunteers but we have the same aims – “to further the cause of Irish liberty” and we’re being trained to use armed force, if necessary. So, yes, actually, I have fired a gun.’

‘Have you, indeed? I’ve been underestimating you, my feisty friend.’

‘Maybe you have. I’m every bit as capable of fighting for my country as you.’

‘Me? I’m not part of this. I’ve only been helping out. From now on I’m keeping my head down. But, it’s all off, anyway. I’m sure it is.’ Will managed to take hold of Maeve's hand again and pulled her arm around him. He hugged her and she responded.

With her head against his breast she said, 'Somehow, I'm not so sure. Let's make the most of today; who knows what tomorrow may bring? I have a bad feeling. Why did Ryan not come home for dinner?'

'He'll be fine. But I'm with you that we should enjoy this evening, whatever the future may hold. It's been a wonderful weekend.'

'It has, starting with you taking me to the theatre last night,' said Maeve as they turned their feet in the direction of the Conyngham Road exit from Phoenix Park.

'And staying up to the wee, small hours just talking.'

'Hmm. As I recall there wasn't all that much talking,' she squeezed his hand.

'Well, euphemistically speaking…'

'You're a bad man, Will Dillon.'

'Me! It takes two to – talk.'

Maeve laughed and slid her arm around his waist. With a hand on her shoulder he pulled her closer as they walked on, making their way down to the Liffey. They watched a couple of youngsters struggling to bring their rowing boat in to the side. A rusty tug chugged past pulling a barge full of coal upstream and a pair of swans glided gracefully out of its path. Will and Maeve ambled along the north bank listening to the sounds of the river in the gathering dusk until Maeve gave a little shiver. Will slipped off his coat and put it round her shoulders. She hugged him and raised her face to his. They embraced and kissed long and deep in the twilight and a moorhen called from the reeds across the water. Above them the moon appeared, pale in the darkening sky.

'The moon,' they both said together.

Maeve smiled and held up her little finger. Will looked at her and then remembered what he used to do as a child. He linked his own little finger in hers. They were supposed to make a silent wish. You do it when you speak the same words simultaneously, but you mustn't speak aloud before wishing, or it won't come true.

They stood in silence, little fingers linked and Will wasn't sure what to wish for. Safety for them all in the days ahead? The satisfactory fulfilment of his mission of revenge? The blossoming of his new relationship with Maeve? In the end he wished that whatever Maeve wished for would come true. Technically, a wasted wish, he thought and smiled at his own foolishness in indulging the superstition.

The hour was growing late by the time they got back to the Doloughan home and Maeve's mother had already retired for the night. She had left them a supper of slices of bread and butter with a pot of homemade blackberry jam and some little cakes. Maeve boiled the kettle to make tea. Either Ryan was still not back, or he'd had such a long day that he'd gone off to bed, too.

The pair enjoyed their meal and lingered over a second cup of tea until by silent, mutual consent they rose and made their way upstairs. On the landing they paused. Maeve gave Will a quick kiss and whispered, Goodnight.

'Goodnight, my love,' said Will.

He sensed her fleeting reaction to what he had called her before she was kissing him again, ardently, fervently, passionately and all the while they were, somehow, moving closer to Maeve's bedroom door. She must have reached behind her to get the handle for the door opened. Still entwined in each other's arms Maeve stepped back, bringing Will with her into her room.

It was his turn to feel behind him for the handle. As he closed the door gently, it occurred to him that perhaps both their wishes were coming true.

* * *

Will awoke early and took a moment to remember where he was. He turned his head and saw Maeve's naked back and, on the pillow, her auburn hair close to his face. He listened to her even breathing remembering how it had been a long, long time before they had both finally dropped off to sleep, happy but exhausted. He remembered mutual declarations of love. And then he remembered what day it was.

Easter Monday.

His wedding day.

The day he and Annie were to have sworn their faithfulness to each other for all time until separated only by death. He blinked his eyes hard and the dampness on his cheeks seeped into the pillow. A wave of guilt engulfed him, pulling him down; down to a despair he had never known. How could he have betrayed his beloved Annie? Abandoned her. He looked again at the back of Maeve's head in the half-light of dawn. An emptiness in the pit of his stomach competed with a fluttering in his heart and his mind refused to intervene.

He closed his eyes and lay still. "Until death us do part" is what he should have been promising Annie in a few hours' time. But that spectre had already done its worst and parted them forever. He told himself that he was released from the ties represented by the beautiful solitaire ring he had placed on Annie's finger. He opened his eyes and looked again at Maeve. Maeve, who had helped heal the wounds inflicted upon him by that release.

As he gazed upon her he felt as though he was slowly being lifted back from the depths. He wiped his hand across his cheeks and got out of bed, careful not to awaken the sleeping girl. He slipped on his clothes and silently crossed the landing to his own room where he changed into a clean shirt. It may be a Bank Holiday for some, but he had to get to the Post Office to start work. His emotions were still in a whirl and he dared not talk to Maeve just now. He scribbled her a note and tiptoed into her room to leave it on her pillow. Quietly, he let himself out of the house to catch a tram.

As he was trundling along towards the city centre he imagined Maeve awakening to find him gone. He hoped she would forgive him as she read what he had written. He repeated it to himself as the tram was approaching Sackville Street:

My darling Maeve, thank you for the most wonderful weekend of my life and the most wonderful night of my life. Forgive me for not waking you to say goodbye, but I couldn't trust myself not to have taken much longer with you than a swift farewell. I must get off to work. Thank your mam for me for her hospitality, and thank you, my love, for all you have come to mean to me. I am counting the hours until we can be together again. With love, Will.

* * *

It was a slack morning at the General Post Office. The Bank Holiday crowds were all at the races, or engaged in some other recreational activities. Only a few were on the streets of Dublin and of those, but a small percentage had business to transact in the Post Office. Will used the morning to catch up on paperwork. He thought he might take an early lunch break and stood up to return the ledgers he'd been working on to the secure room. As he picked up a large bunch of office keys, he heard a commotion in the street. The door burst open and a gang of men rushed in, some in uniform, some not, but all in one shade of green or another – and all carrying rifles.

Will froze. Were they being robbed?

The first man in shouted at them, 'Nobody move!' as he panned his rifle from left to right taking in all the counter staff. 'The General Post Office is now the property of the provisional government of the Republic of Ireland.'

God preserve us, it's started after all, thought Will. It's the Rising.

The gunmen spread out and covered the whole concourse with their weapons. The one who had already spoken barked an order, 'Stains. That one, standing up with the keys. You know what to do.'

Will saw the man who had been addressed as Stains turn round. He was ten feet away. Will stood and watched as Stains raised his German Mauser. The rifle was aiming directly at his chest and at that range he couldn't miss.

Chapter 21

Padraig Pearse stood under the colonnade in front of the GPO and for a moment surveyed the scene before him. A scene, he felt he had been preparing for throughout most of his adult life. The fulfilment of his extravagant dreams for his beloved country now lay in the hands of the gallant soldiers of the Citizens' Army and Volunteers loyal to the Irish Republican Brotherhood who had marched with him from Liberty Hall. They filled the pavement in front of the Post Office and some were taking up positions around their leaders. Michael Collins was helping Joseph Plunkett take his place beside Pearse and they were followed by James Connolly, Thomas Clark and Seán MacDiarmada. Others carried bundles of pamphlets to be handed out that were still hot off the printing press at Liberty Hall. They bore the words that Pearse was about to declare from the front of the grandiose building that symbolised all that he hated about British rule in Ireland.

These were the five leaders assigned to hold the GPO until Volunteers all over the country rose up in support of their stand to drive the English out of their land. Around the city hundreds of their comrades had marched from Liberty Hall and other marshalling points to take over further prominent locations.

Ned Daly led the 1st Battalion to capture the Four Courts and guard against attack from the west, while Seán Heuston, commanding D Company of the 1st Battalion, took over the Mendicity Institute just upstream on the opposite bank of the Liffey. Commandant MacDonagh headed up the 2nd Battalion to take over Jacob's Biscuit Factory to the south of the city; Commandant Ceannt led the 4th Battalion to the

Workhouse, known as the South Dublin Union, in the southwest to defend against soldiers marching in from the Curragh barracks; Michael Mallin, with Countess Markievicz as second in command, marched with a force of Citizens' Army soldiers to establish themselves in St Stephen's Green and the nearby College of Surgeons. These and a number of other buildings being commandeered were all strategically positioned to allow the occupying rebels to pin down any British Army troops emerging from their various barracks in an attempt to approach the city centre.

Éamon de Valera was in charge of men from the 3rd Battalion that took over Boland's Mill near the docks at Kingstown. Any English reinforcements would land here and it was his job to keep them hemmed in and prevent them joining up with the rest of the British forces.

Standing in front of the GPO, Pearse could imagine the scene at these carefully chosen locations around the city. Their reduced numbers, due to MacNeill's treachery, had meant they had to abandon their intentions to occupy Trinity College and some other key places but he was pleased with their revised plans and satisfied with the level of support they had received. Even The O'Rahilly had turned up at Liberty Hall that morning and Pearse knew he had been helping MacNeill distribute his countermanding orders. But O'Rahilly said to him, 'I helped wind up this clock; I might as well hear it strike,' and he placed his motorcar at the disposal of the revolutionaries for the transport of arms and supplies.

Throughout the morning Liberty Hall had been a hive of activity and a main marshalling ground for men arriving from all over to receive their instructions; including hundreds of Volunteers who had chosen to ignore the countermand. There was much banter and bravado. Optimism prevailed amongst the lower ranks. Those higher up, however, were more pragmatic. They were equally determined to make their stand, but as to the outcome, they knew they were facing an almost impossible task.

Pearse glanced over at James Connolly as he joined him outside the Post Office. As they had been about to march off from Liberty Hall, he recalled overhearing Connolly's parting words to William O'Brien, his deputy at the Irish Transport and General Workers Union. 'Bill,' Connolly had said, 'We're going out to be slaughtered.'

* * *

'Right you! With the keys!' Staines barked. 'Come with me.'

He was leading a contingent of the rebels, some with guns, some carrying Hurleys and one had a pike. Relieved not to have been shot, Will did as he was commanded. Stains said, 'Unlock the doors and take me through to the Telegraph Instrument Room. And don't try any tricks.'

Will wasn't about to try anything except stay alive, if that were possible. He heard more orders being shouted out for the rest of the counter staff and the few customers to leave the building as he proceeded to lead Stains and his men up to the Telegraph Room on the first floor. They kept him covered by at least two rifles at all times so he felt under no compunction whatsoever to mention that there were seven British soldiers guarding it.

He was surprised, when he got there, to find the door locked.

'Open it,' demanded Staines, raising his own rifle.

Dillon fumbled with the keys but couldn't insert the right one in the keyhole. 'There seems to be a key in it from the inside,' he said, as he realised the soldiers must have heard them coming and were making a stand against the rebels.

'Step back,' Staines shouted and fired his gun directly at the lock.

It splintered and the insurgents burst into the room. All seven soldiers surrendered. The telegraph girls' supervisor showed more spirit than they did. She was a Scottish woman who was always pleasant to Will when he brought her telegrams to be sent. Staines ordered all the operators out and she, bold as brass, said she'd finish sending some telegraphed death notices before she left, and Stains could wait, thank you very much.

Will admired her pluck, but he was hustled off again with half the soldiers, under the command of some young red-headed urchin he judged to be barely out of short trousers. They called him Sergeant O'Malley and he told Will to take them up to the roof. Will thought at first they were going to throw him off as some sort of a demonstration. His mind was spinning; he didn't know what to think. He just did as he was told – for the moment, but he was trying to learn as much as he could of what they were up to and listening to any snatches of conversation when he could. He picked up that there were other groups of insurgents taking buildings all over Dublin. The main aim of this lot was to secure national and international communications and deny it to the authorities – but they didn't seem to know about the local exchange up the road in Crown Alley.

'Hurry it up, you!' O'Malley poked him hard in the ribs with his rifle, 'we haven't got all day.' They had reached the top floor and Will was fumbling with the keys to find the one that opened the door to the roof. O'Malley turned to his corporal, 'Once we're done up here, and the rest have the building secure, we join the group that's to take the Crown Alley exchange so we need to make this quick.'

So they do know about it, Will thought, as he stepped out onto the leads ahead of the band of rebels. I need to warn them. Got to get free of this lot somehow. He watched as the rebel soldiers headed straight for the nearest corner where they proceeded to haul down the Union Jack from its flagpole. They hoisted a green flag in its place that bore the words, *Irish Republic* in gold lettering. On the flagstaff at the other front corner of the roof they raised a different one. Will saw that it was like the flag the French poet and politician, Lamartine, had presented to Thomas Meagher, leader of the Young Irelanders, following the French Revolution – a tricolour. Green for Irish nationalism and orange for the protestant unionist minority, with white for peace between them – a grand gesture at the time, he thought, but somewhat ironic in the circumstances.

Four floors below, between the great columns in front of the building, Padraig Pearse began reading out his proclamation that would go down in history as a pivotal moment for the Irish nation. A small crowd, with bemused expressions on their faces, was gathering in Sackville Street to listen to him. Such was the secrecy behind the planning of the uprising that the populace had no inkling of its imminence, nor any particular fervour for its support.

On the roof, Will couldn't see Pearse and the others, who were directly beneath him, but he could hear snatches of the speech. Pearse started off, 'Irishmen and Irishwomen: in the name of God and of the dead generations from which she receives her old tradition of nationhood, Ireland, through us, summons her children to her flag and strikes for her freedom…'

The men on the roof were gripped, cheering and clapping. O'Malley seemed to be trying to look important and grown-up. He was cutting a ridiculous figure standing at attention and saluting the flag. More of Pearse's words drifted up: '…We declare the right of the people of

Ireland to the ownership of Ireland and to the unfettered control of Irish destinies…' Right now Will was more concerned about the unfettered control of his own destiny. The rebel soldiers were loving it, though. '…Standing on that fundamental right and again asserting it in arms in the face of the world, we hereby proclaim the Irish Republic as a Sovereign Independent State…'

Will hung back, not so caught up in the excitement of the moment as his gun-toting companions. They were all intent on seeing as much as they could of the reaction of the crowd in the street to what was going on below. The last snatch of Pearse's voice Will caught was '…the Provisional Government, hereby constituted, will administer the civil and military affairs of the Republic in trust for the people…' That was when he stepped back smartly through the door and slammed it shut. He had the key in the lock and turned before the sergeant and his cronies had covered half the distance back from the flagpole.

Will dashed down the top stairs two at a time. O'Malley's voice bellowed after him about how he would personally string up his guts on the flagpole and throw the rest of him, a bit at a time, to the dogs in the street. Will could only hope that none of the other rebels was near enough the upper floors to hear the racket their comrades were making battering on the door from the roof. He reached the second floor out of breath in time to see Staines and four riflemen coming up from below. He dived into a store room before they could see him. The banging from the roof sounded very distant and there was a lot of noise and shouting going on from various parts of the Post Office; with luck Stains wouldn't hear.

But just then a shot was fired. It came from the top floor. Hiding in the store, Will realised nobody could have missed that. O'Malley must have blasted the lock. Staines and the others raced off up the next flights of stairs. Before they could meet O'Malley coming down Will nipped out of his hiding place and made it right down to the ground floor in record time. He wheeled round and was running towards the rear of the building before the shouting started somewhere above him. There was a tremendous clattering of feet as men rushed down the stairs. Others were coming through from the front Post Office to see what was happening.

Will had reached a rear corridor that ran parallel to Sackville Street. He tuned left and dashed down it. But he'd been seen. There was a great shout and he could hear men pounding down the passage he'd just left. It was obvious he wasn't going to have time to make it to the exit at the far end of the corridor. He grabbed a door handle on his right and rushed inside just in time to avoid being seen again as the crew from the front careered round the corner.

He was in the women's lavatory. The rumpus out in the corridor had increased and he could hear both Staines' and O'Malley's voices. Doors were being flung open and slammed again, and they were getting nearer. Will was thinking two things. That the rear exit he'd been aiming for was bound to have been guarded anyway. The other was, what a good job he hadn't barged into the Gents instead, for the little window there was encased by an aging metal grid on the outside. If the Ladies' window had ever had one, it had long since rusted away.

He was across to the outside wall in a fraction of a second and pushing to try to raise the sash. It was small and placed high in the wall so it was an awkward reach, but the frenzied shouting of the rebels getting nearer by the moment lent him added determination. He managed to raise the sash and grabbed the sill to pull himself up. He got his head and shoulders out as he heard the door behind him burst open. He struggled to push the rest of his body through.

'Stop or I fire!' – a voice he didn't recognise.

'Shoot, you fool!' That was O'Malley's strident brogue.

There was a deafening explosion as Will started to fall headfirst out into the inner courtyard that lay behind the front part of the Post Office building. His shins were gashed on the stonework as they came over the sill, but he managed to break his fall with his hands and landed heavily on one shoulder in a crumpled heap. He didn't pause to glance up. He raced across the courtyard to the left where he knew there was an archway under the first floor of the rear wing of the building. It was all part of the Post Office block and there was a short tunnel in the corner big enough to allow vehicle access to the inner courtyard. He reached the archway as the second shot was fired. It was followed quickly by two more and at least one of them knocked chippings from the wall by his head before he was under the archway and shielded from the line of fire.

Will ran out into the rear yard and on to where the ramp led up into the back end of Prince's street. He paused at the bottom and peered round the edge of the building. Brian's head and shoulders were silhouetted in the gatehouse. If he was still at his post it must mean none of the insurgents had come round here yet; they were all still declaring the republic for all they were worth at the front.

Will ran up the ramp. No good turning left, back to Sackville Street. He saw Brian open his mouth to speak, but he was long gone before any words came out. Will charged into a little dark alley between the high buildings at the bottom of the cul-de-sac and prayed it wouldn't be a dead end. It twisted right and then left and then, praise be, opened into Proby's Lane. That took him out into Liffey Street where he turned left and didn't stop running until he got down to Abbey Street.

Now he slowed to a walking pace so as not to draw attention to himself as he turned right, away from Sackville Street and the GPO. He eventually made his way down to a river bridge and back round to Crown Alley off Temple Bar. He went straight up to the entrance of the Exchange to raise the alarm, but before he could even get into the building he heard a clamour of shouting and the tramp of many boots marching. Round the corner came a contingent of rebel soldiers. It was obvious where they were heading, intent on taking control of Dublin's only remaining communications.

It was too late to warn what few staff there might be at this automatic exchange. If he went in now he'd just get caught again, himself. But what could he do? He daren't risk being spotted by the soldiers. If that jumped-up kid, O'Malley, were with them, as he had intended, his life wouldn't be worth two ha'pence. An old woman was walking past, heading in the direction of the fast approaching insurgents.

Will rushed out from the front of the Telephone Exchange calling to the old lady, 'For the love of God, woman, warn the lads not to come any closer. The place is crawling with soldiers, they'll be massacred.'

The woman saw that he'd apparently just emerged from the exchange and blessed him for his courage. She hurried towards the advancing rebels, shouting, 'Go back, boys, go back. The place is crammed with military!'

The rebels stopped and Sergeant O'Malley conferred with some of the others. They asked the old woman how she knew this and she told them about the man who had dashed out of the building, probably risking his life, to give the warning. Looking back, he was no longer anywhere to be seen, but young and inexperienced as he was, O'Malley still knew they couldn't afford to lose any of their number; they were precious few as it was. Neither was he inclined to risk his own neck. He thanked the old woman and ordered the troops to withdraw.

Five hours later the British military took over the automatic telephone exchange at Crown Alley – after it had stood empty all day.[5]

It was sheer bad luck that led to Will's downfall. Exhausted, he had stayed south of the Liffey to keep some space between him and the centre of operations at the GPO. He had avoided the Trinity College area, thinking that such a strategic establishment was bound to be one of the rebels' targets, and worked his way further south. After a few blocks he reached the welcoming stone arch that gave access to the trees and gardens of St Stephen's Green. There were plenty of people milling around and as he drew closer he realised with some alarm that they were watching the activity of yet more of the rebel army setting up their defences in that area. But he was too exhausted to go further. He reckoned he'd be safe among all the casual onlookers. He flopped down on the grass with his back against a convenient horse chestnut tree and sat facing the lake.

His shins were sore and his right shoulder hurt from his earlier precipitous exit from the lavatory window, but above all, now that the adrenalin was used up, he felt utterly shattered. He closed his eyes for a moment, and they remained closed for some considerable time. He thus missed the arrival of a runner bringing messages from the GPO Centre of Operations to Michael Mallin, Commanding Officer at St Stephen's Green. Had he not done so, he could not have failed to recognise the adolescent features and self-important stance of his recent adversary, Sergeant O'Malley.

The first he knew of any danger was a great kick in the ribs which took all his breath away and knocked him sideways. Then a voice he recognised, to his consternation, yelled, 'Bring the bastard over here!'

Will was hauled to his feet and frog-marched to where O'Malley was standing with a bunch of rebel soldiers. While he was being dragged, an officer was questioning O'Malley. 'And who exactly is he, do you say?'

O'Malley was explaining, 'He's an English spy, sir. We caught him at the GPO, but he escaped. I'm not about to let that happen again.'

'How do you know he's a spy?'

'He tried to sabotage the taking of the Post Office. Managed to confine some of our men behind a locked door, costing precious time and

[5] It is well documented that rebel troops did indeed turn back at the last moment, having been "warned" by an elderly woman of non-existent British soldiers lying in wait at the Crown Alley exchange.

imperilling the whole mission. He's a very dangerous agent. Lend me these two men and I'll take him off your hands. I can see you're busy.'

'Yes, Sergeant, we are extremely busy and I can't spare any of my men for bloody traitors.' Still half winded and supported between two of the IRB men, Will saw the officer looking him over. His expression suggested that he didn't think the prisoner looked particularly dangerous. 'There's no time for any in-depth enquiries. One extra "casualty of war" will make no difference in the grand scheme of things. I've already wasted more time than I should. Deal with him here, Sergeant, and be on your way. The despatches you have there from Mallin must reach Connolly and Pearse without delay.'

Before Will had a chance to say a word in his defence, the officer turned on his heel and was calling to other soldiers who were coming and going in every direction. He said something about having to report to the Commanding Officer and headed off towards the little hump-backed bridge where Will met with Bradshaw.

O'Malley glared down at his prisoner, now forced to his knees by his captors. The red-head's youthful eyes had a penetrating look that seemed to see right inside him. 'Well,' he said, 'I'd planned something a lot slower and exquisitely more painful for you, you English bastard – but needs must.' He un-slung his rifle and stepped back a pace, squinting down the barrel at Will's head.

Will realised that in locking the patrol out on the roof he had probably made O'Malley look something of a fool in front of his men, which could account for his exaggeration, but he said, 'Now hould on there, man, I'm no spy! I'm not even English. I'm from County Down, working here in Dublin in the Post Office.'

'There you are. He's admitted it.' The triumph showed on O'Malley face. 'He works for the English government.'

'I said I work for the Post Office!'

'Same thing,' said O'Malley.

So Will tried a different tack. 'I'm not a traitor, I love my country.'

'You're a bloody spy. That makes you a traitor in my book.' O'Malley's interpretation of events entertained no alternative.

'I'm not the one threatening to shoot an honest Irish citizen. You're the traitor!' Will blurted out. Not a remark best calculated to appease the sergeant. The youth grinned at him and glanced at his comrades holding him rigid, 'You see? He's no friend of the Revolution. He calls us traitors. Condemned from his own mouth. Do you want a blindfold, traitor? – 'cos you can't have one!' The sergeant laughed at his little joke.

Will couldn't move; he could only stare up into the Sergeant's murderous gun barrel.

He could hear soldiers, but all of them some way off, now. Commands barked by officers came clearly to his ears, but none was paying any attention to the drama unfolding under the spreading branches of the chestnut tree. Perhaps not surprisingly, all civilian onlookers were now conspicuously absent from the vicinity.

Will scanned the soldiers within his vision. 'I demand to speak to an officer,' he said, trying to sound much more authoritative than he felt, 'You know the rules of war.' He was banking on O'Malley not knowing. *He* certainly didn't, but it sounded like a good rule to him.

His captor hesitated. Will saw him glance over his shoulder in the direction of some distant officers and then back at him. He could see fear in the sergeant's expression but the gun barrel was still pointing straight between his eyes. O'Malley moved it a fraction and it was at that moment Will realised it wasn't fear he saw, but hatred.

'Shut your English gob and die, you bastard.' His finger tightened on the trigger and Will watched in fascinated horror as the hammer pulled slowly back.

Chapter 22

All over the city the insurgents were busy carrying out their assigned tasks, digging in, consolidating their positions, establishing strongholds.

In Phoenix Park, Ryan Doloughan and Paddy O'Daly led a group of about thirty that included many youths from *Na Fianna Éireann*. Kicking a football around on the lower slopes of St Thomas' Hill, their "game" gradually took them closer to where the sentries stood, guarding the Fort.

It didn't take much to overpower them and seize the complex. They commandeered as much weaponry and ammunition as they could carry, but when they came to the section that should have contained the gunpowder, it was empty. Ryan's heart sank. This was to have been the focus of their demolition; blowing up the British supplies in an almighty explosion that would rock Dublin and announce in no uncertain terms that the Rising had begun. Shipped off to England for the war effort, Ryan had to assume. He carried on, overseeing the laying of six of their own explosive charges to blow up the remaining weaponry and ammunition and render it useless to the British. His job was to ensure the boys laid continuous trails of black powder with no lean bits that could fizzle out.

When all was ready he signalled to O'Daly, who shouted, 'Go lads! Get out of here, fast.' Ryan lit the fuses and chased after the others running down the hill. They were well away from the park precincts by the time the explosions were due. Everyone stopped and looked back over the treetops in the direction of the fort.

And waited.

'Give it another minute,' someone said.

They gave it another minute.

Then it came: a great billow of smoke and flames, followed instantly by the sound of a series of small explosions but nothing more. They'd denied the British their store of guns and ammunition but Ryan doubted the sound of the blast would have carried to the Four Courts, never mind the General Post Office or St Stephen's Green.

Ryan ran an appreciative eye over all the stolen guns his unit was carrying but it was with mixed feelings he said to O'Daly, 'Sure, the lads will just have to get things under way without the starter's pistol.'

* * *

A popular actor at the Abbey and other theatres in his spare-time, Seán Connolly, was also an ardent nationalist, along with his five siblings, although the family were not at all closely related to James Connolly. Easter Monday saw Seán leading out the second company of the Citizens' Army that comprised ten men and ten women. The force included three of his brothers and his sister. His other brother was fighting under Michael Mallin on St Stephen's Green. Seán's company marched on City Hall where they were joined by eight more insurgents. Connolly had a key to the building due to his position in the Motor Tax office.

He sent six men on up the road to overpower the sentries at the gates of the Castle so they couldn't hinder him entering City Hall. These rebels were confronted by an unarmed, Dublin Metropolitan Policeman, who attempted to bar their progress. He was shot dead for his troubles and became the first British casualty of the uprising. The rebels tied up the three sentries in the guardroom. Alerted by the gunfire, Castle officials rushed to swing closed the inner gates. Connolly's men occupied the outer guardroom for several hours before withdrawing to re-join the rest of the company. That no attempt was made to invade Dublin Castle further was down to the belief that it would be strongly manned by British soldiers, although the fact of the matter was that most of the garrison had gone to the races and those that remained could never have withstood any determined assault.

Once established in City Hall, Connolly deployed his troops to various firing positions. Those on the roof commanded views in three directions, including over Dublin Castle where the plan was to use sniper fire to hinder any troops getting in or out of that stronghold. Others, including his second in command, Dr Kathleen Lynn and other women, helped to barricade the doors. He sent four units to take over some strategically positioned buildings encircling the castle. Two commandeered the premises of the "Evening Mail" and a gent's outfitters, Henry and James on the corner of Dame Street and Parliament Street; a third occupied the Synod House adjacent to Christchurch Cathedral whilst the last unit took up positions at Werburgh Street at the back of the castle.

The sound of gunfire was coming from many quarters of Dublin and it wasn't long before the company at City Hall came under fire from British riflemen high up in the Bedford Tower of the castle. Connolly took an early bullet but carried on after some swift First Aid from Dr Lynn. On the roof his soldiers were becoming increasingly pinned down by sniper fire from the castle tower and he joined them to encourage them to fight on. By then the British soldiers had found their range and deadly fire rained down on the insurgents. Again Seán Connolly was wounded, and this time mortally so. He became the first of the rebel forces to die since the start of the rising. He would not be the last.

* * *

On St Steven's Green, the sound of firing from divers parts of the city did nothing to alleviate Dillon's rising panic. The movement of the hammer on O'Malley's rifle seemed to Will to be in slow motion. He felt that the sadistic sergeant was deliberately squeezing the trigger as unhurriedly as he could to prolong the agony and increase his own enjoyment.

In his peripheral vision Will was aware of officers and soldiers still passing by ten or twenty yards away. One wearing a stylish hat along with the regulation army-style jacket and trousers caused his heart to miss a beat.

He yelled out at the top of his voice, 'Give my best regards to Eva when you see her – when all this is over!'

The outburst startled O'Malley. His finger froze on the trigger, the rifle still half-cocked. The woman officer looked startled, too – at what she'd heard and probably even more so at what she saw. She called out, 'Sergeant! Hold your fire! Stand back,' as she strode across.

Will imagined the thoughts running through O'Malley's head. He'd been on the very verge of killing him, doubtless thinking it was no more than he deserved. Now he couldn't go ahead and shoot his prisoner against the direct order of a senior officer, and that none other than the second-in-command at St Stephens Green, the Countess Markievicz. With obvious reluctance, he lowered the rifle and Will felt his body start to relax for the first time since he'd received the soldier's boot in his ribs.

When the Countess had been informed of what the prisoner was accused she told the sergeant that she desired to question him further. She assured him that there was no requirement for him to remain and he could return to his Unit.

'Bu…but ma'am…he's my prisoner. I can't just leave him. He's dangerous. I must stay with him.'

'No, Sergeant, he is the prisoner of the Republican Army and here, he is under my jurisdiction. Didn't I see Mr Mallin giving you dispatches to deliver to Mr Connolly?'

'Yes, ma'am…but…'

'Then why are you still here? Go, man!'

'I was ordered, first to – '

'Go!'

The wretched O'Malley slung his rifle back on his shoulder and with a last glare at Dillon that seemed to hold a mixture of hate, frustration and despair, turned and trudged out onto Grafton Street and made off in the direction of Trinity College, the Liffey and the General Post Office.

Constance Markievicz dismissed the remaining two soldiers and took her recent new acquaintance aside to the comparative seclusion of a nearby copse by the lakeside.

'What *have* you been up to, Will?' she asked. She was feeling weary, but she gave him her full attention.

'Och well, now, it's not as bad as it looks.'

'Well, I'd say it looks pretty bad!'

'They made me unlock all the doors for them at the Post Office and after a while I got bored and decided to shove off. They didn't seem to want me to go and I had to lock that oaf of a sergeant and his platoon out on the roof in order to take my leave of them. That's all.'

Constance threw back her head and laughed heartily, 'You didn't! I can see why he could be annoyed with you! But hardly worthy of the death penalty, I think. I hereby grant you the first pardon of the Irish Republic!'

'Well I take that as a signal honour, Countess – though I confess I'm not convinced it will be worth a whole lot by this time next week.'

The Countess grimaced. 'I fear you may be right. Less than thirteen hundred Volunteers have mobilised in Dublin; nothing like the three thousand we could have expected.' She stopped. She was very tired. She realised she shouldn't be talking like this to an outsider, even if he was a friend. 'But that's for me to worry about,' she said. 'For my sake as well as your own you'd better get out of Dublin. Don't let that sergeant run into you again. Go back to – where was it? Donaghadee? – until things quieten down again.' She touched his hand and looked him in the eye, 'You'll go, Will?'

'Oh aye, I'll go, and you have my deepest gratitude for coming along when you did. Things were beginning to look a mite tricky.'

Constance smiled. She had grown fond of this young County Down man who had just turned up at Eva's soirée. She hoped they would meet again in happier times. Will turned to go. She saw him stop and step back. He kissed her on her cheek and said, 'Stay alive, Constance.'

He was walking away again, and somehow she felt it was not to catch the first train for Belfast. She watched him until he was out of sight beyond the trees. 'You too, Will,' she said, 'you too.'

* * *

The crowd cheering *All Star* to victory at the Irish Grand National at Fairyhouse racecourse that Easter Monday was somewhat thinner than it had been earlier in the day. The arrival of military dispatch riders in the early afternoon to inform the British officers about the insurrection in Dublin caused quite a commotion in the reserved grandstand. All public transport at the isolated location was commandeered by the army to convey scores of its men back to Dublin; all leave cancelled. Hundreds of racegoers were left stranded with no means of getting home and some had travelled long distances to be there. One 33-year-old man from County Clare took a week, travelling on foot to make it back home to Ennis. His wife, who by then had heard of the uprising and feared the worst, fainted when she saw him back home on their doorstep.

There was disruption in the city, too. The rebel soldiers were erecting barricades all over town. Many buses and trams stopped running. Shops closed. After two more Metropolitan Police officers were shot dead the Commissioner withdrew his men from the streets. Now unrestricted, elements among the crowds, particularly those from the poorer, slum areas, started looting.

For the most part, Dublin's law-abiding citizens were appalled at what was going on and denounced the revolutionaries as criminals.

* * *

When Dillon emerged through the arched gateway from St Stephen's Green he found himself confronted by a ring of upturned carts, commandeered motor vehicles, even bicycles and items of furniture. They formed a barrier that the Mallin's men were building around the park.

He turned right and headed along the north side of the Green to where rebel soldiers were still working on the barricade. Opposite the Shelbourne Hotel he found a gap that the insurrectionists were intent on plugging using a commandeered truck.

As Dillon approached, the driver was being forced out of his vehicle at gunpoint.

'Ireland needs your truck,' said the gunman.

'Well, Ireland can't bloody well have my truck,' said the irate driver; 'I bloody need it.'

Another soldier started to climb into the cab and the owner grabbed him to pull him back down. Without hesitation, the gunman shot him and he fell dead at Dillon's feet. Will avoided making eye contact with the shooter and stepped round the man's body. He walked on through the line of the barricade as the second soldier started to manoeuvre the truck into position to seal the gap.

How many more civilian casualties will there be before this craziness has played its course, he wondered. Will realised he had nearly become one, himself, and he could yet, if he wasn't extremely careful. The Countess's advice to go back to Donaghadee was sound and he'd meant it when he told her he would; he just hadn't specified when. There were a number of reasons he couldn't go straight away even though that would be the sensible course to take. Firstly, he still had an assignation with Higginson to arrange. Second, he couldn't just run off without seeing Maeve. And thirdly – and currently the most urgent reason – he had that bit of information Constance had let slip about the number of rebel soldiers that had turned out. The British forces would no doubt find that very useful to know.

He needed to contact Geoff Bradshaw and he wondered if that was going to be a problem. First he needed a phone. The answer to that was right in front of him. The Shelbourne Hotel would surely let him make a call. It was only as he was entering the foyer that his stomach reminded him he had had no dinner. He'd been hi-jacked as a turnkey in the GPO before he could take his break.

He asked the pretty black-haired receptionist if he could maybe get a meat pie and champ with a pint of Guinness.

'Sure, that'll be no problem at all. Is there anything else I can do for you?' Her smiling eyes and moist, red lips would have tempted a bishop.

Will said, 'As a matter of fact, there is.'

She tilted her head in a coquettish manner.

'I need to make a phone call.'

The girl pointed to an instrument at the end of the reception desk. 'You're welcome to use that,' she said. 'I love your accent; are you from Belfast?'

'County Down; a little place called Donaghadee.' Will moved towards the telephone.

'Donaghadee? I've been there. It's got a big lighthouse on the harbour wall.'

Will stopped. The girl must be bored, and grateful for someone to talk to but he had to place his call. He said, 'Well, well. Small world. Now… I must…' He indicated the telephone.

'Ah yes, sure. I'll let you make your call.' That smile, again, that would have melted the heart of Nelson on his pillar.

Will dialled the number in Dublin Castle and waited. Silence. Finally, it started to ring. Well, that was the first hurdle over; at least the local exchange is still working, he thought, blessing the old woman for conveying his message convincingly to O'Malley's platoon. He gave an involuntary shudder at the thought of O'Malley. He saw again, the rifle muzzle, the cocked hammer. He felt a cold sweat on his forehead. The instrument in Dublin Castle was still ringing. He gave it a little longer. He recalled the fine figure that Countess Markievicz had cut in her Citizens' Army uniform and wondered how many other women were involved in the fighting. Thoughts of Maeve and her defiant attitude when they discussed her membership of *Cumann na mBan* filled his mind. He hoped she was still safe at home.

The burring in his earpiece continued. He decided to let it ring three more times before hanging up. After the second ring someone answered.

'Yes?' was the unhelpful response.

'I need to get a message to Geoff Bradshaw,' said Will.

'Who?'

'Bradshaw. Mr Geoffrey Bradshaw.'

'He's not here. What's this about?'

'Can you get a message to him?'

'What's the message?'

'Please tell him there's a really great show on at the Abbey tonight.' Will wondered whether the unhelpful voice at the end of the line would be bothered to pass on such a message so he added, 'He particularly wanted me to let him know when Yeats' play was being performed. Can you tell him, please?'

'I'll see what I can do.'

'Thank you, so much,' said Will. 'Oh! And tell him we can meet at the box office.'

The line went dead. Had the person in the Castle heard his last request? Will had just realised that their old rendezvous in St Stephen's Green was no longer available to them. He glanced at the clock over the reception area. 4:25. It would take about twenty minutes to walk to Abbey Street so he had just over an hour-and-a-half to fill.

The friendly receptionist directed him to the first-floor dining area where he eased his weary frame into a seat at a table by the window. He could see across the road, over the barricade into St Stephen's Green where soldiers and officers were busy carrying boxes of supplies, digging trenches, giving orders or obeying them. He thought he caught sight of Countess Markievicz's distinctive hat as the waiter brought him his meal. Will took a long, satisfying draft of the oul black stuff and tucked in to his long-overdue dinner.

Will followed up his pie and buttery mashed potato and scallions with a leisurely cup of coffee. He decided he would do well to keep off the streets as much as possible while rebel soldiers were still rushing around between their various bases. He had no wish to encounter Sergeant O'Malley for a third time. So it was ten minutes past six when he ventured out of the Shelbourne and turned right. Straight away he heard the sound of distant gunfire.

On his left, armed rebel soldiers were manning the barricade every few yards but the firing wasn't coming from them. He observed them with his peripheral vision; he had no desire to become a person of interest to any of them. He pulled the peak of his cap well down and hurried past, keeping straight on rather than turn up Grafton Street. That would have taken him past Trinity College to O'Connell Bridge. Dangerous territory.

He still heard sporadic firing from across the river but now there were more shots coming from over near the Castle. He veered away and made his way round the north of City Hall on Dame Street and turned up Parliament Street heading for Grattan Bridge.

'Hey Mister!' a voice from above his head startled him. He looked up to see a young lad leaning over the parapet of the roof of a gent's outfitters. The boy shouted down to him, 'You should get off the streets, it's dangerous around…'

Will saw a bright red mist appear behind the boy's head as another shot rang out from the direction of the Castle. The boy crumpled like a puppet with cut strings. Unseen hands hauled him back behind the parapet and Dillon quickened his pace. He hugged the wall, sickened by what he had just seen. The lad couldn't have been more than fifteen or sixteen.

Grattan Bridge was deserted. He could hear firing to his left and across the Liffey he saw a tram on its side up near the Four Courts. Gunshots were coming from the Mendicity Institute up on his left in answer to shots from the far bank. But he had to get across if he was to keep his appointment. He could stroll over and hope that no trigger-happy soldier – rebel or British – would notice him and decide to use him for target practice. Or he could sprint across and minimise the time he was exposed but certainly draw attention to his presence on the bridge.

He decided to run. He dashed across the street and kept on going, head down and weaving erratically so as not to present an easy target. Firing starting up again spurred him on. Almost across. A dive round the end of the right-hand stonework of the bridge. Ducking behind the low wall to regain his breath. He was intact. No holes leaking blood. After a minute he peered round the pillar. British soldiers were lying full length behind the overturned tram, their weapons trained on the opposite bank. None was looking in his direction. Will stood up and strode off along Ormond Quay, leaving the gun battle behind.

He took the first side street north and then turned east along Abbey Street. He was very aware he still had to cross Sackville Street to reach the theatre. He had turned away from the quay in case there were pickets at O'Connell Bridge. It would be just his luck to find O'Malley stationed there. Crossing further up on Abbey Street would avoid that possibility, although it did take him closer to the GPO. He could hear firing again. When he reached Sackville Street he noticed quite a few civilians around, all staring in the direction of the Post Office and the gunshots. Will saw someone bend down to pick up one of a number of discarded pamphlets lying in the road. He retrieved one himself before continuing across. On the far pavement he stopped for a moment to take in the scene further up.

In the distance he saw a large body of soldiers, many mounted, advancing down Sackville Street and approaching the Post Office building. Even as he watched there was a burst of fire from the windows of the Post Office and two soldiers fell from their horses. Their comrades returned fire but Will could see they had nothing or no one to aim at. The advancing battalion were like ducks in a fairground shooting gallery.

Will glanced at the pamphlet in his hand as he entered the east end of Abbey Street. "*POBLACHT NA H ÉIREANN*," he read, "THE PROVISIONAL GOVERNMENT OF THE IRISH REPUBLIC TO THE PEOPLE OF IRELAND. Irishmen and Irishwomen, in the name of God..." Will recognised the words as those he had heard Pearse proclaim outside the GPO this morning while he was on the roof. He shoved the text in his pocket and took out his watch. Six thirty-five. He was late. His circuitous route had taken longer than he had allowed. He hurried down the side road to the Abbey and went in, scanning the few early theatre-goers for any sign of Bradshaw.

He wasn't there.

Dillon's heart sank. Had he not been given the message? Or had Will's last-second instruction about where to meet not been heard? Or had he been on time and given up on Dillon when he hadn't shown up at the set time?

Will was about to check his pocket watch again when he felt a hand on his shoulder.

'You couldn't have picked somewhere south of the river to meet, I suppose? It's taken me an age to get here. Let's find a pub where we can chat over a pint.'

Geoff ordered some sandwiches for them both along with their drinks and by the time they had finished their snack Will had updated his contact with his latest information.

‘No more than 1300 of them, you say. That is good news. It’ll be useful to British intelligence. And you can take a lot of the credit for their low turnout.’

‘Och well, who knows?’ said Will. ‘MacNeill might have found out about their plans anyway.’

‘And he might not. You’re doing a grand job, Will. Boyd is pleased with your efforts and so, I might add, are the top brass in Dublin Castle – though they don’t know who you are, of course.’ Geoff touched the side of his nose with his forefinger.

‘Well, I’m glad everyone’s so happy. It’s been a mite tricky at times, I can tell you. I’m just glad it’s over with. I need to be getting out of here soon; it isnae safe to walk down the street. Are the trains still running?’

‘The army are controlling all rail transport. I doubt civilians will get a look-in. But… ’

‘But what? Can you get me a ticket?’

‘No. No, I’m afraid not. I was going to say, But we’d like you to stay on a bit longer.’ Geoff held up his hand as Will was about to speak. ‘Now, hear me out before you answer. You’re great pals with James Connolly. He and Padraig Pearse seem to be leading this debacle. We want you to see what he’s up to in the GPO. You’ve worked there; you can offer your services to help them find their way around, or as a bodyguard or whatever. Just as long as you get close enough to find out their plans. What do you say?’

‘I say I’m staying well clear of the Post Office until I get out of Dublin. I told you, that sergeant fellow wants me dead. If he finds me inside the GPO I’m a goner.’

Geoff drained his glass and raised an interrogative eyebrow, ‘Another?’ He signalled to the barmaid, ‘Two more.’

Will said, ‘I value me life more than a pint of Guinness. That idea’s a non-starter.’

Geoff waited until their fresh drinks were delivered. Then he said, ‘I understand. A toast: To a job well done.’ They clinked glasses and Geoff continued, ‘I can see it’s been quite a strain. Perfectly understandable that you haven’t the stomach for any more. You’ve earned the right to take the safe option and call it a day. Cheers.’ He raised his glass in salute once more. 'I grant you, it's getting scary out there. Don't blame you – wanting to quit.'

Will knew exactly what Geoff was doing and he smiled inwardly. But he also knew that he couldn't go back to The Dee yet anyway. Unfinished business. He said, 'I expect I could fix things with O'Malley somehow or other. He's only a kid.'

'I'm sure a resourceful man like you could do that,' said Geoff. 'You'll stay on board?'

'Aye, though I'll live to regret it, I'll be bound. I'll find out what that gang of poets and intellectuals is up to, although it seems fairly clear, I think.' He fished the pamphlet out of his pocket and put it on the table. 'They're making us a republic.'

'I somehow don't think that's going to happen.'

'It already has, according to this.'

'On paper. It's their tactics, short-term plans that would be useful to know. Two things.'

'Yes?'

'Where to meet now we can't use St Stephen's Green. Do you know where The Book of Kells is on display in Trinity College?'

'I do, aye. But won't that be overrun with insurgents by now, too?'

'No, they've left that alone for some reason, although there were only about a dozen loyalist students, cadets in the university's Officers Training Corps, ready to defend it had they tried to take it over. They could have just walked in. Anyway, if we need to meet that's where it will be. Same times.'

'You said two things.'

'I did. As I mentioned, you're not known to the British authorities or military. If you find you need to contact anyone on the British side I've been authorised to give you a password that should identify you to most of the army officers.'

'Most?'

'Passwords are disseminated daily, but there'll be a lot of extra battalions arriving over the next few days and there's always a chance that some of them will not get told about you.'

'Marvellous. So what's the password for the two or three who'll know it, then?'

'It's not as bad as that; most will be aware of it. We picked one that would be easy for you to remember: "Abbey Players". Got it?'

* * *

Abbey Players, Will thought as he made his way westward through the darkening city. Sounds like a pack of cigarettes. And not every officer will know it. What a game. Am I a fool for agreeing to continue this espionage lark? Probably am.

It was starting to rain. Sporadic firing could still be heard from various quarters. He had agreed with Geoff that he wouldn't attempt to make contact with the rebels that night. Less chance of any misunderstandings in broad daylight. Besides, he was anxious to get back to see Maeve.

There were no trams running and it was a long walk – made longer by having to make detours every once in a while when he found barricades or pickets blocking his path.

Up ahead he noticed a flickering glow over the trees in Phoenix Park and immediately thought of the Magazine Fort. It must be on fire. Will remembered what Maeve had said about Ryan having to find out all about the fort and wondered if there was a connection.

He trudged on and it was after nine o'clock when, soaking wet, he finally knocked on the Doloughan's front door.

It was opened with minimal delay by old Mrs Doloughan.

'Ah Will, is it yourself? I'm so pleased to see you. What in the world's happening? Come on in out of the rain; you'll catch your death. Have you seen Maeve? Or Ryan?'

'Is she not here, Mrs Doloughan?'

'Ryan went out soon after yourself, this morning. Maeve got a telephone call while she was having her dinner. She went straight out without her pudding. That was about one o'clock. She promised to telephone me if she was going to be late for her tea, but I've heard nothing – only all sorts of rumours down at the corner shop. Whatever can have happened to her, Will? I've been worried stiff.'

Chapter 23

Tuesday was dull and the rain that had stopped sometime in the early hours had left hundreds of insurgents who were on sentry duties or positioned on rooftops feeling damp and dispirited. But the republican propaganda machine was in full swing spreading rumours of nation-wide support and even of international aid expected imminently from Germany. Padraig Pearse issued a further proclamation by pamphlet, headed:

"The Provisional Irish Government
TO THE
CITIZENS OF DUBLIN
The Provisional Government of the Irish Republic salutes the CITIZENS OF DUBLIN on the momentous occasion of the proclamation of a Sovereign Independent Irish State
now in the course of being established by Irishmen in Arms."

It was one of these pamphlets that Will Dillon was reading in a crowded café near the river. Some of the "Citizens of Dublin" who, like him, were enjoying an early morning coffee, had their own copy of the pamphlet to peruse – and discuss.

Unusually for such a place, the conversations hummed.

Will was glad to sit down. He had spent a fitful night. Before retiring, he'd tried to reassure Mrs Doloughan that her daughter was doubtless involved in helping behind the scenes with packing up supplies and so on and probably had no access to a telephone so the old lady mustn't worry. Maeve's mother thanked him but didn't sound very convinced. And Will certainly hadn't convinced himself. He worried long into the small hours about what could have happened to her. Ryan, he wasn't concerned about. He had no doubt been assigned to occupy and hold some building and he would take his chances with everyone else. From what he knew of his friend, he could take care of himself. But before Will finally drifted off, he determined he must find Maeve and ensure she came to no harm.

Bright and early he departed the Doloughan home on his bicycle that he had left there on Saturday. Before leaving he told Mrs Doloughan that he would do his best to return in the evening.

'There is a possibility, though,' he said, 'what with rebel and British army road blocks, I might not be able to, so don't worry if I have to stay in the centre at my digs. And be assured I'm going to find Maeve and make sure she's safe.'

'God bless you, Will. You're a good boy,' said Mrs Doloughan, as she waved him off.

He crossed the Liffey nearby Kingsbridge Station and cycled towards the city centre, and Trinity College. Since he now knew it was clear of insurgents, that's where he left his bicycle in a rack with others belonging to the academic staff or undergraduates.

There were more people about town than he had expected; quite like a normal back-to-work Tuesday after the bank holiday. Except that not many seemed in any hurry to be going to work. They were congregating on street corners; gathering in small groups. Strangers were talking to each other, sharing what little they knew and making up what they didn't. The well-to-do and the shabbily dressed were even conversing with each other.

Will went first to Liberty Hall, hoping to find someone who could tell him which premises the women of *Cumann na mBan* were most likely to be helping at. However, he found it deserted and abandoned. He took one of the new pamphlets that were in a display box outside the door and went to the cafe to have a think.

'What do you make of all this, then?' asked an older man in workman's overalls who was sharing Dillon's table.

'Well, if we're to believe it,' said Will, glancing at the pamphlet, 'what's it say...? "The country is rising in answer to Dublin's call, and the final achievement of Ireland's freedom is now, with God's help, only a matter of days." '

'Do you think it's not true, then? I can't see it, myself. Any folk as I've spoken to think they're a bunch of loonies – or worse. Deport the lot of them, that's what my missus says.'

'It does read like propaganda to me. "All citizens of Dublin who believe in the right of their Country to be free will give their allegiance..." " Citizens can help by building barricades in the streets to oppose the advance of the British troops." '

'Aye, and get themselves shot for their trouble. You'll not catch me building barricades.'

A young man, maybe a student, standing by their table holding his mug of coffee in one hand and a copy of the pamphlet in the other said, 'Have you seen the last bit, though?'

The workman looked down, 'What? "Signed on behalf of the Provisional Government, P. H. PEARSE, Commanding – " ?'

'No, no. The paragraph before that' – he adjusted his spectacles to read – 'where it says, "We have lived to see an Irish Republic proclaimed. May we live to establish it firmly, and may our children and our children's children enjoy the happiness and prosperity which freedom will bring." Isn't that worth fighting for?'

'You think so? Aye, well maybe – if there was the slightest chance of success, which there isn't, my missus says.'

An elderly man with an ex-military appearance at the next table addressed the young student. 'So you're one of them, are you? A *Sinn Féiner*. Taking the law into your own hands and putting the whole country at risk. People are being shot out there because of what your pals are doing.'

'No, I didn't say I was – '

'A *Sinn Féiner*, is he?' A burly chap behind them got to his feet.

His companion, another hefty individual rose, too. 'We'll have no lousy republicans in a respectable coffee house. Let's get him!'

The student, still with mug in hand, looked startled as the second heavy aimed a punch to his gut. Dillon's hand shot out and grabbed the fist before it connected. He jumped up, twisting round, and in less than a second the big guy's arm was bent up behind his back.

The whole café had gone quiet. Dillon pushed his captive off-balance and released his arm so he plonked back down on his chair. Stepping between the student and his other would-be attacker, he said, 'I think there's enough violence out there without bringing it in here, don't you?'

The first guy eyed his mate, who was rubbing his twisted arm, and then looked back at Dillon. He spat on the ground and sat down without a word.

The student's mug shook as he placed it on Will's table. Will said, 'Are you all right?'

'I… I think so. Thanks to you. Thank you.'

'Don't mention it. Perhaps a strategic withdrawal might be in order, though. Finish your coffee. I'm done with mine; I'll come with you.'

With a nod to the workman Will left the café with the student and before they'd got to the door the buzz of conversation had regained its previous level.

The two walked along Custom House Quay past moored barges and a few forlorn-looking yachts whose presence seemed somehow incongruous against a background of gunfire across the city. They strolled on along Eden Quay and past Liberty Hall and Will thought again about his quest to find Maeve. He decided the only way of discovering her whereabouts was to get into the lion's den, infiltrate the nerve centre of the uprising; to do as Bradshaw had requested and enter the GPO, whatever the risk.

'Do you think they have any chance of success?' Will asked his companion as they walked along the riverside.

'I think Mr Pearse is a very fine poet and a visionary, but I'm not so sure about a President much less a military Chief of Forces. We shall have to wait and see.'

'Aye, that's about the size of it. In the meantime, my advice to you would be to keep your head down. Be careful what you say and who you say it to.'

The student gave a mirthless laugh, 'I shall. I think that's probably good advice.'

They had reached Marlborough Street, one block before Sackville Street. Will made to turn right and the student said he was heading for O'Connell Bridge and back to Trinity. With further expressions of gratitude the young man went on and Will headed up behind Clery's and the backs of other buildings that fronted onto Sackville to cross Talbot Street and pay a brief visit to his digs.

Once there, he changed his clothing and pocketed a few toiletries and other items he might need before popping his head into Mrs Gilpin's kitchen.

'Just collecting a few things, Mrs G. Not sure when I'll be back. I'll see you when I see you.'

'Right you are, Mr Lynn,' said Mrs Gilpin, and then, 'You know it's strange. Two people have called here looking for a Mr Dillon.'

'Yes?' said Will

'It's just that I couldn't help noticing the initials on your pyjamas as I was making your bed when you were still sleeping here.'

'Oh yes?'

'And I wondered what WD stood for; that's all.'

'I've no idea, Mrs Gilpin. I picked them up in a jumble sale. Walter Dunwoody? William Drake? Who knows? I must dash, now. Bye.'

With all that had been going on Will had forgotten about Higginson's men staking out the street where he had his lodgings. As he came out now, he gave a casual glance up and down the road but saw no one suspicious. He stepped out hoping for the best and set his face towards the General Post Office and whatever fate might await him if and when he made it inside to join the insurgents.

* * *

Colonel Cowen, Acting Military Governor of Dublin while his seniors were at the races, on hearing of the uprising the previous day, had systematically set about strengthening his garrison. By the early hours of Tuesday morning he had brought in 800 infantry from the Curragh barracks and 150 troops from Belfast. Some heavy artillery was *en route* from Armagh and together with troops already based around Dublin he had 3500 men to face, what he had been reliably informed were no more than 1300 insurgents.

Nevertheless he felt relieved and more than happy to hand over to Brigadier-General William Lowe when he arrived with the men from the Curragh. He passed on intelligence he had been given that the Shelbourne Hotel had not been occupied by insurgents.

'The hotel commands uninterrupted views over St Stephen's Green, sir, where a substantial number of rebels have entrenched themselves. I would recommend making that an early objective. If we control the hotel, we'll control the Green.'

As a result at 5:40 a.m. on Tuesday, silently and unnoticed by the rain-soaked lookouts on St Stephen's Green, a platoon of General Lowe's men started to take over the hotel. They cleared guests from the front rooms on the higher floors and took up positions with their rifles at the windows.

* * *

It was around mid-morning the same day that Dillon now joined the crowds on Sackville Street and made his way up towards the Post Office. Distracted by the smell of soot and charcoal, he turned and spotted the smouldering remains of a newsagent's. Looters had torched it the night before.

The closer he got to the GPO the thinner grew the crowds. People were curious, but not foolhardy. Occasional shots were being fired from the front windows that Will could see had all been knocked out and cleared of any glass. Around the building on the street were great coils of barbed wire inhibiting access by British troops and civilians alike. As he watched, a big shire horse pulling a cart laden with boxes stopped by the great fluted columns at its driver's command. A band of men appeared from the entrance. Ten with rifles formed a pathway from the entrance to the cart, their guns pointing outwards at the crowd. Four more found an opening in the coils of wire and pulled them apart to make a gap. Others ran down this protected passage and unloaded one box each. In less than a minute the cart was empty, the barbed wire was back in place and the men, including their armed escort, were all back inside the building. The old shire horse plodded on, oblivious to the drama in which it had just played a part.

It had all been so quick that Will had not had time to react. He doubted whether he would have wanted to step out of the crowd to seek to gain entrance with those menacing rifles trained on him anyway.

'That's the second load already, this morning,' Will heard a lady with a shopping basket say to her companion. 'And there were motor lorries and all sorts coming and going yesterday afternoon.'

'Is that a fact?' said Will.

The woman with the shopping bag half turned to include Will in the conversation as though the interjection of a stranger was normal, and continued, 'And they've taken over other places, too, you know.'

'I gather they've occupied St Stephen's Green,' said Will.

‘I know. And Jacob’s Biscuit Factory not far from there. That’s where our Mary works. They marched in as bold as brass and ordered everybody out. Just like that. Only not everybody. Mary says they forced a few staff to stay to show them where things were and how everything worked. They’re a bunch of criminals.’

‘Ought to be shot, the whole lot of them,’ said her companion.

‘And some of the women are as bad. You can understand the men – sure they haven’t the sense they were born with. But to see a whole parade of women march up to those doors yesterday… *Cumann na mBan*, they call themselves. Wanting to help, I suppose. The more fool, them. It makes me ashamed to be a woman. Whatever are they thinking?’

‘Aye, what indeed? It’s a sorry state of affairs.’ Will needed to get away from these women. ‘Anyway, keep safe,’ he said and headed back up the street. He turned down Henry Street at the side of the Post Office until he came to Upper Liffey Street. From here he found the little twisting alley that he had emerged from yesterday while escaping from O’Malley. When he had wound his way through to the Prince’s Street end he stopped and peered out. The street was deserted except for two sentries in green, posted by old Brian’s hut at the top of the ramp. They were both smoking and keeping a watch down towards the open end of the cul-de-sac.

Will crept out from the alley and covered the few yards that separated them without the men turning round. He paused for a second or two and then shouted, ‘Atten…shun!’

Their reaction was instant. Prior to taking up arms yesterday these rebel soldiers had done little else but parade ground training; they dropped their cigarettes, stamped their feet and stood erect, not daring to turn their heads to look at the “officer” who had caught them smoking on duty.

Will stepped smartly in front of them and took hold of the one rifle they had between them. The man released his grip on it without a thought. A look of confusion replaced their disciplined straight-ahead stare as Will stepped back and pointed it at them.

‘Into the hut. Now!’

Still in a state of shock, the men opened the door of the wooden guard box and entered without demur. Dillon slammed the door behind them and flipped the large hasp into place. He secured it by dropping the rifle barrel through the staple.

He moved down the ramp and peeped round the corner. The courtyard was empty. Keeping close to the walls to try to avoid his movement being spotted from upstairs windows he gained the archway through to the inner courtyard. From there he could see the doorway opposite – the one he had avoided yesterday as likely to be guarded. For the same reason he avoided it now and ran his eye along the ground floor windows until he spotted the one he had escaped through less than 24 hours ago. As he expected, the gunmen hadn't wasted time closing it. He sprinted across, jumped up to catch the sill and scrambled through.

Being back in the ladies' lavatory raised his apprehension, as he recalled the last time he was there. He crossed to the door and was about to open it a crack to look out to the corridor when he heard a slight noise behind him. Before his brain could identify it as the links in a chain clinking together, it was followed by a much louder and unmistakable sound of a toilet flushing.

Will froze. Rush out into the corridor before he was seen and possibly straight into some armed rebel soldiers? Wait and face whoever was in the stall? Presumably a woman. What would her reaction be? Attack? Scream? The former, he could deal with, but he couldn't risk the latter.

There could only be one decision.

He heard the lock on the stall click open as he slipped into the next cubicle, pulling the door to. He heard footsteps cross to the wash hand basin and he peeked out.

He had forgotten that there was a large mirror on the wall above the basin. The woman happened to glance up and couldn't fail to see his masculine features watching her from the other stall.

Her face registered shock at first. Then astonishment. Then disbelief. Will stepped out of his hiding place as she turned to face him. She opened her mouth. To scream?

He pulled her towards him and covered her lips with his own and she clung to him.

After a moment the woman spluttered, 'How…? How did…? Will! I can't believe it.'

'Maeve, my darling, I've found you.' He held her tight and kissed her again, long and hard.

* * *

'We've found our way through to what we're pretty sure must be the north wall.'

James Connolly was taking a break from his explorations of the labyrinthine corridors of the basement under the Post Office.

The dull look on Padraig Pearse's face broke into a brief smile. 'And that's going to aid our patriotic stand?'

'It's a precaution. In case we have to evacuate the building. My men will tunnel through to the cellars of the shops on Henry Street.'

'Ah, I see. Yes, a wise precaution. So you think we may have to abandon our trophy?' Pearse waved his arm in an expansive gesture to include all the finery of the magnificent interior of the General Post Office.

'Well, let's hope not, Padraig. Let's hope not.'

The door to the rear of the building opened and Pearse recognised Ryan Doloughan's sister, who had been making herself useful with a bunch of other *Cumann na mBan* volunteers. 'Is there something you need?' he asked, noticing a man had followed her through the door. He had about a week's growth of stubble, but looked familiar.

'I've brought you a new recruit,' said Maeve.

'You've what?'

'It's Dillon!' Connolly recognised his erstwhile unarmed combat instructor. 'How the Dickens did you get in here?'

'Och, it wasn't that difficult. You might like to send a couple of your men to relieve the guards at the rear ramp, though. They're locked in yon wee wooden hut.' Will gave a modest shrug at the look of incredulity on Connolly's face.

Pearse said, 'But what are you doing here? Why have you come? You must realise this isn't the safest place in Dublin just now.'

'Aye well, it's not a whole lot safer out on the streets, thanks to the little party yous have started. Anyway, since I helped a wee bit in the run up I thought maybe I could lend yous a hand. This is where I work, you know; did I tell yous that? So if you want to know anything about the layout or where stuff is kept... You found the telegraph room; I know that.'

'You do? How do you know?' Connolly this time.

'It was me who showed it to Staines and his merry crew.'

'That was you, was it?' said Connolly. Then more slowly, with menacing frown, 'Does that mean it was you who led Sergeant O'Malley's section onto the roof to hoist the Irish flags?'

‘Yes, that was yours truly,’ said Will. He knew what was coming.

‘Young Jake wasn’t at all pleased at being locked out on the roof.’ Pearse’s tone gave nothing away.

‘Jake?’

‘Sergeant O’Malley,’ said Connolly. ‘Can you explain yourself?’

‘Well it was plain enough, Mr Connolly. They forced me up there at gunpoint, which I didn’t take kindly to. You know me. I didn’t know whether they were planning to throw me off the roof like some pagan sacrifice, or shoot me when they’d done with me. You’d have done the same in similar circumstances. I left them to it and ran.’

‘But you locked them out there, damn it, man.’

‘I needed a bit of a start. If I hadnae locked the roof door they’d have shot me before I’d reached the next landing.’

‘Both Staines and O’Malley were reprimanded for letting you escape.’

‘That was bit harsh,’ said Will.

‘Harsh? They failed in their duty.’

‘Aye, but they’re both young, inexperienced. They were never going to hold me, now, were they?’

‘You’re a very resourceful man, Dillon, and I dare say you’re right. We could use more like you.’ Connolly reached out his right hand, ‘Thank you for joining us. You can be my adjutant.’

Will took the proffered hand and shook it, wondering just what he was getting himself into. ‘And… er, the little misunderstanding with Jake O’Malley? You’ll have a wee word with the lad that I am now *persona grata*? Otherwise I think he might shoot me the first time I bump into him.’ It seemed, Will realised, that the sergeant hadn’t mentioned their second encounter on St Stephen’s Green. Understandable, in the circumstances.

‘Don’t worry about him; I’ll sort that out. First task. Come with me to the basement and tell me if we’ve found the right spot to start tunnelling.’

‘Tunnelling?’ said Will.

‘I’ll explain as we go.’

As Connolly and Dillon went off, with a nod of farewell to Maeve, Pearse said to her, ‘If you happen to find any more of his calibre breaking in, Miss Doloughan, feel free to bring them straight to us. You’ve cheered me up, considerably. Now, you’d better be about your duties.

Pearse was left to ponder on his own. He watched Maeve go but his eyes were soon downcast once more and a frown creased his forehead.

Chapter 24

It was fortunate that Connolly checked with Will before they started breaking through the basement wall, for what they thought was the peripheral stonework of the basement was still several yards short of the actual boundary which could only be reached by a different corridor.

He had just put them right when a messenger from Seán MacDiarmada found them to ask if Dillon could be spared as his commander had an urgent task that Dillon could carry out. Which was why he again found himself in the inner courtyard, this time having exited more traditionally through the door at the end of the back corridor. He also had the password to gain re-entry. He carried a dispatch for Michael Mallin. All MacDiarmada's Volunteers in the Moore Street area beyond the Post Office were working hard at their assigned tasks and their Commandant was reluctant to spare any. Pearse had suggested he use Dillon.

Will made his way up the ramp and discovered the same two guards on duty. They weren't smoking and were on the alert. They spotted him at once. The one with the rifle raised his weapon and Will gave the password for the day.

'Relax, lads. I'm sorry I had to lock yous up when I came in earlier. I couldn't for the life of me remember the password and I knew a couple of good soldiers like you would never have let me past without it. I'm away off, now but I'll be back later.' Out of devilment, Will saluted them and they both snapped to attention and returned his salute.

Ireland's finest, Will thought as he made his way through the alley once more and wondered what chance the Rising had of achieving anything more than a heap of dead bodies.

Long before he got to St Stephen's Green he was assailed by the sound of gunfire. The single shots of rifles like he had heard the night before were joined by an intermittent rattle that Will guessed must be machine gun fire. In the time it took him to come within sight of the barricades surrounding the park, the intermittent rattle had become almost continuous.

Edging closer and hugging the buildings, Will tried to spot the source of the firing for little seemed to be coming from St Stephen's Green. The shooting was from the far north corner, about where the Shelbourne Hotel was situated. It was as though a great lead cloud of firepower was raining on Commandant Mallin's troops, pinning them down and making retaliation virtually impossible. They were all going to be annihilated if this continued. Will realised it would be quite impossible to get into the Green and find Michael Mallin without getting shot himself. He considered working his way round to the south entrance, furthest from the Shelbourne, but knew as soon as he ventured onto the Green he would be at severe risk of catching a stray bullet.

The pavement along St Stephen's Green North was deserted. Any of Dublin's good citizens in the area were keeping well indoors while this fusillade continued. Will retraced his steps and made his way round the back of the properties overlooking the Green until he reached Kildare Street. Turning down it he could see the side of the Shelbourne at the far end. He had decided not to waste his journey and was soon standing in front of the reception desk and being greeted by the same black-haired young lady he had met yesterday.

She favoured him once more with her sweet smile and said, 'How nice to see you again. I'm very sorry, sir, but we're not allowed to let any non-guests in today;' and added in a low voice while glancing at the two uniformed men standing by the stairs and lift, 'we've been taken over by the army.'

Matching his voice to hers, Will said, 'Well, as a matter of fact it's army business I've come about. Would you know where the officer in charge might be?'

'They've taken over all the front rooms on the upper floors. But I don't think they'll allow you to go up. They've already turned several people away.'

'Thanks. I'll try my luck.'

Will approached the men guarding the stairs. 'I have urgent business with your commanding officer.'

'Are you a guest at this hotel, sir?'

'I'm… no, I'm not a guest.'

'Sorry, sir. We have strict orders not to allow anyone upstairs who is not a guest.'

'It's about the *Abbey Players*' Will emphasised the password he'd been given.

'If you have a general enquiry relating to the current situation you'd need to contact Dublin Castle, sir.'

'No it's… Never mind. Thank you, Corporal.' So the password hasn't been passed on to the lower ranks. Not yet, at least. Will strolled back to the reception desk.

'It seems you were right. Not allowed up.' Then in a low voice, 'Is there another way? A service lift, maybe?' He winked at the girl.

'Yes I can tell you how to get there,' the girl said in her normal voice and produced a street map of the centre of Dublin. As they huddled over the map she pointed out the rear of the hotel off Kildare Street while saying, 'It's not far from here; you need to go up this road,' followed by a whispered, 'there's a service entrance. I'll let you in. Two minutes.' And back to her normal voice, 'and it's on your right. You can't miss it.'

'That's very helpful,' said Will. 'Thank you so much.' And, with another wink to the girl, he left the hotel.

He found the service entrance in under a minute so he had to wait until eventually he heard the lock being turned and the door opened. He slipped inside and planted a swift kiss on the girl's rosy cheek. The rose deepened a shade as she pointed out a rather utilitarian service lift that was in need of a good cleaning.

'Go up four floors; try there first,' the girl said, as Will closed the metal trellis doors.

Noting that the lowest button was labelled 1, he pressed the button marked 5 and the lift began to ascend.

Will heard her call, 'Good luck,' as the receptionist's shapely ankles started to disappear from view.

The elevator creaked and shuddered its way up the shaft until it stopped with a jerk. Will slid open the inner and outer trellis doors and could only assume he was on the right floor. He headed toward the front of the building and was soon rewarded by the unmistakable sound of military orders being given and acknowledged. That and the incessant cacophony of gunfire. He emerged into the front corridor to see most of the doors to rooms facing the Green wide open and soldiers entering and leaving. Will stopped one.

'Your CO. I need to see him.'

'Who are you?'

'Doesn't matter. Please take me to him.'

The soldier drew his Webley revolver and covered Dillon. 'This way,' he said.

They entered a bedroom. The bed and other furniture had all been shoved back against the corridor wall to leave plenty of space by the window. It's lower frame was now devoid of glass and two marksmen were positioned with their Lee-Enfields trained on St Stephen's Green across the road. As Will entered the room one of the rifles let off a deafening report and he saw it's owner flinch with the recoil.

The soldier who had brought him in saluted a senior officer who was standing reading through some papers. 'Sir! Someone to see you, sir!'

'At ease, Corporal.' The officer turned an annoyed glance on Dillon. 'What is it? How did you get up here?'

'It's about the *Abbey Players*, sir.' Will hoped the significance of the phrase would not be lost on this officer, too.

'About – ? Oh... Right, thank you, Corporal. That'll be all. So,' he turned back to Will, 'You're... Daly.'

'Dillon, sir.'

'That's right. What can I do for you?'

'Maybe I can do something for you. I've got a dispatch from Seán MacDiarmada back at the GPO supposed to be delivered to Michael Mallin at St Stephen's Green. It's impossible to deliver it with all this shooting going on, but I thought you might be interested in seeing it anyway.'

'Indeed I might. Where is this dispatch?'

Will handed over a sealed envelope. The officer was about to rip it open.

'Eh – might it be an idea to steam open the envelope – in case you should decide to let me deliver it?' A ghost of an idea was developing in Will's mind.

'Good thinking.' The officer stuck his head into the corridor and called to a passing private. 'Take this envelope to the kitchens and steam it open. Do not look at the contents and guard it with your life.'

'Yes, sir!' The private dashed off.

One of the snipers at the window called out, 'I can see her again.'
'Where?' his companion demanded.
'Across the bridge, near the bandstand. Wait. She's ducked down again.'
'You're right. I think I caught a glimpse of her. There's no mistaking that wide brimmed hat.'
The two riflemen had suddenly got Will's full attention. He ambled over to stand between them.
'Get down, man!' shouted the officer. 'We're not taking much return fire but no need to present them with a perfect target.
At his first words, Will dropped to his knees and peered over the sill. 'Yous have got a grand view from up here, lads. Who did you spot ducking down?'
'It's Mallin's second-in-command, a women officer.'
'She's a big fish,' said the other sniper; 'worth going for.'
'Hang on. I can see her again… I have her in my sights. Three… two… '
The loud retort drowned out the 'One!' and also the sound of Dillon's slap on the gunman's shoulder. 'Good shooting, soldier. Great shot.' He had seen Constance Markievicz's hat fly off as the soldier's bullet narrowly missed its target.
The soldier in question rounded on Dillon, 'Get back out of the way, you dolt! You made me miss my shot! Keep away, will you.'
'Oh, did I? I thought you got her. I'm terribly sorry.'
'Just stay back. And keep down.'
'I will. I'm really sorry,' said Will. And I trust that Constance will heed that warning and stay down herself in future.
The private returned at that moment with the opened envelope and handed it to the officer.
'That will be all, Private. Thank you.' He scanned the single page of writing and stood for a moment deep in thought. He turned to Will. 'You were right, Dillon. I do want you to deliver this.' He inserted the folded paper and re-sealed the envelope. 'MacDiarmada is asking if Mallin can afford to release any of his men to help in the area round the GPO. If the numbers on St Stephen's Green can be reduced at all, that suits me fine. And, with any luck, forewarned as we are, we'll be able to pick up the contingent before they get anywhere near the Post Office.'
This couldn't have been better, Will thanked his lucky stars. He said, 'Trouble is, I won't be able to get anywhere near Mallin under your

continuous barrage.' Will had been keeping one eye on the window watching to see if Constance was foolhardy enough to show herself again but she seemed to have learned her lesson. Then, incredibly, he saw a figure appear by the lake wearing some sort of uniform. For a moment he thought it was a suicidally stupid Volunteer until he realised it was the Park Keeper and he was feeding the ducks.

'But I think I know what you could do,' said Will.

Chapter 25

Two minutes later Dillon was rushing up St Stephen's Green North towards the entrance to the Green. There was an eerie silence. The guns from the hotel had stopped firing and the last echoes of a message broadcast through a loudhailer had just died away. The message had suggested a brief ceasefire while the Park Keeper carried out his daily duty of feeding the wildlife on the lake. The returning silence from the park confirmed the rebels agreement.[6]

As he climbed over the barricade by the arched entrance, Will hoped Mallin would have the sense to see the opportunity this gave him. He jumped down from an upturned cart and almost landed on a soldier who's left eye was a bloody, gaping hole with a large chunk missing from the back of his skull. He tried to expel the image from his mind and entered the Green only to come upon more dead bodies: one lying in a freshly dug trench and another sprawled half in and half out of a dugout who had been almost cut in two by raking machine gun fire. The stink of spent cartridges hung in the air and the sickly smell of blood and fear.

Will shuddered. Broke into a sprint for the bridge. Passed the keeper, oblivious to the drama unfolding around him. Crossed the bridge, veered right. Headed for the area around the bandstand.

It was a hive of activity. Keeping low, dozens of men and not a few women, many dressed in Red Cross uniforms, were grabbing what they could and moving over to the path along the west edge of the Green. Some were supporting the walking wounded and Will saw two stretchers

[6] It is on record that a ceasefire at St Stephen's Green was indeed called, to allow the ducks on the lake to be fed safely by James Kearney, the park keeper.

being carried from the bandstand which seemed to be being used as the First Aid post. He gasped when he saw the number of prone bodies lying to one side who would not be joining in the evacuation. Not now, not ever.

Will caught sight of the Countess leading the way through a gap that had been forced in the park boundary out onto St Stephen's Green West. Looking round, he recognised Michael Mallin hurrying everyone along and preparing to bring up the rear. Will joined the mass exodus and by the time he got to the gap he saw that those in front had already gained access to the comparative safety of the College of Surgeons across the road.

It was then that the firing started up again, like a hundred squibs being let off on Guy Fawkes night. Whether the Park Keeper had finished his act of mercy to the aquatic residents under his care, or whether the CO had realised what was going on, Will couldn't tell. The effect of the renewed firing, however, was to revitalise the tail-enders to unprecedented speeds, before the snipers could find their range again. A Citizens' Army soldier running beside Dillon was suddenly spun round; he clasped his left shoulder. Will grabbed his right elbow and steered him back on track. A dark red stain was spreading on the soldier's upper sleeve. The doorway loomed in front of them. Other hands grabbed the wounded man. Dillon staggered in only moments ahead of Mallin. Someone slammed the door closed as a hail of bullets thudded into it.

Michael Mallin surveyed his troops all crowded into the foyer of the College of Surgeons. He was grateful he'd had the foresight to take it over when they first arrived at the Green the day before, but he cursed himself for not having thought of taking over the Shelbourne as well, though, in reality, he hadn't the manpower for both. He saw that Countess Markievicz was already allocating duties to those around her as he scanned the foyer to get an idea of how many troops he still had to carry on the fight.

As his eye passed over each face in turn, taking a rough count, he did a quick double take and focused back on a man in a cloth cap with thick stubble on his face. Isn't that…?

'Dillon! What the devil are you doing here? How did you get in?'

'People keep asking me that,' said Will. 'Point is, I'm here. I've been waiting for a lull in the shooting to give you this dispatch.' He handed over the envelope.

'The "lull," as you put it didn't come a moment too soon. We were in a desperate situation out there. It's not like the English to go all sentimental over a few ducks and a coot, but the ceasefire was just what we needed to get out of there.' Mallin ripped open the envelope and read the contents. He gave a mirthless laugh.

'The answer is, Not a chance in hell! Do you know what this says?'

'No, Mr Mallin,' Will lied, 'Mr MacDiarmada didnae confide in me.'

'He asks if I can spare any men. All my *spare* men are lying dead out there on the Green, God rest their souls. It was a bloody slaughter. So you have my answer. You can rephrase it, if you like.'

On second thoughts, Mallin decided to give Dillon a written response that provided some detail of the situation south of the river. He sealed it and had someone show Will the way through to the rear of the College. Sporadic shooting was still coming from the hotel and Will had no desire to venture out anywhere near St Stephen's Green while that continued. His route back towards the river took him up Williams Street and when he reached the crossing with Exchequer Street a sudden burst of gunfire to his left caused him to look up towards City Hall. He recalled the firing of the previous evening when he had realised that the rebels must have occupied the civic building and surrounding premises.

He ventured further down Exchequer Street until he had a clear view of City Hall and was just in time to see a British platoon launching an onslaught on the front of the building. At the same time there was a deafening fusillade of fire down onto the roof, coming from the tower inside Dublin Castle. Any rebel soldiers up on the leads had no chance of firing down on the attackers on the ground without being shot to ribbons themselves.

As Will watched from a safe distance, he saw the English troops storming into the building at several points using windows as well as doors. Small arms fire from inside told its own story as the sound of the shooting gradually reached them from higher and higher in the building. The rebels weren't giving up without a fight and seemed to be making a last stand on the roof. The barrage from the castle tower stopped, presumably at some pre-arranged signal, lest British soldiers should be hit.

The sound of gunshots became increasingly intermittent and Will could imagine the hand-to-hand fighting that was going on before the hopelessly outnumbered rebels must be forced to surrender. He wondered with a grim smile, whether any of his recent unarmed combat students were up there and how they were faring. Eventually he saw a sullen succession of soldiers of the revolution being led out under a heavily armed guard. At their head was a woman who conducted herself with dignity under the menacing threat of fixed bayonets on British rifles.

'I know her. That's Dr Lynn,' said another onlooker. Will hadn't noticed him stopping by his side to see what was going on. 'What's she doing with those malcontents? I'd have thought she'd have more sense.'

'It's hard to know what motivates them,' Will replied, anxious not to arouse any antagonism.

'The sooner the army has them *all* arrested, the better for the rest of us.'

There were other civilians in Exchequer Street who had also been watching the unfolding events at City Hall and now that the fighting had stopped there was a general edging forward to get a better look at the prisoners. Will found himself in a small group out on the pavement on George's Street looking across as the British started to march their captives in the direction of Dublin Castle. Three young men hurried over the road to get a closer look.

A British soldier spun round to face the lads and without hesitation thrust his bayonet into the stomach of the lead runner. The other two stopped in their tracks, staring in horror at their companion bending forward as the soldier withdrew the bayonet, dripping in blood. The wounded man fell to his knees. One of his friends rushed to help him. The soldier raised his rifle and fired, hitting him in the chest. He swivelled his aim to the third one, who hadn't moved, and fired again.

At the sound of the shots other soldiers swung round and trained their guns on the little crowd across the road. A woman near Will screamed and started to run. Someone else followed, others remained rooted to the spot. Will flung himself flat on the pavement.

The Royal Dublin Fusiliers had fought their way into Dublin Castle the night before to reinforce the garrison there and had taken a number of casualties from rebel sniper fire from City Hall and the surrounds. They had been itching for a chance to re-take the civic building and get their hands on the republicans. The general instructions they received prior to launching their assault on the City Hall were to assume that anyone in the area not in Army uniform was a rebel. 'Only way to play safe,' was how their CO justified it. So the private who had reacted instinctively to the fast-approaching young man and used his bayonet had no qualms about dispatching the other two possible assailants as well.

His comrades-in-arms had a little more time to consider their action when they aimed their rifles at the small crowd on the opposite pavement. After a few moments, one of them raised the elevation of his Lee-Enfield and fired a shot over their heads. Two of his colleagues followed his example and the onlookers dispersed with amazing rapidity.

Will picked himself up, feeling slightly foolish, but not a little shaken. Three innocent bystanders were lying dead or dying in the road. Such were the horrors of war and that's what this was; nothing less. He hurried off in the direction of the Liffey thinking about how his job in telegraphic communications had prevented him joining the British army to go and fight in France. He'd little thought then that within two years he'd be caught up in a struggle against that same army on his own soil.

He really ought to be getting out of Dublin – if that were still possible. But having found Maeve, safe for the moment inside the GPO, he was reluctant to leave her. He had witnessed how the British had managed to retake City Hall; how many insurgents now lay dead within? Would the Post Office be next? City Hall would have been a priority as it was hampering their access to the Castle. Nevertheless they wouldn't be prepared to leave the rebels occupying the Post Office and the Communications Room for any longer than they had to.

Will crossed the river by the Ha'penny Bridge and was about to turn up Liffey Street. He was intending to use his hidden alleyway back to the GPO when he heard distant cheering or shouting coming from the direction of Sackville Street. He supposed his duty lay in delivering the dispatch as soon as possible – except that he wasn't a member of the republican forces. He owed them no allegiance other than what was necessary to maintain his cover. After a moment's pause, he allowed his curiosity to get the better of him and walked down to O'Connell Bridge where he was relieved to find no rebel pickets.

He turned into Sackville Street. Up ahead, about where the Post Office stood, a large crowd was gathered. There was little or no traffic and people milled around on the street as he walked up as far as Clery's and, with his attention on the crowd, failed to notice a familiar figure emerge from an office a few doors further along.

Buster Gregson noticed Dillon, though. He had been talking business with the Boss in his swish city-centre office and the fact that he had as yet failed to apprehend Dillon had come up.

'I'm becoming annoyed, Gregson. If Moore didn't have a busted knee he'd have had that bastard down in the cellar long since and his slow and excruciating demise would be under way.'

Gregson bridled. He was itching to say that if Éamonn didn't have a broken knee they wouldn't be after Dillon in the first place, but he didn't dare.

Now, out on Sackville Street he couldn't believe his luck to spot the man no more than twenty feet away joining the back of a crowd watching something going on at the GPO. He rushed toward him with the intention of dragging him straight back into the offices of Michael J Higginson.

As Will drew closer he realised the shouting wasn't cheers but jeers. He elbowed his way through the body of people until he could see the object of their scorn.

Weapons were being unloaded from the boot of a motorcar. There were more piled on the back seat and the passenger seat. Unlike before when the early morning onlookers simply watched with bemused expressions, this crowd was hostile. The people knew more now about what was going on and they didn't seem to like it.

A company of Volunteers who looked like they had just arrived, escorting the weapons, had formed a protective semicircle around the motorcar and were facing outwards to the crowd. Leading them, Will realised with a start, was Ryan Doloughan. Behind him, more Volunteers from the GPO were unloading the guns. Those at the front of the crowd were trying to keep a healthy distance between themselves and the armed rebels, but from further back people were pushing forwards. They were intent on making their feeling clear to these self-appointed Soldiers of the Republic and all the time kept up the jeering, taunts and insults.

A sudden surge from behind forced the people at the front right up against the rebel guards. The proximity of bodies made it impossible for them to use their rifles other than as clubs to try to drive off their attackers.

Will found himself, purely for self-defence, grappling with a Volunteer intent on knocking him senseless with the butt of his rifle. In a crowd situation the one imperative is to stay on your feet. Once on the ground, apart from any intentional kicking you could receive, you are likely to be severely trampled and find it impossible to regain your feet. This was running through Will's head when he saw out the corner of his eye one of the rebels duck to avoid a wild, swinging fist. The man missed his footing and fell. That was when Will saw that it was Ryan.

Dillon's own assailant was between him and his fallen friend. He grabbed him in a ferocious bear hug, pinning both his arms to his side. Then he half lifted him, half shuffled round until they had swapped places. He released his grip and shoved hard, forcing the republican away from him and himself backwards through flailing arms, hard heads and resisting bodies.

Through a tangle of lower limbs he glimpsed Ryan struggling to turn over into a kneeling position. A booted leg appeared from the crowd to land a ferocious kick on the side of his head. Ryan collapsed back onto the road. Will twisted round and stepped across his body, straddling him with his back to the crowd. He braced himself, leaning back into the thrusting wall of people to keep them from trampling his friend.

'Over here!' he yelled; 'Dolougham needs assistance. Here! At the double.'

Dillon found that he was taking blows to his body from angry citizens but they were harmless. Another Volunteer reached them and, slinging his rifle over his shoulder tried to grab his Commanding Officer under the arms but in the crush he could only get a grip under one shoulder. He couldn't lift him, lopsided like that, so Dillon leaned forward and got a hold under Ryan's other shoulder. Together they started to raise him.

'Slowly does it, lads. My head's swimming,' came the familiar voice.

Will grinned in relief that Ryan was all right, as in the corner of his eye his earlier assailant loomed into view. The man had reversed his rifle and the wooden butt was crashing down on Will's head.

The sound of shouting and jeering stopped at once as if Will had plunged underwater. He felt himself sinking deep into darkness. His arms floated uselessly at his side. Agonising pain and unknown depths engulfed him. No bottom. Just an eternity of floating down. Where no sound reached. No light penetrated. And all thought ceased.

Chapter 26

Buster Gregson reached the back of the crowd in under three seconds but in that brief time he could see that Dillon had managed to make his way between bodies and was now embedded among the jeering onlookers. Gregson pushed and shoved his way through, trying not to lose sight of his quarry. Can't snatch him now, he thought; too many people. Watch and wait. Me and the lads have been doing a lot of that on this bastard's account. It'll make removing his fingers one at a time all the more rewarding.

He saw Dillon grappling with one of the rebel soldiers and shove him aside as he went to the aid of another one who had fallen. And then he saw the first soldier clubbing him viciously with the butt of his rifle. Steady, man; we want him alive.

Dillon collapsed as the fallen Volunteer was helped to his feet but as Gregson watched, this man immediately dropped on one knee to examine Dillon's unconscious form. For some reason he ordered two of his men to lift Dillon and carry him away from the crowd. Frustrated and angry, Gregson could do nothing but watch as Dillon was taken, along with the last of the weapons, inside the GPO.

* * *

Hours later, Will was swimming through murky waters.

Dark waters.

Deep, dark waters.

There were voices; too far away to be of significance. Except – had one just mentioned his name? He kicked out and struggled to rise towards the surface where the darkness grew pale. And the voices came nearer. All he had to do was open his eyes. All he had to do… So much effort. Strength eluded him. The depths were calling.

'Will! Will! Wake up.'

Calling. Calling his name. He drifted downwards. The voices grew faint. Distant. Insignificant.

'I saw a flicker behind his eyelids. Will!'

'Ah, I think maybe you imagined it, Maeve. Wishful thinking.'

'I didn't. I'm sure I saw something.' She was sitting, holding Will's hand where he lay on a truckle bed in a large room that the insurgents had turned into their First Aid post. A lady in her thirties and wearing a white apron and white flowing head gear had checked him over when he was carried in. She had greeted Maeve as soon as she arrived:

'I've made him as comfortable as I can. Now we wait. I'm Elizabeth, by the way, Elizabeth O'Farrell.

'Maeve… Doloughan. Thank you, nurse.' Maeve looked around the room. There were a few other women there, some of them in nurses' uniforms, ready to attend to wounded Volunteers. Two were busy with a couple of men, both with superficial injuries from gunshots, but Maeve feared the room would be full before all this was over.

She had arranged to exchange her current duties in order to help in First Aid as soon as she heard from Ryan about Will's injury. Her brother had led a successful raid on the British army training camp on Bull Island. They had sneaked in from the seaward side in small boats while the bulk of the garrison were engaging a battalion of rebels on the mainland, whose job it was to keep the British bottled up and unable to get into the city. Ryan's small unit had stolen all the spare weapons and got away in their boats again, without loss. They landed a little further up the estuary and transferred their haul to land transport. The O'Rahilly had allowed them to use his motorcar to bring the guns to the rebel headquarters.

'I'll look in again, later,' said Ryan, who was standing at Maeve's side. 'Don't worry. He's a tough old boot. He'll come round when he's ready.'

Maeve didn't answer. She gazed at Will's face where he lay, as if in slumber. A bright red splodge at the top of his right cheekbone that was already the size of a golf ball was all that suggested he was not simply asleep. She squeezed his hand and prayed that he would "be ready" soon.

* * *

While Will lay comatose, the skies over Dublin gradually darkened. Looters roamed the city centre. Children broke into the toy shop on Sackville Street whose window display Will had admired a few days earlier. They emerged triumphant with a treasure-trove of fireworks that they proceeded to let off at the foot of Nelson's Pillar that had already survived an earlier brush with gunpowder when the rebels had tried and failed to blow it up. Grim watchers on the rooftops of the Post Office and other nearby buildings saw rockets streak skywards and they eyed their stockpiles of homemade bombs made from paint cans filled with explosives. They could only hope that none of the trailing sparks would drift their way.

Whether inspired by the youngsters' pyrotechnics or not, some of their elders, having cleared out another shop of its more portable goods, decided to torch it. The blaze brought a macabre illumination from Cleary's at one end of Sackville Street to the Gresham Hotel at the other, for none of the street lighting, gas or electric, was working anywhere in the city centre.

With the Metropolitan Police confined to barracks for their own safety and the looting in the darkened streets already out of hand, to say nothing of the mayhem being caused by the insurrectionists, Lord Wimborne was about to make a far-reaching decision that would ultimately determine the very fate of Ireland, itself.

'We cannot sit back and allow Dublin to become a den of lawlessness just because a bunch of *Sínn Feiners* think they can hold us all to ransom.' The Lord Lieutenant of Ireland was addressing Brigadier-General William Lowe in his office at Dublin Castle. He twirled the points of his handlebars very deliberately, before continuing. 'I am, hereby, declaring martial law until further notice. You have complete authority, William. Do whatever it takes.'

Sometime in the early hours, when the darkened and empty window frames in the Post Office showed the first faint signs of an approaching dawn, Will Dillon came round and was violently sick. One of the *Cumann na mBan* women cleaned him up. She didn't want to disturb Maeve who had only just got off to sleep herself, having maintained a vigil by his side until she could stay awake no longer. In any event

Dillon's eyes were soon closed again and this time his breathing was even and steady. He seemed merely to be sleeping.

About the same time a former fisheries patrol vessel, the *Helga*, now, due to the war, part of the British navy, left her moorings at Kingstown and began to steam up the River Liffey. She dropped anchor midstream opposite the Custom House and trained her two 12-pounders on the nearby Liberty Hall. As the headquarters of the Transport and General Workers Union in Ireland, the building had long harboured dissidents who were constant thorns in the flesh to both the Irish establishment and their English overlords. Now it was clear that the planning for the Rising had emanated from within these same seditious walls. General Lowe took great delight in ordering the *Helga* to open fire.

Throughout Wednesday morning the Trade Union headquarters took a pounding from the artillery on the river. Relentlessly, shells blasted into the erstwhile spawning ground of the Citizens' Army and the secret rendezvous of the Irish Republican Brotherhood. Yawning gaps were blown in the roof and walls of Liberty Hall that had been the hub of the insurrection, the epicentre of the rebel planners right up until the start of the uprising. A much traumatised caretaker managed to get out unscathed, but unknown to the British, he was the sole occupier of the abandoned building. The shelling had no effect whatsoever on the conduct of the Rising, but Liberty Hall would never again be a haven for far left socialists and communist agitators. By the time the *Helga's* guns fell silent it was reduced to a mere shell, filled with rubble.

The ship was then ordered to turn her artillery towards Boland's Mill where de Valera's small contingent were doing their best to hinder British reinforcements arriving at Kingstown from making their way into the city. However, early on, de Valera had ordered a few of his men to raise the rebel flag over a nearby empty building and so it now took the brunt of the British shelling. Nevertheless, while the rebels were under attack, 2000 men of the Sherwood Foresters did get ashore and marched on Dublin. They planned to cross the canal by Mount Street Bridge but de Valera had anticipated this and placed a few of his men in number 25 Northumberland Road and in St Stephen's School and the parochial hall to cover the southern approaches to the bridge. As a fall-back position, Clanwilliam House on the north side of the bridge was also occupied.

Two days previously, when they had first taken up their positions, a company of veterans from the Irish Rugby Football Veterans Corps were marching down Northumberland Road returning from a training expedition. Their arm bands with *GR* for *Georgius Rex*, or King George, had earned them the affectionate nickname of the Gorgeous Wrecks. The rebels saw these uniformed soldiers, although unarmed, as legitimate targets. Gunfire from the balcony of No. 25 wounded thirteen veterans, five of them fatally. It was an early skirmish which helped fuel the initial antagonism of the Dublin populace to the Rising. It prompted Padraig Pearse to issue a general command that no unarmed individuals, whether in uniform or not, were to be fired upon.

However now, two days later, around midday there was no doubt in the minds of the men in No. 25 as to the legitimacy as targets of the advancing column of British troops. As they drew near to the canal they came under heavy fire from the rebels. A number of troops fell dead in the road before they had a chance to take whatever cover they could find. A raging battle ensued. Only after severe and prolonged fighting which lasted several hours and resulted in many further losses did the British manage to overpower the rebel strongholds south of the canal. Finally, they started to cross the bridge.

It was now the turn of sniper fire from Clanwilliam House to take a terrific toll on the advancing troops. Their first volley dropped ten Tommies on the bridge. Each successive surge forward saw more wounded and dying, but General Lowe's telephoned orders to their CO were to take the bridge "at all costs." For many of the young soldiers this was their first taste of battle, having been shipped off from England straight from their training camps. Some assumed they were in France, but they fought bravely. With machine gun fire and grenades supporting their rifle attacks, their superior numbers inevitably won through in the end but the final "cost" was 234 dead or wounded – almost half of the total British army casualties throughout the whole period of the insurrection.

Two rebels and two fifteen-year-old boys had manned 25 Northumberland Road in the opening skirmishes. One was killed, while the other, and the boys, escaped from the ruined building that was later described in British despatches as "a strongly held post." Of the seven insurgents in Clanwilliam House, who held the 2000-strong Sherwood Foresters at bay for three hours, three lost their lives. The other four escaped to continue the fight elsewhere.

The British army was short of heavy artillery and the guns on the *Helga* were kept busy. They did, however have several twenty-pounders newly arrived from Athlone. Some of these were set up at Trinity College in Westmoreland Street, commanding an uninterrupted view across the Liffey up Sackville Street ready to attack the rebels headquarters in the Post Office and the Imperial Hotel above Cleary's that the rebels had occupied on Tuesday. Other big guns were sited at Philsborough to the north of the city so fire could come from both directions.

1000 Royal Inniskilling Fusiliers had arrived by train and more reinforcements were on their way. The British deployed their troops to engage with the insurgents wherever they were established. South of the river a number of battles were raging. The rebel-held South Dublin Union repulsed repeated grenade and machine gun attacks and even hand-to-hand fighting at some stages. There were rebels there who owed their lives to what they had learned at Dillon's unarmed combat classes.

The College of Surgeons was constantly being raked by machine gun fire from the upper floors of the Shelbourne.

The Mendicity Institute, opposite the Four Courts came under intense fire from British soldiers who worked their way along Usher's Quay, going from house to house, knocking holes through the adjoining walls to get close to the rebel stronghold whilst still under cover.

The insurgents who had taken over Jacob's Biscuit Factory were having a fairly easy time of it so far with little to do but look after the few hostages they had taken when they first moved in, and snipe at any soldiers who came within range. But they caused little hindrance to the nearby British troops who were systematically clearing the buildings around City Hall of any remaining rebels, to safeguard the Castle.

Passers-by and reckless onlookers were not immune to the hails of bullets. There were civilian casualties from random fire from both sides. For some, however, the shooting was not random. A British private reported to his NCO that he had shot two girls who were about twenty, because they acted suspiciously. In another part of town three men were arrested on suspicion of being *Sínn Feiners*, one of whom was actually a well-known pacifist by the name of Francis Sheehy Skeffington. The arresting officer was anxious to impress upon the insurrectionists the zero-tolerance approach being taken by the British. Under the powers of martial law, he had all three shot at dawn the following morning. News of Skeffington's death, while not promoting the rebels' cause among the

Dublin populace, certainly opened their eyes to the ruthlessness of the British soldiers and caused a public outcry.

People caught looting were liable to be shot on the street and no distinction was made between opportunist thieves and the desperately poor scavenging for something to eat. One unlucky thief emerged from a shop with his plunder and received a fatal wound from an army sniper on a distant rooftop. The mob with him scattered, though a few risked their lives to pull their friend's body away. Once the body was removed, the mob returned to carry on ransacking the shop.

* * *

About the time the Sherwood Foresters were taking such a hammering from across Mount Street Bridge, Maeve let out a little squeal when she popped into the First Aid room to check on Will and found him awake. She rushed over to his truckle bed.

'He's just this minute opened his eyes,' said Nurse O'Farrell, who was by his side.

'Will! How do you feel? We've been so worried about you.' Maeve knelt at his bedside and took his hand.

Will sat up and put his free hand to his head. The lump had gone down quite a bit but the violent purple on his cheek around his right eye told its own story. He took in his surroundings at a glance and recognised the room in the Post Office. 'Bit of a headache' he said. 'Otherwise fine. I'm starving; is there anything to eat in this place? Don't suppose the staff canteen's open?'

Maeve laughed. 'Oh, Will it's so good to hear your voice. Are you really feeling all right? We're running the canteen now. You can have something to eat if you're sure you feel up to it.'

Will swung his legs off the bed and stood up. And promptly sat down again. Maeve helped him to his feet once more. 'My legs feel a bit wobbly,' he said. 'Lead me to the trough, I'll be fine in a moment. How long have I been asleep?'

'Over twenty-four hours.'

'Blimey! No wonder I'm light-headed. Is your brother all right?' Will was remembering now what happened.

'He's absolutely fine – and very grateful to you for helping him back on his feet, or it might have been a different story.'

'Well, I'm guessing he returned the compliment. Was it Ryan who got me in here after I lost consciousness?'

'It was the least he could do. He knows how much you mean to me.'

'Oh, I see. If it had just been his oul pal, Dillon, he wouldnae have bothered. But anything for his pretty little sister.'

'No, I didn't mean it like that. He'd – oh, you're teasing me, aren't you?' Maeve dropped his hand and pouted her lips.

'Hey! Don't let go. Not yet. I'm still a bit giddy. I'm sorry, my darling. Just kidding.'

Will and Maeve joined others in the Post Office canteen and Will was tucking into a plate of ham and eggs and boiled potatoes when a green uniformed corporal approached their table.

'Begging your pardon, sir, but Commandant Connelly would like a word as soon as you're finished.'

Sir. Dillon found that amusing but didn't say anything other than, 'Right ho, then. Won't be long.' Then, as the corporal shuffled his feet and didn't seem to be leaving, he added 'Was there something else?'

'Only, sir… that I… wanted to apologise.'

'Apologise?'

'For knocking you out.'

'That was you, was it? I thought you looked familiar. I hope I didn't break anything when I had you in that bear hug.'

'Oh no, sir. I'm fine. But – '

'But nothing. You were protecting your CO, or so you thought. The perils of war, me lad. I should have been more vigilant. I won't make that mistake again.'

* * *

'Mr Connolly. Reporting for duty.'

'Dillon. You're a day late. Not the most auspicious start to your role as adjutant.'

'Indeed it's not. I had a wee bit of a contretemps with one of your corporals or I'd have been back sooner.'

'Ha! Is that what it was? Not to mention saving Captain Dolougham from the mob out there and bringing back the dispatch from Mallin.'

'Oh, you found that in me pocket, all right?'

‘We did. Thank you. And my apologies for the crack on your head. You seem none the worse for it now – apart from that shiner.’

‘Och, it wasn’t much worse than being out sailing and forgetting to duck when the spar swings across; I’ve had a few of those in my time, I can tell you. I’m fine – now I’ve had something to eat.’

‘So you’re ready for another mission?’

‘What have you got in mind?

‘It’s getting increasingly difficult for my men to move around the city centre; the British Tommies are everywhere. I can still relay orders to the Imperial across the road – we’ve got a wire rigged up roof to roof so we can pass notes in a tin box hanging from it; we pull it across by an endless loop of rope. But I need to know what’s happening at the Four Courts and south of the river.’

This suited Will fine. He couldn’t stay confined to barracks if he was to be any further use to Bradshaw and his contacts. He wasn’t happy that Maeve was serving in the rebel headquarters but at least she was safer inside than on the streets.

‘I’ll do my best to find out for you.’

‘I know you will. You’re a good man, Dillon. Come back in an hour and I’ll have dispatches ready for you to take, and a pass to identify you to my commandants throughout the city. Are you armed?’

Will patted his coat pocket where he had placed the revolver he had picked up when he went back to his lodgings the previous day. He also had spare bullets for it, courtesy of the ammunition drawer in Higginson’s gunroom.

With an hour to kill, Will found Maeve again and got her to take him on a brief tour of the defences before she re-joined her allotted post. Her task, along with some other *Cumann na mBan* women, when she wasn’t helping in the First Aid room, was to re-load rifles and keep the sharpshooters at the windows supplied. The background sound of continuous firing followed them wherever they went. Will noted the riflemen stationed at strategic intervals at windows all around the outer-facing walls of the building. All the glass had been knocked out to prevent injury from flying slivers. At each position a loader was standing by and Will thought he recognised one or two of the women from the ceilidh where he first met Maeve – that would be two weeks ago, tomorrow, he thought, with something of a shock. Only two weeks. Back then he was preparing for the long haul, ferreting out information about a possible summer uprising and now here he was, in the thick of it. He glanced at Maeve who was chatting to one of her colleagues and keeping well clear of the line of sight through the window; he thought of Annie.

Maeve finished her conversation and grasped his hand. 'Come up the stairs,' she said and pulled him after her. A tingle, as she touched him, brought his thoughts right back to the present.

More snipers at more windows on each floor. Some with bloodied bandages covering wounds already received. Bandages, some of which had been applied by Maeve while Will was still unconscious.

'This is me. Where I'm stationed,' she said.

They had entered a long room on the fourth floor overlooking Sackville Street. Will took in the scene at a glance – a sergeant with six soldiers manning the windows. One had just discharged his rifle and was swapping it with a re-loaded one from one of the woman there. She called out, 'Oh, am I glad you're back Maeve. My stomach thinks my throat's been cut. I must get something down me.'

The men remained vigilant at their posts under the watchful eyes of their sergeant. Eyes which now widened with instant recognition and astonishment.

'You!' was all the man managed to utter as he grabbed a rifle from one of the women.

'But sir!' the woman exclaimed.

He ignored her and levelled the barrel at Dillon's head.

The recognition had been mutual. Dillon said, 'Och, this is getting boring, O'Malley. Would you point that thing someplace else before you hurt somebody.'

Sergeant O'Malley recovered his power of speech, 'What are you doing walking free, never mind being back in the headquarters of the Irish Republic?'

'I'm – '

'Never mind. Move away from the woman.'

'Wait!' said Maeve. 'Don't shoot him!'

'Step aside!' O'Malley ordered her, keeping his rifle trained on Dillon

'It's all right, he's not going to shoot me.' The calmness in Will's voice denied the look of hatred in the sergeant's eyes.

'Oh he isn't, is he not?' said O'Malley. 'You're not getting away a second time.'

The sergeant's trigger finger tightened. No slow motion this time. He squeezed.

The hammer clicked down – on an empty chamber.

Will was covering O'Malley with his revolver before the sergeant fully realised what had happened.

'I… I tried to tell you, sir,' said the woman from whom he had snatched the rifle.

Will had seen straight away that his old adversary had taken the rifle that had just been fired as they came in the room.

'As I was about to tell you,' he said, 'I am now adjutant to James Connolly. He was supposed to have told you but I guess he's had other things on his mind. If I put this gun away, will you promise to be good?'

Without waiting for a reply, Will pocketed his revolver. O'Malley glanced sideways to where another woman was finishing her loading task, but didn't move.

Maeve said, 'He's telling you the truth. He's not a risk. He saved Captain Doloughan's life.'

'Hmph,' O'Malley's face was priceless. Will saw a mixture of the hate and frustration along with something else. Fear? Relief. Relief that he hadn't just shot the adjutant to the Commander of Republican forces in Dublin. 'Right,' the young sergeant looked at Maeve, 'back to work, you. And you,' he addressed Dillon, 'get out of my command post. If I never see you again, it will be too soon.'

Will grinned at Maeve and winked as he withdrew.

He went to check out the roof before going back down to Connolly. The door he had locked to leave O'Malley's platoon stranded out there on Monday opened to his touch, its lock shattered. From the safety of the doorway, Dillon surveyed the scene. Riflemen lay close behind the parapets out of sight of the enemy snipers positioned on other rooftops. Stockpiles of old paint tins with fuses attached told their own potentially explosive story. As he watched, Will saw distant gun flashes from the tower over Amiens Street Station and heard bullets ricocheting off the Post Office stonework.

He heard a man yell out and saw him fall, grabbing at his calf. Blood was already staining his trousers. A comrade rushed to his aid and pulled the wounded man's arm round his shoulder. He managed to get him up onto his good leg while remaining bent low. They struggled awkwardly like this towards the door. Will didn't hesitate. He dashed out and grabbed the casualty's other arm, the sound of bullets all around.

Between the two of them they half dragged, half carried him into the safety of the building.

As they crossed the threshold they heard a thunderous crash from the direction of the street followed, a fraction later, by a more distant explosive report.

'That sounded like heavy artillery,' said Will and, as though to confirm it, another shell burst further up Sackville Street, followed almost instantly by the crump sound of an eighteen pounder being fired.

'They're shelling us? Mr Pearse said they would never do that; they'd not want to damage all their fine buildings.' The rebel soldier sounded quite indignant.

'It seems the English value Irish buildings a mite less than Pearse was hoping. Less than gaining a victory over republicans, at any rate.' Will looked for the first time at his fellow-rescuer, as they lowered his wounded companion to the ground.

Will was shocked to find himself looking at another face he recognised. The last time he had seen it he was sprawled on the pavement outside his old digs in Mary Lane and the face, full of aggression, was the owner of a heavy boot that had just landed in his ribs.

Chapter 27

When Ewan Moore told Éamonn, he had joined the Irish Volunteers he took a lot of stick from his elder brother.

'Whad'ya want to go and do that for? You've got a perfectly good job working for the Boss.'

'This isn't a job, it's voluntary, and it's protecting our country,' said Ewan.

'Sure it is. You're all playing soldiers when you should be working.'

'We train in our spare time.'

'Spare time? We mustn't be giving you enough work to do.'

When Éamonn had had his knee dislocated a fortnight ago it had definitely reduced Ewan's spare time and he was secretly glad when he read in the Sunday paper that the manoeuvres had been cancelled. But then, on Monday, it was all on again. He had screwed up his courage and told Buster Gregson that he had to report for duty at Liberty Hall and wouldn't be available for work for a while. Gregson had sworn at him and told him he needn't bother coming back; he was fired.

Moore lowered his wounded comrade to the floor and tried to hide from his face any sign that he had recognised the man who had just risked his life to help him. His mind was racing. This was also the man who had crippled his brother. The man Gregson, and Higginson even, were desperate to find. And he needed to score points somehow if he was ever to get his job back.

'Thanks for helping us in.' He forced himself to hold out his hand. 'I'm Ewan; Ewan Moore.'

'Dillon; Will.' Will shook the proffered hand and Ewan saw no sign that he had been recognised.

'Yeah, thanks, Mr Dillon. Thanks very much,' said the guy with a bullet in his leg. 'I'm Pat.'

Will shook his hand. 'You're welcome, Pat,' he said.

'Let's get you down to the First Aid room.' Ewan was wondering how best to further this relationship with Dillon and learn his movements.

Another shell whistled past, this time at roof height. Instinctively, the men inside ducked back from the doorway but they both saw it skim past the flagpole, the tricolour flapping wildly in its wake. A fraction to the right and it would have snapped the staff clean in two as it continued on towards Henry Street. As it was, after the merest touch as it sped past, the pole fractured and started to topple. Two men, heedless of their own safety, grabbed it and found a splint to lash on to hold it upright. The tricolour was destined to remain flying throughout the Rising.

* * *

Will was pleased that Ewan did not seem to remember him. They had last met in very different circumstances so it wasn't surprising. He was still well aware that his personal mission was yet to be completed, although getting to grips with Higginson would probably have to wait until all this shenanigans was over. However, it could be helpful to cultivate his new acquaintance. He might prove a useful link later on.

'Can't be much fun up there on the roof,' he said as they sat Pat on a chair next to where one of the nurses was patching up another gunshot wound to a man's hand.

'It's no picnic,' said Pat. 'Under constant fire. The British are slowly advancing this way. They seem to have Abbey Street all sealed off.'

'And machine guns, murderous contraptions' said Ewan. 'They have them mounted all over: north of us in the tower of the Rotunda Hospital, east at Amiens Street Station tower and on the Castle to the south. Anywhere there's a high vantage point. They can rake the streets, but they're able to pin us down on the roof, too. We've got to keep below the parapet.'

'It can't be easy.'

'Indeed it's not. So what's your role, Will? '

'Me? Oh I'm only a message boy. I've got to take some dispatches from Connolly to the other republican strongholds and report back.'

‘I hope you’re not planning on going out there just yet,’ said the nearby nurse. Then her patient spoke up:

‘It’s hell out there. They’ve really stepped up the shooting. Before I got this they’d started launching shells at us, too.’

‘Aye, we heard those, right enough,’ said Will, ‘But I’m due to see Connolly now and he’ll expect me to be off straight away.’

‘I doubt if he will. I’m not the only recent casualty,’ said the wounded man indicating with his good hand four others receiving the ministrations of the women with red crosses on their aprons. ‘He’ll have been appraised of the change in circumstances. You’ll be stuck here for a while, I’d say, and I’d not be ungrateful for that, if I was you.’

Ungrateful or not, Will needed to get away if he was ever to report to the British on conditions inside the GPO.

* * *

The predictions of the man shot in the hand proved to be correct, however. Heavy shelling, once started, continued relentlessly. Rifle and machine gun fire never let up. Further sorties that afternoon were deemed to be much too dangerous.

Will tried to persuade Connolly that he could sneak out the back and down the alley, but random shells were exploding all around the GPO district and Connolly wouldn’t hear of it. Nor, given Dillon’s recent concussion, would he allow him to make his way out as soon as darkness fell.

‘I don’t want you going the whole night without any sleep. You’re not fully fit again yet.’

Will told Maeve what Connolly had said as they chatted in the canteen over some bread and butter for their tea. She said, ‘And quite right, too. If you’ve got to go out there, go after a good night’s rest.’

‘Good advice, Will,’ said Ewan, who had wandered over with a cup of tea in his hand and joined them.

‘Aye, I dare say. But I’ll slip out at first light and try to get round the back streets to the Four Courts. If I can get over the Liffey, there’s the Mendicity and I’ll see if I can make contact with the South Dublin Union. Then into the centre to check if there’s any action still going on at City Hall and the College of Surgeons and Boland’s Mill, if I can make it out there. Connolly wants me to leave the Jacob’s factory to last.’

‘Why’s that, I wonder,’ said Ewan.

‘Och, he’ll have his reasons, I dare say.’ Will had got the impression that he might be asking – or ordering – some troops to transfer to the Post Office but he wasn’t about to discuss that with anyone else. Connolly hadn’t said it in so many words but earlier he had speculated on the need to protect Dillon on his journey back with the answering dispatches. Perhaps that was why he suggested leaving Jacob’s to the end.

Sleep was hard to come by that night. Will found a space in the main concourse of the Post Office propped up against one of the island writing desks. Maeve joined him later and they snuggled together to try to keep warm. Dozens more were lying on the floor all around them, exhausted from constantly being on the alert and not having had much sleep on Monday or Tuesday nights. Others, who were still on duty were continually passing to and fro and gunshots still shattered the night both from without and within. The smell of sulphur and burnt charcoal was ever-present mixed with the unsavoury odours of unwashed individuals.

In spite of all this, Maeve was so weary with fatigue that she dropped off quickly, her head resting against Will’s shoulder. He lay with his eyes closed but sleep eluded him. The feel of the contours of her body against him was comforting and he remembered the wonderful night of bliss they had shared on Sunday. Will we ever have another, he thought? Survival in this crazy war isnae guaranteed. There’s already many a loyal Irishmen who willingly joined in the Rising who willnae be enjoying the touch of a loved one again.

It is a sweet and beautiful thing to die for one’s country. Who said that? Somebody who spoke Latin, wasn’t it? Whoever he was, he was an idiot. There’s nothing sweet and beautiful about having your eye shot out, or your head blown off, or having to have a leg amputated, or an arm. Having your skull bashed by the stock of a rifle is no joke either. Will touched his bruised temple with gentle fingers. His headache was almost gone, he realised, and the swelling, too.

His right arm, which was wrapped around Maeve, went to sleep before the rest of him, but a few hours before dawn he finally drifted off.

Will had arranged to be wakened at first light on Thursday morning and it was Ryan, who was on early shift, who gently shook him awake and put a mug of sweet tea in his hand.

'Five more wounded overnight,' was his grim greeting; 'and we've had structural damage from the shelling. Things are looking none too good.'

Maeve stirred and opened her eyes. 'Do be careful, Will. I wish you weren't going out there.'

'Isn't it in this place people are getting injured? The sooner I'm out of here the better.' Will made light of his mission.

James Connolly, himself, strode up and proffered his hand.

'God go with you, Dillon, and bring you safely back to me.'

Will shook his hand and then Ryan's, who wished him luck.

He turned to Maeve a little awkwardly and was about to hold out his right hand when she stifled a sob and flung her arms around him. She tilted her head and her lips found his for a passionate kiss. When they came up for air, Will was amused to see that Connolly had turned aside and found something very urgent he needed to discuss with Captain Doloughan.

'Right. I'll be off then,' he said.

'Come with me,' Connolly motioned him to follow. 'I'll show you the tunnel we have made. It will be a little safer than going out into Sackville Street or Prince's Street.'

Maeve was due a stint in the First Aid room and Ryan had to head up to the roof, so they waved goodbye. Will trekked after Connolly down to the basement and through its maze of corridors until they came to a couple of sentries guarding the newly hewn passageway through the foundations. Connolly gave the password, although the soldiers had already stood to attention at his approach, and he and Will bent their heads to negotiate the tunnel.

It came out in the basement of a shop in Henry Street. On climbing the steps to the ground floor, Will found himself in a hardware store full of tools of every description. He saw that a hole had been knocked in the wall to allow access to the next building. There were a number of men stationed here to hold the buildings and protect the covert access to the Post Office.

'What's it like out there?' Connolly asked.

'The British have a barricade further up Henry Street. Cross over and up Moore Street's your best bet. We can give some covering fire while you sprint across.'

Will peered out the door and in the dim, pre-dawn light he could just make out in the distance a number of carts pulled across the road and lots of other bits and pieces piled up to form a barrier. Everything was quiet, so he was all the more startled to hear a sharp report and a bullet shrieking as it ricocheted away off the wall behind him.

'Blimey! Their snipers are up early.' Will ducked back inside.

'That's why you need the fire cover. Are you ready? To your posts, men.' Their sergeant stood nearby behind Connolly. Will was in the doorway poised to make a dash. 'Ready! Fire at random!'

Will ran out into the road and heard shooting all around him. From the rebels? From the army? He couldn't tell. He kept on sprinting. He heard a stifled yelp as he flung himself into Moore Street and pulled up behind the protection of the corner building. A quick mental check confirmed that he had sprung no leaks on the way across. He looked back and was horrified to see Connolly half slumped in the arms of the sergeant being pulled back inside. He must have leaned out to have a better line of fire and taken a bullet for his pains.

The pounding in Will's chest intensified. That could so easily have been him. But how badly hurt is Connolly? No way to find out. Hopefully not bad. Will turned and hurried along Moore Street.

He slipped into an alley on the left, anxious not to remain on open roads any more than he had to. The alley ended in a T and he turned right and kept on making his way north and west until he came out on Parnell Street. He tried to appear casual as he glanced up to his half right at the tower on top of the Rotunda Hospital, visible over the rooftops of the intervening buildings. It was now a British machine gun turret, according to Ewan Moore, who had also told him that when the Rotunda was built in 1745 it was the first maternity hospital in the world. He shuddered at the use to which it was now being put as he crossed the street into the protective cover of the buildings there and headed west. For the first time since leaving the GPO he began to feel like a normal citizen making an early start on his way to work.

Except for the sounds of gunfire and artillery.

With full light the sporadic shooting had intensified. At first it was mostly coming from Dillon's rear, as he walked westward leaving the GPO and the fighting in Sackville Street behind. But the more ground he covered, the more he was picking up the sound of battle ahead. On his circuitous, backroads route to the Four Courts he was making his way through the side streets up to North King Street where Commandant Ned Daly was defending a well-barricaded position after successfully raiding the Linenhall barracks.

Dillon turned out of a narrow alley into a street that led in the direction of the firing. He had only gone a few paces when two uniformed soldiers stepped out from a doorway and levelled their British army issue Lee-Enfields at him.

* * *

Colonel Taylor of the South Staffordshire Regiment had taken two days to advance 150 yards in his attempt to overthrow the rebels' strongholds in the North King Street area. It had cost him eleven men with 28 more, wounded. So he had been obliged to use civilian property as cover knocking his way through adjoining walls in the houses to advance along the street. The fact that some 15 innocent men and boys living in the area had been killed, some by bayonet was regrettable but acceptable.

The colonel was eagerly awaiting the arrival of the first "armoured" vehicles to be used in Ireland. He had high hopes they would swing the battle his way. As soon as they arrived the final assault would commence.

In the meantime British Tommies were posted all around the area ostensibly to ensure no rebel reinforcements could get through, but in effect halting everyone they came across – mostly civilians – and making sure they kept out of the way using whatever force might prove necessary.

* * *

Behind the barricades, the troops under Ned Daly's command – the 1st Battalion, Dublin Volunteers – were fulfilling a similar role keeping civilians away from the fighting. The two pointing their captured British rifles at Will Dillon were surprised when he handed them his pass and asked to be taken to their CO.

They knew the name of James Connolly, of course, but had no idea whether the signature was genuine.

'Stay here,' said the one with a corporal's stripe. 'I'll check this out. Guard him,' he ordered the private, spinning on his heel and marching off.

'I'll keep my pass, thank you!' Dillon called after him but the man didn't even turn round. There was nothing for it but to wait as ordered.

The wait grew from five minutes to ten, to twenty. Dillon was sorely tempted to pull out his revolver and disarm the private; or he could probably have done it quite easily without his gun but if he absconded now he wouldn't get his pass back and he needed that. So he continued to wait.

45 minutes...

50 minutes... and at last the corporal appeared at the top of the side street with another soldier and marched back to where Dillon was now sitting on the pavement, his back against a wall.

'You two, resume sentry duty. You,' he addressed Dillon, 'come with me.'

Will stood. 'My pass, if you please?' He held out his hand.

The corporal hesitated and then fished the pass out of his pocket and handed it back.

Will was taken by means of more alleyways through to Church Street near its junction with North King Street. They emerged from a narrow lane between two houses and the corporal, pointing to a figure up ahead, said:

'There's Commandant Daly. Follow me.'

Just then they heard a fusillade of shots ring out up at the cross-roads. Will saw Ned Daly rush to join a crowd of Volunteers surging forward along King Street.

'You better stay back for the moment,' shouted the corporal as he rushed up the road to join the fray.

Will followed at a more cautious pace and remained by the cover of a plane tree growing near the junction. It was hard to see exactly what was going on but it was clear from the urgency of the rebels' shooting that they must be trying to repel an attack by the British.

Dillon glanced up to the branches above him and on an impulse grabbed a low one and hauled himself up into the tree. Now he could see over the tops of the insurgents. He saw their barricade spanning the road. A couple of overturned motorcars and several carts were backed up with dust bins, an old sofa and sundry other pieces of furniture and mattresses. Men were taking cover behind the barrier, shooting through it where they could, or over it when they had to, and ducking down as British bullets whistled back at them.

Will could see the 'enemy' troops taking cover, themselves, in open doorways all along North King Street. One of the houses was on fire and smoke billowed across the road which was clear of soldiers as it provided no cover. From where he was perched in the tree Will's view was of the far side of the street only but, judging by the shooting, there were more troops making their way down the near side, too. It was a slow process, though, and the rebels were holding their position.

A new sound caused Will to raise his gaze further up the road where two trucks had driven out onto North King Street. As they approached he saw they both bore the Guinness name on their cabs. What looked to Will like giant boilers had been bolted onto their flatbeds. Slit windows cut in the sides allowed rifle muzzles to protrude. Will reckoned there could be a dozen or more soldiers in each truck, all able to fire their guns with impunity. The cabs had sheet metal reinforcement around them and bullets pinged off this as the rebels' attempts to stop their progress proved futile. Will watched the relentless advance of these, presumably, commandeered and hastily adapted vehicles. They approached the barricade. It became obvious that they didn't intend to stop. With shouts of fear and anger the rebels scattered. The leading truck struck one of the upturned carts and swept it aside. It continued to plough through the rest of the obstructions while a hail of bullets from its slit windows on both sides rained on the fleeing insurgents.

The second truck followed, causing further damage to the barricade and inflicting more devastation with its firepower. Behind it the British troops came flooding out of their doorways and, using the trucks as cover, followed up on the advantage they had now gained.

It was a rout. The British had split the rebel forces. Will could see some of the insurgents running to the north, while others who had been manning the south end of the barrier were fleeing down the road under his tree. Ned Daly was among these.

Separated from half his troops, he rallied those around him into an orderly retreat. They fired at the pursuing English soldiers while they backed down the road running from cover to cover in doorways. Will reckoned Daly's intention must be to fight his way back to his colleagues who were holding the Four Courts.

Below him, the street was now full of British soldiers pursuing their quarry. Right at the base of his tree a young private suddenly spun round and fell. He lay on his back and moaned. Will could see blood staining the breast of his tunic.

He could also see the man's eyes – staring straight up into his.

Chapter 28

Ewan Moore sneaked up the stairs in the GPO and carefully turned the handle of the door to the telecommunications room. It was mid-morning and many of the Volunteers who had been up since the small hours were having a meal break, which was what Moore was supposed to be doing. Instead he was taking this first opportunity to try to contact Buster Gregson and win back his place in the team.

The communications room was deserted, as he had hoped it would be. He slipped in and closed the door behind him. He was relieved to find that the lines were still live as he dialled his boss's number.

* * *

'Up there! There's one of them!' The wounded soldier managed to lift an arm and point up to where Dillon was concealed by the fresh green foliage.

Two of the man's comrades had come to his aid and they followed the direction of his pointing finger. One of them immediately trained his rifle up into the tree.

'You there! Come down, and don't try anything funny.'

Dillon had no alternative but to comply. He shinned down the trunk and addressed the man with the rifle, 'You can put that down, for a start; I'm on your side.'

'Yeah? And you can pull the other one. You're another *Sinn Féiner*. Hoping we wouldn't spot you hiding up there.'

'No I wasnae, I was about to come down, myself, so I was, when your man, here, spotted me. I was waiting until you'd chased the last of the rebels off. I need to see your CO without delay.'

A sergeant had come over. 'Keep him covered, Morton,' he said to the rifleman, and to Dillon, 'Who are you and what's your business with Colonel Taylor?'

'That's between me and the colonel. Just mention *Abbey Players*; he'll see me.

'You've come into a battle zone to invite him to the theatre!' Added to Dillon's unorthodox entrance upon the scene, the sergeant probably thought he was dealing with a lunatic.

'Say those words and tell him I'd be obliged if he'll see me.' Will was banking on this Col. Taylor having been briefed with the code words.

The sergeant told one of the other two to get a medic over here and said to the second, 'Tie this man's wrists. And search him for weapons.'

'There's no need for that,' said Dillon, 'haven't I told you, I'm here to see the colonel.'

'That remains to be seen.'

Dillon was forced to submit to having his hands tied behind his back and a quick frisking soon had his revolver and spare ammunition confiscated.

'Carrying concealed weapons,' said the sergeant, 'Right. Take him up to the cross-roads and put him with the other prisoners.'

'It wasn't "concealed," it was in my pocket. You don't expect me to be wandering around the streets of Dublin unarmed, now, do you?' Dillon was glad that his pass signed by Connolly was out of sight in an inside pocket.

'I don't expect you to be wandering around the streets of Dublin at all – unless you're a *Sinn Féiner*.'

Dillon said, 'Please tell the colonel I wish to see him, and mention *Abbey Players*.'

'If I see him, I'll tell him.'

'If! The matter is urgent, Sergeant.'

'All right, when.'

And Will had to be satisfied with that. He was marched off with the private's rifle barrel in his back and his bonds biting into his flesh, to be corralled into a holding area the troops had made using parts of the demolished barricade. Will slumped in a corner away from the main group of captured rebels and tilted his head forwards so the peak of his cap concealed his eyes. It would take an unlikely coincidence but he didn't want to risk being recognised by a captured rebel soldier who may have taken part in his unarmed combat classes.

Six British soldiers all armed with rifles with fixed bayonets stood guard over the prisoners and Will could see no obvious means of escape for the present. A full hour ticked by and he was thinking that he would have to try to get away somehow. He stood to his feet to stretch his legs and get the circulation going again, still with no definite plan of action.

As he stood, he saw the sergeant who had captured him. He was coming in the prisoners' direction and stopped to have a word with one of the armed guards. The soldier looked towards him and signalled him to accompany the sergeant who produced a lethal-looking knife. He stepped behind him and cut through Dillon's restraints.

'Follow me,' he said, with no apologies or explanations.

It turned out Colonel Taylor did know the significance of "Abbey Players," and welcomed Dillon into his temporary new headquarters in a house not far from the breached barricade. He explained that his delay in sending for Dillon was down to everything that he had to sort out after his success in breaking through the rebels' lines with his new and devastating armoured vehicles. He hoped Dillon had been well looked after while he was waiting.

'Ah, your men took great care of me, so they did,' said Dillon, rubbing his wrists.

'And what can I do for you?' asked the colonel.

Dillon proceeded to pass on all that he knew of the rebels situation at the GPO and the various outposts along Sackville Street and the surroundings. How and when he would have been able to do this had been exercising his mind right up until his hiding place in the plane tree had suddenly come to be behind "enemy" lines. He had thought he might be able to revisit the Shelbourne Hotel after delivering most of his dispatches so he could report, too, on how the various rebel-held positions were faring, but his most important information related to the GPO and he was relieved to have passed that on. The colonel thanked him for the intelligence that he assured him would be relayed to HQ by dispatch rider without delay.

'Now that we've broken through here we shall soon have a cordon around the whole of the north side from Parkgate Street to the North

Wall. Other infantry brigades are doing the same south of the river from Kingsbridge to Ringsend.'

'So yous'll have the republicans completely surrounded,' said Dillon.

'We will. Practically have already. Then it's just a matter of closing in on the General Post Office. Every last man of them – and woman, from what you tell me – will be arrested and spend the rest of their rotten lives in jail where they belong; those that aren't shot for treason.'

'May they all get what they deserve, by the grace of God,' said Will, aware that his prayer for the misguided but well-intentioned rebels may not have the meaning that the good Colonel understood from it as the military gentleman added a profound, 'Amen.'

Dillon then explained that to preserve his cover he needed to get to the Four Courts and Colonel Taylor provided him with an escort through to their new front lines just north of those premises. From there he made his way west and turned south into Church Street and as soon as he could he got into the grounds of the Four Courts to his left and sprinted to a side entrance and out of sight of any snipers on the roof.

He banged on the door and waited a few seconds before banging again. He had no idea whether any of the rebels holding the building would be within earshot but he kept on rapping on the door and eventually heard footsteps approaching from the inside.

'Who's there?' came a voice.

'My name's Dillon. I have a dispatch from James Connolly for Commandant Daly.'

'Have you some form of identification?'

'I have.'

Will heard stiff bolts sliding back and the heavy door opened a crack.

'Let me see.'

Will handed over his pass and after a moment or two the door opened further and he was ushered inside.

'Dillon! My dear man, I'm glad to see you're alive. The sergeant told me you were looking for me. You must have witnessed that debacle up by the Linenhall Barracks.'

'I did. I was on my way to see you, Mr Daly, when those mighty Guinness trucks crashed through your barricade.'

'Damned unfair that. How are we supposed to fight back if their men are shooting at us from inside a bloody oil tank? Cowardly tactics. That's the British all over. Can't trust them to fight fair.'

Will commiserated with the beleaguered commandant and explained his long delay in reaching the Four Courts by saying he'd had no choice but to flee in a different direction entirely and spend a long time making his way by a circuitous route back round to the Courts buildings.

'I hoped I'd find you here. It's good to see you made it back safely, yourself, Mr Daly,' he said.

'Call me Ned. Please.'

'Aye, right you are. I'm Will.'

'Well, I'm pleased to meet you, Will. Pleased we're both still alive. I made it back here with about half my men. The others were cut off by the British on the north side of King Street. I hope they managed to get away.'

'I hope so,' said Dillon, envisaging again the dispirited bunch of Volunteers huddled in the makeshift prison by the barricade.

He gave Daly the dispatch from Connolly and the commandant suggested Will should join his men in the mess hall and get some lunch while he was reading it and writing his response. So it wasn't much before two o'clock in the afternoon when Dillon was again preparing to brave the streets of Dublin.

Daly had told him that the men in the Mendicity across the river had held out courageously for two days but had eventually been forced to surrender. So Will wouldn't be including that venue on his whistle-stop tour of the rebel strongholds. But he needed to get down to the South Dublin Union in the Rialto district. That was south-west of the Mendicity.

Ned's advice was to stay north of the Liffey as far as Kingsbridge where it should be safer to cross, rather than risk sniper fire on a bridge closer to the centre. So Will found himself once again walking along Arran Quay and on to Albert Quay, retracing the journey he had made in the opposite direction exactly a fortnight before on his way home from the ceilidh.

During that late evening stroll the only sounds had been the lapping of the water against the moored barges and the occasional disturbed duck. Now, as his stride quickened along the riverside, the predominant sounds were of gunfire and heavy artillery, mostly behind him from the direction of O'Connell Bridge. The regular crump from the shells was more frequent than Will remembered from earlier; he fervently hoped Maeve and the rest were still safe. His thoughts turned to the last time he had walked on this quay. It seemed as though it was in a different lifetime. Had it really only been two weeks since he met Maeve? Ryan's pretty little sister. Beautiful, he had come to consider her, but so much more. Intelligent, determined, brave, thoughtful, loving, caring. She's soft and yielding, he thought, but strong and strong-willed, as well. He marvelled at how she could have overwhelmed his heart in just a few short days.

Another shell exploded somewhere closer, pulling Will back to the realities of the present. And he wondered how the Empire's second city could have come to this – blowing herself apart and murdering her own citizens, all in the space of the same few short days.

* * *

The South Dublin Union was a large complex of buildings on a fifty acre site with plenty of open space, but it included the city workhouse, a hospital and infirmary, a bakery, staff living quarters, churches and a morgue all connected by a maze of narrow streets and alleyways. The place was home to over 3,200 people, including patients, doctors, nurses and ancillary staff. Commandant Éamonn Ceannt and Vice Commandant Cathal Brugha, heading the 4th Battalion of the Irish Volunteers, took over the Union on Easter Monday and came under severe attack from soldiers of the Royal Irish Regiment. There were running battles through the corridors of the hospital and in the grounds, resulting in many casualties on both sides and including innocent patients and staff, too, caught in the cross-fire.

The rebels retreated to the Nurses' Home, a substantial, stone-built edifice which they fortified with barricades and made virtually impregnable. They hoisted the green Republican flag and made it their HQ.

The British had still not managed to dislodge them by Thursday when a column of Sherwood Foresters, many of whom had seen battle the day before at Mount Street Bridge, were escorting a consignment of ammunition to the Military Headquarters at the Royal Hospital in Kilmainham. At a quarter past two, Lieutenant Colonel Oates, leading their advance guard, came under intense sniper fire from the Union as he tried to cross a nearby canal bridge *en route* to his destination. He pulled back and his troops took cover as he considered what was to be done.

* * *

It was after two by the time Will Dillon reached the arched vehicle entrance on James's Street that led through the front of the workhouse and into the Union complex. He soon saw evidence of fighting – pock-marked walls where bullets had hit, broken windows, damaged doors, railings knocked flat – but all was quiet at the moment. He advanced, unchallenged by any of the men in white coats that he passed or young women hurrying about their duties; doctors and nurses fulfilling their obligations regardless of the trauma surrounding them.

A group of nurses emerged from a building up ahead on his right and he turned towards it, giving his best smile to a rather pretty young woman with blonde hair who blushed as he passed. He heard giggles behind him as he opened the door they had used moments earlier. It was marked "Infirmary".

He glanced along a corridor and saw doors leading off on both sides. He tried the first two or three before finding what he was looking for at his fourth attempt – a lavatory and cloakroom. A number of white coats hung on pegs. Will chose a large size and slipped it on over his coat before making his way back out of the building.

He was wondering what had happened to Éamonn Ceannt and his Volunteers when he turned a corner and spotted the green republican flag on a large stone building. He strode towards it, purposefully but not hurried, hoping that his "disguise" would protect him from any trigger happy, shoot-now-ask-questions-later Volunteer.

He reached the main entrance without incident and knocked loudly. He waited, as he had done at the Four Courts, wondering if anyone would hear him. He banged with his fist again and was about to continue when he heard what sounded like boots on a stair case. He then had to go through the whole Who's-there-and-handing-over-his-pass routine again before he was admitted by none other than Cathal Brugha, whom he had met at one of his unarmed combat sessions.

'Dillon!' the man grasped his hand. 'What brings you here? And when did you become a doctor?' he added, with a grin.

Will helped to bar the door again and looked around. The windows, too, were barricaded and an archway opposite was blocked, almost to the top of the arch, by a substantial barrier of bedsteads, mattresses, office furniture and sandbags. A staircase led up to a half landing that was also barricaded. Will could see gunmen in position, covering the entrance. Brugha led the way up the stairs and they made their way through the barricade and on up to the second floor. They passed a sickbay where Will saw that some Union nurses had been coerced into attending the wounded. Commandant Ceannt's top-floor HQ was right next door.

Will was handing over Connolly's dispatch when there was shout from a Volunteer by the window:

Ceannt swung round. 'What is it, Cosgrave?'

'Soldiers, sir! Hundreds of them coming across the green.'

A sergeant yelled, 'Battle stations! Fire at random.'

A fusillade of shots rang out and, through the window, Will saw a number of British soldiers fall dead or wounded. The rest continued to advance in the face of further volleys from the rebels and sustained additional losses. Then a machine gun opened up to their rear, firing shots at an angle through the windows of the Nurses' Home that forced the Volunteer riflemen to take cover. From the trajectories, the Commandant told Dillon, it must be positioned on the roof of the Royal Hospital, beyond the canal.

This knowledge was of little comfort to Will who was doing his best to keep out of the way of the Volunteers but more so, of the incoming bullets. With a full-on attack by the British, he was wondering how he was ever going to get out of the rebels' HQ to deliver his remaining dispatches, much less get back to the GPO, which he knew he must. The British Colonel Taylor's prediction about the fate of the embattled insurgents there was not a vain threat. Will knew it was inevitable and he had to get Maeve out before it was too late.

Chapter 29

In order to get across the canal, the strategy Lieutenant Colonel Oates had decided upon was to detach 100 of his men to occupy as much of the Union as they could and hold the rebels full attention while the rest of his troops negotiated the bridge and got the consignment of ammunition across. Under the joint command of his son, Captain John Oates and Captain Micky Martin the British troops spotted the republican flag which gave away the rebels' position but soon realised that a frontal assault on the building was not going to work.

While the bulk of the Sherwood Foresters kept up fire on the Volunteers' HQ from the cover of a building opposite, Captains Martin and Oates led a small band through an adjacent building and used a coal pick to hack a way through the adjoining wall to the Nurses' Home. The sound of their labours was masked by the noise of the battle, but the first man through the hole they created was shot dead. They lobbed in a grenade and in the immediate aftermath of the explosion Martin crawled through and found himself in the lobby with the barred front door on his right and the barricaded archway on his left. A satchel of hand grenades was passed through the hole in the wall and as other troops followed, Martin lobbed a grenade over the barricade onto the stairs – just as an Irish officer was descending.

* * *

At the sound of gunshots from the lobby, Commandant Ceannt rushed down to the first floor landing. Dillon followed and saw that Cathal

Brugha was there ahead of them. Below, in the lobby a number of British troops were taking cover and firing up the stairs.

Brugha, brandishing his automatic, yelled, 'Let's get the bastards!' He negotiated the barricade and started down the stairs.

'Wait!' Dillon shouted. He'd spotted a British officer pulling the pin of a grenade and lobbing it onto the staircase.

His warning was too late. The explosion lacerated Brugha's body and even as he fell, he took a bullet from the same British officer's pistol. His comrades could only watch as Cathal crawled round the foot of the stairs and into the cover of a small kitchen. They heard him firing wildly through the barricade pinning down the British. More grenades were thrown by the British and the rebels dropped canister bombs down to the lobby in return. Each explosion rocked the building and threatened to bring the ceiling down on attackers and defenders, alike. Smoke, dust and the acrid smell of gunpowder filled the air.

It wasn't long before they saw the British start to withdraw back through the hole they had made. Between the bombs and Brugha's valiant pistol fire they had had enough.

* * *

Lieutenant Colonel Oates got a message back to his son in the Union to say that the main body of Foresters had crossed the canal without further losses and congratulated him and his men for distracting the insurgents and achieving their objective. His orders were for them to continue their assault until evening.

* * *

Will hung, suspended midway between a first floor window and the ground beneath. And then he was falling.

Earlier, Cathal Brugha had been made as comfortable as his catastrophic injuries could allow and Éamonn Ceannt finally had some time to read Connolly's dispatch and formulate a reply. His men continued to return the relentless fire from their attackers.

It was clear Will could not leave the way he had come in, which was why he'd come up with the suggestion that he should be lowered down from a window on the far side of the building, all the ground floor windows being barricaded. Ceannt and Cosgrave held his hands and lowered him as far as they could reach before releasing their grip. Will relaxed his limbs and rolled as he touched the ground. He sprang to his feet and hurried towards the corner of the building. The machine gun on the hospital roof opened up again. Bullets thudded into the wall behind him as he flung himself round the corner and out of its line of fire.

He could hear the shooting from the other side of the Nurses' Home and made his way cautiously to the front corner. Not surprisingly, doctors in white coats were conspicuous by their absence. Will stepped from his cover and hoped that his own 'doctor's' garb would serve its purpose. He could have sprinted the thirty yards or so to the alley between two buildings where he was heading, but there was no guarantee that such an action would not draw down heavy fire from the British soldiers.

His heart was pounding as he walked briskly across the open ground. Firing continued but as far as he could tell none of it was coming his way. Nevertheless, it was with the utmost relief that he entered the safety of the alley and started to make his way back through the labyrinth of little roads towards the exit to James's Street. His heart rate was approaching something like normality as he dumped the white coat in a dust bin and went out through the arch.

* * *

Already south of the Liffey, Dillon chose a route that avoided main roads until he approached the vicinity of Dublin Castle. Two things surprised him on his journey. One was the number of ordinary citizens still on the streets going about their normal business. The other was the pall of black smoke low in the sky north of the river in the neighbourhood of Sackville Street. The crumps as each high explosive shell was fired had been growing louder the further east he walked. Will was imagining the devastation they must be causing. He thought about the sturdiness of the Post Office's construction. Can it withstand this sustained shelling, though? It must. It has to. Oh please, may Maeve and the others be safe.

His mind in torment, Will skirted the castle from the south and noticed British soldiers guarding the entrances with more standing sentry outside City Hall and a number of other buildings in the area. No more rebel activity here, then, Will said to himself, carrying on in the direction of Trinity College.

He had walked quite a few miles throughout the day and time was getting on. He decided he had better pick up his bicycle if it was still there in order to visit the remaining strongholds that Connolly was anxious to hear from. There was still the College of Surgeons, Boland's Mill and Jacob's Biscuit Factory.

There was a lot of military presence in Westmoreland Street near the entrance to the college. Will saw a puff of white smoke rising from a cannon and heard a loud detonation as it rocked back on its big cartwheels. A second or so later he heard an even louder explosion followed by the sound of tumbling masonry across the river. What are they doing to old Dublin town? Will turned away to seek access to Trinity by a side entry.

He entered where some students were emerging and strolled across the quadrangle unchallenged until he drew close to the buildings at the far side near the bicycle racks. He thought he could see his own bike still where he left it. Another group of undergraduates in their gowns and mortarboards were approaching a little way off and a soldier on guard duty by an imposing doorway was watching them as Dillon strode past.

'You! Halt.'

Dillon turned and saw that the soldier now had his rifle aimed squarely at his chest.

'You're not a student. State your business,' said the soldier.

Dillon gave his most disarming smile and said, 'Just picking up my bicycle and I'll be on my way.'

But the rifle remained in business mode. 'The college is no longer open to the public. Turn around and go out the way you came in.'

'Abbey Players,' said Will.

'I don't care if you're Marie bloody Lloyd. Out. Now!' The soldier cocked his rifle.

'Hey, Tommy, leave him alone. He's all right.'

Without moving his rifle the soldier glanced over at the bunch of students who had now drawn level.

'You know us,' said the one who had spoken before. 'We're on your side. So's this chap. Nothing to worry about.'

The soldier looked doubtful, but he was now surrounded by seven or eight hefty students and whatever valour he may have possessed soon gave way to discretion. He lowered his weapon.

'Much obliged, young man,' said Will. 'I guess that makes us even.'

The student replied, 'You're more than welcome, sir. I could have had a nasty beating yesterday morning in that café, but for you.'

'Well, thanks for showing up when you did,' said Will, taking his bicycle from the rack. 'Hope it goes well with yous, when we see an end to all this nonsense.' He rode off back across the quadrangle.

The ride out to Boland's Mill was uneventful. There were plenty of other cyclists around, no doubt due to the trams not running. Dillon's pass got him in to see Éamon de Valera who peered at Connolly's message through his wire-framed spectacles and provided Will with his response right away. The ride back to the city centre was equally uneventful but he anticipated getting into the College of Surgeons would prove difficult.

And so it did. The sporadic, but nevertheless insistent firing on the front of the rebel stronghold, with occasional bursts of machine gun fire, made a direct approach foolhardy in the extreme. Dillon rode around to the back and saw that even though there was some firing on this side, too, there were a few pedestrians risking being out there. Most hurried past the College building on the other side of the road.

Dillon left his bicycle against some railings and walked, on the near side, towards the College. A young woman up ahead, struggling a bit with a bundle she carried in front of her, stepped off the kerb and started to cross as though she might be going to the Royal College of Surgeons. Dillon was still a little way off when she appeared to trip and fall forwards, face down on the road. She lost hold of her bundle, which fell in front of her.

Only vaguely could Will recall hearing the gunshot, but there was no mistaking the bright red stain showing on the woman's back. Other passers-by rushed to her aid. As Will drew level someone was retrieving the bundle. He saw the tiny pink face first, and then the scarlet patch spreading on the shawl. One bullet, two lives; extinguished.

Sickened, Will forced himself to take advantage of the lull in firing caused by this atrocity and entered the cover of a back porch of the college.

When he came out again with Michael Mallin's reply the bodies were gone; only the dark stains on the tarmacadam remained, like some macabre map of a pair of desert islands in a slate-grey sea.

Will collected his bicycle from the end of the street and debated whether he should try to pay a visit to the Shelbourne to update the

British with what he had learned throughout the day. It was nearly six o'clock, however, and on reflection he decided there was little he could pass on that would be of much use. To the north, the bases of the black plumes of smoke were tinged with orange. Fires must be raging on Sackville Street. Will turned his cycle and headed west, in the failing light, to his last port of call.

Gaining access to the Jacob's Biscuit Factory was the easiest of the day. There was no firing in the vicinity when Dillon arrived and the few citizens hanging around or passing by did not seem to be unduly concerned for their own safety. Will produced his pass and was taken straight inside where he was seen by a military-looking gentleman.

'Major John McBride,' he said holding out his hand to Dillon. 'What can I do for you?'

Will recognised the name. As he shook his hand he was recalling some things that Willie Yeats said about him that were none too complimentary. Irish, and an ex-British army officer who fought in the Boar War, this was the man who had married Maud Gonne, W B Yeats' muse and the love of his life.

'Will Dillon, sir. I carry a dispatch from James Connolly at the GPO, which I must deliver to Commandant MacDonagh, personally.'

'Of course. Wait here and I'll tell him you have arrived.' The Major left the room and Will leaned back against a heavy table that took up a good third of the room space.

He didn't have long to wait. The door opened and Thomas MacDonagh entered. This earnest young man was another who remembered Dillon's combat lessons and greeted him with a warm handshake.

'Have you eaten, Mr Dillon?' he asked and Will realised that in spite of a lunchtime snack at the Four Courts his day of exertions had made him hungry, and said so. 'I'll send for something as we talk. You do like biscuits?'

Will gave a polite laugh, unsure if MacDonagh was joking or not. But he needn't have worried.

'We've kept on a few of the Jacob's employees who know the run of the place. One of them knows his way around the kitchen pretty well. Food's getting a bit short, but he should be able to rustle up some scrambled eggs and bacon. Would that suit?'

'That would suit just fine. Thanks,' said Will.

'Talks like you do, too,' said MacDonagh. He issued an order and indicated a chair at the table before sitting down, himself. 'So how is Tom Clarke and Padraig and the boyos? Is old Jo Plunkett still with us?'

Will assured him that he was and that everyone's spirits were high. He sat down, grateful to be able to take the weight of his feet after traipsing across Dublin all day long. They talked some more about conditions at the Post Office and then Will handed MacDonagh the last despatch. He waited as the commandant read what Connolly had written, trying to determine from the man's facial expressions if his suspicions were correct about Connolly asking for reinforcements.

MacDonagh finished the letter and placed it aside as the door behind Will opened. The delicious aroma of fried bacon and coffee wafted in.

'Ah, Maguire, just put the tray on the table here.'

Will glanced up as the man placed the appetising food in front of him. 'Thank–' his heart missed a beat, '– you.' He turned his head away, his mind in a whirl.

Maguire. *Talks like you do, too.* A Jacob's employee. Two years ago, the night of the UVF gun-running, in the telecommunications room at Donaghadee Post Office. Jude Maguire complaining how hard it was becoming to make a living from fishing. Whose brother had already left and got himself a good job with Jacob's in Dublin. "*Sometimes I think I could do worse than go and join him.*" And only a few weeks ago the last harsh words Will had spoken to the man who had so unexpectedly appeared with his supper tray: "*Next time be quicker off the mark. Away off back to your missus with you.*"

Maguire was as stunned as Dillon.

'You!' was all he managed to say as he recognised the man he held solely responsible for the breakup of his pretence of a marriage to Peggy and his forced migration to the South. Addressing MacDonagh, he demanded, 'What's Dillon doing here?'

'He is adjutant to James Connolly. What's the matter with you, man?'

'Well the more fool, Connolly, then. This man is one of the staunchest Loyalists I ever met. He's held in the highest regard in the Orange Order – *and* he played a significant role in arming the UVF.'

Chapter 30

Earlier on that Thursday morning, the First Aid room was quiet when Maeve turned up for duty. She was busying herself with some tidying up when she was surprised to see James Connolly slipping into the room unaccompanied. His face was as white as the nurses' starched aprons, and as rigid.

'Need a bit of patching up,' he said, as he walked a little unsteadily to a chair.

Elizabeth O'Farrell came over at once and called Maeve to assist. They worked well as a team, swiftly, methodically.

'Well,' said Elizabeth, 'the good news is that it's a clean wound – just under your right shoulder. The bad news is, there's no exit wound. The bullet really should be taken out.'

'That can wait,' said Connolly. 'Put a bandage on it. And keep that information to yourself. I want no fuss. There's work to be done.'

'But you're in no fit state to be working.'

'Nonsense, woman. Where's that bandage?'

With his wound thoroughly cleaned and dressed as best they could, Connolly thanked the women and went to consult with Pearse and Clarke on the state of affairs in the Headquarters of the Irish Republic.

Throughout the day the constant shelling continued to take its toll and the building was starting to sustain significant damage. Some shells were of the shrapnel variety, invented in the early nineteenth century by British army officer, Henry Shrapnel, and designed to cause havoc in the open battle field by each discharging hundreds of ball bearings or other metal fragments at bullet speeds into massed columns of troops.

However, when these exploded within the confines of a room in the GPO, their devastation was contained and their damage limited.

Much worse were the HE shells. Their high explosive nature was causing immediate structural damage to the building; anyone within range of the blast was either killed or injured, depending on their proximity. Others were hurt by falling masonry, but perhaps worst of all, the explosion often caused fires to break out that demanded immediate attention. By the afternoon a team of Volunteers was on permanent standby for fire duty.

Connolly remained in command and few realised that he had been badly wounded. It was ill-luck in the extreme that one of the shrapnel shells penetrated the building near to where he was issuing further orders. A number of fragments shattered his shin and ankle and he fell to the floor in agony.

This time there could be no hiding his wound. He could no longer stand. Little could be done apart from binding up his lower leg and giving him aspirin. Reluctantly, he allowed himself to be laid down on the truckle bed where Dillon had recovered from his concussion, but he insisted on its being carried to the nerve centre and, with help from Pearse, he continued to direct operations as best he could.

The GPO was not the only target of the British shelling and whether by pin-point accuracy or indiscriminate inaccuracy – Connolly believed the latter – many other buildings at the southern end of Sackville Street were succumbing to the bombardment. Some had completely collapsed. Many caught fire and many of these became infernos, raging unchecked as the Fire Service would not risk going inside the army barricades. In places the heat was intense. By the late afternoon, silver and gold jewellery in *Hopkins and Hopkins* at the corner of Sackville Street and Eden Quay melted in their window – before the windows, along with the walls, were blown in by the 18-pounders.

* * *

In Jacob's Biscuit Factory MacDonagh was sounding incredulous: 'Is this true, Dillon? You're an Orangeman? And in the UVF?'

Will's right hand shot to his coat pocket, only to find it empty. Then he remembered. His gun had been confiscated in the morning and he'd never got it back. So in response to MacDonagh's question he said, 'Of course it isnae true, what do you think? I know this man; he's from

Donaghadee, same as me. He helps crew the lifeboat sometimes, but the last time we were called out he got there too late and I gave his place to a young lad. I guess he's holding a grudge for loss of pay.'

MacDonagh looked at Jude. 'Maguire?'

'That's got nothing to do with it. I'm telling you the truth. I don't know what he's told you, but he's no republican. He's even cut his hair and trimmed his beard short in the hopes no one would recognise him; it used to be big and bushy.'

'These are serious allegations Dillon, which I'm glad to hear you deny. But it's just your word against his. What am I to do?'

'Ignore the man's blethers. Wasn't I teaching you how to defend yourself against a British soldier only last week?'

'Sure, you were indeed.'

'It's all part of his act,' said Maguire. 'He's a British spy; that's what he is.'

MacDonagh stood. He drew his revolver. 'Look here, I'm sorry, Dillon. If I thought for a minute you really were a spy, I'd shoot you on the spot. But I find it hard to believe this man's allegations.'

'Thank you,' said Dillon.

'They're not allegations; they're the truth.'

'However,' MacDonagh continued, ignoring the interruptions, 'I've got to act upon the information I've been given. It's ironic, actually. Connolly has asked me to give you an escort to see you safely back to the GPO. So that I shall do. But I'm afraid you will have to accompany them as their prisoner. I shall send Connolly a full account of this conversation, including my own feelings on the matter, and he can decide what to do with you.

'Sorry. Best I can do. But take your time. Enjoy the bacon and eggs while I write my dispatch.'

It was getting on for eight o'clock by the time Thomas MacDonagh had prepared his carefully worded message and arranged a detail to escort the prisoner. Rope, binding his wrists behind his back, dug into his flesh for the second time that day as Will left the Jacob's factory. He was flanked by two privates, while a corporal called Kildare walked in front; all three were armed.

Dillon peered around in the dark. There were still a few people hanging about or rushing past, anxious to be home and safe. He was envisaging the route they were likely to be taking down to the River

Liffey and trying to decide the most suitable place for his getaway. He needed a wall on his left where he could lurch sideways into one of the privates and smash his head against the brickwork. With his next step he would slam the heel of his shoe into the small of the corporal's back, probably break his spine. Then he'd come from underneath and ram the top of his head into the other private's jaw before he had time to react with his weapon.

He was thinking that the ideal spot could be just ahead when a shot rang out. The Volunteer on his right stumbled and slumped forward to the pavement. The corporal swung round at once, his rifle raised, but before he could see who he should be aiming at another shot was fired and he, too, fell to the ground. Almost simultaneously a third shot took out the remaining soldier.

At the sound of the first shot, Will dropped to the ground himself and curled up small. If this was a distant sniper he wanted to present as minimal a target as he could; the gunman might even assume he was already dead. But he quickly realised this was small arms fire, close-range, not from high-powered rifles. As the third shot was still ringing in his ears, he felt hands lifting him back onto his feet. He wasn't to be shot, he was being rescued.

Who could be doing this? Who knew where he would be? He'd find out soon enough. The thought uppermost in his mind was the death of the three soldiers had killed off any risk of his unmasking coming to the ears of James Connolly.

He heard the sound of tyres brushing the kerb as a motorcar pulled up behind him and the person helping him to his feet turned him towards it.

It was an open-topped green Crossley and Buster Gregson was holding open the rear passenger door.

Dillon found himself bundled into the back with Gregson beside him holding a pistol in his ribs. He reassessed his position. Not rescued; a change of captors – and these were infinitely worse than the rebel soldiers. But he realised, now, how they knew where he would be. Ewan Moore. He'd shown a great interest in Will's plans. Somehow he'd managed to get word to Gregson, who was now calling out to the bloke who had got him to his feet.

'Will you hurry up and get in the front, Liam.'

The man called Liam slammed the passenger door and Kelly, who was behind the wheel, lost no time in driving away. He took a circuitous route avoiding army road blocks by keeping within the cordon that now ringed the city centre. First he drove west to cross the river upstream and then continued north a little way before swinging east. They eventually turned south and Will recognised Amiens Street Station on their left as they turned west again into Talbot Street. Up ahead and left, the great billows of black smoke at the lower end of Sackville Street were tinged with more streaks of red and orange as sparks and flames licked skywards.

One block before reaching the main thoroughfare Kelly swung the motorcar left into an alley and pulled into the right behind an office building. The air was pungent with the smell of burning and the heat was palpable.

'*Higginson Enterprises* – tradesmen's entrance,' Kelly announced in a mocking tone.

For the first time since the journey started Gregson removed his pistol from Dillon's ribs and got out. Will found it difficult to alight with his hands still tied behind him, but as soon as his feet touched the ground, bending slightly, he charged Gregson and butted him in the stomach. He swerved left and dashed into the alley heading back towards Talbot Street.

Out of the corner of his eye he saw that Kelly had anticipated his possible flight and was right behind him. He felt the chauffeur using his long reach and grabbing at his coat collar. The next moment he was pulled off his feet and fell sprawling on the ground.

* * *

Corporal Kildare remained face down on the pavement until he heard the motorcar pull away. His ribcage felt as though he'd come second in a boxing match with a kangaroo. With some difficulty, he got on his hands and knees. Drawing breath was hard. He saw his two comrades lying still on the pavement and checked each in turn. Both dead. He managed to pull himself to his feet. His breathing came a little easier. His hand went to his pocket and confirmed the dispatch from MacDonagh was still there. With grim determination he turned and walked slowly in the direction of the Liffey and the General Post Office beyond.

* * *

Maeve completed changing the bandages of another wounded Volunteer as the door to the First Aid room opened and two men came in supporting a third between them. He was dressed in the dark green of the republican uniform.

'Quickly, this man's been shot at least twice,' said one of his supporters.

'He was already wounded when he caught another bullet out on Sackville Street trying to get in and we managed to rescue him,' said the other.

'Right, lay him down here,' said Maeve; the two other women in the room were both busy treating more wounds. 'Gently, ' she said, as the patient let out a groan. 'All right, you can leave him with us. We'll do all we can. Thank you.'

The man's rescuers left him to Maeve's tender ministrations.

'Well, Corporal,' she said, noticing his stripes, 'what do we call you?' He looked to her to be in a very bad state. She leaned over with her ear close to the soldier's mouth to hear him.

'... Kildare... Jos...eph Kil... dare.' He was struggling to draw breath, but he caught her arm as she was about to straighten up and she saw he had more to say.

'Mess... age... Mac...Donagh.' He let go Maeve's arm and his hand tried to get at his breast pocket. '...Conn...oll...y.' He gasped for breath and tried to speak again. 'Spy... Dill...' His eyes closed. His hand stopped moving and then his arm slid to his side.

Maeve felt for a pulse in his neck. Nothing. He was gone. She slid the dispatch out of his pocket, her mind in turmoil. What had Corporal Kildare said? MacDonagh – wasn't he in charge at Jacob's Biscuit Factory? And Dill... Was he talking about Will? She stared at the sealed dispatch in her hand as though it were some horrible instrument of torture. She glanced round at the other women. Both still engrossed in their own missions of mercy. The dispatch slipped easily into her pocket as she stood up.

'I'm afraid we've lost this one,' she said. 'I'll go and get someone to move the body.'

* * *

Four long leather straps, one round his neck, one round his chest and upper arms, one round his waist and forearms and one round his ankles held Dillon's body rigid, binding him to a square wooden upright about eight inches wide that was supporting the low ceiling in some sort of vaulted cellar. A couple of oil lamps on wall brackets were burning to provide a dim illumination. It was enough for Will to see a wooden stairway ascending to his right – presumably to the offices of Michael J Higginson – a workbench with tools and the stone steps over to his left that he had been frogmarched down from the alleyway after his abortive escape attempt had come to an abrupt and premature end.

In order to secure him to the wooden pillar Gregson had untied his wrists, but Kelly had him in such a tight hold he had no chance of trying anything. He could now barely move a muscle. He could flex his wrists and knees very slightly and turn his head a little, but apart from wriggling his fingers, that was it. Which was all the more frustrating since Buster Gregson had gone off with Kelly to pick up Higginson leaving only Liam behind to keep an eye on the prisoner.

The sound of machine gun fire and shells exploding was muffled down in the cellar, but the heat from burning buildings not far along the road was making the atmosphere in the underground prison stifling. Will looked around him once more. The place seemed to be a mixture of workshop and dumping ground. There were abandoned wooden crates and cardboard boxes lying around and a number of piles of old newspapers. The area round the bench was clear so work could be done. A tool rack with saws and hammers and drills – all the usual stuff – was attached to the brickwork behind the bench under a wall clock that had lost its minute hand. The small hand pointed a little after the IX. Will's eyes were drawn back to the tools. He couldn't stop his imagination running riot as to what use some of them might be put in the wrong hands. The sweat on his forehead wasn't just due to the air temperature.

Liam was sitting on the bench gazing at the wall opposite. He hadn't spoken since the others left. Dillon decided to break the ice: 'Aren't you worried being so close to where all those shells are exploding?'

His captor interrupted his fascination with a spot on the wall to glance over at him and then resumed his contemplation of the infinite, in silence.

'I mean, it must only be a matter of time before Higginson's place takes a hit. Or the fires reach this far.'

Liam shifted his position. He didn't look at Dillon this time. Remained silent.

‘Not a job I’d relish. I mean, who knows when Higginson’ll get here. Might decide to wait ’til morning. You happy to be here all night? Haven’t got to be somewhere?’

‘You shut up!’ Liam stood up and grabbed something off the bench. In two strides he was face to face with Dillon and holding a chisel against his throat. ‘How about I make a start before they get here and cut out your voice box?’

‘Oh, Higginson wouldn’t like that, spoiling his fun, now would he?’

There was doubt in Liam’s eyes. He lowered the chisel close to Dillon’s hands. ‘Perhaps I’ll just take a finger. The Boss wouldn’t begrudge me that.’

The fingers of Dillon’s right hand snapped closed round the metal and gave the chisel a violent twist. The handle was torn from Liam’s unsuspecting grasp. Will flicked the chisel round so he could take the handle in his left hand as Liam made a grab for it. Will twisted it forward and stabbed Liam in the fleshy part of his hand between his forefinger and thumb.

The man jumped back with a yell. In a reflex action he delivered a backhander to Dillon’s cheek with his left before clutching at his right which was shedding copious amounts of blood. Will wriggled his jaw that stung from the blow, and saw Liam glancing wildly around for something to wrap round his wound. He found nothing and made a dash for the stairs. First Aid kit in the office, Will supposed.

As he climbed the wooden steps he said, ‘You’ll be sorry you did that. Just you wait; you’ll be sorry.

Will had no intention of waiting. As soon as Liam was out of sight he went to work with the sharp end of the chisel, trying to cut through the belt that held his wrists and waist. He had so little movement in his wrists that it was difficult to get any pressure behind the blade once he had it in the right position. It kept slipping and he had to manoeuvre it back into place each time before trying again.

The solitary hand of the clock on the wall pointed mid-way between the IX and the X.

The bevelled blade didn’t have the sharpest edge and progress was painfully slow, but for the time being Liam remained somewhere upstairs. Trying to bandage your own hand can be tricky, Will thought, as the chisel slipped once more. Careful, Will lad.

By the time the one-armed clock showed a quarter to ten, he had managed to cut more than halfway through the leather. Then two things happened at once. He saw Liam's feet as he started back down the stairs. And he heard a motorcar pulling up outside.

Reluctantly, he held the chisel near its tip and let it swing between his fingers before releasing it. The weight of the handle carried it in an arc to fall amongst some cardboard boxes to his left. He didn't want to be caught with the blade and draw attention to the cut he had made in the belt.

Liam reached the floor of the cellar as the door from the back alley opened and footsteps began to descend. The injured man glared at Dillon. Round his fist he held a towel that was soaked in blood. He circled around Dillon and moved to the bench.

Michael J Higginson reached floor level. He was wearing a mohair overcoat and silk scarf. The toecaps of his shoes reflected the two flickering flames on the wall. Behind him came Kelly who was followed by someone else making heavy weather of the steps because of the crutch he was using. No sign of Buster Gregson this time.

'So this is the annoying bastard who's been interfering with my business interests,' said Higginson.

That was when Kelly spotted Liam's hand.

'What in the world have you done to yourself, Liam?'

Higginson turned with an annoyed look towards his employee. 'You're dripping on the bench. What happened to you, man?'

Avoiding looking at the prisoner, Liam said, 'I was just doing a bit of whittling when the chisel slipped. I've stabbed my hand real bad. Couldn't find any First Aid stuff in the office.'

He doesn't want to admit what really happened, thought Will. I guess I don't blame him.

'You're a fool,' said Higginson.

'Let me see the wound, Liam.' Kelly sounded rather more concerned than their boss.

When Liam unwrapped his hand there was a sharp intake of breath from Kelly and even, to a lesser extent, from Higginson.

'That needs stitches,' said Kelly, 'as soon as possible.'

Liam looked at the boss, his eyes asking the question.

'Oh, go on, you good-for-nothing. Kelly, take him to the Rotunda. It's not far. Pick us up back here in an hour. We're going to enjoy the next sixty minutes, are we not, Éamonn?'

The man with the crutch smiled. 'Oh, I think we are,' he said moving forward. 'Thank you for including me in the party.'

As he stepped into the light Will recognised the man whose knee he had dislocated a fortnight ago.

'Get off you two. We'll be fine playing here on our own.'

'Thank you, sir.' Liam headed up the stone steps and Kelly followed.

Higginson went to the tool rack and selected an item. 'Secateurs. My favourite.' He moved over to where Dillon stood, unable to move. 'Just right for fingers.' He touched the blade against Will's pinkie. 'It's the little crunchy snap that they make as the blade closes that I find so satisfying. Do you not, Éamonn?'

'Oh, I do indeed. Although... I was thinking of starting with something else.'

'Well now, I think in the circumstances, it's only right that you should get to play first. What had you in mind?'

The two turned back to the bench and Will took the opportunity to strain as hard as he could on the belt round his waist. He felt it give slightly as the cut lengthened a little but he had to relax as his torturers turned back to face him again. The clock on the wall behind them single-handedly proclaimed the time to be ten o'clock.

Moore came up close to Dillon and bent slightly. He had a club hammer in his hand.

'I think the right knee first. Poetic justice and all that.'

Will winced and stared down in horror as Moore put the face of the heavy hammer against his kneecap and then started his backswing.

* * *

Ryan Doloughan crouched by the parapet on the Post Office roof. He had a pair of field glasses trained on the Imperial Hotel above Cleary's trying to assess the damage. It was late, getting on for ten, but Connolly, despite his injuries, had insisted his men do a recce to see where they stood. The overhead wire that had been so useful in carrying messages had been snapped by bullets. Connolly had sent others to the rear of the Post Office and through the Henry Street tunnel to assess the positions there, as well.

To Ryan it looked as though the whole of Sackville Street was on fire, at least at the lower end. Bright orange tongues of flame leaped high into the night sky from many of the taller structures. He could feel the heat radiating from them and was grateful for the protection of the parapet, not just from the shells and incessant gunfire. Through the glasses he saw down near the Liffey some buildings had collapsed. Then, panning back to Cleary's, he paused on one of the big shop windows. It gave the impression that it was somehow moving. As he watched, he realised that the glass was melting in the tremendous heat. The great pane appeared to be dissolving into the pavement and molten glass was running down the gutters.

The flames had not yet reached as far as Talbot Street, but Ryan reckoned they could before the night was over and, as though to confirm this, he saw fire burst out in Hoyte's Druggist and Oil Works just across from the GPO. Somewhere in the distance a church clock started to chime the hour but it was drowned out by an almighty explosion as scores of drums of motor fuel in the works yard ignited in the great heat. An immense fireball bellowed into the sky above Hoyte's and myriad drums containing methylated spirits and turpentine were blown high into the air to land and explode on nearby buildings. Burning debris was falling everywhere.

On the GPO roof Ryan whipped off his coat and used it to try to smother patches of burning fuel, but fires were starting all over quicker than he could extinguish them. One was now blazing out across the doorway. His only way off the roof was blocked.

* * *

Across the road, in the cellar under *Higginson Enterprises*, Éamonn Moore swung back the club ready to smash it down on Dillon's kneecap.

At the same moment, Will heard the most tremendous explosion and the building rocked to its foundations. Moore hesitated and looked to the Boss. Higginson said nothing; the blood drained from his face. At that moment there was another huge explosion right above them, as though a bomb had been dropped into the building. This time, as the structure shook a huge crack appeared in the vaulted ceiling. The wooden post that Dillon was strapped to snapped in the middle as though made of matchwood. He felt a terrific wrench on his neck as the lower portion to which he was still bound by three straps pitched backwards while the belt round his neck was dragged off the upper part of the post still attached to the crumbling ceiling.

A great chunk of masonry, no longer supported by the wooden post crashed on top of Moore and another, still with the upper half of the post attached, tumbled down where Dillon had fallen back. No longer held upright by the ceiling, the side wall with the oil lamps collapsed inward, catching Higginson a sickening blow to the side of his head and shoulder. Looking stunned, he fell and an avalanche of rubble piled on top of him, trapping his legs and lower torso. Burning oil from the lamps spread over the floor. Cardboard boxes burst into flames and newspapers ignited.

Will was aware that the belt around his neck was no longer restraining him. He watched Moore go down under a huge slab before seeing to his horror the second slab coming away from its supports and falling right where he lay. The upper half of the post slammed into the floor by his feet and the great slab of masonry came to rest like the side of a ridge tent, with one edge behind his head and the other supported by the post. It was actually protecting him from any further falling debris.

He flexed his arm muscles and strained against his waist restraint. He felt the cut he had made tear some more. He strained again with gritted teeth, a prolonged effort, until he felt it give way. With his lower arms free he started to wriggle, raising his arms as much as the upper belt would let him. Gradually he worked it upwards until it came off his shoulders and hung loose around his neck. With his arms now free, he slipped his head out from under both the upper restraints and bent to his ankles. The belt was tight and he couldn't reach behind the post to find the buckle. He set about manoeuvring it down the rough wood a tenth of an inch at a time.

While working to free himself he could smell burning and realised that the light in the cellar was no longer coming from the lamps but from flames of burning paper and card. A box near his feet caught alight and he increased his efforts to slide the belt down. One corner was nearly off the stump of the post. He tried to twist his ankles a little to flatten them against the wood and slacken the belt. He pushed at the leather near the corner again – and it slipped over. At last he could withdrew his feet from the loop and crawl out of his 'tent'.

Some of the wooden crates were on fire now and flames were climbing up the remaining walls fanned by draughts blowing through where the collapsed wall had been.

A quick check confirmed that Moore was very dead. Will moved over to where Higginson lay prone under the rubble. Flames were already licking around the feet of the wooden bench next to where he lay. As he approached, the Boss opened his eyes. Will could see him start to struggle to free himself but he couldn't budge the lower part of his body.

'I'm stuck. Help me out of here,' he said.

Will stepped over Higginson and stood at the foot of the steps up to the back alley looking back at him. The irony of the situation was not lost on him.

'I wonder if you remember,' he said to the trapped man, 'a while back up in Bangor? Your motorcar mounted the kerb and knocked down a young lady. I asked you to drive us to the hospital to save her life. You ignored me and ordered your chauffeur to drive on. She died.'

Will paused.

'Now you die.'

He turned and climbed the stone steps.

'Come back! I can pay you. Name your price.'

Will kept climbing.

'You can't just walk off and leave me!' Flames were licking close to Higginson's face, now.

Will turned at the top of the steps and looked down at him. 'Pretty much what I said to you as Annie lay on the pavement.' Without another word he stepped out into the alley and closed the door. As he hurried towards Talbot Street a loud rumbling started behind him. Looking back, he saw the upper stories of the offices collapsing. With a tremendous roar of tumbling bricks and masonry the entire building crumpled in upon itself to become a giant heap of rubble that filled the space where the cellar had been.

Will felt a grim satisfaction as he turned left towards Sackville Street. The inferno up ahead was not the safest place to be venturing but he knew he had to get Maeve out of the Post Office if he was to save her from capture and incarceration. Or worse.

Chapter 31

Fire now had a substantial hold on the roof of the GPO and Ryan could no longer control it. Added to the heat from the street his situation was becoming desperate. He looked at the door, engulfed in flames. His scorched and blackened coat would have to be his protection somehow. He draped it over his head and shoulders as he estimated the position of the door handle that was completely obscured by the flames. Holding the coat closed across his face with his left hand, he thrust his right hand through the flames to grasp the handle. The searing heat of brass knob burnt into the flesh of his palm as he pushed open the door, flinging himself through the barrier of flames, all in one swift movement. He tripped and fell in a heap in the corridor inside as flames were sucked in through the open doorway. He jumped to his feet, pushed the door closed and used his coat once again to smother the flames on the inside of the frame.

'Fire! Fire on the roof,' he yelled, racing down the stairs. By the time he reached the first floor the fire-fighting squad were already on their way up with buckets of water.

'Be careful of the door handle; it's red hot,' Ryan shouted to them as they passed on the stairs.

He wrapped a handkerchief around his hand to protect his burnt palm as he went to report back to Connolly. He found him in a frustrated frame of mind, wanting so much to be up and helping but forced to lie on his stretcher bed and depend on others to move him around. Pearse was becoming despondent again, too.

'We can withstand any amount of shelling,' he said, but if fire takes hold all could be lost.'

‘The lads are fighting valiantly to bring the flames under control,’ said Ryan.

‘I hope they win, Captain. I do hope they win.’

* * *

‘I’m really worried about Will,’ said Maeve.

She was applying a salve to her brother’s burnt hand in the First Aid room.

‘It *is* getting very late,’ said Ryan, who had come to her immediately after reporting back to Connolly. ‘He’ll have been held up and decided to spend the night at Jacob’s or one of the other places we’re still holding.’ He said this to try to reassure Maeve rather than out of any sense of conviction.

‘Maybe,’ she said, and he knew he hadn’t convinced her.

There had already been numerous casualties amongst his friends and comrades; he hoped that Will hadn’t become another statistic of the uprising.

Maeve was winding a bandage around his right hand when the door opened.

‘They said I’d likely find you two here. What have you been doing to yourself, Ryan?’

Maeve jumped up. The remainder of the bandage unrolled onto the floor. ‘Will! We’ve been so worried about you. You’re safe. Where have you been to this hour?’

She ran to him and hugged him close.

‘Ah, well it isnae easy to get about the city any more. It took me a lot longer than I’d have thought to deliver all Connolly’s dispatches. But sure I’m here now; isn’t that all that matters?’

‘I’m so glad you’re safe.’

‘Me too – I mean, that *you’re* still safe,’ Will added, though he realised, as he said it, how relieved he was that he, too, had somehow survived the day virtually unscathed. And on top of successfully handing over all the dispatches, he had finally fulfilled his private mission. There had been a moment when he thought he was going to be crippled for life – even if “life” was only going to last another hour. But Annie’s death was avenged and in a most befitting manner. Oddly, he felt a bit flat now that it was over.

‘What’s that mark on your neck?’ Maeve gently lifted his collar away from where the belt had hauled at his skin before it came loose from the broken post.

‘Och, it’s nothing. Had a wee bit of a contretemps with some British soldiers. One of them tried to throttle me with his rifle strap,’ he lied.

Maeve gasped, ‘But you got away.’

‘Aye, but the three Volunteers who were supposed to be seeing me safely back here, weren’t so lucky. Shot. All three.’

Ryan spoke up from where he sat. ‘Our lads, shot?’

‘I’m afraid so. I was lucky to get away. The guy with the rifle strap wasn’t, though.’

Will had used this fabrication to explain to Connolly why he had no answering dispatch from MacDonnagh at the biscuit factory, claiming (truthfully) that it had been carried by the corporal in charge of his escort. With the three Volunteers killed, as he believed, by Higginson’s thugs, there was only MacDonnagh who was privy to Jude Maguire’s accusations against him and Will thought any further communication between Jacob’s and the Post Office now was very unlikely.

He had managed to cross Sackville Street well up to the north end and, by keeping to the shadows and taking a number of detours to avoid army barricades, make his way back to Moore Street and the final dash across Henry Street. Since his return, from what he had seen of the situation in the GPO, the scores of republicans defending their position were still coping. But only just. If the fire hazard was to worsen he doubted whether they could hold out. However, beyond the walls of the besieged headquarters, the streets of Dublin had become hazardous in the extreme.

Will was exhausted, physically and mentally. Connolly had thanked him sincerely for bringing him back his Commandants’ replies and told him he wouldn’t require him again until the morning.

‘These dispatches from all around the city will be invaluable to us as we decide the way forward. Now, do get some sleep, Mr Dillon; you look terrible.’ This, from a man lying on a stretcher bed, his bullet wound inflamed and his shattered ankle liable to be turning gangrenous.

‘I’ll do that, and right readily. Thank you, Mr Connolly,’ said Will.

A contingent of the insurrectionists was bedding down in the concourse to try to snatch some sleep but there were always many more bustling around going about their various tasks until it was their turn to go off-duty for a few hours. Will found a corner which, while not exactly quiet, was at least a little apart from where men and officers were passing to and fro. Maeve said she'd join him once she'd cleaned up in the First Aid room and Ryan set off to aid the fire-fighters on the roof.

Will closed his eyes and tried to block out the sounds. Officers shouted commands, corporals delivered oral messages from their captains, groups of Volunteers chatted quietly but every now and again a loud peal of laughter would break out. Gallows humour. From various directions Will could hear low moans, too. The number of wounded was rising. But over all this was the noise of the shelling; endless continuous explosions throughout the night.

Exhausted as he was, Will was soon drifting in that half-conscious state just prior to falling asleep. He barely registered that Maeve had come and snuggled in beside him, nor that a messenger had rushed down to report how the fire on the roof was still raging and parts of the burning timbers had collapsed into the floor below.

* * *

Old Mrs Doloughan stood at her bedroom window, unable to sleep. It seemed to her that the whole city was on fire. An orange glow canopied the night sky and flames of yellows and reds blazed, hundreds of feet into the air, the sparks flying higher still. She could hear the distant roar of the inferno right out where she was, near Phoenix Park. But over the sounds of the raging fires she recognised the dull, percussive explosions of the big guns shaking the night air and rattling her windowpanes, and the insistent staccato of machine guns spitting out their deadly stream of lead to wreak havoc amongst the brave republican soldiers.

She pleaded with the Blessed Virgin to keep her son safe, and her daughter. 'Bring them back to me, Holy Mother. You know what it is like to lose your son. Please don't make me experience that. Bring Ryan home and bring Maeve home, I beseech you.'

Her fingers worked at her rosary beads as she gazed again at the awe-inspiring sight of the heavens on fire over Dublin. Finally she left her window and returned to bed. Sleep eluded her for a long time.

* * *

Friday morning saw many of the military and political top brass gathered in Dublin Castle. General Sir John Grenfell Maxwell, just arrived from England as the newly appointed commander-in-chief of the forces in Ireland lost no time in declaring his intentions.

'The most vigorous measures will be taken by me to stop the loss of life and damage to property which certain misguided persons are causing in their armed resistance to the law. I shall not hesitate to destroy any buildings within an area occupied by the rebels and I warn all persons within those areas, now surrounded by HM troops, forthwith to leave such areas.'

His statement was printed on handbills and distributed round the city centre without delay.

It was sunny and although few shops were open – there were no newspapers, no bread, no milk – yet a fair number of Dublin's citizens had ventured out to see what was happening. Few were talking, as they had done earlier in the week; they were mostly keeping their own council, but they read the new GOC's declaration and many heeded the warning.

Elsewhere in the land, contrary to Padraig Pearse's prediction, very few Volunteers had taken up arms in support of their city comrades. One group that did, the 48-strong Fingal Volunteers under Commandant Tomas Ashe fought tenaciously for five hours on that same Friday and roundly defeated a force of 70 Royal Irish Constabulary at nearby Ashbourne in County Meath.

The largest rebel force outside Dublin was in Galway where Liam Mellows led over 600 Volunteers in abortive attacks on a number of police stations. They had 25 rifles and 300 shotguns between them; the rest were armed with pikes. The cruiser, *HMS Gloucester* sailed into Galway Bay and shelled the rebels' position, while British troops were making their way westward from Dublin. By the time they arrived, however, the rebels had given up the struggle and dispersed.

Another outbreak was 80 miles south of the capital, in Wexford. There Volunteers held the town of Enniscorthy for five days, blocking roads and the railway line and preventing troops getting to Dublin.

Despite the efforts of these few bands of rebels, however, many British reinforcements did make it through via the ports and railway stations and by the end of the week General Maxwell had in excess of 16,000 troops at his disposal. They faced a republican force in Dublin that had grown a little over the first few days of the Rising, but amounted to no more than 1,600.

Outnumbering the enemy ten to one, Maxwell was determined to bring the insurrection to a swift close and with the country under martial law he had no qualms about using all the powers that gave him. Not every captured rebel became a prisoner of HM Government; some lay dead in the street within moments of being seized. The unofficial penalty for looting was often to be shot, children and adults alike, and quite apart from stray gunshots from both sides, not a few innocent civilian bystanders lost their lives to British bullets as well.

* * *

James Connolly called Dillon to his bedside and asked him to help gather all the *Cumann na mBan* women together. Pearse had heard about the new military commander's warning for non-combatants to leave the areas where rebels were still holding out and he was insisting that the woman should leave.

'You have served us and your country magnificently,' he told them when they were all present, 'but now is the time to depart. Go safely to your homes and pray that God may spare us who remain to carry on the fight.'

With much emotional leave-taking, they all left – some reluctantly, others less so – except for Nurse O'Farrell and three others, who refused to abandon the menfolk. Maeve was one of them.

Ryan pleaded with her to go. 'You know it is quite possible I may not make it out of here.'

'You mustn't say that.' Maeve's eyes were glistening and moist as she took his hand in both of hers.

'But it's true; it's a possibility. And we don't want to leave our poor mother childless, with you gone, too.'

'I'm not planning to 'be gone' but I shall not abandon you and Will and all the others.'

'You wouldn't be abandoning us; you've already been a tremendous support to us.'

'And I shall continue to be so, as God gives me strength.'

Ryan looked to Will who was standing a little aside, not wishing to intrude on their sibling dispute. 'Will?' he said.

‘I doubt there’s a man here could persuade her to leave, Ryan. The same girl. Stubborn as a mule. But,’ he added, to Maeve, ‘I’d feel so much easier if you would decide to go with the other women. March out with your head held high.’

Ryan shot him a grateful look – short-lived as Maeve pouted. She said, ‘Well, maybe you could do worse than having a mule at your side before all this is over. I’m staying.’

Her brother could see there was no changing her mind and Pearse, too, was forced to accept the four women’s determination to remain.

The fire that had started on the roof of the GPO the night before had taken hold on the top floor by the early hours of Friday morning. Valiant efforts were made to control it but in the end the entire storey had to be abandoned. This was another reason Pearse had been anxious to give the women Volunteers a chance to withdraw

‘I fear that our time in this ill-fated headquarters of the burgeoning Irish Republic is running out,’ he said, when the second storey began to burn in multiple places during the afternoon.

‘We may have to consider a strategic withdrawal,’ Connolly admitted from his stretcher bed. ‘I hope my pall bearers are up to it.’

Clarke and Plunket, MacDiarmada, The O’Rahilly and some from the lower ranks, too, were gathered for this conference. They included Plunket’s right-hand man, Michael Collins, Ryan Doloughan and Will Dillon, as Connolly’s adjutant.

Will said, ‘Never fear, Mr Connolly, as I’m sure you’ve said yourself in your trade union days, “One out – all out;” you’ll not be left behind.’

This brought a ripple of laughter that lessened the tension briefly before things turned serious again. Will could tell they all knew they would soon have to abandon what had been their home for the last five days, and then…what? That was the big unknown.

Pearse again: ‘We know from Dillon, here, that Daly is still in a strong position at the Four Courts. I say, when we have to leave the GPO, we fight our way through the back streets to link up with him.’

This met with a mixture of approval from some and doubt from others. From what Will had seen last night of the British army cordon encircling the city centre, which would be growing stronger and tighter as time passed, it was unlikely that the rebels could sneak past even singly, in an effort to escape, never mind win through in an open attack, but he held his peace.

Michael Collins, on the other hand, was all for it.

'I can lead the lads through whatever the English have got out there. Our boys are worth ten of those conscripts. If we're going down, it won't be without a fight, I can tell you.'

Pearse asked Dillon to brief Collins and The O'Rahilly on conditions in and around Henry Street and Moore Street as of late last night. A contingency plan was developed that would see the whole garrison exit via the tunnel and make a dash for premises on Moore Street to use as a temporary re-grouping area. From there they would commence their fight to get through to the Four Courts. The toughest part would be dodging bullets on Henry Street but they could see no alternative.

The only decision remaining was when to start the exodus.

* * *

In the event, that decision was largely taken out of the hands of Pearse and the other leaders.

Anyone not manning a ground floor window, taking pot shots at British military rash enough to show themselves, or on current fire-fighting duty, was grabbing something to eat from the limited rations still available. Like many of the Volunteers, Will was in the main concourse. He was sharing a catering sized tin of cold baked beans with Maeve, Ryan, Elizabeth Farrell and the other two nurses.

The sound of distant gunfire and occasional shots from the street outside had become just part of the background noise, along with the constant chatter of scores of pent up insurgents and, more recently, the ominous crackling of flames and sparks from many parts of the building. Even the detonations of shells, which couldn't be ignored, were by and large taken for granted and Will and Maeve didn't intend to let them spoil their meal. They were all hungry and the beans tasted delicious.

The whistle of an approaching shell sounded over the background noise.

'This one's going to be close, ' said Ryan.

Fired from the direction of Trinity College, the trajectory of the HE shell took it high over O'Connell Bridge to fall in an ark to the left side of Sackville Street. It cleared the Prince's Street wall of the GPO and dropped through the burnt out roof, its path taking it by chance through great gaps in the two floors beneath. It detonated when it hit the first floor near the front of the building.

They all heard the tremendous explosion and Will saw a great crack open up in the ceiling of the concourse. It started near the centre and rapidly zigzagged out towards one corner. Little bits of plaster were falling like snowflakes and then came a tremendous rending as the centre gave way. The snowflakes became an avalanche. Ceiling joists, lumps of plaster, floorboards, desks, chairs, filing cabinets crashed down from the floor above.

Will and Ryan rushed the girls to the far side of the concourse. As they ran, Will felt a violent shove from Ryan followed by a glancing blow on his left shoulder from a falling rafter. Without the push it would have caught him full on the head.

'Thanks,' he yelled.

'Down!' Ryan shouted to the women. 'Under the counter.'

Everyone else was fleeing the devastation, too. Those, like Will and Ryan who had escaped the tumbling rubble without serious injury were starting to reach out to others who had fallen beneath some of the treacherous debris. This was made all the more hazardous as further portions of the ceiling showed danger of collapse.

With admirable efficiency all the men worked together and very quickly everyone was at the safe side and out of danger. Many had scrapes and bruises and there were a few broken limbs. Will saw Sergeant O'Mally help free one man's body from under a heavy metal filing cabinet and carry it to the side. Just one more whose Rising had come to a premature end.

Burning material that landed amongst the falling timbers from above caused numerous fires to break out. It was clear to Will that the area had to be abandoned and Captain Doloughan was already barking orders as the Volunteers made their way through to the back, some assisting any of the walking wounded who needed help. Will and Maeve made sure the three older women got through with the rest.

'I doubt we'll be in the oul GPO much longer,' Will said to Maeve. 'I just hope we can make it out alive.'

* * *

By eight o'clock on the Friday evening virtually the whole GPO garrison was crowded into the basement, finalising their plans by the light of hurricane lamps. It was the one part of the building that was still intact, by and large. Many more areas on the ground floor had become untenable either from flames spreading or ceilings collapsing. The decision had been taken to evacuate via the tunnel.

The O'Rahilly volunteered to lead the first group across the killing ground that was Henry Street, now, itself, a picture of devastation as errant shells had destroyed buildings on both sides. Covering fire to try to help them would be laid down from the occupied shops on the Post Office side, still undamaged. The plan, then, was that this first group would take up positions in Moore Street and add the strength of more covering fire from their side, as each successive group attempted the crossing.

The size of the groups was dictated by the capacity of the hardware shop above the tunnel exit. One shop-full could dash out of the door and across the street at a time. Will accompanied The O'Rahilly through the tunnel first, not to be part of the vanguard but to try to see if the situation had changed any since the previous night and to report back on how O'Rahilly's group got on.

'Over there,' he pointed out Moore Street to O'Rahilly in the failing light. 'Make for the near corner first to get out of sight of the troops up Henry Street.'

'But you say there's more of them at the far end of Moore Street?'

'There could be. There were last night. You'll need to take cover in the doorways opposite as quickly as you can.'

'Right. We'll occupy the end building and fire from there to provide the extra cover for the rest of you coming across.'

The O'Rahilly opened the street door.

'Start your cover fire! Come on, lads, follow me!'

He raced out over the pavement and across the road.

There was a burst of machine gun fire, which promptly stopped under a hail of rifle shots from the rebels.

About twenty more men were right behind O'Rahilly when Will saw him staggering onto the far pavement and into Moore Street. One of his comrades grabbed his arm and put it round his own shoulder as he half-helped and half-dragged him across the side street and lowered him to a sitting position in a doorway some way up, away from the shooting.

Will had no time to speculate on how badly O'Rahilly might be injured. The shop was already filling up with more evacuees and he had to get back through the tunnel to report to Connolly and Pearse. But news that The O'Rahilly was down soon spread to the waiting men and there was a distinct reluctance amongst them to venture out.

'How goes it, Dillon?' James Connolly asked from his prone position on the truckle bed as Will emerged from the tunnel.

He reported on what had happened; how The O'Rahilly had been shot and how the others were now less than anxious to leave the safety of the shop.

'Get me through there!' said Connolly to his stretcher-bearers. 'Pearse can be in charge back here, but I can see I'm needed through the tunnel.'

Will was looking around. 'Where is Mr Pearse?' he asked.

It was Michael Collins who answered as Connolly was being picked up. 'He's still up on the ground floor making sure no one is left behind up there.' He added, 'Look, I'm going through, too, to spur the lads on. Could you make sure Joe Plunkett gets across all right, Will? He's not a well man.'

'I shall indeed. Go easy, Michael' said Will.

From the mouth of the tunnel Connolly called back, 'Dillon, come through, again, so you can report back to Pearse on our progress.'

Will quickly attracted Maeve's attention where she was helping Elizabeth Farrell adjust a wounded man's dressing. 'Can you keep an eye on Mr Plunkett. I've promised Michael Collins I'll help him out of here. I've got to go through to the shop again, but I won't be long.'

'Sure, I can do that. Be careful,' said Maeve.

Will joined Michael Collins and followed the stretcher party through the tunnel.

From a position near the door onto Henry Street Connolly, weakened though he was from his wounds, was propped up on one elbow and giving a rousing pep talk to his men that equalled any of Padraig Pearse's rallying calls when the poet was at his best.

'So we're not retreating,' he concluded. 'We're moving on. On to join up with Daly and the boys at the Four Courts. On to victory!'

No resounding cheer echoed in the shop as Connolly sank back on his bed, but there were voices raised in agreement and at least some that called out, 'Let's go, lads.' Nevertheless, Will could see those at the front hesitating to open the door and step outside. From beside him Collins pushed his way forward and grasped the door handle. He pulled it open and then produced two revolvers from his coat pockets.

'Come on!' he yelled and dashed out into the semi-darkness. Firing both guns, one in each hand, towards the British position up the street, he ran across the road with the others at his heels. Not until the last man passed him did he stop firing and duck into cover himself. Collin's own efforts, with added covering fire now from both sides of Henry Street, limited enemy shooting. This time they all made it across, unscathed.

Collins directed the men into the first building that their comrades had already occupied, but he stayed on the corner and reloaded his guns, ready to assist the next lot across.

Will returned to the basement and gave the signal for more men to go through. He saw Pearse had joined the others, so all his men must now be accounted for. Will told him the situation and that Connolly was staying in the shop to encourage each batch as they left.

The evacuation continued smoothly and efficiently. Reports came back of further successful crossings and, inevitably, of a few being shot dead or wounded. Pearse sent the women through fairly early on – all except for Maeve, who refused to go without Will, but the other three all made it over safely. Seán MacDiarmada and Tom Clarke went across, each leading a group and Ryan Doloughan was one of the last to head out with his group.

He left with a cheery, 'See you on the other side,' to Maeve and Will.

'Good luck, Ryan,' Will called, looking around. There were now only enough left in the basement to make up one last group.

Will helped Joseph Plunkett into the tunnel with Maeve behind him followed by the rest, Pearse insisting on being the last to leave. They climbed the steps from the cellar and all congregated in the hardware shop where they found Connolly had already been taken across, without further injury. The last of the covering riflemen joined the final group and Maeve held the door as, first the gunmen rushed out, firing their weapons and then the others. Returning fire from the British was intermittent, pinned down, as they were, by the rebels firepower. Will held back as he didn't want Plunkett's slower progress to hinder the others, but it was only a matter of moments as the rest cleared the doorway.

‘Come Maeve,’ he called as he helped Plunkett out to the darkened street and was aware of Pearse bringing up the rear. He saw at least two bodies lying, sprawled in the road and heard some sporadic shots from the army barricade, but just kept going as fast as Plunkett could manage. They made the far pavement and headed for Moore Street. Plunkett stumbled but Will supported him and got him round the corner to safety. Pearse was right behind him. Will turned to grasp Maeve’s hand and pull her into the cover of the corner building.

She wasn’t there.

He strained his eyes to look back across Henry Street, searching the shadows. Then he saw her. Lying, crumpled in the road, her head against the far kerbstones. She wasn’t moving.

Chapter 32

Will didn't hesitate. He rushed back over the road and flung himself down low at her side, with his body between hers and the British guns. It was difficult to see what injuries she had in the dim light of a waning moon and the lurid orange glow that hung over the city.

He carefully lifted Maeve's head off the kerbstone as shots whistled past above them. Out of the corner of his eye he saw Michael Collins across the street firing back with a two-handed volley from his revolvers. When he paused to re-load, the machine gun opened up but it was aiming too high like the rifle fire. Will had to get Maeve off the street, and quickly. Back into the hardware shop would be much safer than trying to carry her across the road.

Still crouching and cradling her head as best he could, he slid his hands under Maeve's arms and started to drag her over the pavement. More covering fire from Moore Street silenced the machine gun for the moment but then a flurry of rifle shots rang out as a crouching figure raced through the darkness and halted at his side. Without a word spoken Will felt Maeve's weight lessen as her legs were lifted by the newcomer. Keeping low, the two men struggled to reach the safety of the shop doorway as more bullets ricocheted above their heads.

They crossed the threshold and laid Maeve down inside the empty shop. A hurricane lamp was still glowing where it had been left on the counter. It revealed the features of the other man. Will was still protecting Maeve's head on his lap. 'Can you bring the lamp over, Ryan. Was I glad to see you turn up!'

As he fetched the light, Ryan said, 'I was at an upstairs window across the road and saw her falling. She sort of spun round and collapsed in a heap. I think she hit her head on the kerb when she went down.

The girl gave a low groan, which was a sweet sound to Will's ears; she was alive. He took off his overcoat and made a pillow of it for her head, avoiding the lumpy pockets containing stuff he had brought from his digs. Her brother straightened her legs and then opened her jacket. The ever-widening crimson stain on her once white, but now distinctly grubby shirt was centred under her right breast and told its own story. Gently, they rolled her onto her side. The back of her jacket was intact. No sign of blood.

'The bullet's still inside,' said Ryan. 'It needs to come out.'

'She's losing blood,' said Will. 'We need to stop that first.' He was looking around for something to act as a bandage and could see nothing.

'The next shop up, or the one after that, is a drapers; I'm sure I remember seeing skeins of cloth and stuff from early on when we were establishing ourselves in here. Hang on, I'll go and look.'

'You'd better take the lamp.'

'Will you be all right without it?'

'Yeah, we're not planning on doing much. Hurry.'

Will watched his friend scramble through the rough hole knocked in the dividing wall and disappear into the next shop. He heard his footsteps getting fainter and reckoned he was having to go on into the next one along.

Maeve groaned again and he caressed her cheek. For a moment, in the darkness, he was holding Annie lying there, unconscious and he spoke out loud, 'We have to get her to the hospital.'

'Will? Is… that you? Where…'

Not Annie. Maeve. Her voice, weak and hesitant.

'I'm here. We're back in the shop. You're safe. But you've been shot.'

'In my head?' said Maeve, starting to sit up. 'The back of my head hurts.'

'Try to stay still for now, my love,' said Will, but he put his arms around her in her half-sitting position and gently held her close. 'We think you hit your head when you fell and knocked yourself out for a few minutes, but you took a bullet in your chest. We need to bandage that up to stop the bleeding before we decide what to do next.'

With that Ryan emerged through the hole in the brickwork carrying a bundle of cloth and filling the room with light again from his lamp. Maeve smiled up at Will and then glanced down at herself.

'Oh no! This shirt's ruined,' she said. 'All that blood will never wash out properly.'

Will and Ryan couldn't help smiling over the Maeve they both loved.

They got her out of her jacket with some difficulty.

'Ouch! You're wrenching my shoulder off,' she said. 'And I hadn't noticed the pain in my chest until you two started in; it's like a broken rib. I wish Elizabeth was here.'

'I'm afraid you're stuck with us. Sorry, old thing,' said Will, bundling up some clean cloth to act as a pressure pad while Ryan tore another into strips for a bandage.

'Just you be careful, then. I'm very precious, you know.'

As they worked they talked.

'She must have the bullet removed as soon as possible,' said Ryan.

'I know. I'll take her to the nearest hospital. Isn't there one off Henry Street?'

'Jervis Street Hospital. Aye, sure it's just up the road. But it's practically on top of the army barricade. You'd be arrested as soon as you put a foot in the place,' said Ryan.

'I doubt there'll be many of us who aren't prisoners of the British by this time tomorrow,' said Will. 'It's more important we get her the treatment she needs than we avoid arrest for another day.'

'Would you two stop talking about me as if I wasn't here!' said Maeve, lifting her arm to facilitate the bandaging. Will saw her wince at the pain.

'Sorry,' he said. 'Gently does it, Ryan.'

'We're trying to decide what is best for you, sister, dear. What *would* be best, as a matter of fact, would be to take you to Finnegan's Nursing Home at Portraine.' To Will, he added, 'Dr Finnegan is an Irish League man and a strong republican. He lets us use his facilities on the occasions when it's better that the police don't get involved, if you know what I mean.'

'That sounds just the place. Where is it?'

'Outside the city; north of here. Right on the coast opposite Lambay Island. They've even got a wee jetty and take convalescing patients over to the island for a change of scenery. Sure, but it's no use for us, now.

It's the best part of 20 miles and even if you got The O'Rahilly's motorcar you'd never get through the army cordons.'

Will considered that for a moment and quickly concluded that his friend was right. Even a 20 mile journey would delay the treatment Maeve needed for too long.

'No, she needs treatment right away to stop the bleeding and get that bullet out.'

'Well, I'll take her to Jervis Street, then. You've helped us tremendously, Will. This is your chance to try to get away before the British move in. Because I've a horrible feeling you're right; we won't last another 24 hours, even though Michael Collins and Padraig Pearse are urging us to fight on.'

'But Ryan, your place is with your men. Maybe you *will* make it through the back streets to the Four Courts, who knows? But I'm not needed any more. I think poor old Connolly is on the way out. He rallied himself magnificently to spur the men on to cross Henry Street, but afterwards he looked deathly.'

'Will's right, Ryan,' said Maeve. 'I'm ever so grateful to you for coming to help me, but you need to go back now. I'll be fine if Will can get me somewhere near the hospital, but I agree with you; after that he must try to slip away in the dark and see if he can sneak past the barriers. No point in us both being taken prisoner.'

'I'm not leaving you,' said Will. 'If there's any slipping past barriers to be done, it'll be the two of us, once you're patched up. Help me get her through the tunnel to the GPO basement, Ryan and then you go back. And thanks for helping me get her to safety; I doubt if I could have managed on my own keeping low to dodge bullets.'

'I'm fine; I can get through without help.' Maeve stood up, wobbled a little and grabbed Will's arm to steady herself. 'I feel much better with this bandage strapping me up. It's just my ribs ache. And the back of my head.'

Ryan hesitated, but Will could see that he knew he ought to report back. As a member of the Irish Republican Brotherhood he needed to be in this to the finish.

He looked at Will, who was putting his coat back on. 'If you're sure, then. Do you have a gun?'

'It was confiscated yesterday.'

'Here, take this. I'll get another one.' Ryan offered Will his Webbley revolver, but Will shook his head.

‘Thank you, but we’ll be safer unarmed. If we do meet up with any soldiers our best chance will be to try to convince them that we are innocent bystanders caught in crossfire. If I’m carrying, that would look a mite suspicious.’ Will crossed to the counter. ‘What I will take are these,’ he said, picking up a pair of bolt cutters that were on display and slipping them into the deep inside pocket of his overcoat.

‘Well, if you’re sure,’ said Ryan. ‘You’ve been a good friend, Will. I hope we shall meet again in happier circumstances.’ He stepped forward and embraced him and Will found himself wondering whether their next meeting would be in this world or the one to come. Ryan turned to Maeve. ‘You’ve been absolutely wonderful, my pretty little sister,’ and he hugged her very gently.

‘Don’t call me –’

‘I know, I know. I’m sorry.’ But her eyes were smiling at him.

‘Do take care, big brother’ she said, as Ryan stepped to the open door.

‘God speed,’ Will called and his friend dashed out into the darkness. They heard two rifle shots fired – too late to catch the speeding Ryan. Will turned and saw a tear glisten in Maeve’s eye before seeping onto her cheek. He knew, like him, she was wondering if she would ever hear her brother tease her like that again.

* * *

The maze of corridors in the basement were difficult to navigate even when they were all lit by electric light bulbs. With the electricity long since cut off and the dark passages only illuminated a few yards ahead by the hurricane lamp, Will struggled to find a way to the other side of the building. He wanted to lead Maeve to his old exit by the ramp up to Prince’s Street. He figured with so much concentration of activity at the Henry Street side, what surveillance there may still be on the other side may have become lax. He was relying on it.

They had considered going back up to the ground floor but there was a fire raging at the top of the stairs that ruled out that idea. Will knew there were back stairs near the rear exit door; it was just a case of finding them.

The passage they were on turned sharp right and led to an old store room. A dead end.

‘I’m sorry, I could have sworn this was the right one,’ he said as they retraced their steps to a wider corridor; ‘it must be the next one. How are you doing?' He gave Maeve a little squeeze with his right arm round her waist.

'Oh! Be careful, my love. I'm all right. A bit tired, my head aches and I feel as if all my ribs are broken so please don't squeeze. Hey, but other than that, I'm fine. I can walk; that's the main thing. Is this the one?'

They had reached another passage branching off.

'Ah! Yes, this is it. I remember that poster on the door opposite. He held up the lamp – was the light getting dimmer? – to reveal an image of Lord Kitchener saying "Your country needs you." His outstretched finger was pointing straight at the passage opposite.

'You see, he's showing us the way,' said Will. He paused to pump up the pressure in the hurricane lamp. 'I don't think there can be much oil left in this. We need to hurry.'

He felt Maeve reach for his hand and they set off again a little faster. Ahead they could see the passage turned right like the previous one.

'Oh, it's not going to be another dead end?'

'No, this is the right one; I'm sure of it,' said Will.

As they approached the corner the lamp spluttered. The flame sparked for a moment and went out. They were in utter darkness.

'Will!'

Maeve's grip tightened, squeezing his fingers but he couldn't see her. He could see nothing, not even his other hand carrying the now useless lamp. He put it down and took a tentative step forward. His hand holding Maeve's didn't move, his arm stretching backwards. Maeve was transfixed.

'Don't leave me!' she screamed.

'I'm not, but we must go on.'

'I can't.'

Will moved closer and held her against him as gently as he could. She was shaking from head to toe. She sobbed against his shoulder.

'I'm sorry,' she managed to whisper between gulps of sobbing. 'It's… it's the dark. I can't stand...'

Will could sense her panic rising. 'There's nothing to worry about. Hold close to me.'

Maeve clung to his right arm as he shuffled forward a short step. She stifled another sob and moved with him.

'Good, now two more steps and we can turn right. Ready?'

They shuffled again. Wills eyes were beginning to adjust to the darkness and as they reached the spot where he knew the turn must be he thought he could see in the distance a slight greying of the stygian blackness. It was where the rear stairs ought to be.

'We're on the right course,' he said to Maeve. 'The stairs are along this way. You're doing fine. One step at a time.'

With his free hand he felt for the wall to his left and they began to make steady progress. Maeve's shaking eased and she kept pace with Will. The greyness ahead was lightening with each step they took.

'I'm sorry for being so silly,' Maeve said, still clinging to Will's arm.

'Hey, anybody who's just been shot in the chest, banged on the head and plunged into darkness is entitled to be as silly as they like.'

It was a relief for both of them to be in the open air once more. When they'd climbed the stairs they saw that the fire had reached the far end of the rear corridor but they had passed safely underneath it and come up by the exit door to the inner courtyard.

They paused for Maeve to gather her strength and then crossed to the archway and on to the corner of the ramp to Prince's Street.

Will peered round the edge of the building. In the orange glow he could see there was no one on the ramp. He signalled to Maeve to move out and, together, they made their way towards the wooden hut at the top. As they drew near Will suddenly held up his hand and stopped. He had seen a wisp of white smoke rising from the open door. He signalled for Maeve to stay where she was and, keeping right over against the opposite wall he inched forward until he could see into the hut. Two soldiers were enjoying a quiet smoke to relieve the monotony of sentry duty.

Will made his way back to Maeve. He figured they wouldn't be in there smoking if there were any other soldiers or officers nearby, at least he hoped they wouldn't. He had a quick word with Maeve before creeping forward again, this time on the hut side of the ramp, until he was crouched behind the open door.

Maeve started on up the ramp and walked past the hut out onto Prince's street.

'Halt!' came an English voice from the hut and the first soldier stepped out, raising his rifle to point at Maeve.

In one swift movement, Will rose from his crouching position, grabbed the rifle and twisted it out of the surprised Tommy's grasp. He clubbed the Lee-Enfield and rammed the butt into its late owner's face, before swinging round and covering the second soldier with the business end.

‘Drop your weapon.’ Will’s tone demanded obedience and got it. ‘Now kick it out here. You stay where you are.’

He turned and grabbed the first soldier who was still spitting out teeth and shoved him back into the hut. He slammed the door and did his trick with the barrel of the rifle to hold the clasp in place. He was tempted to keep the second gun but wiser caution prevailed. Out of sight of the prisoners in the hut he swung the rifle like he was throwing the hammer and flung it far down the ramp and into the courtyard.

Back with Maeve the two set off down the narrow alley at the end of Prince’s Street. Will hoped he could remember the twists and turns from his previous jaunts but they looked different in the eerie orange light. There was shell damage, too. It was like being back in the GPO basement. They came to dead ends because of collapsed walls and rubble blocking the path and had to retrace their steps and try another turning. Finally they were in sight of Liffey Street, but the passageway was blocked by a collapsed building. There was nothing for it but to pick their way through the remains of the ruined house.

Will helped Maeve climb over bits of masonry and piles of rubble. They made slow progress but at last they stood on the pavement on Liffey Street. Will made as if to cross over.

‘Wait,’ said Maeve, ‘I need a rest.’ She was breathing heavily and leaned forward slightly as she held onto Will for support.

‘You’re bleeding again,’ he said. The bandage was now steeped in red. ‘We must get you to the hospital.’

‘Wait… just a… bit more.’ Maeve’s breathing was difficult.

‘Let me carry you.’

Will lifted her in both arms and they made their way to Abbey Street and on to where it crossed Jervis Street. He put her down for a brief rest on the corner but saw a patrol of soldiers coming up from the direction of the river so picked her up again and headed up to the crossing with Mary Street, which was the continuation of Henry Street. The hospital was on the opposite corner. He managed to keep ahead of the soldiers and crossing Mary Street, he looked to his right and saw the army barricade, this time from behind. The barricade from where the shot had been fired that was now in Maeve’s chest.

He carried her through the gate in the wrought iron railings and entered the building through a large black door.

'Can somebody help me please?' he called out putting Maeve down by a chair. Her legs wouldn't hold her. It was only then that he realised she had fainted.

* * *

A private in British army uniform stood guard outside the room where Maeve was recovering from having the bullet removed from her chest. It had lodged between her first and second ribs. She was lucky in that hitting the ribs had stopped it penetrating further and possibly puncturing a lung; unlucky, that it had broken both ribs in the process. But it also made extraction relatively easy as it was near the surface. Her blood loss, which was why she had fainted, didn't cause the doctor undue worry. He did an excellent job of closing the wound; he'd had a lot of practice over the last week.

As he finished strapping her up he said, 'You'll make up the blood loss soon enough,' and to the nurse, 'Give her some hot sweet tea and she'll soon be feeling much better.' He went on to test her eye coordination by getting her to follow his finger in front of her face and shining a light into each pupil. 'There's no sign of any aftereffects from your bump on the head.'

Maeve was now sitting on the edge of her recovery bed sipping the tea the nurse had brought her.

'What's going to happen to me?' she asked.

The nurse didn't look her in the eye. She had helped the doctor fix up the patient; they had done all they could for her, medically speaking, but they were powerless to protect her from the British army.

Shortly after her patient had been brought in by a rather disreputable looking young man, a patrol of soldiers had pounded on the door and demanded to see the couple that had arrived just before them. The doctor had insisted they wait until he had finished cleaning up the wound, but as soon as they saw through the window in the door that he was starting to bandage her up a sergeant and an enlisted man entered. The NCO started to question her.

'I really must protest,' the doctor started.

'Be quiet,' said the sergeant and proceeded to address Maeve.

'Where is the man who brought you here?'

'I don't know. Gone home, I suppose,' said Maeve.

'Did *you* see where he went?' the sergeant asked the nurse.
'He was here when you arrived, but with all the fuss you created I didn't see him leave. Sorry.' The nurse looked anything but sorry.
'Describe him.'
'Well, he looked rather dishevelled; dirty, unshaven. Above average height.' The nurse paused.
'Hair?'
'Oh yes. He was only in his thirties, I'd say.'
'Hair colour, you stupid woman.'
The nurse smiled inwardly. 'Can't honestly say I noticed. He was wearing a cap.'
'Right. We'll be on the lookout for him. In the meantime, we've got the girl. Name?'
'Ma… Mary. Mary O'Neill,' said Maeve, almost forgetting the name they'd given the doctor.
'Which battalion are you with?'
'What?' said Maeve.
'Which unit? Where have you been fighting?'
'I haven't been fighting. That's your job, isn't it?'
'Don't try to be funny with me, girl. I want to know where were you shot?'
'In the chest.'
'What location! Are all Irish women thick? – oh, never mind. We'll do this back at the barracks.'
The sergeant and private accompanied her to the recovery room and the private took up his post outside the door. 'As soon as she's passed as fit, bring her straight down. We'll be in the foyer.'
'Yes, sarge!'

* * *

Will had stayed with Maeve while the doctor started to work his magic on her, but when he heard the commotion down at the entrance, as the soldiers arrived, he nipped out into the corridor and heard their demand to see him and Maeve. He made a quick decision and instead of returning to Maeve he found the stairs and went up to the next floor. There, he located a lavatory and locked himself inside.
From his coat pocket he took out his shaving kit that he'd picked up from his lodgings on Wednesday and ran the basin tap to get some hot

water. He lathered his face and proceeded to remove all his stubble. He had a thorough wash and brush up before emerging from the toilet with his cap folded in his coat pocket and his coat over his arm. He strode along the corridor looking through the little windows in the doors until he found what he was looking for and slipped inside.

* * *

The young private guarding Maeve's room held the door for the white-coated orderly with the wheelchair and followed him into the room. The nurse had gone to check on another patient and the prisoner was alone.

'I have to take you for your post-op check before you can be declared fit to leave,' the orderly said to the girl on the bed.

She looked surprised but just said, 'Oh. All right.'

The orderly helped her into the wheelchair, while the soldier stood by. 'I come with you. She doesn't go out of my sight.'

'Fine. You can hold the door for me again,' said the orderly.

The three went out into the corridor, turned left and stopped by the lift. The soldier obligingly pressed the call button and opened the trellis door when the cage arrived. He slid back the inner trellis and the orderly reversed Maeve's chair and pulled her in after him. The soldier stepped in and closed the outer and inner gates.

'Which floor?' he said over his shoulder to the orderly.

'Four.'

The soldier pressed the button with a 4 on it and the lift began to ascend with a judder and a clank. The orderly stepped behind the soldier. His left arm shot out and tightened round the private's neck. He gripped his own left wrist with his right hand to strengthen the squeeze on the man's windpipe. He kept up the pressure until the soldier's knees buckled and then lowered him, unconscious, to the floor.

The lift stopped at level four. Maeve was already on her feet. She slid open the double doors.

'What now, doctor?' she asked, stifling a giggle.

'Hold the doors while I hide this bloke somewhere where he can sleep it off and then we get you out of here. Is the corridor clear?'

Maeve checked both ways. 'Clear,' she said.

It took him but a few moments to drag the soldier into a storeroom and get back to the lift. 'Bring the chair out, my lovely,' he said, 'we'll leave the doors open to stop the lift. Now sit in it.'

Maeve couldn't hold back the giggles. 'Oh Will, I hardly recognised you myself, all clean-shaven and spruced up in your white coat.'

'You played along brilliantly. We're a good team.'

'How are we going to get past the other soldiers?'

'I noticed a back corridor when I was exploring the second floor. It appeared to run the length of the building. Hopefully it will be the same up here. Did you notice as we came in there was another entrance at the far end of the hospital frontage? We'll need to check when we get back down, but I expect the soldiers will be waiting in the big entrance foyer where we came in.'

Will wheeled Maeve on down the corridor to the rear of the building and, sure enough, on the left was a long passageway that ran the length of the hospital. As they turned into it a door opened about halfway along and a doctor started to walk towards them. Will kept up his steady pace, head down. As they reached the medical man Will mumbled 'Doc,' and kept going. There was no challenge for them to stop. They reached the end and turned left again until they found the stair well next to another lift.

'Time to abandon the wheelchair,' said Will, bending down to retrieve his overcoat that was folded up in a recess beneath the chair. He slipped off the white coat and left it over the back of the wheelchair. 'Can't risk being caught in the lift anymore. You all right for the stairs?'

'I'm feeling fine. The doctor has strapped me up well. My ribs don't hurt at all. Oh!' Maeve gave the involuntary cry as she brushed against the handle of the door to the stairs. 'Well, hardly at all. They gave me aspirin.'

'Good. Let's go. We'll no have long before they find out you're missing, if they havenae already.'

They hurried to the ground floor and checked the corridor was clear before leaving the stairwell. Since it was approaching midnight there were no staff around – and no soldiers, either. Will donned his coat and cap as they stepped through the other front door and Maeve pulled her jacket close against the night chill.

They turned right, going north from the hospital, but in the distance they could soon make out figures in uniform milling around. It looked as though they were building another barricade.

'How ever are we going to get through the army cordon?' Maeve voiced the question that had been uppermost in her mind ever since Will had turned up with the wheelchair.

‘I think I know how we can do that and it involves going south anyway, but I didn’t want to go past the other hospital entrance where the soldiers are. It looks like we’ll have to risk it.’

They turned round and crossed to the far pavement. As they approached the south door, they forced themselves to slow to a stroll, arm in arm, like a pair of late-night lovers heading home. As they passed, the hospital door opened and a soldier stepped out. A match flared as he cupped his hands and lit a cigarette.

Will and Maeve strolled on.

A moment later, they heard muffled shouting behind them. Will glanced back and saw the smoker turn and open the door. The shouting grew louder, as if someone had turned up the volume on a wireless set. The soldier at the door called something to his comrades inside and then turned and looked straight at Will.

‘You there! With the cap!’ he shouted. ‘Stop, in the name of the King.’

Chapter 33

Leaving his sister with Will, Ryan Doloughan sprinted across Henry Street in the dark. Two shots rang out but not before he reached the comparative safety of Moore Street. His momentum carried him further on up the road before he stopped, leaned forward with his hands on his knees and took in great gulps of air. When he recovered from his mad dash he straightened up and was about to turn back to the house on the corner when he noticed someone slumped in a doorway.

Cautiously, he approached the prone figure.

The man sat leaning back against the door and the first thing Ryan saw, black in the dim, orange light, were some words scrawled on the door in what must have been the man's own blood. His right arm lay across his lap and the tip of his forefinger looked black, too, with the blood the brave man had used to write his own dying words. With a great sadness in his heart, Ryan read:

"Here died The O'Rahilly. RIP."

He wondered how many more stout-hearted Irishmen and women were to die before this was over. Was he to face the same fate, himself? He thought of his sister and Will Dillon and silently wished them all the luck of the Irish.

* * *

The soldier's command for Will and Maeve to stop outside Jervis Street Hospital had the opposite effect on them. They started to run.

Shots whistled over their heads as they reached Mary Street and swerved right, out of sight of the hospital. Behind them, angry shouting and the rapid clumping of a dozen army boots caused their adrenaline levels to soar – enough to speed them on, faster still.

At the end of the block they dived south down Wolfe Tone Street, but as they did, an English voice behind yelled out, 'There they go!'

Will had a tight grip on Maeve's hand, helping her to keep up. They had to keep a block ahead of their pursuers or risk being shot at, but before they reached the next intersection with Abbey Street they heard the soldiers in Wolfe Tone Street behind them. Four shots shattered the night before they could turn right along Abbey Street.

'Come on, stopping to shoot will have slowed them down. This is our chance to give them the slip.' Will could hear Maeve's breath coming in short gasps but they couldn't afford to let up. His plan was to turn south again towards the river at the next junction. At the last moment he changed his mind and they raced straight on across Capel Street. Will prayed that they'd make the alleyway up ahead before the soldiers could spot them.

It was something he'd just remembered Mrs Rafferty, his first landlady, had told him about. One of Dublin's hidden secrets close to his first digs. The narrow entrance to Meetinghouse Lane appeared on their right and Will pulled Maeve into it. A moment later they heard the pounding feet of the soldiers come out into Abbey Street and stop.

The two fugitives stopped, too, exhausted. They stood in the dark lane panting for breath, their hearts thumping in their chests. They heard the British soldiers run up to the Capel Street junction and, not seeing them on that street, call out to each other asking where their quarry could have gone. After a few more moments they heard the sergeant barking an order:

'You three! Down there. We'll carry on along here. Find them!'

More boots clomping towards them, only three pairs now, but getting closer.

The little alleyway where they were hiding could easily be overlooked in the dark, but Will couldn't rely on that. He whispered in Maeve's ear, 'Come.'

Their brief respite had done them good and it helped now that they didn't have to run.

‘There’s the remains of the old chapterhouse of the abbey up here on the right. Abbey Street – that’s what reminded me. My landlady told me all about it. Said hardly anyone knows it’s here, it’s so well hidden.’

‘So we can hide there until the soldiers give up? Because I don’t think I can go much farther; my ribs are really hurting now.’

‘I’m sorry, my love. It must have been much worse for you, so much running.’

‘It’s all right. Hanging onto you added wings to my feet.’

They came to a narrow opening and Will said, ‘It must be through here. Take my hand and mind your footing.’

The darkness took on a deeper resonance in these confines, but what little suffusion of the orange glow in the sky that reached them was just enough for Will to make out stone steps leading down from the level of the alley.

‘What’s that strange smell?’ Maeve asked as they started down.

Will had noticed it, too, and remembering what Mrs Rafferty had said, he told Maeve how after the ancient building was re-discovered in the 18th century it had been used, and still was, from time to time to store grain or potatoes. What they could still detect in the stale air was the damp, earthy smell of honest-to-goodness Irish spuds.

When they reached the floor, Will was thinking they had descended, not just through six feet of earth, but through 750 years of history to when the Cistercian abbey was first built in the 12th century. But Maeve cut short his mental excavations.

‘Will, I can’t go any further. Please! There’s no light down there. Don’t make me.’ Maeve hung back on the bottom step.

‘We can’t stay here. In case the soldiers do find the passage. We must go in a little way, so the darkness can be our friend.’ He stepped back and held her close. ‘Close your eyes; tight. Now, keep them closed and walk close with me. We won’t go in far; I promise. Just enough to be hidden from the entrance.’

They moved down together off the last tread. Will carried on, a step at a time, inside the structure. He could hear Maeve’s teeth grinding. She clung to him, her muscles taut. Her palm felt sweaty against his. He guided her away from the steps until they reached the wall on the right hand side. There seemed to be another opening with a few steps going up, but he leaned against the wall beside them.

‘We’ll be safe here. Let’s sit on the floor.’

They slid down with their backs against the wall.

'You can open your eyes now.'

'No. I don't want to.'

'You'll be fine. I can actually see a little now my eyes have grown accustomed. It's not like in the basement.'

'Ooooh…'

'Have you opened them?'

A tiny whisper, 'Yes.'

'You all right?

A gulp for air and another 'Yes.'

Will put his arm around her and felt her rigid body start to relax a little.

In the faintest trace of light that penetrated into the chamber he sensed, rather than saw, the vaulted ceilings of the ancient chapterhouse, all that now remained of a once great Abbey apart from an adjacent slype, or covered passageway, which must be up the steps beside them. Pervading everywhere was the stench of old potatoes.

Will kept alert for the sound of footfalls from the alley above while he spoke in a low voice to try to take Maeve's mind off her fear of the dark. 'It's appropriate enough that we should be hiding here,' he said.

'It is? Why?

'Well, according to my landlady, the oul Abbey in its heyday played a big role in the affairs of state. A few years before the Dissolution of the Monasteries when it was destroyed, it was in this very chapterhouse the ill-fated "Silken" Thomas Fitzgerald started his unsuccessful rebellion against Henry VIII. You could say he was the Padraig Pearse of his day.'

'Gosh. And that happened right in this room where we're sitting.'

'It sure did. Almost four hundred years – '

'Shh! Do you hear that?' Maeve breathed the words, for they could both now discern the sound of footsteps approaching in the alley.

The clomping of army boots on the cobbles was unmistakable. Sounds of the soldiers speaking came muffled to where they sat. They caught snatches.

'…goose chase.'

'…no-one…go.'

Then a closer voice. 'What's through here?' and a flickering light shone from the direction of the steps to the alley.

Will froze.

But for an instant, only. Silently, he stood and helped Maeve to her feet. He took her arm and spoke in a low tone – not a whisper, because that can carry – 'There's a couple of steps here. We're going up them.'

He could imagine poor Maeve's terror but she clung to him and kept by his side as they moved a little way into the inky blackness along the slype. Looking back, Will saw first a hand carrying some sort of oil lamp. That was followed by the whole body of a soldier, who stood at the entrance of the chapterhouse. He held the lamp high and looked around, left and right. The blackness within the slype lessened, before the lamp swung away again. What little light it gave must have been enough to assure him the fugitives were nowhere to be seen.

'It's empty. The place stinks of rotting vegetables. Let's go.'

The light retreated. The sounds of footsteps diminished. Will's heart rate began to return to normal.

'Still all right, my love?'

'I was petrified they would see the passage.'

'It's pretty dark over in this corner.'

'Er… I had noticed.'

'You're doing brilliantly.'

'Maybe, but can we go now?'

'Not just yet. Got to give them time to get clear.'

They sat down again against the wall in the passage and he took her hand in his. He was silent for a moment and then he said, 'Maeve, you know I will do my very best to get you – to get both of us, away from the clutches of the British army.'

'But how can we get through their lines?'

'You'll see soon, I hope. But the thing is, no plan is foolproof. We must face the possibility that one or both of us could be killed.' He felt the clasp of Maeve's hand tighten but she said nothing. He continued, 'You know how fond I have become of you; you've made me fall in love with you in the so short time I've known you.'

'Only because you made me fall in love with you. You are – '

'No, let me finish. I hope we have all the time in the world ahead of us, but… well, we might not. And I need to tell you something.'

Maeve's voice was very quiet, 'Yes?'

'Maeve, I'm not… I'm not exactly what you think I am. For a start, I'm not a Roman Catholic – '

'I know.'

'And I'm not – What? You know?'

In spite of their circumstances, Maeve gave a little laugh, 'I've known ever since you didn't eat the Host on Easter Sunday.'

'You saw me! But you never said anything.'

'Because I was falling in love with you. You must have had your reasons for telling everyone you were Catholic, but it didn't bother me. It's you, not your religion, that I love.'

Will felt ashamed, but forced himself to carry on. 'Maybe you won't for much longer. I'm not a republican, either.'

'But… but you've been helping us ever since we first met at the ceilidh.'

'I have, in a sense, because you're all such great people, but I've also been reporting back to a Unionist contact and through him to the British.'

Maeve was silent again.

Will felt miserable. 'Please say something. Even if it's that you never want to see me again.'

Maeve said, 'So it's true.'

'What?'

'You're a member of the Orange Order? And you helped to arm the UVF?'

'How…? Why do you ask that?' The pitch of Will's voice was raised.

And she told him all about her time with Corporal Kildare and his heroic arrival at the GPO with MacDonagh's dispatch.

'But… Connolly said nothing to me,' said Will when she had finished.

'Connolly doesn't know.'

'He doesn't?'

'Somehow the message fell out of my pocket when I was scrambling past some burning debris. I think it must have got burnt up.'

'You think…? Maeve – thank you. I probably owe you my life. Thank you, my love, but I don't deserve your protection. I've betrayed you.'

'You rescued me on Henry Street; you saved Ryan on Sackville Street; you got Joseph Plunkett safely out of the GPO. You even saved James Connolly from being robbed by those thugs out near Eva Gore-Booth's house. Whatever else you've done in secret, you are a hero of the Rising, Will. You're my hero.'

She buried her head against his chest and he hugged her close, but carefully. She raised her face to his. In the darkness his lips found hers and parted slightly as their tongues took impish delight in each other, teasing and tasting. Their kiss, though gentle, was long and ardent.

* * *

The sergeant and his two men spent a fruitless twenty minutes searching the streets in the area. They called out to their three comrades and eventually managed to meet up with them again, only to hear that they, too, had been unable to find the two fugitives.

'It goes against the grain but we'll have to call it off. They could be anywhere by now and it's twenty past two, we should be reporting in shortly anyway. Let's head back to the Shelbourne.'

'Sarge.'

'At least being garrisoned in a hotel we can look forward to a decent kip. But not yet. Keep vigilant. Keep looking out as we go; we could still spot them.'

'Will do, Sarge.'

The men turned east along the ruins of Abbey Street. They passed building after building that their shells had reduced to piles of rubble, but saw no sign of their quarry. It wasn't until they were about to cross O'Connell Bridge that the sergeant thought he saw someone loitering near the boats moored a little further downstream.

* * *

The dark waters of the Liffey flowed swift and strong past the barges tied up at Custom House Quay. At half-past-two that Saturday morning, the 29th April, the tide was still on the ebb and adding to the flow of the river to make the smaller boats tug at their moorings.

Will cut a furtive figure in his peaked cap searching along the waterfront. He and Maeve had left the sanctuary of the abbey chapterhouse after giving the army patrol plenty of time to move on and made their way back east, mostly along the riverside. Will wanted to be downstream of the last bridge, the railway crossing next to O'Connell Bridge, and when they got to the Custom House he left Maeve in the shadows of the big doorway while he went to find what they needed.

At the quayside he stopped by a sleek 25 foot yacht that he recognised as one of the lead-keeled Seaview Mermaids out of the Isle of Wight and wondered who had brought it over to Dublin. Whoever it was, he thought, they'd sure picked the wrong year for an Easter sailing jaunt. In the orange glow reflecting from the water he could just distinguish the white lettering on the hull, *Molly Malone*. So someone with a heart for the Emerald Isle, then. He untied the painter and threw it into the yacht. Now held only by the aft mooring line, she started to drift round with the tide to face downstream. The security chain clinked against the side of the quay.

He signalled towards the shadows of the Custom House and Maeve emerged to hurry towards him.

'Do you ever know how to sail one of these things, Will?' Maeve couldn't hide the anxiety in her voice.

'Didn't I grow up on the water around The Dee? I could sail before I could ride a bike,' Will chuckled.

'In the dark?'

'Sure, many's the time I've taken the *William and Laura* out at night. The lifeboat,' he added, at Maeve's questioning look. 'Welcome to the *Molly Malone*, our cordon-busting ride to freedom. Get you on down into her in case them soldiers turn up again.'

The bolt cutters that had been weighing down one side of Will's coat since they left the hardware shop on Henry Street made short work of the chain and rendered its padlock superfluous. Will untied the remaining mooring line, looped it round the bollard and got down into the yacht. He cleated the line to hold them while he got the sail up. The Mermaids were gaff rigged boats with squarish mainsails. So he would have to haul on the throat halyard first to raise the canvas and get the luff tight, before hauling on the peak halyard to lift the gaff up at an angle and tension the sail.

'Can I help?' asked Maeve, standing behind Will as the great sailcloth started to unfurl and climb the mast in time with Will's pulls on the halyard.

'I don't think there's anything at the moment, thanks. Hauling like this would do your ribs no good at all. Best sit down in the cockpit for now.'

Before Maeve could reply they heard a shout.

'Hey! Over here! The bloke in the peaked cap and the woman. I've found them!'

The devastating sound of the English sergeant's voice ripped through the night air and they could hear answering shouts from further off. At once, Will cleated the halyard with the sail only half up and grabbed at the mooring line, but he was too late.

The sergeant had rushed to the quayside, bringing up his rifle as he ran. It was now covering then both from only six feet away.

Chapter 34

The all too familiar sound of the other soldiers' running boots filled the air. Will glanced down and then, in one movement, scooped up the heavy bolt cutters and swung them out and launched them straight at the sergeant's face. Caught completely off guard, the soldier took the blow on his mouth and lower jaw. His rifle dropped as he staggered backwards. Shouts from his comrades rang out as Will let the mooring line go.

As soon as it freed, the flow of the river pulled the boat out into the current. A volley of shots rang out from the receding quayside. Maeve promptly sat herself down, bending low, and Will ducked. More shots followed but the *Molly Malone* was already downstream and the soldiers were firing wildly into the darkness.

Will's more immediate problem was to control the boat. They were at the mercy of the current. The yacht was slewing round and since she was simply moving with the flow, the rudder was useless. They had to make headway. Will started to haul up the mainsail once more, a task made difficult now, with the boat swirling about in the swiftly flowing river. He managed to get the luff tight and tied off the throat halyard leaving the long edge of the sail loose and flapping in the breeze. Next he got the Genoa up, the Mermaid's headsail, and ran the two sheets back to cleats on the gunwales either side of the cockpit. Then he turned his attention to the peak halyard and raised the angle of the gaff until the long edge of the mainsail had enough tension to stop it luffing. Finally, he released the boom and at last he was able to sit down opposite Maeve as the sail filled with the light sou'westerly and swung to port. He grabbed the tiller and, with wind in the sail, he could feel the boat responding to the rudder.

He set her on a steady course thinking what a mercy it had been that the current had held them in mid-stream all the time they were out of control, so they were well clear of the moored vessels along North Wall Quay. He was near to exhaustion. He'd been on the go since the start of the evacuation of the collapsing General Post Office almost seven hours ago and up for thirteen hours before that, but he had to remain alert. They were sailing, silent as a ghost, down the Liffey, but another British military night patrol could yet spot their sail in the diffused glow from the still raging city-centre fires. He tried to relax, sitting with one hand on the tiller and pulling gently on the main sheet with the other. Soon the river opened out into Dublin Bay. He kept close to the northern shore looking across to the lights of Kingstown away over to the south.

'All right, Maeve?' Will said, after a while. He had been so busy trying to handle the *Molly Malone* and so worn out, that he'd almost forgotten his passenger sitting, hunched, across from him.

'Mmm.' Her quiet response seemed fitting to Will, as the yacht now skimmed effortlessly over the water and through the night. Before them, the inky canopy was perforated with myriad-starlight. Looking back, any stars over the city centre had long since fought a losing battle with the clouds of dense smoke that hung over the environs of Sackville Street.

But they were leaving that behind. Two people in love, sailing off into the sunset. Well, the sunrise actually, in a few hours' time. Slipping through the ring of machine guns and barricades that sealed off the centre of Dublin. Escaping to safety. The silver sliver of the waning crescent moon looked to Will like a benign god shining his approval on them.

Maeve sat with both arms folded across her middle and Will reached for her hand. He wanted her to share the exhilaration he was feeling with the wind on his face and the hissing of the water, and the romance of the moon and stars collaborating in their bid for freedom. She gave him her hand but kept her other arm where it was.

Her fingers felt damp to his touch. Not cold with spray. Warm. Slippery.

Will raised her hand to try to see it better. 'Maeve! Are you bleeding?'

'I... I think so.' Her voice sounded tiny, distant.

'But how? Has your bandage come undone? It was all that running. I'm so sorry. I should never have made you do it.'

'No… It's not my… ribs. My tummy.' Maeve withdrew her hand from Will's and pressed it against her stomach again.

'Maeve, what's happened? Is it bad?'

'I didn't… sit down… quickly enough… I… was hit… another bullet. I'm afraid I'm… making… a bit of a habit… of that. Sorry.' Her breathing was shallow.

'My darling! Why didn't you say? Oh... are you in much pain?'

'Didn't want… distract you. Important… you get away. Your unionist… friends don't seem… able to protect you… anymore.'

'We both need to get away, but that's not more important than your health. Oh, my love, what are we to do? You need urgent medical treatment.'

'I'll just sit here. I'm… all right if … I don't… move.'

Will was frantically weighing up options. Going back and having to tack all the way against the wind was out of the question. Putting ashore at the nearest suitable place was not much better. (a) How was he to find a suitable place in the dark? and (b) once ashore, how were they to get to a hospital? Could Maeve make it all the way to Donaghadee – a good twelve hour sail? He doubted it very much. Then he remembered something Ryan had talked about. A Nursing Home. Dr Finnegan's? Opposite Lambay Island – with a landing jetty. It was perfect. But could they get there in time? Will reckoned they'd already covered nearly half the distance but it would still be a good hour away.

'We'll head for Finnegan's Nursing Home, the one Ryan mentioned. Remember?'

'Mmm… Good.'

'You just sit quietly. We'll get you fixed up in no time.'

They must be passing Clontarf, Will thought, and sailing along the seaward shore of Bull Island because up ahead, he could see the regular flashing beacon of the lighthouse on Howth Head. He calculated it wasn't far off 3:30 and there was the merest hint that the blackness of the sky was becoming less intense. Sunrise wasn't until nearly six o'clock but the astronomical twilight was beginning. Once they rounded the head it would be due north until he spotted Lambay Island. That should be about 4:30 and they'd be into nautical twilight, just enough light to make out the bulk of the island and to find the jetty on the mainland opposite.

The next hour was the longest of Will's life. Once clear of the lighthouse he found the constellation of the Plough and followed the line of its last two stars upwards to locate Polaris, the Pole Star. That gave him his northerly direction and the boom swung a little as he set the new course. He adjusted the Genoa's sheets to get maximum speed from wind which was a bit fresher now they were out at sea. Maeve spoke little, and only when Will spoke to her. Except once, when she said she was cold and he wrapped his overcoat around her.

'That's nice,' she said.

The *Molly Malone* hissed through the water, rising and falling in the slight swell. The horizon was becoming faintly discernible. Will checked his pocket watch but couldn't make out the hands; probably about 4:15.

'Not long now,' he said and then a little later, 'The island! I can see it looming up ahead, to starboard. Maeve didn't answer but to encourage her he added, 'About ten more minutes and we'll have you in the Nursing Home.

He steered a course to port that would hit the shore line about level with Lambay Island. A few minutes later, it was the building he saw first, silhouetted against a pale grey sky on a low cliff top. A short wooden landing stage at the side of a cove under the cliffs confirmed it was the right place. He adjusted their course to bring them to the end of the jetty.

The *Molly Malone* was coming in too fast. He loosened the peak halyard and lowered the Gaff. The mainsail started flapping and they lost momentum, but he tightened the Genoa's sheets and brought her in on the foresail alone. The gunwales scraped the wood of the jetty and he released the sheets. With both sails flapping the yacht stopped and Will was able to get a line looped around a cleat at the edge of the jetty. He jumped ashore with the painter and soon had the boat secure alongside.

Back in the cockpit, Will gently lifted Maeve's head. 'We're here, my love. Do you think you could stand? I'll take your weight.'

Maeve didn't answer. Her head was heavy between his hands, her eyes closed. 'You need to wake up, darling. Can you hear me?' Will's concern was growing. 'Maeve! Wake up, Maeve!' Her face was expressionless; her eyes remained closed. She looked very pale.

He felt the side of her neck. She still had a weak pulse. Facing her, with his hands under her armpits, Will lifted her until she was sitting on the gunwales. Her arms dropped to her side and he was aghast when he saw how much blood had soaked through her clothing. He climbed out of the yacht and slipped his hands under her armpits again, this time from behind. He lifted her right up and then adjusted his grip so he could carry her, trying to tuck the overcoat around her to keep her warm.

Will glanced about in the pale light, which was enough, now, to extinguish many of the fainter stars, and saw some stone steps leading from the back of the jetty up to a steep path that wound its way up the sharply sloping cliff face. Maeve wasn't heavy, but Will's arms began to ache before he was halfway up the path.

He struggled on. The cliff sloped back more towards the top, so the climb became slightly less arduous. At last he stepped onto a level sward that had already had its first cut of the season and stretched like a lawn at the back of the nursing home. Will staggered across it to what looked like a rear entrance and banged on the door. He felt his knees giving way. The strength in his biceps was gone. He collapsed to the ground, trying to let Maeve's body down gently. She was half on top of him as he succumbed to utter exhaustion and he, too, lost consciousness.

* * *

Will opened his eyes and saw a magnolia-coloured ceiling supported by magnolia-coloured walls. His first thought was to close his eyes again and continue to rest his head on the goose down pillow and remain lying on the soft mattress. His second thought snapped him wide awake.

Maeve.

Where is she? How is she? He must go to her.

He swung his legs off the bed; he'd been lying on top of the bedclothes. He found that he was still fully clothed apart from shoes and his overcoat, which he saw draped over a chair. Standing up, his stockinged feet touched a shoe and he bent down to put it on along with its pair.

The room he was in, although small was tidy and well equipped with a basin, armchair, upright chair and table by a bright, sunlit window and even a carafe of water and a glass on a small table at the bedside. As Will stood again, now fully shod, the door opened and a white-coated individual entered who introduced himself as Dr Finnegan.

'Good to see you are awake, Mr Dillon. I trust you feel well rested,' he said.

'I do. Thank you,' said Will. 'Em… might I ask how you know my name?'

'When we found you last night – well very early this morning, that is – you and the young lady were both in a state of collapse. We took the liberty of searching your pockets and found in your coat a letter signed by James Connolly, naming you and introducing you as his adjutant. In my book that entitles you to all the medical care we can provide. You probably know that we are sympathetic to the cause since you went to such trouble to bring the injured women here.' He took Connolly's letter from his pocket and passed it to Will. 'You'd better have it back. Am I to assume that the pair of you are fugitives?'

'I'm afraid so. The British army has us down as a pair of republicans. Can you believe it?' said Will.

The doctor smiled, 'Well, I'll ask no more questions. The less I know the better, when any soldiers come calling.'

'Is that likely? I thought this place was safe – well outside Dublin and all.'

'It always has been, but since martial law was declared we've had several unwelcome visits from the military – at all times of the day and over the past week, especially, to see if we're treating any wounded Irish Volunteers or members of the Citizens' Army.'

'I'm sorry to hear that,' said Will.

'We've managed to satisfy their questions so far. Hopefully we shall continue to do so.'

'Er... Maeve – the girl I brought in – can I see her? How is she?'

'I'm very much afraid she is far from well, Mr Dillon.'

'But she'll be – '

'She lost a lot of blood. She had internal bleeding, too. We've operated and managed to stop any further exsanguinating. The bullet caused considerable damage. We've done our best, but – '

'But? Tell me she's going to be all right, Dr Finnegan. She is, isn't she?'

'I'm very sorry, Mr Dillon – '

'It's Will.'

'Will. I'm very sorry, Will. She – Maeve – had already lost consciousness when you got her to us. She has remained in a deep coma ever since. Realistically, I don't expect her to come out of it. The trauma has been too much, and coming after an earlier gunshot wound, I see.'

'The earlier one was fixed. She was fine after the bullet was removed.'

'I'm afraid the second wound was worse; a lot worse. You must prepare yourself for the worst, Mr – Will. The reason I don't expect her to come out of her coma is… She's dying, Will. She won't last the day.'

'No! There must be something you can do.'

The doctor shook his head. 'Sadly, she's lost too much blood, quite apart from the internal injuries. I've read that over in the field hospitals behind the trenches in France and Belgium, army medics are transfusing donated blood back into badly wounded soldiers with encouraging results. Maybe one day we'll be able to do that here. But right now all we can do is make her comfortable until...' Dr Finnegan's voice trailed off. After a suitable pause he added, 'Maeve is not in any pain while she is in the coma, so that's a mercy.'

Will's mind was spinning. Maeve. Ryan's pretty little sister. Sweet Maeve. It can't be true. 'I must see her,' he said. 'Please, can I go to her?'

'Of course. She's in the next room. Come with me.'

He picked up his coat and Dr Finnegan led the way to an identical room, also filled with bright sunlight. Will noticed the sun was already high in the sky. Lambay Island looked green and inviting, bathed in its light. He checked his pocket watch. 11:45. He must have slept for over seven hours. He realised the doctor was speaking.

'… won't be able to respond.'

Maeve was lying in a bed identical to the one next door. She was under the blankets, all except for her arms and her head, resting on the pillow. Her russet hair framed her face and emphasised how pale her skin had become. Gone was the usual rosy bloom on her cheeks. There was a deathly pallor about her that made Will gasp when he saw her.

He stretched out his hand and caressed her cheek, half expecting it to be cold and clammy, but it was warm to his touch. Yes. She is still alive! Thank you. Please keep her alive. Let her live. Will wasn't sure who he was addressing, but he realised he hadn't voiced the words aloud, so it must have been to Someone higher up the chain than Dr Finnegan.

The doctor was holding her wrist between his fingers and thumb. He nodded and laid her arm down again. 'Her pulse in weakening, I'm afraid. She hasn't got long. I'll leave you to say your goodbyes.'

The door clicked closed behind him but Will didn't hear. Maeve's face became blurred as his eyes filled. He lowered his head onto her breast and slipped an arm under her shoulders to hold her close to him. He lifted his head and gazed down at her pale cheeks. She still looked so pretty. He remembered the first time they had kissed, when he gave her the little kingfisher he bought in Killarney. He lowered his lips to hers now. They felt soft, yielding, tender – unresponsive. It was as though she was already gone.

'Goodbye, my darling. I'm so sorry. I'll be right here beside you to the end.'

Someone was shouting in another part of the nursing home. Will glanced up, annoyed at the disturbance. Then the door burst open and a girl wearing a nurse's uniform rushed in.

'Soldiers! They're coming to check our patients again. Dr Finnegan says you should leave immediately. The back way. The way you came in.'

'I can't leave Maeve. Not while there's – '

'Mr Dillon, there isn't. Any hope. She'll be gone before your sailboat clears Lambay Island. You need to go. Now!'

Will hesitated. He lifted Maeve's hand, her seemingly lifeless arm dragging it downwards.

'Please hurry,' the nurse was becoming agitated. 'If they find you here they *will* take you prisoner, or worse. They won't bother your friend in her condition. We'll say she was in a motorcar accident. You mustn't worry about her. You must save yourself.'

The door opened again. Dr Finnegan appeared.

'You're still here! You should have gone, man. The soldiers are checking every room; they're already at the head of this corridor.

* * *

Ryan Dologhan was looking out through the shattered window of O'Hanlan's fish shop, No. 16 Moore Street. They had spent the night knocking through party walls and working their way along the road from house to house, but they were no nearer a position where they could break out with any hope of success. The British had them pinned down. Pearse and Collins still hoped they might, somehow, escape and get through to the Four Courts. Connolly and the other leaders, aware from the dispatches Dillon had brought that they weren't the only group of insurgents reaching the end of their tether, were ready to admit defeat. Joseph Plunkett was penning a letter to his fiancée, Grace Gifford; he dated it, "6th Day of the Irish Republic. About noon."

Pearse came to the window and stood alongside Ryan. 'How is it looking?' he said.

'It seems to me like there's more British soldiers behind that barricade than there was this morning. They're getting reinforcements.'

As Pearse leaned closer to look, they both saw a man – a publican, with his wife and daughter emerge from their besieged premises further up. The man carried a white flag. A hail of gunshots erupted from behind the barrier. Pearse and Doloughan instinctively ducked back. When they looked again the bodies of the little family lay dead on the road.

'No!' said Pearse. 'The brutes.' It was some minutes before he spoke again. He addressed Connolly, but spoke to all in the crowded room: 'James, I think we've done enough. At any rate, I cannot justify prolonging the battle while more innocent victims fall to the indiscriminate bullets of the British tyrants.'

Lying on his stretcher bed Connolly said, 'My friend, for the first time in 700 years the flag of a free Ireland floats triumphantly in Dublin City. That is no mean achievement.'

'Aye, we have blazed a trail where others may follow,' said Pearse. 'It was never ours to see the fulfilment of our dreams, but without what we have done this past week, no fulfilment could ever be realised. Ireland shall be free. The tricolour shall fly throughout the land. For us, though – our part is played and played well. We can all be proud and hold our heads high – for as long as we have left to do so. We shall not all see the final act of our drama, but know this: wherever an Irishman raises a glass to Ireland's freedom, the Easter Rising of 1916 will be remembered.'

Elizabeth O'Farrell volunteered to take a message to the commander of the British troops in Moore Street to ask for terms of surrender. At 12:45, in her full nurse's uniform and carrying a stick with a white flag that Ryan made for her with the handkerchief he had earlier used to bandage his burnt hand, she marched from number 16 up the street towards the barricade. She was received and listened to and sent back with a message for Padraig Pearse. He was to present himself by three o'clock at a shop just up the road that Brigadier-General Lowe was using as his HQ. The general would accept no terms other than unconditional surrender.

At three o'clock on Saturday 29th April, Padraig Pearse, Commander-in-Chief and President of the Provisional Government, accompanied by Nurse O'Farrell, handed over his sword to General Lowe in a symbolic act of surrender. Three-quarters of an hour later he was taken before General Maxwell to sign a general order of surrender. It read:

"In order to prevent the further slaughter of Dublin citizens, and in the hope of saving the lives of our followers now surrounded and hopelessly outnumbered, the members of the Provisional Government present at headquarters have agreed to an unconditional surrender, and the commandants of the various districts in the City and County will order their commands to lay down arms. Signed, P.H. Pearse, Dublin, 29th April 1916."

Ryan Doloughan was given the job of acting as bodyguard to Nurse O'Farrell and a priest who accompanied her, delivering copies of the surrender order to all the other strongholds around Dublin. Persuading the various commandants that it was genuine wasn't always easy and there were times when they were dodging bullets, themselves, before their job was finished.

'It's a great pity it has all come to this,' said the priest, as they left Thomas MacDonagh at Jacob's Biscuit Factory.

'Ah, it is, Father,' said Elizabeth. 'Sure I never dreamt when I was entering the Post Office last Monday that we'd be defeated by Saturday.'

Ryan said to them, 'Ach, sure being beaten doesn't matter a whole lot in Ireland; we're good at it. But not to have fought at all, now that would have been a tragedy.'

* * *

In the nursing home, Will cried out again, 'I can't leave Maeve.' The little dams of his lower lids breached and tears spilled down his cheeks.

'You can and you must. There is nothing you can do for her. We shall make her remaining time with us very comfortable. Please be assured of that. But she wouldn't want you to stay and be arrested.'

Will allowed himself to be hustled over to the window. Finnegan and the nurse got it open and helped him climb through onto the flat roof over the rear entrance.

'Your coat!' The nurse grabbed it and thrust it out after him.

Will heard a sharp rapping on the door of Maeve's room and then the handle turning before the window slammed shut. He scrambled to the edge of the roof, threw his coat down and lowered his body over. Hanging from the guttering with his arms fully extended he had a three foot drop to the ground. He let go and rolled on landing, snatching his coat as he picked himself up. Without looking back, he ran to the start of the cliff path.

Not until his head dropped below the top of the cliff as he descended, did he let up and take a more cautious pace on the steep path, but he heard no hue and cry behind him. Thanks to the good offices of the doctor and nurse he was not now under arrest, but approaching the *Molly Malone* once more and facing the loneliest sail ride of his life.

As the yacht sped over the water towards Rockabill Light off the Skerries, clouds built up and Will felt the sun had chosen to abandoned him just as he had abandoned Maeve. On passing the light an hour or so later it was time to say goodbye to the coastline to port and head into open sea. It seemed this was a day for saying goodbye. In the daylight he was able to use the yacht's compass that was in a binnacle set into the decking. He set a course for St John's point at the edge of Killough Bay and settled back for the five hours or so it would take to get back within the sight of land again. This time, his own County Down. It would be good to be home.

Maeve filled his thoughts. Each time a sweet memory popped into his mind – dancing at the ceilidh, riding in the jaunting car, their picnic in St Anne's Park, staying over at her mother's place – each time, the images he conjured up would morph into Maeve lying, pale as death, in the nursing home. Maeve left all alone, as he climbed through the window to escape arrest.

Arrest by soldiers of the army he was supposed to be helping. Have I helped? he wondered. I suppose I helped stop the German guns landing. How many lives did that save? And I helped ensure Eoin MacNeill countermanded the order to mobilise. That must have saved thousands. But the rising still went ahead. Not something one man could stop. And having got to know many of the leaders, Will wasn't sure how much he would have wanted it stopped. Much as he didn't want to see Ireland, or his corner of it, at least, ruled by an independent Catholic government he could understand, now, how Irish poets and visionaries, not to mention ardent republicans and nationalists, would want to see the back of England having the final say in how their country is run.

But did that justify the terrible cost of the past six days? So much of Dublin's fair city reduced to wreck and ruin; so many people killed or horribly injured; so many loved ones gone for ever. Maeve filled his thoughts again and stayed there.

From St John's point Will set a course for South Rock Lightship with the daylight beginning to fail. Then on to the Skullmartin Lightship from where he could follow the coastline in the twilight, past Ballyhalbert, Ballywalter, Millisle and finally sail round the lighthouse on Donaghadee pier and into the harbour.

It had started to rain, but he was home. The church clock was striking nine as he made his way up from the harbour to his house that he had left exactly three weeks previously. He bought a fish supper on the way and when he got in he cracked open a bottle of Guinness to wash it down. It was good to be back, but he had an empty feeling in the pit of his stomach that no amount of fried cod and chips would ever fill.

Two days later an unseasonal storm blew up and his evening meal was interrupted by the old familiar sound of the maroon booming out its distress call from the harbour. As volunteer lifeboat coxswain again, Will left his Guinness half-finished and, glad to have his mind distracted, he grabbed his oilskins and dashed out into the night.

AFTERMATH

General Sir John Maxwell, GOC Ireland, was determined to make an example of the insurgents. He had all the commandants arrested and over the next days and weeks, thousands of others, too – people who were not even Gaelic Leaguers, never mind members of the Irish Volunteer Force or Citizens' Army. He ended up incarcerating more than twice as many people as the 1600 or so who played a part in the actual Rising.

64 rebels had lost their lives in the fighting and those wounded amounted to about 200. Civilians fared worse with over 2000 wounded and 254 killed and 40 of these were children. The military lost 116 dead, a third of whom were from Irish regiments, and 368 wounded; the police, 16 dead and 29 wounded. So in all, the fighting killed 450 people and wounded 2614. A vast 550,000 square feet of buildings in central Dublin were destroyed and £2,500,000 worth of damage was caused. A third of the city's population was reduced to living on relief – all in the space of six days.

With all of this it was, perhaps, no surprise that when the rebel leaders were marched off to jail, they were jeered by the people and pelted with rotting vegetables and the piss from chamber pots.

Although some of the British army's actions had sickened Dublin's civilians, they mostly held the insurgents responsible for the terrible carnage. The GOC held them fully responsible. He had been put in complete charge of Ireland under martial law. He could do virtually as he pleased. He ordered every one of the seven signatories to the Proclamation to be court-martialled and shot. In all, 90 trials resulted in the verdict, "Death, by being shot." A few weeks later the executions commenced. Joseph Plunkett was allowed to marry Grace Gifford in

Kilmainham Gaol just a few hours before his execution. But as the death of each leader was announced over a nine day period, there was growing public reaction – particularly because it was all carried out behind closed doors – secrecy was needed to protect the witnesses, it was claimed. This didn't smack of fair play, and the people never believed so many could have deserved the death penalty.

The leader of the Home Rule Party, John Redmond, spoke out in Westminster against the executions, very much reflecting public opinion and in the end they were stopped. James Connolly was the fifteenth and last to be shot. He had become so ill from his gangrenous wounds that he couldn't stand up to face the firing squad. Lying in the military hospital just across from Kilmainham Jail, he spoke his final words to his wife.

'Wasn't it a full life, Lilly, and isn't this a good end?' and to his daughter, Nora, he added prophetically, 'We shall rise again.'

Soldiers carried him across the road to the inner courtyard of the jail where most of the executions were performed. He was strapped to a chair, to hold him upright, and shot, the last of the seven signatories who had proclaimed an Irish Republic in front of the General Post Office on Easter Monday. And thanks to the Lord Lieutenant's declaration of martial law and General Maxwell's subsequent ruthless exploitation of the powers it gave him, all seven leaders had been turned into martyrs – Irish heroes to a man.

Eamon De Valera was due to be shot the next day and became the first to have his sentence commuted to life imprisonment. Constance Markievicz had also been condemned to death but Prime Minister Asquith had already declared that no women should be shot and she had her sentence commuted to penal servitude for life. Cathal Brugha was released because of his catastrophic injuries, which he wasn't expected to survive. But he recovered and lived to fight another day. Sir Roger Casement was the last to die for the cause. He was held in Pentonville prison until August, when he was stripped of his knighthood and hanged for treason.

Ryan Doloughan along with hundreds of others was taken into custody and sent to England to serve a long prison sentence. However, the following year, the new Prime Minister, Lloyd George, declared a general amnesty and by June 1917, DeValera, Markievicz and all the other political prisoners had been released and returned to Ireland, this time to great popular acclaim by the people.

Men like Michael Collins and Ryan Doloughan were encouraged sufficiently, by their newfound popularity and their freedom, to start planning straight away on how to further their cause. Collins worked to build up *Sinn Féin* and the Irish Republican Brotherhood which he later merged with the Citizens' Army to become known as the Irish Republican Army, dedicated to upholding an Irish Republic.

It was the IRA who, within a few more years, fought the War of Independence that ensured the fulfilment of Connolly's prophecy that they would, indeed, rise again. In 1922, W. T. Cosgrave, the man who had helped Dillon escape from the South Dublin Union, became the first leader of the newly established Irish Free State.

* * *

Will Dillon followed all the events in the immediate aftermath of the Rising with a keen interest as they unfolded in the national press. It saddened him to learn of the deaths of people he had come to think of as friends – Padraig Pearse, James Connolly and the others, although he knew they were expecting nothing less.

For himself, he met up with Edmond Boyd soon after he got back, who told him that those he represented were well satisfied with his efforts.

'Things could have been a whole lot worse. You did well, Dillon. Perhaps you can be of use to us again.'

'I shouldnae think so,' said Dillon.

'Why not? You've been well paid, haven't you?'

Will looked Boyd in the eye for a long moment before turning away and saying, 'Sure there's no Post Office any more. I'd have nowhere to go.'

Once life in Ireland had begun to return to what passed for normality in the Emerald Isle, Boyd arranged for the *Molly Malone* to be sailed back to Dublin where its mysterious reappearance on the Liffey, moored at Custom House Quay was soon relayed to its owner in England. That individual's pleasure at being unexpectedly reunited with his lost yacht was turned to a curious wonder the first time he unfurled the Genoa and found a typed sheet that simply said, THANK YOU, pinned to the sail, together with a crisp, white five pound note.

As the summer months passed, accounts of the fallout from the Easter Rising faded and were replaced in the broadsheets by news of what they were calling the Somme Offensive and other harrowing accounts of the Great War along with more mundane items demanding the attention of the readers.

On a balmy day in early October, when Ireland had been enjoying a brief Indian summer, Will Dillon was reminded of his adventures of the previous April by a letter he received addressed in a flowing script and with a Dublin postmark. The envelope contained three sheets of paper, the first of which was a brief covering note signed by Eva Gore-Booth.

"I write at the request of our mutual friend, Mrs Dolougham, who has been anxious for some time to show her gratitude to you for the great efforts you went to on behalf of her daughter, Maeve. I believe Dr Finnegan relayed to her the role you played at the end of April, last. Now, a suitable means of thanking you has presented itself and she engaged my assistance in procuring it for you. Willie Yeats has written an excellent poem that he's calling simply, *Easter 1916*, which he says he may publish eventually in an anthology, but he has produced twenty copies for close friends and when I asked him, he was delighted to let me – or rather Mrs Doloughan – send one to you. I know how you appreciate his work. I do hope you like this very moving piece. With kindest regards, Eva Gore-Booth."

Will eagerly looked at the next sheet and found written upon it, in W. B. Yeats' own hand, the verses he had penned to immortalise the momentous events of Easter 1916. He read it through a number of times, reliving the memories it kindled. The poignancy of the last lines kept drawing him back to them:

Was it needless death after all?
For England may keep faith
For all that is done and said.
We know their dream; enough
To know they dreamed and are dead;
And what if excess of love
Bewildered them till they died?
I write it out in verse –
MacDonagh and MacBride

And Connolly and Pearse
Now and in time to be,
Wherever green is worn,
Are changed, changed utterly:
A terrible beauty is born.[7]

And Yeats had signed it and dated it, 25th September 1916.

Such a wonderful present that Mrs Doloughan had thought to obtain for him, but Will felt so undeserving. He was a fraud being given this matchless gift when he had failed so miserably in his attempt to save her daughter. He turned, reluctantly, to the last sheet to see what she wanted to say to him.

It was a rambling sort of letter. Mrs Doloughan started off clearly enough by thanking him for getting Maeve to the nursing home. She went on to write about memories of "her little girl" growing up. She talked quite a bit about comas and how some people stayed unconscious for years and how grateful she was that that hadn't happened to Maeve. She talked about her sometimes as though she were still with her and at others, as though she was in her coma. It was a very confused letter that Will imagined had come from the heart of a desperately grieving woman. The last line before her signature didn't make any sense to Will. She wrote, "I'll sign off now, to leave her room."

Someone had added another couple of lines after Mrs Doloughan's name; perhaps some words of explanation, Will thought. He read them with tears in his eyes.

"It is a strange feeling, indeed, to lose four-and-a-half months of one's life, but strength slowly returns, if not memory. I am told I owe you a very great debt and I thank you from the bottom of my heart."

It was signed, "Yours affectionately, Maeve."

~ ~ ~

[7] From "Michael Robartes and the Dancer" by W. B. Yeats (1921) Macmillan

APPENDIX – WHO'S WHO

A-M list of real historical people who play a part in *Dillon's Rising*

Ashe, Thomas – republican who led the uprising at *Ashbourne, County Meath*
Birrell, Augustine – British Chief Secretary for Ireland (Sir Matthew Nathan's boss),
Brugha, Cathal – Member of the IRB and the Irish Volunteers; severely wounded at the *South Dublin Union*
Casement, Sir Roger – British diplomat of Irish extraction, humanitarian activist, Irish nationalist, and poet.
Ceannt, Éamonn – a founder of the Irish Volunteers who held the *South Dublin Union* with Cathal Brugha as his deputy; a leader of the Rising and signatory of the Proclamation
Charlie Monaghan – IRB radio operator
Clarke, Thomas – a member of the Fenians, leader of the IRB, chief instigator behind the Rising and signatory of the Proclamation, fought at the *GPO*
Collins, Michael – republican, Plunket's aide (and future founder of the Irish Republican Army), fought at the *GPO*
Connolly, James – Secretary of the Irish Transport and General Workers' Union (ITGWU), co-founder of the Irish Citizen Army (ICA), poet, a leader of the Rising and signatory of the Proclamation; fought at the *GPO,* Commandant in charge of military operations in Dublin,
Connolly, Seán – civil servant, actor, member of the ICA; CO at *City Hall* during the Rising (not closely related to James Connolly)
Cosgrave, William Thomas (W. T.) – Irish politician who fought at *South Dublin Union*; and in 1922 was to become the first leader of the Irish Free State
Cowen, Colonel – British Assistant Adjutant General
Craig James – Unionist MP for East Down
Daly, Ned – led the fighting at the *Four Courts* during the Rising
de Valera, Éamonn – republican maths teacher who established a stronghold at *Boland's Mill* during the Rising
Friend, Major-General – British Head of Armed Forces at the start of the Rising
Gore-Booth, Eva – poet and dramatist, suffragette, social worker and labour activist
Heuston, Seán – republican who took over the *Mendicity Institute* during the Rising
Hyde, Douglas – led the Irish language revival, founding chairman of the Gaelic League
Kearney, James – Park Keeper at *St Stephen's Green*
Keating, Con– IRB radio operator
Larkin, James (aka Big Jim) – trades-unionist, founder of the ITGWU, co-founder of the ICA
Lowe, Brigadier-General William – British Officer in charge at the Curragh barracks
Lynn, Dr. Kathleen – Irish Medical Officer at *City Hall*
MacBride, Major John – republican, fought at *Jacob's Biscuit Factory* under Thomas MacDonnagh during the Rising
MacDiarmada, Seán (aka Seán McDermott) – member of the Gaelic League, Irish Volunteers and the IRB, a leader of the Rising and signatory of the Proclamation, fought at the *GPO*
MacDonagh, Thomas – Irish political activist, poet, playwright, teacher, occupied *Jacob's Biscuit Factory*;

APPENDIX – WHO'S WHO

M-Z list of real historical people who play a part in *Dillon's Rising*

MacNeill, Eoin – co-founder of the Gaelic League and Chief of Staff of the Irish Volunteers

Mallin, Michael – Irish socialist, CO at *St Stephen's Green* during the Rising

Markiewicz, Countess Constance – Eva Gore-Booth's sister, revolutionary nationalist and suffragette; second-in-command at *St Stephen's Green* during the rising and future Sinn Féin and Fianna Fáil politician

Martin, Captain Micky – British joint leader of attack on the *South Dublin Union*

Maxwell, General Sir John Grenfell – new British C-in-C of forces in Ireland from Friday 28th April, 1916

McInerney, Tommy – IRB driver

Mellows, Liam – republican who led the uprising at Galway

Nathan, Sir Matthew – British Assistant Secretary

Nelson, Alexander (aka Alec, aka Kicker) – young lifeboat crewman, who in later years would become the cox of the Donaghadee lifeboat

O'Brien, William – Irish nationalist journalist, Connolly's deputy at the ITGWU

O'Daly, Paddy – republican carpenter who worked at the *Magazine Fort* and subsequently led the attack on the Fort at the start of the Rising

O'Farrell, Elizabeth – member of Cumman na mBan, nurse at the *GPO* who carried Pearse's surrender message to the British

O'Rahilly, Michael Joseph (aka The O'Rahilly) – Irish republican and nationalist and a founding member of the Irish Volunteers; fought at the *GPO*

Oates, Captain John – British son of Lieutenant-Colonel Oates; joint leader of attack on the *South Dublin Union*

Oates, Lieutenant-Colonel, Sherwood foresters – British senior officer who ordered attack on the *South Dublin Union* while Dillon was there

Painter, H. E. – Donaghadee coastguard

Pearse, Padraig – Irish teacher, barrister, poet, writer, nationalist, political activist and a leader of the Rising and signatory of the Proclamation, fought at the *GPO;* in overall command throughout Ireland during the Rising

Plunket, Joseph – Irish poet, journalist, member of the Irish Volunteers and IRB, a leader of the Rising and signatory of the Proclamation, fought at the *GPO*

Sheehan, Donal – IRB radio operator

Skeffington, Francis Sheehy – radical writer and leading pacifist

Staines, Michael – Irish republican who was prominent in the initial attack on the *GPO*

Taylor, Colonel, South Staffordshire Regiment – British officer who led the attack on the Volunteers at North King Street

Weisbach, Lieutenant – German U-Boat Commander who landed Roger Casement off the coast of Kerry

Wimborne, Lord (aka Ivan Churchill Guest) – British Lord Lieutenant of Ireland)

Yeats, W. B. (aka Willie) – Irish poet and dramatist, friend of Eva Gore-Booth

APPENDIX – WHO'S WHO

A-Z list of fictional characters in *Dillon's Rising*

Annie – Will Dillon's fiancée
Boyd, Edmond – Leading 'Shadow', influential Ulsterman high in the echelons of the Royal Arch Purple
Bradshaw, Geoffrey – pro-British Clerical Officer at Dublin Castle (Will's contact)
Brian – Gatekeeper at the GPO
Dillon, William James (aka Willie James, aka Will) – GPO Telegraphic manager, volunteer lifeboat cox and reluctant spy
Doloughan, Maeve – member of the Cumman na mBan, sister to Ryan, fought at the *GPO*
Doloughan, Mrs – elderly republican, mother of Ryan and Maeve
Doloughan, Ryan – member of the Irish Republican Brotherhood (IRB), fought at the *GPO*
Gibson, George – Worshipful Master of Donaghadee Lodge of the Orange Order and the Royal Arch Purple
Gilpin, Mrs – Dillon's 2nd landlady
Gregson, Buster (aka Rugby Shirt) – one of Higginson's thugs
Higginson, Michael J (aka the Boss) – a Dublin racketeer
Kelly – Higginson's minder-cum-butler-cum-chauffeur
Kildare, Corporal Joseph – Irish Volunteer at *Jacob's Biscuit Factory*
Liam – one of Higginson's thugs
Lieutenant-Commander – Coastguard Divisional Officer at Donaghadee
Maguire, Jude – fisherman and lifeboat crewman
Maguire, Peggy – Jude's wife
Maguire, Seth – Jude's brother
McBride, Sergeant – Royal Irish Constabulary (RIC), Donaghadee
Moore, Éamonn – one of Higginson's thugs
Moore, Ewan – his brother, another of Higginson's thug
O'Mally, Sergeant Jake – republican Volunteer soldier locked out on the roof of the *GPO* by Dillon
Pat – Volunteer, wounded at the *GPO*
Rafferty, Mrs – Dillon's 1st landlady
Shorty – one of three Force Erin extortionists
Walsh, Gerry – Higginson's handyman/gardener
West, Corporal Geordie – Ulster volunteer
Wilson, Harry – UVF dispatch Rider

About the Author

AG Lyttle grew up in County Down and graduated from Queen's University before moving to Surrey with his English wife to take up a career in Management Services, keep dogs and cats, and grow apples, blackberries and three children. The latter have now reaped him a fine harvest of grandkids.

He writes:
I hope reading "Dillon's Rising" has brought as much pleasure to you as it did for me to write it. If so, do, please, take a moment to leave me a review on Amazon.co.uk and Amazon.com or at your favourite online retailer. Many thanks for that!

As you know, Ireland's bid for freedom did not end in 1916. So who knows, perhaps we'll see "Dillon's War" one of these days, covering the War of Independence and the short Civil War that followed. That's if Boyd's shadowy group can manage to persuade Will Dillon to risk his neck again and return to Dublin.

If you liked the snippets of history in "Dillon's Rising", you'll love my current work in progress, "Starlings in the Corn". It follows the adventures of an impoverished protestant boy who vies with his best friend from a well-off catholic family for the attentions of a beautiful girl, as they grow up in fifties and sixties Ulster. The tale reveals much of Ireland's own struggles through the centuries to free itself of its shackles, mirroring the lad's determination to throw off the restrictions of his background, despite the treachery of an old school bully – and with some unexpected help from the IRA.

AG Lyttle, March 2016

Connect with me

Follow me on Twitter: https://twitter.com/AGLyttle
Friend me on Facebook: https://www.facebook.com/AGLyttle
Or email me: aglyttle@virginmedia.com

Acknowledgements

I am grateful to my wife, Anita, and beta readers, Jill Stedman, Brenda Price, Gail Jack, Susan Baldwyn Roger Lewry and Michael Paterson for their invaluable input that helped to make this edition of Dillon's Rising *what it is, and to Vanessa Wester for her excellent advice and encouragement regarding publishing; to Sean and Rachel Lyttle for being my models for the book cover and to Sean for designing it; and finally to all the wonderful writers on The Word Cloud, the writers' forum run by Writers' Workshop (http://writing-community.writersworkshop.co.uk), whose support and input over the years has been for me, as for many a struggling author, both a delight and an enlightenment.*

CIRCULATING STOCK WEXFORD PUBLIC LIBRARIES
BLOCK LOAN
BUNCLODY
ENNISCORTHY
GOREY
MOBILE NORTH
MOBILE SOUTH
NEW ROSS
WEXFORD 2[illegible]-12-2016 WD 3/2/22
DATE

CPSIA information can be obtained
at www.ICGtesting.com
Printed in the USA
LVOW12s1054301016
510895LV00002B/399/P